Y

U

M

E

YUME

Sifton Tracey Anipare

RARE
MACHINES

Publisher and acquiring editor: Scott Fraser | Editor: Whitney French
Cover design and illustration: Sophie Paas-Lang
Printer: Marquis Book Printing Inc.

Library and Archives Canada Cataloguing in Publication

Title: Yume / Sifton Tracey Anipare.
Names: Anipare, Sifton Tracey, author.
Identifiers: Canadiana (print) 20200373676 | Canadiana (ebook) 20200373706 | ISBN 9781459747371 (softcover) | ISBN 9781459747388 (PDF) | ISBN 9781459747395 (EPUB)
Classification: LCC PS8601.N483 Y86 2021 | DDC C813/.6—dc23

We acknowledge the support of the Canada Council for the Arts and the Ontario Arts Council for our publishing program. We also acknowledge the financial support of the Government of Ontario, through the Ontario Book Publishing Tax Credit and Ontario Creates, and the Government of Canada.

Rare Machines, an imprint of Dundurn Press
1382 Queen Street East
Toronto, Ontario, Canada M4L 1C9
dundurn.com, @dundurnpress 𝕏 f ⃝

To my dad, Victor Charles Anipare,
who showed me my first anime

Ho, ho, fireflies come!
Over there the water [is] bitter
Over here the water [is] sweet
Ho, ho, fireflies come!
Ho, ho, come by the mountain road!

— "Hotaru Koi"
(Children's song from Akita, Japan)

序章
THE WOOD WHERE
THINGS HAVE NO NAMES

万事は夢

All things are dreams

There is a quiet forest upon a mountain on a spring day. The sky is blue, the grass is a lush green, and the sun is shining. A wide dirt path winds through an assortment of trees: thousand-year-old oak, majestic redwood, thick reedy bamboo, baby spruce, short fat pine, many others with no names. There are no sounds except for the occasional breeze that does not affect the foliage. There are no living creatures, save two: a young man and woman down the road. They hold hands as they walk in silence.

The woman's long hair obscures her face as she giggles into her chest. She covers her smile with a small, demure hand. A black dress jacket tailored for a man hangs over her shoulders, shielding her from the cold. Underneath, a skimpy white camisole is visible. Pyjama bottoms two inches too long, a conscious choice or perhaps a current style. Her feet are bare. Tiny white toes poke out from her pants as they scuffle through the dirt. She walks with tiny, pigeon-toed steps, making it hard to keep up with the steady, rhythmic strides of her long-legged partner. The young man wears simple but stylish black shoes, black dress pants, and a white dress shirt that could be designer, a handsome though nondescript ensemble. His face is long and narrow, framed by jet-black hair that flows neatly over his brow, but not enough to cover his ears. He wears two beaded bracelets on his gaunt, pale wrists: one is obsidian, as dark as his own hair; the other is a vivid ruby, the same colour that flows through his veins. There is something in the curve and fullness of his lips and cheeks that is captivating, and his skin, with a natural hint of peach, makes the cold sharpness of his eyes stand out. That is something else unique about him. His eyes are not brown, but an unnatural, pale, icy grey. He stares straight ahead, focused on his intended destination, cool and oblivious to his companion. His demeanour is gentle but serious as he holds the woman's hand and guides her down the road.

The young woman's body shakes harder and harder with muffled titters as she sneaks shy glances at him. Surely such enigmatic beauty would catch anyone's attention; make hearts flutter with minimal effort beyond eye contact and an outstretched hand. However, it was the one next to him who had *really* captivated her, the one who had singled her out. Out of all the women he could have, he had pointed at her. He had chosen *her*. Now, her dream is about to come true.

They continue down the long, winding road in silence. They disappear around the bend, reappear where the path straightens, follow its twists and turns. Suddenly, the man stops in his tracks. The woman stumbles in surprise. Her head twists this way and that as she becomes aware of her surroundings. She looks away from the man, eyes wide, and lets out a wistful cooing sound.

She has just noticed this wide-open space that is their destination. In the middle of this forest, sequestered away from all civilization, stands a large cottage. Pale yellow curtains billow through its open French windows. On the porch an outdoor wicker deck chair for two swings in the silent breeze. Thick brown tiles like slabs of chocolate make up the roof, and the cedar logs glow in the sunny afternoon light. They almost look like they are melting. A long flight of wooden stairs leads to the front door, a solid cocoa-brown panel of wood a full storey off the ground.

Without turning to look at her, the young man speaks, his voice low as if speaking to himself: "Akki-*sama* ..."

His right wrist flexes in pain as his red bracelet glows with heat.

He starts to proceed, but the woman is still dumbstruck by the beautiful scene before her. There is so much for her to take in. She releases his hand and falls to her knees with exaggerated sighs. He stands there for a moment, hoping for her to say something poignant or explain herself. The man clears his throat, a soft yet awkward sound. She does not notice him. She merely gazes up at the cottage with admiration:

"Tash — Tu — ... Tash — Tu — ..."

Over and over she whispers to herself, a garbled, unintelligible noise. The man frowns: something about various tutors? No, various Tudors. No, it is a person's name she is repeating. He suppresses an irritated noise in his throat. She can babble on her own time. He lets go of her and presses on toward the cottage without looking back. The woman gets to her feet and prances after him, begging him to wait for her. The door groans open on its own accord and the man walks in without hesitation; the woman follows. The door slams with a resounding boom that ripples through the woods. It sends trembles up the trees, then trickles down the mountain until, little by little, it fades and everything is still.

Well, almost everything.

Nearby, in the woods, peach trees begin to rustle and stir. A faint giggle emanates from their leaves. Something grows in the woods, swelling in size with each footfall. It has spied on the house for some time, and now it approaches.

Inside the house, the woman reaches out into the darkness. She gropes for the velvety comfort of the young man's hand but only feels the panic that comes with flailing in an empty space. A dim light grows brighter in a corner somewhere above her line of sight, so gradual it locks her heart in suspense. The man is there, a few steps ahead on a narrow stairway. A small candle glows at his socked feet, its light throbbing and pulsing like a heartbeat. There does not seem to be anything else inside the cottage. No hallway, no drawing rooms, no furniture … just a tiny recessed entryway, a single pair of straw sandals, the stairs, and her patient companion, shoes in hand. As she runs up to him, disjointed thoughts flit across her mind: *What was the architect thinking when he made the front door on the second floor? Not like a Tasha Tudor cottage at all.* She thinks about asking … *later, of course.* Not that the architecture matters. This place is romantic and gorgeous. It is as she has always pictured a foreign cottage. Well, almost, because when she thinks about it, it is quite a strange design for a house. She giggles again and sighs with happiness when she regains the comfort of the young man's sleeve. She does not say a word to him. The wide grin on her face is enough to express her feeling without uttering a syllable. She could content herself with walking these steps for the rest of her life were it not for the one with whom she is about to reunite. He is close by; she can feel it. She leans her head on the young man's shoulder, tightens her grip around his arm, and sighs as loud as she dares.

Now the climb is even more awkward for the young man. The flight seems to grow longer with each step. The muscles in his legs burn, but at last the stairs — like all stairs — come to an end, and relief kicks in. *Not much longer now.*

The hallway they reach is long, with one set of doors. The man loosens the young woman's grip and slides the doors open for her. She gasps at the sight of a large, extravagant room. Down pillows lie in the centre, shielded by thin mesh drapes, surrounded by plates of exotic, expensive-looking food: mountains of tropical fruit drizzled with honey, giant cakes covered in flower petals, and a champagne tower. Taper candles line walls that extend far into the darkness. There must be hundreds of them. A giant paper lantern hovers over the blankets in mid-air. The fire glowing within it is deep red, unlike any fire she has ever seen. Ghostlike wisps of incense drift through the air. The room is filled with heat, with warmth, with love. The young woman clasps her hands with a sigh. She throws herself against her companion and kisses his cheek, then enters. She pulls back the mesh drapes and kneels on the silk futons, sweeping her hands over their intricate designs. She turns back to him and pats the spot next to her, inviting him to join her. When the young man waves his hand, she insists. It is the last thing he wants to do.

Keep them warm, his grin tells her. He holds up a finger. He means for her to wait.

The woman giggles again. She turns her back to him, removing his jacket from her shoulders. He slides the door closed. Without hesitation he turns back down the stairs. There are more candles now, but the amplification in lighting does not improve his mood one bit.

"Nice shade of lip gloss you got there," a high-pitched voice snickers. Small peals of laughter join in.

No, don't respond, the young man thinks to himself. He is not in the mood for nightmares right now. He rubs the kiss on his cheek with the back of his hand and wipes it against what must be the wall. It is too dark to tell. However, he does not need light to see fresh burn marks on his skin where the blood-red beads have singed him.

He puts his shoes back on at the tiny front entrance. Every part of him feels heavy as lead. He waits by the front door. It feels like forever. He half expects to hear the doors upstairs slide open and the woman call him. Impossible, of course, for she does not know his name. Instead he hears shuffling noises above his head. A deep voice murmurs for a long time, like a one-sided conversation. He hears the woman giggle. Then, moans of ecstasy, increasing in volume and urgency within seconds, tear through the once-silent house. He feels a twisting sensation in his stomach, an odd combination of nausea and relief.

Now what?

It is a foolish question to ask, he realizes, because there is only one thing he can do. He forces the front door open. His eyes sting with the transition to the outside world, but he jogs down the steps as fast as his legs can carry him, away from the house he feels is always watching him. Tapping quick staccato notes on the stone steps, his spirits lift a little as his shoes readjust to his feet, but grow heavy again as he settles down on a decaying stone bench in the garden. His back to the house, surrounded by withering bonsai trees and mouldy pools that reek of discarded carrion, he sits there, feeling hollow and heavy at the same time. He is already bored with the same few roads and trees he explores when there is nothing else to do until the next enamoured woman his protector manages to sweep off her feet.

A deep, loud moan cuts through the silence. Louder than normal. He clicks his tongue in disgust, but otherwise does nothing. There is nothing he *can* do. He leans forward and rests his chin against the butt of his hand. He is sick of this place. The blood-red sky, the shrivelled brownish-grey grass, the stench of rot that always chokes the air and permeates his clothes when he wakes up. It sticks to his hair, he can smell it on his skin; no amount of showering seems to get rid of it.

What he would not pay to see this whole world disappear ...

A sound wrenches him from his thoughts. Behind him, he hears the splintering crush of wood and infrastructure, like a wrecking ball through concrete, high over his head. He ducks and curls up on the ground just in time to avoid a shower of gold rubble. When he looks up, the colour drains from his face. Sitting cross-legged next to where the cottage stood is the biggest *yokai* the young man has ever seen. It towers fifty feet above him in a hooded white silk kimono, striking and bright against its midnight skin so that it casts a shadow over its face. Every movement of its limbs causes the ground to shudder. The sleeves of its robe are too long, but instead of pushing them out of the way the monster is focused on something in its hands: a sandwich of cedar wood walls, layered with slabs of chocolate-brown roofing and soft, airy clouds. The monster yawns wide. Its jawbone clicks with three explosive pops as it unhinges. It brings the shattered cottage deep into its giant mouth. The man is too frightened and stunned to stop it, not that he can. It is too late. It chomps down with sharp, white teeth and a deafening crunch that echoes even as it takes another gargantuan bite.

All that remains of the cottage are the front door and the stone steps to nowhere. The rest is gone, including its occupants. The woman, the nightmares, Akki. The realization hits the man like a slap to the back of the head. *Akki-sama*. This *yokai* must have eaten Akki, as well. *So that's it, then. He's gone. No one can protect me now.* He had always wondered how his pact with Akki would end — he never guessed it would be in the grip of another *yokai*'s teeth.

The *yokai* continues to chew and swallow. Smiling, head bobbing side to side in a pleased manner, it lets out a deep moan of satisfaction that shakes the air and the ground. The man recognizes the moaning sound from before. The *yokai* brings the house to its lips one last time. Then it sees the man staring up at it from the corner of its eye.

He breaks into a furious sweat. He has been spotted. He cannot outrun a creature this size. He is not even sure if he should move; all this monster has to do is stretch out a hand and squeeze. His head would pop like a grape. Then it could slide out his spine and use it for a toothpick. He would feel every sensation of it. Even in dreams, these things hurt. He must do something.

First, he apologizes for disturbing it. He rises to his feet, palms out in a sign of negotiation, speaks in a gentle voice. With all the canned coffee and Cup Noodles he consumes, he assures the monster that he would be far from delicious. He feels like a child again, grovelling to a creature more powerful than himself, but he has no choice. The bracelets on his wrists are useless, now. No one will rescue him, not this time, perhaps ever again. He keeps his eyes on the *yokai* as he takes his first step, ready to flee.

"Oh, no you don't." The *yokai* twists its body and lifts the giant cottage sandwich higher into the air. "I saw it first!"

The young man feels his heart clench. His arms drop to his sides. Its words were muffled in a mouthful of chocolate, but ... he could have sworn ... "Uh ..."

"What? I'm using plain English, aren't I? You heard me. It's MINE."

He cannot keep his voice from trembling. "I — I'm sorry," he tries again. "I didn't mean to intrude. Please. Take all you want. Just don't hurt me, please."

The *yokai*'s angry eyes now widen. "Is this your house?"

"No! Please. By all means. Help yourself. Just let me go. Please, don't eat me."

"What?! Why would I do that?! What do you take me for, some kind of monster?!"

"It's just ... that house, Akki-*sama* ...?" The name does not seem to register on the *yokai*'s face. "Wasn't there anyone inside the house? It's okay if there was," the man adds quickly. "I mean, I'm sure you had a good reason — unless, it was by accident. Right?"

The *yokai* looks close to tears. Its eyes dart around, making the trees shiver. "It was empty." Its voice is soft. "It *looked* empty." The young man takes a deep breath. "You know what? Never mind. I wouldn't worry. Carry on."

"But — I … I'm …"

"No." He tries not to look so happy. "Please. I insist." As a sign of trust, he backs away, turning when he reaches a safe distance, choosing another bench far away to perch upon. Tears brim in his eyes when he hears the last remnants of the house pulverized in the *yokai*'s mouth. Freedom has never sounded so beautiful.

When the monster, now smaller, plops down on the bench, his old fears return. He braces himself for the attack, but it sits facing away from him, refusing to meet his eye. It stretches a small hand toward him and waits. "You can have it," it says in a soft, forlorn voice.

The front door is so small the man is tempted to take it. "No, I can't," he replies. "Go ahead. It's all yours."

"I feel bad. I didn't mean to eat it — er, them?"

"No, take it!" He allows himself a small grin. "Give it a good home."

The creature does so, breaking off piece after piece, eating much more politely than when it was unaware of being watched. The young man pretends not to look at it. Now that it is almost as tall as he, the *yokai* looks much less threatening, more interested in its barren surroundings than the stunned gentleman gaping at it. The way it spoke, the way it moves — placing every morsel of chocolate door on its long, snakelike tongue with delicacy — is hypnotic. For sake of safety, the man pretends to play along. It is too late to make a run for it now. "You look satisfied."

"I've never had one before." It licks the last traces of chocolate from its fingers and pats its belly. "Whoo … that was a meal and a half. What's the deal with this place, anyway?"

"This is private property. Or …" he looks over his shoulder at the ruins. "It *was* private property."

The *yokai* looks down at its swinging feet. "Oh, I see. It was important to you."

He allows himself another mirthless grin. "No."

"Well, it *looked* edible. If you didn't want anyone to eat it, you shouldn't have made it out of food."

"I didn't. Trust me."

"Yes …" It removes its hood and looks him in the eye. "I think I do."

The man grins despite himself. He can feel a blush coming on. He cannot remember the last time he spoke this freely to anyone, human or otherwise. He narrows his eyes as he tries to determine exactly what kind of *yokai* he is dealing with. He has never seen one that looks and talks like this. It could be a simple shape-shifter taking the form of a woman. It is possible that she is a *futakuchi-onna*, a demon with a mouth in the back of its head. Or perhaps a *nure-onna*, a snake woman. They are not uncommon in this part of the mountains, but if that is indeed what this is, why does this one look so … He searches for the word.

The frustration on the man's face catches the *yokai*'s attention. "NOW what?"

"Nothing. I'm sorry. If … I may ask … what are you?"

The *yokai* narrows her eyes. "What kind of a question is that?"

"Well, forgive me, but I'm having trouble —"

"You make me sound like I'm some kind of freak or something."

"Well, you did just eat a house."

She turns away to hide her grin. "Yeah, well … I wouldn't talk, *Momotaro*."

The young man smiles a little. "Momotaro?"

"Yeah. Your cheeks look like pink peaches. Peach cheeks. 'Peach Boy.' Momotaro. So there."

"Momotaro," he laughs. *Normal.* That is the word he is looking for. Either this thing is far from her home, or she is toying with him. Many *yokai* still do that, he remembers from his former protector. *They like to play with their food before they eat it.* He looks away. "Well, I must go. Again, I apologize for disturbing you. Please excuse me."

She grabs him by the arm. "What's your name?"

"Zaniel," he admits with a sigh. It is pointless and often unwise to lie to a *yokai.*

"Oh. Cool name."

He does not dare relax at her calm tone. *They play with their food.* Perhaps it is safer to talk his way out. "You know," he begins, "there are many places to eat here. There's a whole village just down the road from here. I'm sure you know it. It's where all *yokai* go. It has all the food you could want."

She leans so close he can see himself in her big black eyes. "Food like *that?*" She gestures to the remains of the house.

"Um … maybe?"

The young man blinks. She is gone.

Zaniel leaves the garden, looking over his shoulder now and then, taking careful steps. The *yokai* does not sneak up behind him or leap out from the trees. By the time he reaches the end of the forest, he supposes she did not want to seduce and devour him after all.

The forest disappears at a cliff. Clouds line its face like a border and stretch into the bloody horizon. He hesitates at the edge, clinging to a nearby tree for stability. This place has always frightened him. He never knows what can be down there, waiting beneath the clouds. Is it a straight drop? Or would he roll down the mountain for miles and miles if he fell? *It doesn't matter, now.* He sits down and rests against the tree, closing his eyes. Soon, he will wake up to what he can only describe as a new life. *Everything is going to change — for the better,* he prays.

A rumble of thunder drowns out the last of his prayers. He opens his eyes. The blood-coloured sky is now thick with lavender clouds. Night is falling. He cannot make out the forest, save for a few lightning strikes that illuminate his surroundings, but then the trees in the distance catch fire. He sees the glow of flames brighten and hears a shriek in the distance. A shriek of panic, rage.

"No ... no!" *What's happening? Who could be doing this?* He knows the answers already. It is Akki, and Akki is angry. What he does not know is why. Was this all a test of loyalty, to see if he could stay on his toes? To see if he would throw himself at the first pretty face to come by and try to sway him? Zaniel is certain he will never know, even if he should dare to ask. And for the first time in years, he does not care. It was foolish to get his hopes up in the first place. He should have known better than to trust anything in this place.

That's the problem with dreams: you can't tell the good from the bad, and after a while, they blend into one.

Zaniel closes his eyes again and assumes a comfortable position. He prepares to awaken. The tumultuous thunder, the heat of the encroaching forest fire, the warmth of that *yokai*'s ebony eyes. He can feel them, even now, like a warm kiss.

"Goodnight, Momotaro."

His eyes fly open. The warm feeling on his skin dissipates the moment he does — the only thing he sees is the obsidian bracelet on his wrist, shimmering with cold light. As his body feels heavier and heavier, his bracelets vibrate. He feels creatures' eyes all around him, watching him. He feels relief that he is leaving this world. Then, he feels the regret that he may have lost his only chance to make a friend here. And then ...

"Damn." Zaniel sits upright in his bed, touching his shoulders and chest. "My jacket. I left it in the house."

It is true. The Yokai had eaten a perfectly good jacket.

PART I

one

ORANGE MARMALADE

光陰矢の如し

Time flies like an arrow

"Ima okina-EE-to, okurema-SOO, yo … Ima okina-EE-to, okurema-SOO, yo …"

Ah, the screeching chime of the alarm clock. I finish brushing my teeth before I poke my head out the bathroom door to look around my living room. It doesn't take long to locate the small mint-green robot ramming itself into the wall.

"Ima okina-EE-to, okurema-SOO, yo …"

"Sorry, little friend." I pick it up, pressing the snooze button. "There's no escape for either of us."

"Ohayou gozaimasu! Kyou, ganbatte —"

I toss it into my open closet. The tiny *plomp* of the robot landing on my folded futon tells me it survived the trip. I get dressed, then head to the kitchen to get my lunch and stuff it in my giant purse. Not a lot of room among the giant scissors, glue, markers, and construction paper, but I manage. I give myself one last glance-over in the reflection of the glass in my *genkan* door. The same "polite, professional, playful" businesswoman I always see stares back at me: white short-sleeved polo shirt, black dress pants, black work jacket, stone face. I force her to smile. Forget it. The "playful" part will come when it needs to.

I sigh again. Back to work today. Time to enjoy English.

I brace myself for smiling down the four flights of stairs to my building's front door, where three musical notes chime as the bolts slide out of place with *Star Trek*–like clicks. Outside, the giant constructivist painting that is my neighbourhood is ready for Halloween. The grey and white cuboid and cylinder apartments, once studded with greens and pinks on their balcony gardens, now have tiny orange pumpkins. The canopies of electric cables over the streets have a couple of plastic ghosts dangling from them. And, of course, there's me: the resident monster, emerging from her lair to frighten the passersby.

"*Mite, mite. Meccha gaijin ya na ... Kowaaaai ...*" a schoolgirl whispers to her friend as they walk past me. I unlock my bike and pretend not to notice I'm being described as scary. It's harder to ignore the guy sneaking a picture on his phone. I look up at the wrong moment. He runs away, shouting, "*Kowai, nigero!*" to someone down the street. Good to see the jerk train is right on time, like all trains in this country. Another shouter walks past my apartment with his entourage, which consists of five dudes dressed like they're going to the baseball stadium up the street. Surprisingly, there's one tall African American in their company. I can tell he's American by his accent.

"Hey! A SISTER!" he points at me. "How you doing?"

I manage a small shy wave in return. Others stare and whisper as I mind my own business and get my rusty, trusty bike unlocked. The sidewalk looks clear now. I wheel out from my parking space, ready to pedal, and almost run down a tiny man blocking my path.

I recognize his traditional outfit from the shrine down the street from my building. He must be a caretaker there. "Good morning." His words are slow, with sharp, pronounced consonants.

This is new. I'm wary, but more relieved that he isn't pissed off I almost mowed him down. "Good morning."

"How ... are ... you?"

"Um. I'm fine, thank you. Uh, how are you?"

"I ... am fine. Thank you." His face crinkles with laugh lines as he spreads his arms. "Welcome ... to Japan!"

"Oh. Thank you." I smile as I swing one leg over the bike. *"Ittekimasu?"* I offer, unsure.

"Itterasshai," he says, bowing, and continues down the street. I watch him go, clapping two blocks of wood behind his back. Okay, so most trains run on time in this country. Ninety-nine percent. No country is perfect, but Japan, sometimes you come close.

I speed past palm trees with makeshift scarecrows wrapped around their trunks. Looks like the shops have deemed it safe to break out the fake plastic leaves they all use over their marquees for fall, too. A 7-Eleven employee on a stepladder hangs up a sign for special autumn food out front. The City of Nishibe Post Office has also put up its Halloween stuff. Yagi-*sama*, the cartoon goat mascot, poses in the window with a witch's hat on its head and a pumpkin in its hands. Along the stadium and station approach, food vendors are setting up. The smells hit me as I read the signs over each stand: chicken yakitori, Kobe beef, *yakisoba* noodles, *takoyaki* ... my mouth waters as each word twinkles like lights. Farther down the main street, the lineups at Tully's Coffee are so far out the door it's impossible to tell who's there for free pumpkin spice latte samples and who's trying to catch the next train. So much for not getting stared at.

I walk my bike through the crowd, eyes down. Then, I take the detour under the train tracks, past the Tsutaya video rental store, the flower shop, and another row of small restaurants. I take another shortcut by the other shopping centre, bigger but less busy because it's farther from the station. I can smell the coffee from the second Tully's mixed with KFC, the popcorn and cotton candy in the video game arcade, the ramen stands' beer, all the delicious odours that permeate the air. I pop out onto a large intersection with a cluster of squat buildings, health clinics, and real estate agencies that play the company jingles whenever they're open. I lock up my bike at a rack in front of the tallest building and head inside. I take the elevator and press the button for the seventh floor. According to the tiny plastic strip of logos over the doors, there is only one company on that floor:

ZOZO'SSCHOOLOFGOOD ENGLISH
(EIKAIWA)

The elevator opens to a reception area that looks like the set of a 1970s children's education program. *The Electric Company* meets *Polka Dot Door*. Lots of neon orange, yellow, and green; dots and zigzags; identical clown faces with menacing grins; and speech bubbles that scream, "Hi, I'm Zozo! Let's enjoy English!" Sprinkled among photos of grinning children are hundreds of tiny Japanese characters on brochures and posters. My favourite co-worker, Yoshino, stands on a chair, adding Halloween decorations and past photos of students and teachers in their costumes. Two other teachers, Seri and Yuki, alternate handing her pictures and pieces of tape. And, of course, I see myself in a giant blow-up photograph in my good old gothic Tinker Bell costume. It's the one photo of me that goes up on the wall, every year, just in time for Halloween.

For some reason, the lobby is busy for a Tuesday morning. Several parents stand around our school manager as he waxes poetic about the company. Lieko, another teacher, stands behind him and nods after every sentence. She looks me up and down, then looks away. Most of the parents are too busy listening to the manager or whispering about how much Yoshino looks like Kanako Yanagihara to notice my arrival. Those that do stare. The tiny sectional where the guests sit is covered with unfinished foam puzzles and old toys. Somewhere in the melee I see our old malfunctioning Anpanman plush toy on the floor. Why is it even out of the staff room? And who are all these parents? What is going on here today?

Children fresh out of their lesson enjoy their freedom as their parents pick up school bags and gather shoes, chatting away in rapid-fire Japanese. The kids that notice me point and shout: "Ah! Belle-*sensei, ohayou gozaimasu!* Hello! How are you? I'm fine, thank you!"

"Hi, kids! How's it going?"

Lieko and Manager redirect their attention from the small crowd. Their heads follow me like hungry predators as I claim my high-fives from the kids. As always, I feel like I'm in a promotional video about expat *eikaiwa* life. An invisible camera watches me, catching the precise moment my mouth goes from neutral to a million watts when my eyes and those of my co-workers meet. Once again, the time has come to play my part as an essential cog in our corporate machine. I'm ready to greet everyone with my rehearsed morning-toothpaste-commercial enthusiasm in three, two, one ...

"*Ohayou gozaimasu!*" I bow. They don't return the smile, or the bow. Just a quick nod from Manager before he turns back to the parents. Maybe I'm in trouble. Or maybe it's just another Tuesday morning. Who knows with Manager. Lieko, on the other hand, is still talking to students like she didn't hear me at all.

Several kids run up to me for high-fives and go right back to fighting each other. One of the youngest retrieves the filthy Anpanman from the floor. She offers it to Lieko. "*Sensei, hai — douzo!*" she beams.

"Oh, *thank you*, Akiko-*chan*," Lieko sings, showing her pointy white teeth. "But you must say, 'Here you are!'" She doesn't make any gesture to take Anpanman from the little girl.

Confused, Akiko shrugs and runs up to me. "Belle-*sensei, douzo!*"

"Thanks, Akiko!" She's the sweetest, but I'm not touching this thing, either. It's probably from the eighties, maybe even older, and I don't think it's ever been washed. So instead, I smile and gesture every word. "Can *you* put *Anpanman* on the *table*, please?"

"*Hai!*" She throws the wretched toy onto the reception desk and runs over to her mother. "*Ganbatta*, Akiko-*chan!*" her mother says, giving her a giant hug. "*Eigo jouzu desu ne!*"

Lieko glares at me as I remove my shoes and trade them for my giant Tinker Bell slippers. Whatever. It's not my fault the company doesn't allow us to speak Japanese with the students. Doesn't mean there aren't sneaky ways to get around it. Ignoring her, I wade through the children and head for the staff room to stuff my purse into what little space there is in the staff cupboard.

Yoshino sticks another picture of a jack-o'-lantern to the wall before she looks down at me with a big grin. "*Ohayou*, Cybelle-*sensei!*"

"*Ohayou gozaimasu*, Yoshino-*sensei*. You look busy up there."

"It's Halloween!" she says with her light British lilt. "We can finally stop talking about EIKEN exams and celebrate. By the way, I like your shirt! Short sleeves — *very* brave."

I look down. "What? I haven't even taken off my jacket yet."

"I guessed. It is nice outside. And I don't see you switching to 'warm biz' anytime soon." She hops down, light-footed, from her chair. "By the way, I want to talk to you about something later. When are you free?"

"I got nothing until my Moms' trial at two."

"Aw. I have classes until then. Okay, I'll nab you around lunch, if that's no bother?" Manager interrupts her next sentence by calling her over. "*Hai!* We'll talk later! Oh yeah, there's a box of tea and maybe some cakes left in the staff room. The water in the kettle should still be hot."

"Cakes?"

"From the open house. There's plenty left. Dig in. 'Second breakfast!'" She adds in a whisper and sprints off to talk to Manager and some stern-faced parents.

BREAKFAST. I could smack myself. I didn't eat a thing this morning. I walked out the door on an empty stomach. *Cybelle, you idiot.* No wonder I'm so hungry. Wait a minute — did she say "open house?" That's new. No wonder I'm getting weird looks from strangers. Since when do we do open houses? What happened to Manager sulking behind the reception desk on a quiet Tuesday morning, grunting at everyone in lieu of words?

I slide the door open and slip into the hidden staff room. Glad to see it's empty, as usual for a Tuesday. I sign in on the computer, which flags me for clocking in over an hour early. Tsk, tsk. No wonder Manager gave me such a weird look when I greeted him. I shrug it off. At least the cupboard is still normal. I squeeze my purse into its usual space among the other giant purses, textbooks, CDs, old cassette tapes no one dares throw away, stuffed animals, the kindergarteners' personal art supplies, puzzles, markers, and crayons for kids in the lobby, and the infinite number of files and binders of track records, invoices, and handouts. I grab one of the stools at the bench (just big enough for three or four people to sit next to each other) with my own binder of English miscellany and jot things down. I have plenty of space to spread out and work. Today I only have three classes, which means lots of peace, quiet, and time to plan for the week. And what luck, there are a few of my favourite *conbini* cakes — lemon Baumkuchen — next to our good old electronic kettle.

As I munch away and sip some green tea, a high-pitched voice rings through the paper-thin walls. Someone shouting about civility? Being civil? The door slides open and bangs against the wall, making me jump out of my skin. Lieko sticks her head in and glares at me.

"*Cybelle,*" she hisses with perfect pronunciation. "*Come outside. Didn't you hear your own name?*" She walks away in the middle of her last sentence. I follow her out to the lobby, anyway, where Manager gestures to a small boy hiding behind his mother.

"Cybelle-*sensei,*" he sings. "This is Sotaro."

From between his mother's legs Sotaro sticks out his tongue. I try to not look as I bow to her. Manager continues to repeat my name in the same three-syllable tune as he talks to the mother in slow, hesitant English.

"Cybelle-*sensei* is the Native English Teacher at our school. She is from Canada. Her English is very good. The students love to enjoy English with Cybelle-*sensei.*"

I nod after each sentence with a nice big smile. When Manager switches to natural-speed Japanese I continue to nod and smile at all the right pauses. Sotaro watches me from his mother's crotch in fascination.

"Sotaro-*kun,*" Manager sings, "say hello to Cybelle-*sensei,* please!"

The moment is gone. His mother pulls Sotaro out from behind her and right away he pretends to pass out on the floor. His mouth hangs open so wide soon there's a pool of saliva soaking the carpet. Manager laughs along with Lieko, now behind him.

"Aw, he is sleepy," she croons.

We all stand there laughing awkwardly until Sotaro and his mother leave. Manager turns to me. "Thank you, Cybelle-*sensei!*" He says it without smiling. He then shakes his head, like he just changed his mind about something, and turns to Yoshino. He tells her in Japanese that she did well to recruit Sotaro, and that she should sum up the details of his trial lesson for me in English. Then he says something about my interview at two o'clock and turns away.

Wait, what?

"Hang on," I call after him, forgetting my contractual obligation to pretend I don't understand Japanese. "I have my Moms' trial class at two."

"Ah, sorry, no. Maybe, no Moms' today. Lieko has Zozo II class today but many students have flu. So, we have to cancel. So, maybe, no mothers will come today. But, good news is, we have interview."

Ugh. Another "riveting" teacher interview. Good news, my ass. "Okay. What's the teacher's name?"

"It's … *nandakke* … one moment."

Manager takes off to riffle through papers behind the reception desk. Meanwhile, Lieko eyes me with her predatory gaze. "Her name is Misaki Wada," she says, her voice stiff. "She studied English in university and lived in Australia for one month. I read her file from Head Office and memorized all of it. Manager wants me to interview her in Japanese, so I must know everything about her. Maybe I should do both interviews, Manager," Lieko raises her voice another octave and shows all her teeth. "To save time?"

"*Fuzaken ja nee yo!*" Manager scoffs. "Native speaker *ga hitsuyou da!*"

Ouch. I don't need to be fluent to understand how pissed Manager is that she even asked. I struggle to keep my attention focused on photos along the wall while he continues to yell in Lieko's face about her having something to prove and, oh shit, where did I put that file, get out of my way. He practically shoves her and disappears into the staff room, leaving the two of us alone. I didn't think this could get any more awkward. I follow after Manager: anything beats standing in an empty lobby with the world's scariest woman. Without my Moms' class, I don't have anything to do before my three lessons except maybe eat my lunch, but it's not even eleven. I'll find something to do.

Ignoring Manager's outbursts at the other teachers, I make a few more self-laminated cut-outs, organize all my work for the week and even for next Tuesday, and attach a fresh interview questionnaire to a clipboard. This all takes about half an hour. I decide to make a sunset with construction paper and coloured foam for my Baby Zero class on Friday: I can teach them "Mr. Sun" and let them touch the picture.

The wall clock says it's almost twelve. *Now* I have nothing to do but eat. I'm the first one to take out her lunch, which gets me a few wary glances from Lieko, but I'm out of ideas. Yoshino and Seri join me a few minutes later. I get up to use the washroom and come back to Yoshino in front of the computer, Lieko in my seat next to Seri, and my bento bag on top of the photocopier with no explanation. Manager offers me his seat and leaves to eat in Room One by himself. He's not one for lunchtime conversation with five women, anyway. I don't blame him. All anyone ever talks about is Zozo-related drivel, like there's nothing else in the world. Lieko starts it off:

"Yoshino-*sensei*. How did your lesson go?"

"Do you mean Zozo Zone 1, or Zozo Zone 3?"

"I mean, how did your Zozo Zone 1 lesson go?"

"It went well."

"I see. What class will you teach next?"

"Next, I have a prep period."

"I beg your pardon?"

"I mean, I have a preparation period."

"I see." Lieko takes another tiny bite of her food. "Yoshino-*sensei*, how is our branch ranking?"

Yoshino takes her time to chew. She looks like she's thinking. "We are doing our best," she says. That can't mean anything good.

"How many more students do we need by the end of the month?"

Seri changes the subject. "I have a question first, Lieko-*sensei*. Where did you buy that teriyaki chicken? It looks good."

"No. It's too greasy, and I should have used more sauce."

"No, no, it really looks good."

"Thank you. You are too kind."

Gag me. *Japanese hornet stings have got to be less painful than this.*

After a few minutes of such pleasantries, all the teachers whip out their smartphones. Not me; I devour my rice pilaf, hamburger patties, and cabbage salad before taking out my trusty old flip phone. With my lunch gone, there's no better time to bury myself in imaginary text messages while I'm really playing Snake or Minesweeper. Today I have an actual text.

Cybelle, it's your mother. We need to talk. BULLY IS GETTING MARRIED. So come home! Love and kisses

"What?!" My outburst disrupts the other teachers from their text marathons. Heads swivel like birds as they stare at me. I don't have time for textbook talk. I squeeze by them all to exit the staff room and find an empty classroom for privacy. It must be almost midnight back home. I try several times, anyway. Every time the machine picks up; it's still my own voice I hear telling me no one is home. Oh well, it was worth a shot. A thousand yen well spent. I head back to the staff room. Lieko is still eating. Yoshino has swapped her lunch for a giant binder and several pens and is now working on the computer.

"You okay, Cyb?" Yoshino asks me. "You have some kind of emergency?"

Aw, someone does care. "No, nothing bad. My baby sister got engaged."

"Whoa! Seriously?! Hey, congrats! ... Or not. You don't look too excited."

"No, no. I am. Just dreading the phone calls between now and this wedding." The word feels like a foreign object lodged in my throat.

"It'll be fine. Just don't tell your mom about 'Christmas cake.'"

"Too late, she googled it ages ago."

The door slides open. Manager steps in, looks at me and Yoshino, waves his hands awkwardly — "Ah! Sorry. *Atode, ne?*" — and leaves the room.

"Say!" Yoshino plops down on the stool next to me. "Cybelle-*sensei*, are you interested in coming with me to a party Saturday?"

No.

"What kind of party?"

"It's this Japanese-English language exchange party at Kappa Garappa, in Osaka; it's run by a networking company that specializes in 'foreign friendships.' They'll have snacks, and a special drink menu. The thing is, all my other girlfriends are too shy to speak to guys, let alone foreign ones. I'd rather go with someone who is confident enough to, you know, talk!"

"Are you sure about this? I mean, yeah, I'm all for socializing, but ... I don't know. You might want to go with someone who isn't, you know ..." I mutter under my breath: "What's a polite way to say 'penis-repellent'?"

Yoshino laughs, hard. "*Uso!* All the guys will be dying to talk to you! You're so cute! If they don't want to look like assholes, they'll have to talk to me, too. And you can bring your friends!"

Lieko makes a snorting sound as she covers her upturned lips. Yoshino and I redirect our attention back to our food, but not before Yoshino widens her eyes and makes stabbing motions with one of her pens, which makes *me* snort in turn. That wipes the grin off Lieko's face quick. By some miracle we hold in our giggles until Lieko picks up her lunch and storms off. Whatever. I turn my mind back to this party. I've never had much success in making friends outside of work. Plus, I haven't spent time with Yoshino away from Zozo in years. Maybe it won't be so bad.

At 1:45 p.m. Misaki Wada steps off the elevator. She's about five foot two and looks young, like she just finished high school. She freezes when she sees me come out of the staff room. Manager greets her and tells her she'll have an interview with Lieko and another with me, in English.

"*Eh?!*" She loses all composure. "*Hontou?! Eigo de?! Iyada, dekinai!*" She goes on and on about how she can't speak English. Everyone assures her that I'm "very nice" and they wish her the best of luck. Manager gives me a pointed look as Lieko takes her into the private room, now cleared of all signs of anyone eating there.

"Another woman. *Mattaku,*" he curses under his breath. He clears his throat and asks me, in English, "What do you think about her?"

"Um, well ..."

He nods. "Yes, I agree. I didn't like her attitude. About English. With you. I think, not a good sign. Don't you?"

"Well, yeah," I admit. Manager stares at me like I should say something more. "You think she's nervous?"

"Hmm. No. I think, no. Last week, remember, your interview with Tabata-*san*. She was very happy to speak English with you. And your interview last last week, Koyama-*san*, also enjoyed English. And I remember Yoshino-*sensei*, when you gave her interview; *very* happy to speak English! Maybe too happy. But this Wada-*san*, hmmm ..." He sucks air through his teeth. "Ah, excuse me." He walks off, still grumbling.

I wait patiently until I see Lieko stand up, shake Miss Wada's hand — an uncomfortable, flaccid handshake I don't look forward to — and open the door for me to come in. I take a seat and after introducing ourselves, we begin.

"So, Wada-*san*, tell me about yourself."

She sits there, staring at me until Lieko sighs and translates for her. "*Anou,*" Miss Wada begins. "I finished university and went to Australia in summer. I came back to Japan two months ago."

"I see. And why do you want to work for Zozo?"

More staring, more silence. Lieko again translates; this time, Misaki Wada answers in Japanese. Lieko gives me a look from the corner of her eye. I skip several questions and decide to ask something from the bottom of my list. "Thank you, Wada-*san*. Um, what three things do you want to do in the future that you've never done before?"

"*Eeto* ..." her eyes search the ceiling. She answers in English this time. "First thing: I want to travel abroad. Second thing: I want to marry — ah, I want to get married. Ah, third thing: I want to have a baby."

"Those are all good answers, but, since you studied in Australia, you've already travelled abroad. Is there anything else you'd like to do in the future?"

Staring at me, Misaki tilts her head back and forth several times until Lieko translates for her a third time. They have a brief discussion in Japanese about how important it is to work, get married, and have babies, until Lieko turns to me and says, "She didn't understand your question. I think we should end the interview here."

I can't help but agree. We all bow and shake hands. Misaki holds my hand like I've handed her a soggy Kleenex. "*Anou ne,*" Misaki says. "May I ask a question? You are from America?"

"No, I'm Canadian."

"Ah. But this Zozo school, has teacher from America?"

"Um ... no?"

"Eh? Why?"

Lieko explains to her that I'm the only Native English Teacher at our branch. They have a brief conversation over the fact that the company hires teachers from other countries, not just the U.S., before Misaki finally bows her thanks to everyone and leaves.

Manager is glad to see her go. He rants in Japanese to every other co-worker who comes close: how will she speak to the students in English, what is Head Office playing at, how will we ever get up to quota, she should get herself a husband and sign her *own* babies up for lessons if she wants to help us out so much ... Oh well. I guess Misaki did not impress him.

Once I clear the bench of all my props and paperwork, I hear the elevator doors open and my two kindergarten girls scream hello. We spend the first part of our lesson singing the "Hello Song" and the "Welcome Song" with my Jibanyan hand puppet, who holds up flash cards for them to shout out English vocabulary. For every word they say correctly, I put a magnetic star on the whiteboard beside their names. Then we make cookies and cupcakes out of pastel-coloured playdough and talk about desserts over cups of imaginary tea. They talk to each other and to me in Japanese and I reply in English. That's how our playtime usually goes.

Momoko pokes my leg. "*Sensei*, jack-o'-lantern *wa aru no?*"

"I don't," I tell her. "But we can get one. Do you want a jack-o'-lantern?"

"Yay, jack-o'-lantern! I love jack-o'-lantern!" Motoka throws her donut in the air by accident. We spend the rest of class having a food fight with our desserts. For earning so many stars beside their names, I award the girls two stickers each.

"Okay, ladies, let's sing the 'Goodbye Song'!" Momoko and Motoka promptly take each other by the hand and extend their chubby digits toward me. We make a circle and sing: "*English school is over, we are going home; goodbye, goodbye, we are going home!* Goodbye!"

"*Sensei*, bye-bye! See you again!"

After the girls leave for Lieko's class, I head to Room Five and teach my bilingual Zone VI students, Riko and Reiji, about different school subjects. We play several vocabulary games with playing cards. Afterward, once my private lesson in Room One with Kennichi is over and I have a friendly chat with him and his mom for a few minutes, I organize my box of toys and lesson props for tomorrow. Then I grab a big City of Nishibe–approved plastic bag to go through all the empty classrooms, as per my Tuesday duty. I bypass Room Five, where Lieko is inside with a group of adults. *Way* too old and far too professional to be students here. They must be from Head Office. This is new. I can only guess what she's talking about, but whatever it is, it is not an exciting topic. One guy is out cold, and the others don't look too far off from joining him in Sleepyland.

Well, that's it. 7:00 p.m. The workday is over. Good; I'm hungry. I'm also a little surprised. Sotaro wasn't all that excruciating, and I half expected one fight between the kindergarteners or at least a complaint or two from Kennichi about how tired he was, but no, everything today was ... well, perfect. I sign out on the computer, yank my purse out from under Lieko's, unsure of how it got there, and pick up my jacket.

Manager is standing right at the door when I slide it open. "Ah, Cybelle! Eh ..." He looks down at my purse. "Are you going home?"

"Yes, Manager. I left the garbage in the usual place — I didn't get to Room Five though, Lieko's still in there now, so ..."

"Ah, ah, yes ..." he pauses, still blocking my path as he looks down the hall at Room Five. We can hear Lieko talking to the office workers. "Okay, you don't have to do it," he decides, like there was ever a choice. "Ah! Cybelle! You have emergency? Go back to Canada? Soon?"

"My sister's getting married."

"Ah, I see ..." Manager hisses with a stern look. "So, maybe ... you have to go back to Canada ... before April?"

"I don't know yet, Manager," I say through a tight, clenched smile. "But I doubt it."

"Ah. Hmm. I see. But ... if you go back before April ... hmmm, it will be, very bad, I think. Your students will miss your lessons. And you."

Behind him, Yoshino squeezes an arm to grab something off the photocopier. She's trying not to laugh at the constipated look I must have on my face. "Manager," she says, "I think we should wait until Cybelle-*sensei* tells us when this wedding is. You know, before we start worrying about it?"

He crosses his arms. "Yes," he says after a while. "*Shou ga nai, na.* It can't be helped." He explains to Yoshino in Japanese, please tell Cybelle to tell me as soon as she knows, but please tell her how bad it will be if she has to take vacation before April. Maybe she should go home during New Year's vacation instead. Yoshino looks like she's trying to think of the politest way to reply but the elevator doors chime with the arrival of a guest or a student, so she leaves us alone. "Ah, Cybelle, do you remember Sotaro?"

"Yes, I do."

"Ah, good, good," Manager nods, rubbing his hands. "Sotaro will come back tomorrow for a trial lesson with … you … and Yoshino-*sensei*, so please … ah, please prepare a trial lesson. For Sotaro."

"Okay, no problem."

"Tomorrow morning. After Zippo and Zappo."

I nod.

"Please."

I have run out of ways to respond. He still isn't budging from the doorway.

"So … when will you prepare for the trial lesson? Before you go home? *Ne?*"

"I already have a trial lesson kit ready." I'm trained to have things ready for such occasions. The other nine times out of ten that he doesn't tell me beforehand about trial lessons I am still prepared. What is this man's problem? I'm *starving*.

"Ah, ah, okay. That's great. Well …" He still doesn't move. His eyebrows are still furrowed as he concentrates on what I hope is my purse and not my boobs. "Ah!" he claps his hands like he just remembered something. "Head Office sent you a form about re-contracting!"

"I know."

"Have you ... thought about it? You must think about it."

Is he serious? "That form isn't due for another three weeks." There's no point in explaining that I haven't decided what to write on it, but he's never been this anal about it before. I'm always the one who harasses him for the form in the first place. Why does he want a decision now? What's the rush?

"Ah, ah, okay. That's great ..." Manager trails off, resuming his X-ray vision again. Room Five opens and a chorus of polite Japanese spills out into the hallways, diverting Manager's attention. Finally, he relinquishes my personal space. I squeeze out from the staff room with a genuine, time-for-dinner smile. I'm free.

"Well, have a great night, Manager! *Osaki ni* —"

"Ah!" Manager cuts me off. "Wait! You stay. I mean, don't go home. I mean, one moment!"

My freedom is short-lived. After he and Lieko bow to the polished-looking office workers, Manager gestures to me and speaks in super-fast, super-polite Japanese. I smile and pretend not to understand a word while I wait for the English translation.

"This is Cybelle-*sensei*, the Native English Teacher." The office workers all take turns saying their names, "nice to meet you," and shaking my hand. "She is from Canada. She is very good at English," Manager continues. They ooh and aah and applaud. "And she is very good at making food."

"I am?"

"Yes! You always have delicious lunch."

"Oh. Yeah, I guess I'm okay."

Our conversation initiates more applause. Manager explains something in more detail to them, again using the politest level of Japanese. Meanwhile, Lieko nods, smiling at the workers and sneaking a deadly glare at me. I think I know what I'm hearing, and I pray I'm wrong because it sounds like he's talking about discussing me with Lieko. Maybe Manager is suggesting ideas to them, maybe it's all conjecture. I know for sure that if he lets me go without translating, I'm in the clear.

"Okay, thank you very much, Cybelle-*sensei*. Now you can say, '*Otsukaresama desu!*'"

"*Ehhh?*" The office workers stare at me, wide-eyed, looking me up and down. "*Nihongo de?*"

Manager nods, hands clasped, begging me with his eyes to respond. I feel like a trained pet being compelled to do a trick. *Son of a* ... "*Otsukaresama desu.*" I bow.

Everyone bursts into applause before returning the courtesy. "*Otsukaresama desu*, Cybelle-*sensei*! See you again!"

I switch out of my slippers and grab my shoes like I'm in a hurry to go somewhere important, then smile and wave at everyone until the elevator doors close on Manager's high-pitched words. I don't want to think about what he might be telling them about me. Manager was saying something about ... damn, what was the word? *Kaku?* Writing? No, that's not right. Unless he meant 'status'? Which is not Lieko's business to begin with. And now that I think about it, what was up with Manager talking about our 'quota' earlier? *What the hell is going on around here?*

As I drown in the hum of the elevator, I concentrate on what to have for dinner. I need to erase all memory of Manager's creepy eyes, Lieko's raptor grin, and this impending trial lesson with a demonic child. As for my re-contracting form, I still have time. I don't know what Manager was getting in my face about. It isn't due until the end of October. Another thing I need to push down into the recesses of my brain, behind this looming headache. I need to eat. What do I have in my fridge? Well, no — Zozo's fridge. In Zozo's apartment. It's not mine. It's a place to sleep and keep my stuff. If I'm not re-contracting, I have to get used to letting these things go. Hmm ... maybe I'll grab the first thing I see on the way home. I don't feel like cooking, but I can't remember the last time I was this hungry. McDonald's it is.

"*An*-punch! *An*-kick! *Sore ike!*"

I jump out of my skin and scream. Somehow, the world's oldest Anpanman toy got left behind in the elevator. Its legs kick back and forth in the guise of flying, but the toy stays in the corner of the tiny floor. How had no one noticed it was here? Strange that no one thought to return it. Well, I have no plans to touch it.

"*An*-punch! *An*-kick! *Sore ike!*"

I shudder. I decide to leave it in the elevator and let it ride back up. The doors slide open and I book it out of there. I can still hear the toy, its gears grinding with the dying battery's efforts to turn out one last recorded phrase. .

"*An*-punch! *An*-kick! *Mata ne!*"

Ew. Creepy. I can't wait for someone to throw that thing out.

Outside, I unlock my bike and head to McDonald's. The bank has changed its flower garden so it's full of marigolds in the shape of a jack-o'-lantern. When I ride under the highway bridge there's a sudden gust of cold wind, carrying that chilly Halloween feeling that gives me goosebumps, even under my suit jacket. I can also detect the telltale fragrance of fries and teriyaki burgers in the air even before I go inside and place my order. Patience, stomach. We're almost there.

"Potato fry, chicken nugget *okyaku-sama!*" the young teller sings to me as I dig out my vibrating phone and flip it open. I figure it's another text from my mother, firing messages at me to call home. Instead, I read: *Dress professionally this week.*

The next one reads: *You have a very important trial lesson tomorrow night.*

And the third: *Wear a skirt from now on.*

I snap my phone closed to get my food and thank the smiling employee. Talk about weird. I'd assume it was a wrong number if these messages didn't sound so passive-aggressive. Who at Zozo could have texted me? Not Manager, there would be a dozen "maybes" thrown in. No way in heck Yoshino would text me like this. Lieko, maybe? She doesn't have my number, let alone the authority to text me this kind of crap. It must have been Manager, telling me what to do like it's still my first day on the job. I'll err on the side of caution, wear a stupid skirt, and try to manage the kids as best as I can in *seiza*. If I want to re-contract, I must continue to play my role as a cog in our efficient corporate machine. Until then, I'm taking this giant bag of fries and nuggets to watch some good old Japanese DVDs. *Rinkan* and *Spirited Away*, here I come.

As if the decorations all over Zozo and the neighbourhood weren't enough, my local convenience store has also primped for Halloween. I park my bike in front of my building and walk back to 7-Eleven to get more food. I'm that hungry. The shelves are covered in black cats, orange pumpkins, purple witches, and white ghosts. I chat with the manager while he heats up my chicken *soboro* and chestnut rice in the microwave. He shows me the new desserts they got. I'm tempted to get the expensive graham crackers (since when do Japanese convenience stores sell those?) but then I see two Halloween Winnie-the-Pooh mugs with cups of pudding inside. The manager asks me if I'm excited for Halloween and whether I'm going to dress up. Last year's costume, like always, which I call "Tinker Hell." I throw in one *nana-chiki* for the road and pay up.

People stare at me as they pass the 7-Eleven, where I devour my fried chicken in under a minute. *"Gaijin, mite, kowai ..."* some of them say. Whatever. I have too much on my mind. Soon it'll be Christmas, and a few months after that I'll be starting a brand-new year with brand-new faces if I don't screw up the courage to haul ass out of Zozo. But ... to do what? Go back home? Prepare for my sister's wedding? Brace myself for the backlash that will come with it all? Or do I sign up for another year of being treated like I just stepped off a plane after a few episodes of *Sailor Moon* with three phrases on my tongue? Do I continue going to work like the star of an expat promotional video series in which every episode is my first day?

My stomach growls.

"All right, all right," I say without thinking. "Let's get some of this food into you."

An elderly woman stares at me, blood-red eyes wide with shock as I walk past her. Maybe she heard me talking to my stomach, maybe not. I don't think about it too much. Japan has seen stranger things than me.

two
EYES OF FLAME

鬼も十八番茶も出花
Everything has its time

In the human world, people are asleep. Most people. Not long after the stations shut their gates and their employees make their way home, the downtown core of Osaka buzzes with life. Like firecrackers lit by unseen pranksters, lights flash and bells and whistles go off along the main streets; those still out and about are overwhelmed with excitement ... excitement, and alcohol. Automatic sliding doors that lead to bars, clubs, pachinko parlours, video arcades, and karaoke establishments swallow up new victims as they regurgitate old ones back out onto the streets, poorer and drunker than before. People stagger from the howling cacophony to cold, abandoned stations, to find that their last trains left half an hour ago. They turn to one another, shrug, laugh, and stagger back to the fray. *"Shou ga nai, na ..." It cannot be helped*. Nothing left to do but move on to other bars until morning. They flood the convenience stores on every corner, stock up on anti-hangover juice, and hit the streets for round two (or three, or four).

The fascinating part of the nightlife is not the salarymen throwing their boss up in the air like pizza dough, or the karaoke employees in *One Piece* costumes and giant electrified sandwich boards, or the tricked-out Lambos flying down the streets, their underbodies lit with violent shades of neon pink and purple. Nor is it the man in a giant Jafar costume handing out flyers for an Arabian-themed restaurant. It is the people in the fray who are completely incongruous with one another, their surroundings and their country, their time in history and location in space. There are the usual symptoms of a night out in Osaka. A young woman dressed like a space cadet sings into a loudspeaker, presumably for money. A man in a Pikachu costume holds up a sign for an *izakaya*, screaming for customers, straining his already-wrecked vocal cords. Snack bar–bound professionals with neckties around their heads bump against young couples in search of affordable love hotels. A game centre blasts ear-piercing pop hits as scantily clad hostesses lining the street dance along. "Where's my samurai? Where?!" they screech to one another.

Then there are the weird symptoms. A young man — a university student, perhaps — comes along in poofy pink pants, a red beret tilted to the side of his face, and real wooden clogs that echo off the granite sidewalk, even in all this noise. A cocky mishmash of European stereotypes that make one wonder what part of his own culture he is trying to disguise. He looks like he is on his way to a very hoity-toity art class. He passes a gaggle of girls — no, full-grown women who look ten years younger than they truly are — all dressed in matching floral *mori* outfits, carrying matching wicker baskets in the crooks of their right arms, running to an unseen destination, as if late to an afternoon picnic in a British forest. Not ten minutes later a teenager sports baggy jeans that sag to his bottom and a brown baseball hat turned to the side that bears the name "Marcus Garvey" in calligraphic letters. As he walks, he turns his head at the last second, showing what is written on the back of his hat in the same font: GANJA. *Quite the ensemble: he must be on his way to jail.*

The *yokai* named Akki chuckles at his own cruel joke. A flush-faced, muscle-bound giant taking up half of the expansive sidewalk with his enormous size, the nightmare demon squats in front of a convenience store ablaze with fluorescents. The frightening creature poses as a human dressed head to toe in midnight: a black *haori* jacket stretches over his broad shoulders, humongous matching *hakama* pants brush the pavement and black *waraji* straw sandals wrap around his massive feet. He dangles a relit cigarette in one large hand and a tiny empty rainbow-coloured poptop coffee can in the other. His eyes are closed beneath two furrowed eyebrows that look more like black flames sweeping across his expansive forehead into a sleek, sumo-style *chonmage* topknot. He stands out far more than the night owls that flock around him, and everyone finds him terrifying, in spite of the friendly tune he murmurs under his breath:

"*Ho, ho, hotaru koi …*" Nothing happens.

Pedestrians who notice him cross the street, or circle so far and wide around him they would rather risk bumping into one another than come within three feet of him. Some mistake him for a lost samurai cosplayer but dare not disturb him to take a picture. They do not notice his chubby fingers are decked with several gold rings that do not match his outfit. Those that dare do anything risk tiny glares over their shoulders but keep their thoughts to themselves, unaware that he can see and hear them all. *Another dangerous thug,* some think with a shake of their heads. A couple of aggressive-looking *obaachans* think, *This city has gone to hell.* Police cruisers slow down, their drivers pretend not to look at him, but they do not stop. *Good,* Akki thinks to himself. Cops make him sick with rage.

"Acchi no mizu wa nigaizo," he sings, *"kocchi no mizu wa amaizo …"* Still nothing.

Across the street, two Matsumoto Kiyoshi employees shout a few announcements about their special deal: fifteen percent off the anti-hangover juice for the next couple of hours. The suddenness of their voices stirs the *yokai*; one eye winks open. Not so many people around now, he opens the other and allows his glowing green gaze to take in his surroundings. An ambush of women run into the coffee shop next to the Lawson behind him. They appear to be brand-name types: A Bathing Ape tote bags, Rodeo Crowns shirts, and it looks like one of their skirts says NEGRO LEAGUE down the side. They move so fast Akki can only catch a glimpse of writing on the last woman's baseball cap: CHUBBY GANG.

The words float on the air and translate, their meaning permeates his mind, like music. He bursts out laughing, scaring the people who have just crossed the street to avoid him. Were it not for the gallons of cheap sake sloshing around in his gullet, he would not be in such a good mood. Deep down, he can feel the decades of anger built up in his veins as he has watched the nation sink deeper and deeper into what he sees as its own multicultural mire. He gulps down the last of the Boss Rainbow Mountain Blend coffee in his hand and wonders if he is the last "real" thing left awake in this city — a sobering notion that sends chills up his Herculean spine.

"Ho, ho, hotaru koi …" Akki sighs.

Across the street, another herd of young women, sweaty and fresh from a nightclub, run toward the drugstore. They could be quintuplets with their matching micro-shorts, stiletto heels, lacy white tops, milk-tea-coloured hair, and runny layers of eye makeup. They stop to examine a display of collagen drinks as two U.S. Marines, far from their base, pass by. *"Mite — gaijin! Gaijin! Ehhh!"* They shriek over the drugstore announcer and the city din, as they dance around the two men, fawning over their biceps. *"Meccha kakkoii!"* the women add once they are out of earshot.

The *yokai's* eyes become daggers. "Fuckin' *gaijin*," he mutters. *That's what these dumb-ass bitches go for, huh? Too drunk out of their skulls to recognize a* real *man when they see one? How can anyone be so stupid? This is what's wrong with society.* He considers throwing his coffee can at them, but it is too small to hit multiple targets. He lets his anger pass; he is too lazy to transform and scrap with anyone tonight. *Fuck these skinny, shriekin' little cunts. Squawkin' crazed hens.* He wishes he were a farmer and it was back in the day. Then no one would question his actions: ripping feathers, snapping necks, crushing beaks under his sandals, taking turns punting them down the street into a giant vat of frying oil. *Cheaper than that KFC crap and better quality to boot. Human flesh: nothin' like it.*

The young women squish together and run across the street, bowing to a stopped taxi. They hobble toward the *conbini*. Their voices drop to hushed whispers. Now they are pointing at him. The *yokai's* head turns as one blurts out an ill-timed, *"Ehhh, samurai mitai — meccha sexy, na?"*

Oh, my. This is unexpected. He nods and raises his can in wary salutation. They wave back but cannot maintain their composure. They scream like immature teenagers — *"Kyaa! Kyaa, ikemen!"* — and run into the *conbini*, knocking down a poor, inebriated salaryman on the way. The salaryman stumbles right into the spot where the *yokai* sits, leaving him with a slurred *"Oh! Suman na,"* unaware that he has phased right through one of the most notorious creatures of the night. Instead, the salaryman chalks that chill up his spine to the seasonal temperature change and continues down the street.

On the other side of the Lawson's giant glass window some of the women jump up and down and watch him while the timid ones pretend to look at magazines. The *yokai* smirks. He feels his cheeks and other parts of his body grow warm. He rises to his feet, drains the last few drops of coffee down his throat, and haphazardly tosses the can at the receptacle behind him (to the chagrin of those passing by, it lands wide of the mark — he does not care; someone will pick it up; Lawson employees know what they signed up for) and rescinds his earlier insults. *Gettin' laid is gettin' laid*, he thinks to himself.

The *yokai* strikes a pose to play cool. He knows better than to go running into the store like a desperate sex addict. *Don't do anythin'*, he thinks. *Don't make the first move. Bitches love a challenge. Any minute now, one of them'll come back out to chat you up.* All he must do is bide his time. He believes that is what Zaniel would do. Without him, there is little else he can do in his current form except hope for the best.

Any minute now ...

It looks like the women have established a plan when someone passes the *yokai* from behind, oblivious to his size and dangerous demeanour. If anyone in the nightlife crowds sticks out like a sore thumb, it is the waiflike, shades-sporting high school student who is, of course, not on her way to or from school but not a working hostess, either. She seems the right size, the right age to be a teenage girl; face and skin like a doll, like porcelain but not as pale, extremely long black flowing hair in a perfect *hime* cut. Her uniform is genuine, complete with the insignia above her right breast, red ribbon, red bow tie, and black jacket designed for autumn weather. As if to confuse people even more, her *seifuku* skirt is hiked up as high as a *seifuku* skirt can go. Her bleach-white fluffy socks billow over blood-red Chuck Taylors, exposing her smooth calves and fleshy thighs to the night breeze. By some unseen power she walks without the dread of cold or fear of night.

She now stands at a crosswalk leading toward a *shoutengai* shopping street that leads deeper into the heart of downtown to where all the bars, nightclubs, and arcades lie, where things get lower down and dirty. She knows her beauty and does not care; her concerns lie far beyond the opinions of those staring in suspicion and awe.

Fuckin' nice legs, too. Real *nice.* The *yokai* would recognize them anywhere. *Damn.*

Now the *yokai* must choose, for the crosswalk lights are about to change. If he waits, he may spend his evening in the company of several women, but he risks losing sight of the teenage-looking girl. The *gyaru* brigade is still in reconnaissance, pushing each other inside the Lawson and swatting each other away. He hears every word: "No, no, I can't! *You* go talk to him!" He looks back at the girl waiting for the crosswalk, then peeks over his shoulder at the women in the *conbini*, stirring up another round of squealing. He groans out loud, his giant head dunking backward to curse the night sky. He has no choice; no one else is coming. *And these matchstick-legged bitches take too long.* "*Immortal*" *don't mean I got all fuckin' day.*

A red flashing hand on the crosswalk cuts off the last electronic notes of a melancholic tune. The *yokai*'s arms pump back and forth as he runs; people clear out of his way to avoid his unintentional haymakers, unaware that they would do no harm.

"Phew! Made it." He stops right beside the girl and looks her up and down. "Hey there. *Hisa-bisa, na?* Haven't seen *you* in a while. You hungry? You *look* hungry."

She does not answer. He offers her the last of his cigarette, first putting it to his lips and lighting it with his fingers. She accepts it, examines it, then places it on her tongue and curls the entire thing into her mouth. She chews three times and swallows. The *yokai* looks on, pleased. The light changes and the tune of *"Toryanse"* plays, cueing everyone to cross.

"*Uwaa,*" he stretches and cracks his neck. A couple nearby leaps at the sound of his popping bones. "Well, *I'm* still starvin'. I found this great place, you'll love it. It's new, but very old school. They got everythin'. I'm talkin', *everythin'.* And *don't* tell me you've already eaten. I won't take that shit for an answer. Tonight's my treat." He pauses, looking her up and down several times with a comical grin. "Don't take this the wrong way, but those shades don't exactly work with that getup. I mean, it's sexy, but ... where's your backpack? Your purse? You at least got a cellphone or any of those stupid knick-knacks girls obsess over these days? Guys around here might get the wrong impression about a chick like you this time of night. All right, you don't gotta say nothin'. You're safe with me, 'kid.'"

The girl walks on, oblivious to the loud brash man walking in step with her as he raves about this mysterious, exclusive restaurant he knows. Back at the Lawson, the young women finalize their plan to chat him up, scan up and down the street, and — after an extensive argument and a lot of incessant whining — confirm that he is long gone. It ruins the rest of their evening. No one who approaches them that night is as good-looking. In time, they fight over what it would have taken to attract a cosplayer *that* good-looking (well, they are almost sure he was a cosplayer) and by the time the first train arrives half of them are not even on speaking terms. One falls asleep on the way home, half-drooling on her friend's shoulder. In her dreams, a beautiful young man — the kind her mother wants her to meet one day, the complete opposite of her type — sits next to her on the train, strikes up a polite conversation. She guesses he may be half-Japanese, but between the train and the hotel in the middle of nowhere, she never thinks to ask. In the penthouse suite, she meets the black-clad samurai, who (as she had expected) gives her the best sex of her life. She wakes up at the end of the train line, miles away from her stop, with an irrepressible grin and a craving for whiskey sours.

"By the way," the *yokai* says to his companion, "I know we got lots to catch up on, but first I gotta tell you: I think I've developed a whole new respect for the way you walk. Let me explain. This chick I met the other night — you had to see it — *could not* walk straight. Fuckin' hell, you should have seen her *run*. She looked like a penguin runnin' to take a shit!

"Not in a talkin' mood, huh? Whatever. Even *you* would have busted a gut laughin'."

The *shoutengai* is loud as midday thanks to the expansive rows of video arcades, convenience stores, and hyperactive night owls. As the giant *yokai* struts, his gaze swings from one side of the street to the other, taking in the scene; his eyes stray like powerful magnets on the cleavage of every woman who passes, despite the thick sweaters and autumn jackets that obscure them. The girl's hands remain buried in deep invisible pockets. Her head stays straight-on, focused; nothing distracts her, not even the occasional eyebrow waggle from her companion. They stride through the crowded shopping street, side by side but never touching each other, despite the tide of night-crawlers and party animals. Instead they create an invisible, seamless divide among the masses, like the parting of the Red Sea. Nothing fazes this pair as they walk with determination to their ultimate destination. Their faces and appearances are impossible to decipher but they succeed at giving off the impression of owning the city and all that resides therein.

"See, the kid takes off, I go in and do my whole 'heroic samurai' speech, and I don't even have time to flash one of my swords around — this bitch is all *over* me, just like that! I think she might've gotten started without me, if you know what I'm sayin'. So, we're done in like two minutes, not that I'm complainin'. Then this chick starts talkin' my ear off about how much she wants to travel and see some other weird famous cottages in the UK or some shit, I don't know, I wasn't listenin'. She goes on for ages, keeps repeatin' a name, 'Tasha Tudor'-somethin'-or-other, so I figure a'ight, we're done here. I get up to head out for a smoke. She does *not* stop talkin'! By now her voice is just cuttin' through me like a rusty knife, so I just fuckin' *go*, I don't even bother puttin' pants on. Guess what? Bitch *follows* me! Waddles all the way downstairs, chases me outside into the back … courtyard, or whatever the hell you call it … and she's still yammerin'! I don't know what to do! So, you know what I do? I panic. I mean, I transform and just fuckin' *book it* over the wall and straight into the bush. Last I see her, she's tryin' to climb over the fuckin' wall after me! What a psycho! Talk about a fuckin' nightmare. Get it? 'Fuckin'?' 'Nightmare?' Ah, you're no fun."

Three boys, high school students, run out of a video arcade and barrel into the girl's path. Without a hint of apology, they heckle her; high-pitched hyena-like cries as they jostle each other, reach out to touch her. The *yokai* keeps walking, oblivious.

"Here's the freaky part. I lose her, take a good strong leak in the bush, and figure okay, it's safe to morph back and put some pants on, so I head back to the house and — you ready for this? It's *gone*. I mean, just *pfft!* into thin air. Nothin' left but dirt and rubble. So now the bitch is gone, my house is gone, the kid's gone, my clothes are fuckin' nowhere. *Weird*. And comin' from me, that fuckin' *means* somethin', you know what I'm sayin'? My thoughts exactly. FUCKIN' weird —" He presses on, notices too late that the girl has yet to follow. "Come *on!* Hino-*chan*, I'm hungry!"

The girl responds: *"You can wait, Akki."* This is not at all what the boys hear. The sound they hear is a horrific snarl from the girl's clenched, razor-sharp teeth. She leaves them with a final, meaningful glance over her shoulder, over the rims of her sunglasses, as the *yokai* waits for her to catch up. With her gaze upon them, the boys feel their elated euphoria drain away until there is nothing left but a sense of how short life is. They are left standing there, mouths open, with a dreadful feeling as if everything they have ever known and loved has been ripped away from them. One of the boys runs away from his friends to wait for the first train alone. He does not want anyone to see the urine stain on the front of his pants.

Akki cannot help chuckling. "Shit, girl, they're just kids. ANYWAY. What I wanna know is, who the fuck thought it was funny to fuck with my place? I mean, once the fires went down and I rounded up my nightmares, the house was back to normal, but what the fuckin' hell?! Everybody knows Akki's territory is *Akki's territory.* When I find out what spineless piece of shit had the grapes to mess with me ... ooh, just wait 'til I get my fuckin' hands on 'em ..."

The mismatched pair steer soundlessly down dirtier, quieter streets with fewer lights. The urban cacophony fades as they go farther and farther from the safety of the populated *shoutengai* toward the glow of the Tsutenkaku Tower and the heart of the slums. Akki leads Hino through a labyrinth of narrow alleyways, past standing ramen shops, shot bars, a pharmacy with blinding fluorescent lights called Love Drug, and a closed shrine where the water of its *temizuya* still trickles and a *shishi-odoshi* can be heard. They come to a dead end between two stumpy derelict buildings. In the darkness they can make out the shape of a small torii gate. It looks as though it was ripped out of the ground and abandoned there. An old man huddles in a corner next to it, warming his hands over a burning trash can, surrounded by garbage bags and stray cats, oblivious to the giant man and long-limbed girl approaching him. The walls are slathered in a colourful assortment of indecipherable graffiti. Four characters painted in crude white brush strokes jut out from among the rest:

自分自身

"Finally," Akki says. "Damn impossible to find anythin' around here anymore. It used to be so easy to find that shrine! Go down past the fishmonger, turn at the *unagi* guy's place, turn at the giant brothel, and bam. Easy as that. Now they're all gone. Anyway, this is it. Here you are, old man," he twists three gold rings from his fingers and tosses them into the fire. "One for me, an' one for the lady. And I might have a friend stop by." Under the cuff of Akki's jacket sleeve black beads shimmer with the light of the flames.

The old man comes to life, like a living statue performer who waits for someone to drop money in front of him. *"Konbanwa, irasshai, irasshai,"* he bows, his smile revealing an absence of teeth. He makes several dramatic gestures to the old torii gate and grabs a handful of the darkness between its legs, lifting a thick black plastic tarp. It is still pitch-dark underneath.

"All right." Akki pumps his fist in the air. "I'm fuckin' starvin'!" He turns back to Hino with a triumphant smile. It fades as he realizes she has not moved from the main road. He shouts back to her. "What?!"

Even with shades on he can tell when Hino rolls her eyes. With a heavy sigh, she walks over, stoops under the tarp and disappears. Akki follows. The old man's cackling already sounds as if he is miles away. The two *yokai* plummet into complete darkness.

"Fuck, it's dark in here," Akki's voice echoes. "The hell we do now? Hino? You still here? Oh, there you are. The fuck's wrong with you? No, don't take off! Can'tcha hold my hand or somethin'?"

A deep, cold voice cuts through the air. *"Don't* touch me, Akki."

A dim light fades into view. A woman in a beautiful kimono materializes before them, candle in hand. *"Irasshaimase,"* she says, bowing low. *"Omatase shimashita. Jibun rashiku ite kudasai."* They follow her through the dark empty space to a set of rice-paper *shouji* doors, which automatically slide open to reveal a tiny courtyard with a giant cherry blossom tree. Illuminated from below, its tiny falling petals twinkle in the light. Hino and the maître d' step inside, but not before the sight catches Akki's attention.

"Whoa, check that out …"

The maître d' notices the *yokai's* admiration. *"Kirei desu ne? Hai, kochira e douzo."*

Another set of *shouji* doors slide open on their own accord to a magnificent traditional restaurant with sky-high ceilings dappled with starry lights. The maître d' announces to no one in particular that two more guests have arrived: *"Ni-mei-sama goraiten desu!"* From unseen parts of the restaurant, a booming chorus of *"Irasshaimase!"* greets them. The entire place is lit with a warm glow from scores of red and gold hanging lanterns. The restaurant must be fourteen storeys high, with a massive stage. Towering gold screens with intricately painted cranes and forests line the stage. Sullen-looking men sit alone at several tables in a large pit below. A sparse number of patrons and servers look down over the wrap-around balconies on every floor to watch the new arrivals. The maître d' blows out her candle as she leads them over a stone bridge that stretches over a giant koi pond, away from a long shiny black bar under a thick bamboo roof, past a sushi bar the full length of the restaurant, where customers make their selections from giant tanks brimming with fish, lobsters, and crabs. The chefs greet them with low, respectful bows as the new arrivals pass by.

The maître d' clears her throat. "You've arrived at a good time. More customers will be here soon, but for now it's still very peaceful."

"Oh, good," Akki snorts. "You speak the language. Tell her *how* peaceful." He cocks his head in Hino's direction.

"Certainly. We are open from sunset to sunrise. Our 'oni only' hours are from two until sunrise. We have a strict policy against allowing humans during those hours; you will not be bothered while you are our guests here. We make sure you can relax and shed your worldly guises whenever you wish." Akki takes a second to stick his long red tongue out at Hino behind their escort.

The lady stops at a booth with a window. She bows a perfect ninety degrees. "Please have a seat. I will return shortly. Relax, and be yourselves."

The girl slides into one side of the booth. Akki collapses on the other with a sigh of relief into his cushioned seat. He rips off his jacket and shirt and chucks them onto the humongous table. The table was not designed with giant boar gods in mind, so he settles for his in-between form: a samurai with a blazing green aura haloed around him. He feels so free. "See? What'd I tell you? The real deal. Pure. Classic. Right out of the old days. None of that newfangled *gaijin* shit you see everywhere. You don't even see *fries* on their menu. Anyway, what was I talkin' about? Oh yeah. I don't even know if the kid made it out of there," Akki goes on. "Haven't seen him since. I left him a message to show up here but no clue if he even got it. Maybe I went a little too far, settin' the whole place on fire. Shit, man, I don't know where I can find a better wingman than that kid. Tail hasn't been this easy to get in a century. All he has to do is bat those crazy eyes of his and bitches come runnin'. Then all *I* gotta do is step into the room. The second they lay eyes on this divine temple they forget all about him. Can't blame 'em. The kid's like a rickety shack next to me. Oh, don't look at me like that. I can say that about him. We all know it's true. The real bonus is he's got both bases covered — the prudes fall for that 'cherry boy' *soushoku-danshi* vibe he gives off, and the sluts who got that *gaijin* fever are too stupid to see through him. Best of both worlds, you know? Never could figure out why he goes through all that trouble to convince bitches he's a '*hafu.*' Hell, whatever gets the job done, am I right?"

The girl faces him for the first time this evening. She speaks in a throaty voice, deep as a man's: "You moron. He *is* '*hafu.*'"

He cracks up. "Please! You tryin' to play with my balls, Hino-*chan*? You know I prefer the real thing."

"He has been dreaming about his American father kidnapping him for *years*. Do you not talk to him? You have been harassing this human for a third of his life, and you do not know anything about him?"

Akki swears under his breath. "Leave me alone. Fuck. Can't we just hang out instead of talkin' about stupid shit nobody cares about? I'm hungry. And DON'T look at me like that. I picked a *good* place for us this time."

He snaps his fingers and the maître d' reappears with a young girl holding a large electronic device. Her kimono is gorgeous: a lavender background with pink *sakura* petals floating over a garden and a pond etched in perfect details at the bottom of her dress. Hino's eyebrow lifts a little as she watches the petals flow in invisible wind. Akki smirks. "See? I told you this is the place for us. No more waitin' all year for the one day we can go out in the human world and do what we want."

"Oh, certainly, if you do not mind people throwing soybeans at you all night."

"Hino." Akki cocks his head at her. "They're just beans. Now, check this shit out." Akki proceeds to bark his order from the paper menu: "Fugu liver and spike dorian, four plates of each. *Aka-chan* sashimi, two plates ... um, the ground bone gratin, four of those, and two plates of your finest horse."

The young server blinks in stunned confusion. The maître d' murmurs Japanese into her ear. After a few moments of quick interpretation, the server nods and taps the screen at record speed to keep up with Akki's requests. *"Hai, kashikomarimashita,"* she confirms. *"Nomimono wa?"*

"A glass of your youngest B-positive blood, and a whiskey sour." He grins proudly across the table. Hino is not amused. "Oh, come *on!* That's the whole reason I brought your skinny ass here! What restaurant in this country do *you* know that has B-positive blood? Name one! See? You can't." She does not respond. Akki frowns. *"Fi-*ine," he whines. "Just the whiskey sour."

"Hai, hai!" The server bows, then flutters to the bar and returns holding a single whiskey sour in both hands as if it is a precious artifact. *"Jibun rashiku ite kudasai,"* she sings as she bows again and disappears.

"I apologize," the maître d' says with a bow. "Our restaurant is still very new; in time, our staff will learn to understand our clients in fluent *yumego*. If there are any problems, please do not hesitate to talk to management. *Jibun rashiku ite kudasai*; please be your-selves." With a final bow she takes her leave to guide new arrivals.

"Yeah, Hino, please be yourself," Akki grumbles before he downs his drink. The girl removes her sunglasses and places them delicately on the table. They glare into each other's eyes — in the light, she can see the pulsing, neon-green flames in his eyes, and he can see her crimson irises. Hino turns away to look about the restaurant. She is not in the mood to argue with him. She never is. Akki signals a waitress for another drink and resumes sulking.

The food comes and goes without another word exchanged. While Akki wolfs down everything that steams and wriggles before him, Hino cannot help but marvel at the voraciousness of his mortal inclinations. Earlier, she had presupposed his attempt at conversation as chauvinistic banter; but, watching him now, she sees there was more to it. Hino always thought *yokai* were above such earthly desires as food and sex. She has never known another to engage in these fledgling behaviours with such en-thusiasm. Then again, she thinks to herself, Akki has always been a bit "unique" and, to be fair, everyone must consume *something* for survival. Even demons. She decides to keep this rationalization to herself, however, and turns to watch the stage, upon which two human girls appear with a large, ancient-looking woman. They lead her to a stack of cushions and a *shamisen* in the centre of the stage and, struggling together, help her sit. One puts a large *shakuhachi* flute in her hands before they bow to the audience and flit back to the wings. The woman's eyes are white, bulging vacant orbs in her slowly decomposing skull. She sings in a scratchy war-bling voice, an ancient song no human would understand. She then brings the bamboo flute to her dry, cracked lips and plays another melancholic tune. During her third song, the woman's kimono twitches. Another pair of long, craggy arms stretches out from once-unseen sleeves and plays along on the *shamisen*. Hino finds herself nodding in time with every piece. When the performance ends in a final dramatic flourish, everyone rises to their feet in applause, clapping long after the four-armed creature is guided off stage.

Maybe this place is not so bad, Hino thinks to herself.

Once the woman is gone, human musicians arrive with *koto* to play for ambiance, and a flood of customers enter the restaurant. Some are as big as Akki, their skin the colour of his ruby bracelet, sporting dark matted hair, horns, and severe underbites. Some are fat, flesh-coloured, and so short they would not be able to stand next to Hino without seeing under her skirt. Others arrive dressed as humans, unzipping their skin and shedding their disguises once seated at their tables. The patrons at the sushi bar greet their long-time friends as they unzip their own uncomfortable facial disguises. Akki pretends to ignore the fact that Hino remains unchanged. She has been stuck-up ever since they met. He does not expect her to relax anytime soon.

"Wow, we really did get here just in time," Akki says, mostly to himself. "Not late enough to enjoy the slogan, though."

The bite in his words seems to be directed at a pale-blond man bumping into the tables and guests, escorted by a group of flush-faced red-haired Japanese women, who laugh as he whirls and topples against them. "Oh man, this place is *sick,*" the man slurs. "Who's up for some sake, baby?! Whoo!"

Akki sucks hard on a post-dinner cigarette with a loathing hiss. "Fuckin' *gaijin.* Never would've thought humans could be any *worse.*"

Hino holds back a snort. "Does your minion not count?"

"'Course not! The kid ain't ... well, he ain't no regular human. Ain't many that can walk through dreams. Least, not like he can. Kid's got a gift, *hafu* or not. That puts him way above humans. 'Specially *these* assholes. This country needs to throw a fuckin' wrench into whatever conveyor belt keeps bringin' 'em in. How'd everythin' go to shit so fast? All these years it's been like watchin' a slow *jinrikisha* wreck. I don't get it. We'd always had it made until *they* showed up. Solid food, soothin' music, nice tight milky-skinned women who knew how to keep their mouths shut … and, of course, we had the samurai. How did this country decide to give all that up?"

Hino scoots deeper into the booth so she can lean her chin against her hand and look out the window next to their table. "You are forgetting about all the things this country *has* retained, Akki. More than that, you are talking about a planet with seven billion people. 'Foreign' influence is inevitable. Everything is so interconnected that even in Japan there are things that people do not realize are from other countries and influences, and people seem to love them fine."

Akki glares at her. "Bullshit. Name two."

Hino's eyes flicker to Akki's whiskey sour glass; she overturns her initial response. "Tempura. Coffee. May I go on?"

Akki gives her a nasty snarl. That had been his first dinner, no more than two hours ago, fresh from the Lawson trash bins. He thought, of all people, she would be the one to agree with him. "I already regret bringin' this shit up with you."

"The point is, if we as a nation want to keep up with the rest of the world, we must hold together, work through our ideals, and get used to change. We must find solutions, not add to problems with our stubborn determinations. We must not think of Japan as 'going to hell' just because things are not as they once were. There are many things that we have held onto, as well. You would not believe how many traditions have been lost in other lands … how much history has been corrupted, the number of races that have gone extinct." Hino's eyes flicker downward with a hint of sadness. "We are very lucky, Akki. You would do well to remember that."

Akki makes a grunt of slight approval. "This might be the most I've ever heard you say since Nagasaki. Where'd you get all that shit?"

Hino does not remove her gaze from a nearby window as she answers: "Japanese history teacher."

"Far out. How is he?"

"Delicious." She spins her shades on the table. "Sometimes I think about *how* lucky we *yokai* are. Still venerated. We have not been reduced to annual Halloween costumes or anime or cartoons on cereal boxes yet. Count your blessings, Akki."

"What? Sorry, I wasn't listenin'. See the chick that just walked in with that blue-skinned dude? Hang on, she'll turn around again ... there! Look at the size of *that*. How do you think she sits on that thing? And shit, check this out — ha, ha, look at this *gaijin* fuck!"

Akki gestures his cigarette to the drunk man now lying across his table. Half of his red-skinned companions are removing his clothes by tearing them in long thin strips. The other half have removed their long red wigs and are giggling at the bite wounds they have made along his arms and throat.

"Well, my point is, we're goin' down the shitter, and I don't mean the *yoshiki*-style. Think about it. Forks and knives. Pants on a woman. *Christmas*. All kinds o' bullshit that were hard enough to take back then, and they're *still* around! Don't make sense for us to replace good shit with all this Western crap. Okay, fair point, their alcohol ain't bad. It's no sake, though. Can't beat the home team. Nah, things oughtta go back to the way they've always been. All this foreign influence is just bullshit dumped on an already hardworkin' society's shoulders. It's 'cause of all the suckin' up we did to 'fit in' and keep up with the world that we had to get rid of things that made this country what it was: perfect."

Hino puts her shades back on and accepts a cigarette from the tray of a passing waitress. Before turning back to the window, Hino mutters in Japanese, *"Boke."*

"I heard that."

The restaurant is in full swing now. Tables on the ground floor are occupied, but the customers are quiet. Their mouths are kept full by a small, efficient army of kimono-clad waitresses, pink, blue, and lavender butterflies flitting up and down and around the restaurant to keep patrons fed and happy. Many of them work in pairs to carry heavy rainbow arrangements of fresh sushi, steaming bowls of noodles, wide platters of sizzling skewers of meat drizzled in warm sauces, and giant ice-cold pitchers of beer dripping beads of condensation. The decor and spotlights overhead make the restaurant look more like a giant kabuki theatre than an exclusive establishment for fine dining. Those who are not eating or drinking wait patiently for another performance. The waitresses only have a moment to take dishes and glasses away and wipe down the tables before another crowd of guests swoop down on the chairs, relieved after an hour of lining up. The room is as dynamic as the city nightlife, but with a much wider assortment of characters.

One guest — a man — arrives alone. He strides right past the long line, ignoring the inquisitive looks of the wait staff who do not have the courage to question him. At first glance he looks like a normal person, but his eyes stop them. They watch him weave through the tables straight to the window seat with the giant *yokai* and the demon posing as a high school student. He has the look of someone who has already put in several hours but still has a long night of work ahead of him. His black suit and blue dress shirt are dishevelled. Hino is not surprised to see something else on his face: a look of dismay masked with the commitment and duty the country has drummed into so many young people she has seen over the centuries. Hino sees his disappointment, his bottled rage, his broken heart. She also notices how puffy his eyes are. Akki, as usual, notices nothing.

"Hey, whaddya know? Zaniel-*kun*. Fancy seein' you here! Glad to see you're still alive!"

The young man stops at their table and bows low, panting. "Akki-*sama* ... I'm sorry. It took ages to get down from the mountains and ... Are you glowing? Sorry. I mean ... you look different."

"Like it?" Akki beams at him in all his fiery-green glory, his grin so wide Zaniel could count all sixteen of his upper teeth were he not staring at Akki's broad naked chest, upon which a large tattooed dragon appears to sleep. It opens one yellow, glistening eye, hisses at Zaniel, and rolls over so its back is turned. Zaniel snaps back to attention again when Akki answers: "Kinda nice, right? I finally found a place outside the mountains where I can let myself go. No shirt, no shoes, no problem."

"Uh …" Speechless, Zaniel turns to Hino, who rolls her eyes behind her shades.

Akki tilts his head back to gulp down the last of his drink and belches. "Yup, the other *yokai* weren't kiddin' about this place. Glad they talk so loud when they're walkin' by the house, or I never would've heard about it! Only issue is all the humans you gotta go through to get here."

"I see." Zaniel remains stoic. He starts to speak again but is caught off guard by the array of empty plates and whiskey glasses scattered all over the table. "Um … Akki-*sama,* how long —"

"You ain't said nothin' to Hino, by the way."

Zaniel catches his tongue and steels himself before bowing again. "Hino-*sama,*" he says. "Greetings. I apologize for my rudeness." The girl continues to look out the window, ignoring them both. "Akki-*sama* —"

"Oh. OH. That reminds me. You're not gonna believe this. Hino-*chan* here thinks you're a *hafu.* Ha, ha! Can you believe that?!" Out of habit, Akki smacks Zaniel in back of the head. The *yokai* laughs, hard. "Oh, cool! Check that out, Hino, I can touch people in here! Awesome! Ain't gonna be no more sittin' around the house for me. I'm gonna be bringin' bitches here all the time!" He interprets the look on the young man's face not as a reaction to pain, but of shame. Guilt. "Wait. That true, kid? All this time, you've been a *hafu?*"

Zaniel pins his arms by his sides to keep from rubbing his head. He is in trouble. "I apologize, Akki-*sama.* It's true. But my mother is Japanese, and I am a full citizen, born on Japanese soil. I have nothing to do with my foreign side anymore, I swear."

"Huh." Akki sneers down at him. "Guess that explains the eyes. And the accent." And a great deal of other things, now that Akki thinks about them. His smile returns. He will not let this ruin his good mood. He is feeling merciful tonight. "Ah, lighten up, kid. We've known each other too long. I ain't gonna hold it against ya. Ain't like you're gonna give me reason to. Gotta say, I've never seen anythin' really *gaijin* about ya, aside from those weird eyes of yours. But I guess it can't be helped. Don't worry, I still think you're one of us — well, not *us*." He gestures at himself and Hino. "Japanese, I mean. *Nihonjin*. You get me."

"Oh." Zaniel exhales. "Um ... thank you? I mean, thank you. Akki-*sama* is too kind."

Akki sighs. "I know."

"I do not mean to question you, Akki-*sama,* but how long have you been here?"

The *yokai* shrugs his giant shoulders. "No idea. Twenty minutes. Couple of hours. Why?"

"A couple of ..." Zaniel pulls at his obsidian bracelet, nervous. The stinging sensation of its potential removal stops him. "But I thought — tonight —"

"And why you still standin' there, kid? What are you, a foot soldier? Take a seat or somethin'. Have a whiskey sour. They're *go*-od."

"Akki-*sama,*" Zaniel says with a little more urgency. "Your guest, um ... she's been waiting for you all night."

"My guest?" Akki's eyes search the bottom of his freshest glass. Realization spreads across his face in a lecherous grin. "Oh, yeah ... well, she can wait a bit longer, can't she? I'm still digestin'. *Oi, omae!*" he barks in Japanese at a passing waitress. "Another whiskey sour, chop chop."

"Akki-*sama,*" Zaniel trembles. "I had to leave her to come and find you. If you don't go now, she might not stay. I'm sorry I left her. I didn't know what else to do. And I'm *very* sorry, about the last one ... that time, I ..."

"Geez, kid." Akki points to him when the waitress hands him his drink. *"Mou ippai, hayaku,"* he repeats. She nods in compliance and runs off for the second time. "Relax. I ain't had a night out in Osaka for ages. You know, if you're so concerned about makin' the woman wait, you can do her yourself. I don't mind. Unless she's real hot. Is she? I don't remember."

Zaniel wipes his brow. Once again, the *yokai's* memory — and concept of time — has shown its fickle nature. "Well, I guess it depends on what you mean —"

"You know what I mean. How hot was she for *me?*"

"Well, she was kinda —"

Akki does not wait for the rest. "Ah, forget it. I don't feel like gettin' up right now, anyway. If she ain't rarin' for me, there's no point. Speakin' of which, I ran into a whole batch of humans at this *conbini.* They were *definitely* feelin' the samurai vibe, beggin' me with their eyes to fuck 'em. Anyway, I want one of 'em for later. I haven't decided which one yet. No, don't take off *now.* They can wait! Have a seat. Order somethin'. Don't be so wound up. They got some pretty relaxin' music here, too, don't they, Hino?"

Zaniel slowly slides into the booth next to her, as if sitting down too fast will trigger an explosion. "But ... Akki-*sama* ... I can't eat food in this realm. If you recall, I'd —"

"Yeah, yeah, yeah, don't remind me. You'll explode. Or whatever it is you humans do. Blah, blah, blah. Always the same shit with you. Anyway, while I have you here. The chicks you've been bringin' up to the house have fuckin' *sucked* lately, you know that?"

Zaniel is surprised, but not at the fact that he is being blamed. "I'm sorry, Akki-*sama.* All I can tell is who desires you. I'm afraid I have no control over their personalities." Zaniel does not add that it is Akki's own choices that have brought such disappointment. Pointing out his own flaws would be the utmost disrespect.

"Yeah, well … you *should*! Save me the trouble! Isn't that what I'm payin' you for?"

"You pay him?" Hino interrupts. "Since when?"

"I, well … I pay him in *protection*. And whose side are you on?"

"Same side I'm always on," Hino murmurs to herself.

"Thank you," Akki says curtly, having not heard her. He sighs and massages his furry temples. "The point is, boy, if you still want my help in this world, you're gonna have to step it up. I don't want any more chatterboxes who lie there like dead fish. I need somethin' worth the effort, y'hear? This bullshit is gettin' *really* exhaustin'. Unless you want things to go back to the way they were. I mean, hey. Maybe I have no idea what I'm talkin' about. Maybe you'll be perfectly safe without my protection. Hmmm. You've been workin' longer hours in the real world lately, haven't you? A *hafu* in your position needs all the sleep he can get if you ask me." He snickers at his own joke.

Zaniel gulps, his eyes fixated on his feet. What on earth can he do? "I apologize again, Akki-*sama*." He bows low. "From now on, I'll do my best."

Akki throws up his hands. "That's all I ask! Save me the trouble of havin' to replace you. I don't blame you, though. Women aren't the same as they used to be." Falling silent, the three of them watch the drunk Westerner's lady friends suckle on his limbs. The lull in the conversation gives Zaniel a moment to think, to imagine the very idea of being replaced by another. He cannot wrap his mind around the image, and wonders if he even wants to.

"*See*, Hino?" Akki smirks. "I told you I picked the right place for us. Take that." He drains his glass in one gulp. After one last drink, with great effort he slides out of the booth, removes another gold ring, and tosses it onto the table. "All right, I'm outta here. Gotta rest up before my next 'visitor.' That's for the tab; order whatever you like. And bring back my change. Oh, and order some *shoujo horumon* for takeout and bring it up to the house. On second thought, nah, just bring back my change." He struts out of the restaurant without a backward glance. The staff chorus-sings at his departure: *"Mata okoshi kudasaimase!"*

Zaniel sits rigid and uncomfortable, silent next to Hino, who continues to smoke and stare out the window, playing with her lighter. The rain has started again. He does not dare touch the ring or even the whiskey sour. A part of him wishes the floor would open and devour him. He had concocted a whole story to relay about the other night, a perfect explanation that gave him an excuse to leave the vicinity of Akki's house but left out the Yokai. The one he cannot get out of his head.

He turns to see Hino's shades are now fixed on him. He clears his throat. "Um, I was surprised when Akki-*sama* asked me to find him here. May I ask, what is this place?"

Turning back to the window, she takes a long, slow drag. "We are in Osaka. This is a real place, in the real world. Did you see the name outside, on the walls?"

Zaniel shrugs. He did, but they meant nothing to him.

"This is 'Jibun Jishin.' Look closely when you go back out. You are smart, so you have probably figured it out that it is a new restaurant for our kind."

"I see," Zaniel nods. "Um ... it seems like a nice place to bring a friend."

Hino's head turns sharply to face him. She lets out two sharp puffs of smoke through her nostrils, like a dragon. "Akki and I are not friends."

"But —"

"I am *his* friend. Does not mean he is *my* friend."

"Yes, of course. I apologize."

Satisfied, Hino returns her attention to the window again. "They will have to kick you out soon. The witching hour is coming, no humans allowed."

"Yes." Looking around the restaurant, he sees Hino's description is accurate. No one besides the two of them and the employees looks human. He wonders if the creature from the other day could be here. If she can breach Akki's private territory and change things, make things disappear, she might end up here. What *was* she? Zaniel cannot figure it out. Aside from being mysterious, and perhaps a little exciting, he is still unsure.

Hino speaks again. "Well, now ... what do you suppose this could be?"

He turns. All this time Hino has been watching a tiny creature no bigger than a sake cup on the other side of the window. Her white kimono looks familiar. She catches raindrops on her long, snakelike tongue. She licks the drops rolling down the window. Then, she notices Zaniel. Startled, she scuttles away along the ledge with quick, fluttering steps. He gasps. Despite its size, it is indeed the Yokai, the same one from the other day.

"That was interesting," Hino mutters. She turns and sees Zaniel is already gone. Her eyes droop closed on her next drag, during which she can hear him excusing himself to everyone he bumps past in his attempt to catch up with whatever is outside. *He will not catch up with her in time.* She leans back against the cushioned booth and surveys the damage from Akki's buffet. She notices the lone whiskey sour in the midst of it. Hino eats the rest of her cigarette with polite, tiny bites. It does not satisfy. She clicks her tongue. What good will it do to waste a perfectly good drink? She reaches for it and takes a sip. It burns her lips, goes down smooth. *Not bad.* She takes another to be polite, but over time finishes the whole thing. It still pales in comparison to B-positive children's blood. She almost wishes she had not turned Akki down.

However, she grins, *it seems this world is* indeed *getting more interesting.*

three

REELING AND WRITHING

三人寄れば苦界
Three people together make for bitter times

"Good morning, Shibelle! Wow! So pretty! You have date?"

Misaki Wada is the first to greet me when I arrive. Her return to our school means we must be mad desperate. Makes me wonder how much say I have in the hiring process. (My guess is none.)

"Yeah, right!" I laugh. She gives me a confused head tilt. "I mean, no. Why?"

"You have a skirt today," she points. "You look so fashionable!"

"Oh. Thank you," I smile. I guess today she's more open to speaking with me. "I need to look good for my trial lesson today. It must be an important one. I'm already shaking."

"Eh?" She tilts her head. "'Shaking?'"

"Yeah, you know. When you're nervous, you kinda …" I demonstrate with my hands.

"Oh, ho ho, I see! 'Shaking!'"

She follows me into the staff room, reassuring me that I look great as I put away my things and get organized. "Eh, by the way, Shibelle," she adds. "Your picture. In the lobby. Halloween. Eh ... Tinker Bell?"

"It's 'Cybelle.' And yeah, that's me."

"*Ehhh! Sugoi!* So, this Halloween, your ... eh, *chotto matte* ..." She whips out her cellphone and types something on it. "Eh? Cos-tume...?"

"Oh, I wear the same costume every year. It's just easier that way. If is still fits, why not, right?"

Misaki goes silent. She stares at me hard, tilting her head. "Eh? I do not understand. One more time?"

"Oh. Um. Yes. I will be Tinker Bell."

"Eh! *Sugoi!* My costume ... I not decide yet."

"It's okay, you still have time. Most of the teachers just buy little things from the hundred-yen store —"

"Eh? Time? *Wakaran* ..." She tilts her head again. "Do you mean, 'one more time?'"

"No, it's okay." So much for conversation. The air in the staff room now feels so stuffy it makes my eyes water, like someone's chopped onions in here. The only new addition I see on the staff room bench are a Yagi-*sama* standee and the now empty cake box from yesterday. No onions in sight.

The door slides open. "Ah, Lieko-*sensei*, does Shibelle look nice today?" Misaki sings.

Lieko ignores her. "I sent you text last night," she says to me. "To 'dress professionally.' But today, you wear short sleeves. Did you not see the text?"

I'm still wearing my jacket over my top. How can everyone tell? "I did. I didn't think it would matter; I always keep my jacket on for trial lessons. And it's, like, twenty-five degrees outside."

"But cool biz season ends this month. Soon, you must stop wearing short sleeves."

Says who? Since when? "Well, I'm comfortable in what I'm wearing now. And to be honest, it's never been a problem with Manager."

"Ah, I see. Well …" She wrinkles her nose, the most emotion I've seen from her since she started working here. "At any rate, you did not reply. So, I must assume you did not receive my texts."

Of course, I saw them. I'm wearing a skirt, aren't I? What is she getting at? "Well, there was no name on them. I figured they were from Manager or …" I trail off before I say, "a random stalker." Probably best not to joke with a pissed-off Lieko.

"No, *they were from me.* You have very important trial lesson today. Every lesson is important, now. It would have been better if you replied to them. According to Manager, you always reply to him or to Yoshino with '*hai, wakarimashita.*' It is not professional to not reply at all. Please consider this for next time. The Zozo company is very important."

Wonderful. The *one* time I don't respond all hell breaks loose. Not sure what hell that would be, it was just three stupid texts. I don't know what business Lieko has harassing me after-hours in the first place. I decide it's better to drop it. I sit down at the bench to get to work. Lieko must be waiting for a rebuttal or an apology because she remains rooted for another moment, staring at me before she goes to the cupboard and riffles through files. She mutters something in Japanese, diverting my attention. Her nose is buried in a binder as she walks out of the room. She takes significant time to glare at me over her notes as she slides the door closed behind her. Now I'm really glad I didn't call her a stalker.

Once I finish a little more prep work for the week, the elevator dings with the arrival of our morning students. For the next forty-five minutes, I play with a group of three-year-olds in the guise of English instruction. My students all sit on their knees in perfect polite *seiza*. My skirt leaves me no choice but to do the same. The kids whip out their Zippo and Zappo colouring books to get their "homework" stickers. I also reward them with the Chicken Dance song and a couple of Sharon, Lois & Bram hits. Overall, my students are a joy to teach, when they're not crying, beating each other up, or kicking the CD player. The helicopter moms at the giant viewing window couldn't be prouder. They even follow along with the songs and repeat vocabulary after me.

After the "Goodbye Song," the moms appear to be happy with how the class went. I hope they feel they got their money's worth, because my calves are killing me.

"Thank you, Cybelle-*sensei*," Yuta's mom bows. "How was he?"

"As usual, Yuta was great," I smile down at him. "You spoke up so much today, big guy. Have you been practising?"

Yuta nods. His mother answers for him, anyway. "Yes! Yuta has been practising. We have stickers — toy stickers — in bathroom! On the wall! So ... we have been practising. Ah, together — at bath time!"

"That's awesome! Way to go!" I deliver the high-fives and help usher the students out. Toshiro's mother also practises a bit of English on me: "Now, your home ... you have snow?"

"No, we still don't have any snow yet. In Canada, it's fall — just like Japan." She looks relieved.

Around the corner from the classroom, the lobby is packed with students. Most of the parents get the play-by-play from teachers about their lessons. Some kids have just arrived and are fighting for puzzles and toys. Sotaro is in the middle of a melee over a Winnie-the-Pooh plushie. His mother and Manager watch with serene smiles as Sotaro decks two kids in the face at the same time. They both drop the stuffed toy, screaming. Sotaro takes his prize under the darkest corner of the desk to play alone.

"Ah, Cybelle-*sensei*," Manager greets me. "Twelve o'clock, right on time. Sotaro is your trial lesson. Only ten minutes. Sotaro ... is here!" He points under the desk. Great.

"Great!" I say out loud. "Room Three is all ready for him."

"Okay!" Manager claps his hands together. "Sotaro, time for lesson! Time to put down Pooh-*san*! Cybelle-*sensei* is exciting for your lesson! Are you exciting?"

From the darkness, Sotaro lets out a shriek and throws Winnie-the-Pooh at Manager.

"Cybelle-*sensei*, maybe let's tell Sotaro it's time — time to enjoy English! Let's say, 'Come, Sotaro! Let's enjoy *English*! Let's enjoy English! *Let's* enjoy English!'"

Behind me, Yoshino stifles a snicker. "Yes, Sotaro-*kun*. Let's enjoy English!" She manages to grab Sotaro's hand and get him into the room. Yoshino is a lifesaver. She knows darn well Zozo doesn't pay me enough money in the world to jump up and down singing slogans and pretend English is the best thing since sliced sushi. I grimace at the giant clown mascot on the wall, then turn to Sotaro's mother and try to assuage her guilt with an enthusiastic smile and bow before I follow Yoshino to Room Three. The mother smiles and bows back; I can tell she is embarrassed. I must put my best foot forward for her sake. For the company's sake. For *my* sake. I close the door behind me, smiling at Sotaro. I must be professional ... *must be professional ...*

"Hello, Sotaro? How are you today?"

Sotaro sticks his tongue out at me. I look him dead in the eye, waiting for a response. After a few seconds, he tucks his tongue back in and looks down at his hands. He sniffs. "I'm fine, thank you, and you?" he says soberly.

"I'm fine, thank you!" I sing. "Now, Sotaro, do you know who this is?" I take out my *Yo-kai Watch* puppet.

"Jibanyan! JIBANYAN! *Choudai!*" Sotaro tries to snatch it from me. I hold it up high and out of reach.

"That's right! Jibanyan, can you say hello to our new friend Sotaro? *Hello, Sotaro*," I say in a gravelly voice. "*Nice to meet you! How are you?*"

"I'm fine," he screams with passion. "Thank you!"

I bring the puppet to my ear. "What's that? You want to give Sotaro a high-five? Okay! Good job, Sotaro! Hey, Jibanyan, let's sing Sotaro the 'Hello Song.' What do you say?" I make the puppet nod. *"Hello, hello hello hello, hello hello hello, hello hello what's your name?"* Sotaro drops to the floor. He snores like a chainsaw, pretending to sleep.

"What's that, Jibanyan? His name is Sotaro? Well, hey there, Sotaro, how are you? Jibanyan, let's say hello to Sotaro and ask him how he's doing! *Hello, hello, hello, and how are you? I'm fine, I'm fine, and I hope that you are, too!*"

Sotaro rolls around on the floor and sticks his tongue out at me during the rest of my usual song-and-dance routines. I give up. "Okay, Sotaro, let's sit down for storytime!"

Sotaro throws all my books and toys out of my teacher box. His mother watches from outside with no aversion to what's going on. After struggling to read my bilingual picture book of Japanese folktales to him, Yoshino comes in with her own box of magic tricks.

"Good job, Sotaro-*kun*!" Manager says when Yoshino opens the door. "'High touch'! Good, good! Now, Sotaro, please give Yoshino-*sensei* and Cybelle-*sensei* 'high touch'!"

Sotaro whacks the hell out of Yoshino's hand, then reluctantly turns to me. I let him wind up and move my hand away on purpose.

"Whoops! Try again!"

He stumbles, laughs, and tries again. When he makes contact, he immediately checks his hand. There's nothing there but he wipes it on his pants, anyway.

"Ah, Sotaro is shy," Manager says. "But, he did a good job with 'high touch'! Good job, Sotaro!"

Is that what we're calling it? A good job? Okay. Whatever. It's fine.

Manager asks Sotaro's mother in Japanese what she thinks. She cocks her head, hums a little sound, then nods and mutters something. The manager claps his hands. He thanks her and bows half a dozen times. We have a new student. Fantastic. Guess now Misaki will have someone to teach. Manager then takes us aside to congratulate Yoshino and me in Japanese on a job well done. His mother was very impressed with my patience. To save face, Yoshino follows his command and translates, "Sotaro enjoyed your lesson." Manager goes on another lengthy explanation about what kind of lesson Sotaro's mother might be interested in and asks Yoshino to talk to her about her options. There's no mention of sticking Sotaro into any of my classes. Thank goodness. At least now I can eat.

It must be raining outside when my Moms' trial class starts. The kids come in with their parents, their adorable umbrellas shaped like frogs and ducks, and their giant ponchos. It takes a while for everyone to strip all the wet gear off and usher themselves into the classroom.

"Hello, ladies," I greet them. "How's it going?" Everyone freezes and exchanges deer-in-the-headlight glances. I wait for a few seconds before I repeat my question with a bigger smile. "How's it going, Fumiko?"

Fumiko smiles back but tilts her head. She doesn't understand.

"How are you?" I ask instead.

"Ah! *Naru hodo!* I'm fine, thank you."

"Good!" I turn to the young, ginger-haired woman next to me. "How's it going with you, Mami?"

"Eh … I'm, so-so?"

"Aw, why 'so-so'?" I ask.

Mami takes her time, smiling all the while. "Because … last week … Taiga … had a fever." Everyone goes "aw" in sympathy. "Yes. Taiga had a fever, and … he had no school … so, I take care of him. He is very … spoiled?" Everyone laughs. "'Mommy, I want this! I want this! I don't like medicine! I don't like doctor!' Every day. Such a pain."

"That's too bad. How is he feeling now?"

"Better, but still … spoiled."

Again, we all laugh a little. I turn to the woman next to me. "How about you, Miyoko? How's it going?"

"It's going … not bad. I went to Kyoto this past weekend."

"Cool! Can you describe to us what it was like?"

"Hmmm …" She thinks for a bit. "No."

"It's okay! Try your best! Um … how is Kyoto?"

"Ah! *Wakatta! Ja* … Kyoto is very beautiful. There are many people and many festivals. And I went with my husband. We enjoy. Eh … *tanoshikatta*."

The other moms all nod, adding, *"Ah, sou desu ne,"* and so on. Then they begin conversing in Japanese about how they never have time to travel, what with their kids and all. Then they start talking about how travel is getting more expensive, and how the things in general are getting more expensive, and how *eikaiwa* schools like Zozo are expensive. I feel like a fly on the wall. If I want to call this trial lesson successful, I need to bring the conversation back to what they're going to pay for.

"Well, I'm glad to hear that everyone is doing well. Let's open our textbooks, shall we?"

The moms fall silent. They look down at their books. No one makes any move to pick them up. I'm not sure what I've said or done wrong. I reach for my textbook but Miyoko has a question. "What about Cybelle-*sensei*? How's it going … you?"

"Me? Oh, thank you for asking! Things are okay. I haven't been doing anything special these days." As usual.

"Eh?" Head tilt. "I beg your pardon?"

"Oh, I mean, um, it's going … so-so?"

My students let out a chorus of compassionate *ehhh*'s. Miyoko nods. "You must always be so busy with school. Do you travel on your holidays?"

"Nope. But I'd like to. I never have time anymore. And I don't have anyone to go with. I've always loved Kyoto, though. Never get tired of it."

Miyoko hesitates. "Why do you like Kyoto?"

"It's just beautiful and historic. Kinda reminds me of home. Well, it used to. Now all the cool places are getting bulldozed to make room for ugly glass condos no one can afford to live in. It's not like Japan; you can still see thousand-year-old buildings, right beside the new ones. They can exist together, in the same place — I mean, assuming they're earthquake-safe enough to live in. I've always loved that preservation of history, you know?"

They don't. All three women stare at me like I sprouted a second head. I know these looks. They didn't understand a word I said. I spoke way too much too fast or used too many words they didn't recognize.

"That's right," Mami remembers. "You are from Canada. You will go back to Canada?"

"Um, no. Not yet." Thinking out loud, I go on: "Maybe, I don't know. I think my family wants me to go back, but then I'd have to find a place to live, get a job, figure out a profession. All that fun stuff. I still really haven't thought that far."

Bad idea. Miyoko is the only one nodding, while Mami and Fumiko stare. It's my fault, really. I forgot myself and stepped out of textbook conversation mode. I need to stop doing that. *It's a trial lesson … a trial lesson …*

"Okay, everyone has their textbooks? Awesome! Please turn to page thirty-two."

Thank goodness, they understand that. We read Dr. Martin Luther King Jr.'s "I Have a Dream" speech; an odd introduction into talking about literal dreams, but it's what we have to do. The textbook breaks down the speech, with a side blurb in Japanese about what dreams mean. The textbook also says that for homework, everyone has to write down things people dream about.

"Oh, *shukudai!* Exciting!" Fumiko laughs. "Cybelle-*sensei*, I am very exciting to know what you dream next week!"

"Me, too!" says Mami.

"And me," Miyoko agrees.

"Next week?" What happened to this being a one-time trial lesson?

"Yes," Miyoko beams with pride. "We will have Cybelle-*sensei*'s class on Tuesdays. Manager say before class. Now, we can see Cybelle-*sensei* all the time! Did Manager tell you?"

I rub my eye. It's twitching again. "Oh. Okay ... yes! Um. Please write down your ideas for homework, and we'll share them."

Fumiko points at my eye. "*Ne, sensei, daijoubu?*"

"I'm fine; it's just itchy." When she tilts her head, I make a scratching gesture.

"Ah! *Kayui desu ne.* Maybe, you should sleep more."

"That's probably it."

"Eh?"

Oops. "Yes, you are right. I will try to sleep more." To salvage what's left of our time together, I reach into my teacher kit and take out a box of playing cards and teach them Slap Jack. They start out hesitant at first but get into it by the end. I'm glad they like it; from what I've heard, playing cards are considered the devil's pastime in Japanese schools, so everyone gets excited that they can play them here.

After the class, Manager confirms our new arrangement with the mothers. He apologizes for the short notice but thanks them for signing up. Fumiko and Mami stand quiet, looking reluctant, but Manager assures them our lessons will help their kids. Miyoko is the only one with the brass to say more than a weekend's notice would have been nice. I'm glad someone said it, whether or not it was on my behalf. Oh well, it's another bonus for me, I guess.

The rest of the day flies by. My private lesson with Keisuke goes well, as usual, and my bilingual students go home with a new appreciation for *Sesame Street* after learning about all the different kinds of toppings a pizza can have besides tuna, mayonnaise, and corn. Then I head to the washroom for the *maipetto* spray and a washcloth. It's my day to wipe all the sticky fingerprints and oily forehead streaks from the observation windows. Which is fine, because I need to do something to burn off steam without ruining my skirt suit. On every clock in the school, the number seven throbs in my vision as I go to each room except for Rooms One and Five, where I can hear Seri-*sensei* and Yuki-*sensei* teaching their private lessons. Manager walks by Room Three, sees me inside, and knocks on the door.

"Cybelle, *otsukaresama desu.*" He bows. "You look so fine today. You have … a date?"

What the…? "I have that important trial lesson tonight."

"Eh? No."

I blink a few times. "Yes, I do. Lieko texted me last night?"

"Eh, no …" He repeats, frozen in the door with a blank look; he then smacks his forehead. "*Shimatta!* Ah, Cybelle … one student, asked for trial lesson, then cancelled."

"Seriously?"

"Yes. He is very serious. He really want to have lesson with you, but today he has important meeting with doctor, so maybe, he will not come tonight. Maybe he will see your lesson next week. Sorry. Ah, but you will go to restaurant? After last classes finish?"

Uh-oh. "Tonight?"

"Yes! We will go to Pepe le Pew, behind the station. I thought that is why you wear a skirt. But this dinner is not fancy. It is not *enkai*. Only dinner. But, nevertheless, it will be very exciting. Now, ah, I want to talk about re-contracting form. Do you have?"

"It's still in the staff room. I haven't taken it."

"Ah, yes, but … Lieko wants to know. She asks me, did you finish?"

I hesitate. "Um … no?" Why the hell would *she* care whether or not I did?

He studies the floor for a long time, sucking air in through his teeth. "Hmmm ... *ja*, maybe, then, it's okay. You can finish it another time, maybe." The phone rings in the lobby. "Ah, sorry! I must go! Ah ... wait in the lobby! For everyone!" He dashes out. I hope he means to wait once the day is over, not to sit there right this moment. Once I head back to the staff room, every now and then I take a stretch break from lesson planning to stick my head out the door and check, just in case. No other teacher is out there this early, so I go back to killing time.

Yoshino storms in and hammers away at the staff computer's keyboard. She does not look happy. "Have fun tonight," she mutters. "You look really pretty today, by the way."

"I got pretty just for *you-oo*," I tease her, pretending to poke her cheek. "You're coming, too, aren't you?"

She sighs. "Manager and I have to call more students for supplementary lessons. He 'claims' it won't take long, but we have so many people to call. It's going to take all night."

I sit down. "Yoshino ... be honest with me. How *are* we doing, as a branch? Because I already know we're not doing well."

"Yeah," she sighs again. "We're really not."

"Shit." The word slips from my mouth.

"Don't worry! We're not going to become another NOVA. It's just our school. Ever since Manager became, well, the manager, our school has been losing money. We can join you as soon as we secure more students ... which won't happen if we have fifty more families to call and the stupid computer keeps FREEZING." She kisses her teeth. "This is BS. I'm not even the full-time teacher! This is supposed to be Lieko's job!"

We poke around at the computer until it unfreezes. I sign myself out. "So why isn't she sitting here ripping her hair out instead of you?"

"'*Someone has to go and make sure we keep our reservation,*'" she whines in a quiet, singsong voice. "*Mendokusai.* You go ahead though, have fun. I hear the buns are good; let me know if the rumours are true."

"Will do." I hear Seri-*sensei*'s voice as she comes out of her classroom. Guess there's not much else to do but head to the lobby. *"Osaki ni shitsureishimasu?"* I shrug.

"Hai, otsukaresama."

"Ganbatte ne."

Yoshino gives me a weak smile. "Ha, I'll try. Between you and me, I might leave early and burn the place down."

"Please save my stuff before you do." We manage to force smiles as we leave the staff room together. I go to get my shoes. My hand reaches down to the bottom shelf. Then I wrench it away in time to miss the old, dirty Anpanman toy. "Son of a —! You know what, forget saving my stuff. Promise you'll start with this little monster first."

"Aw, not Anpanman! He's so *cute.*"

The elevator dings. Several parents stream off the elevator, and the lobby is busy again. Seri, Lieko, and Misaki bid their students farewell and suck up to the parents for another ten, fifteen minutes. Then they take their sweet time cleaning, getting their coats, signing out, and pouting about how sorry they are that Yoshino and Manager have to stay longer and work. Yoshino blows me a kiss farewell. I catch it before the elevator doors close. I'll need it; without her, this is going to be a crappy night.

Outside, I stop to unlock my bike. Even though it only takes two seconds, everyone complains about how cold it is and they start their high-heel trot toward the station where part-timers Yuri-*sensei* and Jun-*sensei* will be waiting for us. I try to think of all the possible excuses to not follow them. Maybe if I had any real friends outside of work it would be easier to come up with some outrageous lie. I already told everyone that I don't have a date tonight. This *is* complete BS, as Yoshino would say. Our Zozo branch must be way down in the rank if we have to call and beg people for more lessons. But if Lieko is the one who's supposed to make these phone calls ...

I shake my head. No. Manager is still the manager. I would know if Lieko was about to replace him. She's been with Zozo for a few years, but she's only been with our school since September. It's fine. I'm worrying about nothing. I should look forward to a boatload of French food and some non-work-related conversation. As we walk, I look around at the palm trees lined up along the station approach and the signs advertising seasonal food. The *oden* stands, the roasting chestnuts, the bakery's curry-filled buns and pumpkin-flavoured *pan*. Everything says autumn is here. Even the sounds of thunder —

Ew, that's not thunder, it's my stomach. "Geez, seriously?" I mumble.

Bells chime as Lieko pushes the restaurant door open. We are welcomed by a chorus of *"Irasshaimase!"* This place is new all right. New and expensive: they've got a grand piano and violin playing, more chandeliers than they need, rich cream walls and furniture, and all the employees are dressed in French waiter uniforms with vests, bow ties, and long white aprons. The kitchen must be nearby because I can already smell something good. I strip off my jacket, welcoming the central heat. Any hint of frustration in my mind melts at the thought of a warm bowl of soup coursing down my throat. My co-workers ooh and ahh and point at everything while Lieko approaches the maître d', who bows and leads the way.

My dream bubble pops when a man steps in front of me and cuts me off from the teachers. *"Bonsoir, mademoiselle."* He bows. *"Puis-je vous aidez?"* His pronunciation is perfect, and he's pretty cute.

"Uh, *bonsoir?* Um ... *ensemble?*" I gesture back and forth between me and all my co-workers, now sitting at a table. *"Issho ni?* We're all together. I'm with them. Uh ... them? Over there?"

"Oh! I'm so sorry. *Pardonnez-moi.* I thought you were alone. Please, follow me." He bows again and leads the way. "May I ask you, where are you from? *Vous êtes française?*"

"Uh, no. I'm not …" No, wait. Maybe I can do this. *"Je ne suis pas française; je suis —"*

"Haitienne?"

"Uh, no …"

"Eh? America-jin?"

I laugh. "Canadian. But I don't speak French. Sorry."

"No, no! You speak, ah, very good. And, you speak Japanese? *Sugoi!*"

"Me? You're the one speaking three languages, dude. Doesn't that make you, like, *pera pera … pera?*"

He cracks up. "No, no. I need lots of practice in French. And English. They are not so good. You are a teacher?"

"Yes, I work at Zozo's School of Good English, on the other side of the station." We reach our table, situated under a chandelier sparkling crystal and warm amber light. "We all work there," I gesture to my co-workers.

He bows again to the other teachers, who now have quizzical *Do you two know each other?* expressions. "I see. Ah! Please have a seat." He pulls out my chair for me and everyone makes small, murmuring sounds in their throats. I don't understand why. The guy is just being polite and doing his job.

Lieko smacks open a menu. "Now that *everyone* is here," she snaps in English, "we can order some drinks." Whatever. I'm happy, knowing I have one person I can actually talk to tonight.

"Chotto matte kudasai, Lieko-*senpai,"* Misaki interjects. She asks about Manager and Yoshino, and about waiting for them. Lieko sighs dramatically and says she doubts they'll make it to the restaurant at all. In fact, she adds, Misaki must be very grateful that we can even have this dinner to welcome her. Our school is doing so poorly in the region that we're losing money and Head

Office is very upset with Manager. Misaki says yes, she is very grateful. Lieko says good; she also apologizes for Misaki having to train at our school at such a difficult time. Well, shit. She just confirmed everything Yoshino said earlier. Makes me wonder why we're still having this dinner.

"*Oolong-cha, hitotsu,*" Lieko tells our waiter. Jun asks for oolong tea, as well. Seri and Misaki order orange juice. Yuki and Yuri will just have water. The waiter jots their orders down, then comes around the table back to me. "Ah," he murmurs to me. "*Et ... pour vous?*"

"Hmm ... um ... *Qu'est-ce que vous osusume?*" It just comes out. At least I make him laugh. "Sorry, I mean *recommandez*? Oh, forget it. What do you suggest?"

"Let me see," he gazes up at the chandelier in thought. "Today, everyone has the 'ladies' menu, which is beef au jus and ratatouille. So, I think red wine is the best."

"Ooh, that sounds good." If anything is going to get me through the next two hours, it's alcohol.

"Excuse me, Cybelle," Lieko leans over the table. "The company does not pay for our drinks. Nor is Manager here to cover our bill. Maybe, order water. You should change to water."

What am I, an idiot? "How much for one glass?" I ask instead.

"Five hundred yen."

"Perfect! Glass of red, please."

"Five hundred yen? How cheap! I'll have one, too, please!" Seri says.

"Ah, I'm sorry," Yuki blushes. "One for me, too." Misaki asks for one also. Everyone giggles except Lieko, who does that creepy smile of hers.

"In that case, if you share a large decanter, it's 900 yen," the waiter suggests. We nod in agreement. He bows his leave with an extra nod in my direction. When he and another server bring our drinks, Lieko leads the toast.

"To Misaki, for joining our school," Lieko shows all her teeth. "And we must also toast to Sotaro, the moms, and all the other trial lessons that will bring our school rank up a little higher. Let's all do our best! *Kanpai!*"

"*Kanpai!*" We all clink our glasses and take polite sips. Well, I take a little more than a sip since it'll take a little more than two classes to make a difference for our school. When the food comes, I dig right in. I devour my pumpkin soup, garden salad, and assortment of free hot buns as politely as I can muster. I nod and smile at everyone's comments, but between my ravenous appetite and the number of times someone says "mmm, *oishii!*" I can't think of anything to say. It's a little hard when I have Lieko glaring daggers at me every time someone comments on how "*oishii*" the wine is.

Our waiter returns with several fellow employees and tiny plates of beef and ratatouille. Both my plates are empty while everyone is still crooning over theirs, so I discretely signal a nearby server for another round of bread. Everyone turns them down but marvels as I make room in my tummy for an orange bun, a matcha green tea bun, another small helping from the wine decanter, and some more pumpkin buns. I pretend not to overhear their comments about how much bread I plan to eat as I slather pumpkin bun number three with butter.

"*Sugoi*, Shibelle-*sensei*," Misaki says with wide eyes. "You are so hungry! So much food! But Shibelle-*sensei* is still hungry!"

"'Cybelle.' And yes, I guess I've worked up an appetite."

She turns the word "appetite" over a few times, then gives up. "Did Shibelle-*sensei* eat lunch today?"

Ugh. "Yes. I ate stir-fried rice." Again.

"And breakfast?"

"I ate scrambled eggs and toast."

"And yet you eat so much bread! *America-jin no shokuyoku wa sugoi deshou?*" She's not asking me. She's asking the other teachers.

I look around the restaurant, pretending not to understand. I feel more and more uncomfortable when I realize that no other customers get their chairs pulled out for them. Well, don't I feel even stupider. Desperate times …

"Mmm, yes, the bread is delicious," I say. "I hope I still have room in my *betsu bara* for dessert!"

Everyone around me laughs. "Shibelle-*sensei*, you say *'betsu bara!' Sugoi!*" Misaki giggles, covering her mouth. "Can you speak Japanese?"

"A little."

"Eh, *sugoi.* How long you stay in Japan?"

"Um, about —"

"Uwaa!" Lieko looks down at her uneaten bun and goes on a loud tirade about how full she is and that she has no room for dessert. The conversation switches back to conversational Japanese as they exchange opinions about portion control and dieting. Whatever, I'm hungry.

Our waiter returns with his co-workers and our desserts — small coffee roll cakes and tiny bowls of chestnut ice cream — which brings everyone's focus back to our meal and how delicious it all looks. Perfect timing for me to stuff my face and have an excuse not to talk about myself anymore. All I want to do is be full and be on my way home. I'm not feeling great. *"Sumimasen,"* I signal a different waiter and order some black tea with honey. I realize I've been talking all day, and now that I've gone a stretch without doing so, I can feel a sore throat coming on.

"Anou, Shibelle-*sensei,"* Misaki asks me, eyes wide. "Will you stay at Zozo one more year?"

Oh, great. The last thing I want to think about. "Uh, well …"

"Please stay!" she cries, leaning so close I can smell the wine on her breath. "I will miss you!"

I smile my thanks. With quick glances to Lieko, the others smile and nod but say nothing. What I wouldn't give to dash from this table as soon as I finish dessert, but no can do. Got to stay until the very, very end. Got to fit in. Must do my very best to play my part in the well-tuned *eikaiwa* machine …

"I don't know yet. My sister is getting married soon, I think."

"Eh? *Kekkon suru?*" Misaki asks. "Older sister? Younger sister?"

"She's my youngest sister."

"*Ehhh* … she is so lucky. I think, it is best if you marry at younger age. At older age, it is difficult."

Yeah, thanks.

"Shibelle-*sensei* is married?"

"Ha —! I mean, um, no."

"*Eh?!* So, does Shibelle-*sensei* live with her sister in Japan?"

"No. My family is in Canada."

"So, Shibelle-*sensei* live by herself? *Eh, sugoi!* Very difficult."

"It's okay, I guess."

"Shibelle-*sensei*, how many brothers and sisters do you have?"

"I have six."

I might as well have said thirty-one thousand and eight. Their sudden outburst of laughter makes everyone at the next tables turn and glare at us — well, at *me*. When the post-meal coffee and my black tea arrive, I'm more than happy to have an excuse to stuff my face again with bun number seventeen (or whatever, I've lost count by now), even if it means giving everyone around me another excuse to marvel and stare.

As we leave the restaurant, the cute waiter stops me. "Ah, excuse me, *mademoiselle*." He grins. Everyone — and I mean *everyone*, staff and customers alike — is staring at me. I smile, bracing myself.

"*Oui?*" I chuckle.

"You teach English?"

Shit. Really?

"Then, maybe, I can take lessons? From you? What time is your school —"

"Um, excuse me," Lieko appears, breaking out her highest English voice. "But Zozo's School is strictly for children and parents of students. I'm sorry. And, before you ask, she cannot give you private lessons. It is not in her contract. Sorry."

He looks crestfallen. I'm not about to give up, though. "That's true! I'm free to do language exchange, though. You can teach me Japanese!" Japanese that I don't need, but I'm not about to tell him that.

"Excuse me," Lieko is still looking to the waiter, "but our English teacher doesn't understand this is not allowed. I'm very sorry for her rudeness; our manager will talk to her about this tomorrow. Now, we must go. Thank you for the delicious meal. *Gochisousama deshita!*"

"Lieko-*sensei*," Misaki whispers. "I think, what Shibelle-*sensei* means is —"

Lieko gives her a look that would stop a bullet train. "*Gochisousama deshita,*" she repeats to the waiter with an extra syrupy smile.

"*Mata okoshi kudasaimase!*" the staff sings. Sexy Server Man ushers in the next group. He's already forgotten me. I'm just another customer to him.

Everyone spends another five minutes standing around outside, yammering about how cold it is. Misaki asks the others how I can stand the cold without a proper jacket, and why am I not worried about getting sick. I fish out my keys and unlock my bike. It's high time I get out of here.

"Ah! Shibelle-*sensei*, you ride bicycle?" Misaki cocks her head, noticing my bike as if for the first time. "But, Shibelle drank wine. Is it dangerous? *Abunai deshou?*"

"*Sou desu ne ...*" the others agree. "Maybe, Cybelle-*sensei* should walk back to the station?"

Lieko clicks her tongue and says something to her train pass holder about how Cybelle must know she cannot ride her bike if she has alcohol. If police see me, I could be charged and Zozo would get in trouble. Well, *duh*. Did I just get off the plane?

"Actually, I live this way. Past the stadium. See that 7-Eleven down there?" I point. "My building is right there."

"Oh, really?" Misaki cocks her head. "*Eh, zannen* ... maybe, we are tired. We should take a rest. But maybe we may see your apartment another time?"

My ass, you will. "Sure." I force my face into what I hope looks like a smile. Misaki, swaying a little, goes in for a hug. "Well, see you all tomorrow!" I bow instead of meeting her halfway. "*Otsukaresama desu!*"

"*Otsukaresama desu!*" the teachers sing in high-pitched chorus. "Goodbye! See you again!"

"*Ah mou, hayaku shinasai!*" Lieko snaps, already several feet away. They high-heel-jog after her. Fine by me. I'm just glad they didn't hug me. Sober as a judge, I hop on my bike and pedal like hell.

I've never been so happy to live within walking distance of Zozo. I've never been so happy to live in Nishibe. No painful, awkward commutes to Osaka for me. If I had to keep up this best friend charade for another hour I'd eat someone's face. The girls are sweet for the most part. Not as conversational as some of our past teachers, but not as stuck-up as others. And there have been *many* others. The turnover rate is so high in this line of work. No wonder my old friends — the ones who all left for their home countries or Tokyo — called it the McDonald's of Japan employment. I should be grateful for my co-workers, thanking my lucky stars we don't have *more* Liekos. Geez, the way she takes over everything. My dress, my trial lessons, my re-contracting, my *bread intake* ... it's like she's in training to take over as manager. Again, that can't be right. I'd know if that's what was happening. There would be signs — major signs. I'm worried about nothing.

My bike swerves several times; it's harder to keep it balanced in this skirt. Guess I underestimated those three glasses of red juice. I wobble whenever onlookers step in my path, and one time I almost hit a dishevelled elderly woman who refuses to step out of the bike lane. I walk my bike the rest of the way home, hop in the shower, put on my PJs, and climb into my futon with a box of Oreos. I'm exhausted but still hungry. I'm also starting to regret not buying those graham crackers from 7-Eleven. I could have s'mores right now, roasting under my little *kotatsu* table. *Cybelle, you idiot.* I'll have to make a Flying Pig order soon, especially if I want to get my hands on a pumpkin for my kinders.

Tucked deep into my squishy bed, I try to count sheep. I have to start over several times. I try other things: donuts, doors in my apartment, days until the next national holiday (seventeen … not soon enough).

Screw it. I turn on the TV and watch an hour of foxy boxing and a prank show where they suffocate sleeping TV personalities. I'm not sleepy. And I'm still hungry. That was the most awkward dinner. *To be fair, it beats my welcome dinner.* I turn off the TV and throw myself on my futon. *Oh wait, I never had one.*

I sigh. "Complete BS."

four

RULE 42

出る杭は打たれる
The nail that stands up gets hammered down

It is night again. The human world has wound down after nine-teen hours of school, work, studying, volunteering, cram schools, shopping, errands, cooking, and cleaning (and preparing to do it all again the next day). Long after humans have departed the cities that never sleep, the steel and cement flatlands buzzing with elec-tricity and adrenalin, time has stopped in a tiny pocket of land in a mountain valley. Wisps of smoke above the treetops collect in the cold violet air. Without wind, they spiral and swirl together, in and out of each other, into curlicues and whirligigs, growing in number until they coalesce to form a giant cloud. At the top of the cloud a single, wet eye bulges out. It slowly blinks a vapour eyelid over its red-veined sclera. It searches the night sky, then scans the forest for a clearing. When it locates what it is looking for, it drifts toward the clearing. It hears whispers become murmurs, becoming words:

"Evening."

"Evening? Pretty sure it's later than that."

A rustle in the grass. "And morning for some of us!"

An impatient sigh. "Yes, *Sensu-sama*, we *know*. Good morning, I guess, if that's what you want to hear."

"It is! So, what's the plan today, gents?"

"Ahem."

"And ladies. Or, whatever it is you are."

"Isn't it obvious? I'm an *umbrella*."

"Oh. I see. Is that plastic?"

"Yup! I'm trying a new look. You like?"

"It's very ... modern."

"And yet you can keep your soul. Interesting."

"I know! Aren't you jealous? Yes, you're jealous. I can tell."

"*Ahem*. Back to the matter at hand. What did you have planned tonight? I'm so bored of chasing humans; this better be good."

Other voices agree, offering their various opinions. The smoky cloud descends and settles on the grass, exposing a humungous red full moon in an indigo sky, the light of which reveals a cadre of monsters, varying in shape and size. Animal-like creatures, mostly, with a few modern-day appliances and accessories that have long been abandoned by human owners and became sentient over the years. A short, squat *yokai* with blue scales all over its body excuses itself between a pair of rice cookers to stand before the group on a large, conveniently placed boulder. It places a hand where its neck must be and makes a sound in the guise of a human clearing its throat for attention:

"Everyone. I've been thinking. The *onsen* is just up the valley. We walk around in our starkers all the time, and we're always robbing humans of their clothes, but that's it. Let's up the ante. What say we strip some *skin* tonight?"

"Don't we already do that?" says a dragon-looking demon.

"Not really. See, I hear a lot of humans are afraid of this thing called Titan, and for some reason people keep attacking it?"

"Ugh, that's so ten years ago," a voice pipes up from a broken fan lying in the grass.

"And it sounds foreign," says the umbrella rolling in the grass.

"No, it's Japanese! I think." The scaly blue *yokai* strokes what must be its chin. "Well, it's some creation of Japan. Anyway, I look in people's heads and all I see are big skinless giants running around chasing and eating humans. And *Sensu-sama's* right — you used to see it a lot in human dreams; then it went away. I guess it's making a comeback?"

"Sounds like fun!" the dragon snarls.

The fan feigns a yawn. "Sounds like something we used to do before people got into all this 'late for a meeting' and 'failing a test' garbage. Come on, those aren't *real* nightmares. Whatever happened to getting home before your face gets eaten off? Now *that's* something to worry about!"

"Yes!"

"I concur!"

The blue *yokai* shushes the crowd again. "All right. So are we going with skin?"

"Personally, I wouldn't mind stopping by a bathhouse or two," says one blotchy, red demon with an extremely long tongue.

"What's wrong with scales?" says a catlike *yokai*. "Because if we're talking about skin, then it has to be fish for me."

"Hmmm ..." The blue demon looks down at its own body. "I don't know."

"No white meat," says the small dragon demon, twirling its whiskers. "Human all the way. Everyone knows that red meat is much more delicious. *Enenra-sama*, you hang around humans — wouldn't you agree?"

"Tobaccooooo ..." The cloud of smoke croaks out a smoker's cough.

The blue *yokai* groans. "Should've guessed. I suppose we're heading to another snack bar, then?"

"No snaaacks …" the smoke *yokai* says. "Mmmmeeeeeeth …"

"Yes, yes, we can get some of that, too. Hey, you there!" The blue *yokai* points to someone at the back of the crowd. "What are you in the mood for?"

Behind the last row of creatures, lying in a large ditch, is the Yokai. She stirs in sleep, then sits upright, awake. She scrambles out of the ditch that has been her bed. The other demons turn around and stare. She looks at their stoic faces, recognizing no one. Her face feels itchy. She wipes her mouth, violently — her sleeves come back sticky and black in the thin veil of moonlight. It appears to be some kind of viscous substance, not unlike congealed blood. "Huh? Wha? What's happening?"

"Hey, relax. You must have been having a bad dream. A little ironic, but I'm not judging. You hungry?"

The Yokai looks around, confused. Everyone continues to stare as they await her response. Some demons nod with encouragement, others glare through narrowed eyes. The minimal light from the moon gives her just enough detail to see the crowd, some no higher than her knee, like the dragon, some as big as cars, like the cat. Slowly she begins to understand they are not ordinary creatures, nor are they to be trifled with. Something about the yellow eyes, the too-long claws and fangs, and the scent of blood in the air churns her empty stomach. She can only think of one thing she wants. "I want to go home."

Half the group throws up their hands, arms, tentacles, and similar appendages in disdain.

"I *knew* she wouldn't pick human."

"Told you so!"

"I didn't hear. Did she say scales? *Please* tell me she picked scales!"

"She didn't choose!" a massive pond turtle in the crowd shouts. "I nominate her! Her skin already looks like it's been burned to a crisp. So tasty-looking is she …"

The blue *yokai* silences everyone with another shushing motion of its limbs. "Everyone, please. We're not here to eat our own. We agreed to meet to come to a *consensus?*"

As voices rise into another heated debate, something rustles in the grass next to the Yokai's leg. She feels something wet lick her leg and cries out. "Mmm, just like honey! Or caramel!" the fan squeals. "Try it, try it!"

"What does it taste like? Human, or something else?"

"Oh, please," the umbrella rolls its eye. "If she were human, she'd have bolted by now."

"Not necessarily," the fan pipes up. "Humans can be quite stupid, you know."

The blue demon shushes the crowd again. "We *know*, Sensu-sama. Now, back to business. I get the feeling the majority of us are craving human. You there, Gigantor. You in?"

The Yokai thinks for a moment. "Hmm. I *am* hungry."

"Good. What would you like?"

"... Something to eat?"

"Well, *duh*. What else do you call human skin? Decoration?"

"Oh," the dragon sighs, "that reminds me of a beautiful story. Quite lovely a tale."

"A story!" The other *yokai* all cheer and get comfortable on the grass. "Let's hear it!"

"Certainly. You'll love it; it's all about skin." The dragon makes a throat-clearing sound as it lies prostrate on the ground. The fins on its back start to shiver, playing a light suspenseful accompaniment:

"Once upon a time there were two friends. The very best of friends. Soulmates, you might say. One day, they went on a journey together. The first went to his grandmother's house to borrow her horse for the day, then he went to retrieve his friend and they departed on their journey. They walked, they talked, they laughed, they sang. They had a grand old time. Then, night began to fall, and the friends grew very tired. So, they parted ways. The first friend made sure the second got safely home, then went to return the horse. On his way home, however, the man got so tired he leaned against a tree and fell asleep.

"Suddenly, a *yokai* appeared. It sat beside the man and, when it was sure the man was sleeping soundly, it stole him to eat up his life and claim his soul. When his friend heard this, he became so enraged that he shed his skin and excuse me, but have you heard a single word I've said or are you being *rude on purpose?!*"

The Yokai bolts upright again, eyes snapping wide open. "Oh, I'm sorry. I can't believe how sleepy I am." She laughs nervously. "You were saying something about eating skin?"

Everyone groans again. A ruckus of arguing voices breaks out. Some side with the dragon, wanting to hear the end of its tale. Others side with the Yokai, saying yes, they *were* talking about skin, and that they are still hungry.

The dragon lets out an angry puff of smoke (which the *Enenra* cheerfully gobbles up). "We're ALL hungry, damn it, but I am trying to make a point here that may be useful to the likes of *you* someday! You know what, shut up. I'm not going to bother finishing my story. I'm out of here. Hmph! Ungrateful little shits ..."

The departure of the dragon *yokai* turns the once-composed crowd into a sea of arguments.

"Wait, *Koto-san*, I wanna hear the rest of the story!"

"I thought we were going with skin!"

"What are you fools talking about?! Speak English!"

"But I don't know any English!"

"I mean, no one gets what you're saying! Speak plainly!"

"*Oh.* Well, why didn't you say so?"

The blue *yokai* holds up a claw. "Wait ... I've heard of you. Aren't you the one who ate Akki's house a while back?"

At the sound of the name, the crowd falls silent. Everyone turns their attention to the giant Yokai now.

"Whose house?" Then the Yokai remembers. The warm, dark chocolate, the sweet delectable crunching ... But the other *yokai* fly into a frenzy.

"What?! *This* is the one who ate the boar god's place?!"

"It must be! No one would lie about that!"

"Forget this! I'm out of here!"

"Me, too! No way am I getting wrapped up in *that* business!"

They scatter, galloping on all fours, rolling in the grass or dragging themselves across it, disappearing into the surrounding trees. Some take a moment to stick out their tongues one last time at the Yokai or call her crazy. The Yokai hesitates to follow any of them, which only makes sense as they traverse in different directions — left, right, up into the air, burrowing down into the ground — until she is left alone in the clearing.

Well, at least I won't be eaten, she thinks to herself along with other consolatory thoughts. The Yokai wanders off in search of other friends and food. Being a giant, she covers ground quickly. The scent of peach mixes with cedar and maple, the silence broken by the sounds of what she hopes are bats in the trees and raccoons in the underbrush. The air reeks of overripe fruit. Her stomach feels funny. She sniffs her hands again: they too smell of rotting peach. Suspicion alleviates. *So it isn't blood.* The trees here appear to be full of the large dancing orbs. She grimaces at the sound and sensation of peach pulp squishing under her giant feet. At least, that is what she hopes she is stepping on.

Someone giggles.

The Yokai whirls around. "Who's there?!" She looks around the trees and down at the ground. No response, except another wave of gentle laughter when the wind blows. Her stomach growls. She is still hungry. She heads deeper into the woods, hugging her stomach as if she can protect it from the chill in the wind.

Something rushes over her naked foot. Startled, she backs into the bush and stumbles against a tree, grabbing a branch that shakes a peach loose. It bounces off the Yokai's shoulder and tumbles to the ground. Instinctively, the Yokai reaches out to catch it. She misses.

"Whee! Oof!" The peach giggles as it lands.

"What the ...?" Wary, the Yokai reaches down to retrieve the peach. She picks it up and turns it over. Rolling her thumb over the surface she feels two soft, fuzzy lips open up at her touch. She drops it with a shudder. "Ew! What the hell?!"

Giggling, the peach rolls around on the ground. Face-down, its words are muffled: "That tickles! Do it again!"

"Ugh!" The Yokai runs away, horrified. *What the hell is this place?*

The Yokai finds herself on the other side of the underbrush. A wide dirt path winds ahead of her. Holding her raging, empty stomach, she climbs up a small hill and follows the path. Her surroundings are just as unfamiliar as before. The now-leafless trees extend high above her like old, scraggly fingers. *Are the trees getting taller*, she wonders, *or am I getting smaller?* She is unsure until she notices a figure on the path, about the size of a normal human. She must be shrinking, she thinks to herself. Maybe it is the hunger. She must find something to eat, somewhere to go, before she disappears altogether. It is not a stressful thought, merely a calm conclusion that spurs her to approach. Despite the darkness she can tell the figure — a man, by the look of it — has his back turned to her. Something also tells her she is about to get a rude awakening when she approaches this person. She braces herself. She hopes this person is politer than those creatures in the clearing.

"Excuse me," she begins. "Hello? Can you help me? I'm lost and ... Hello?"

The person does not answer. She comes closer, ready to tap his shoulder. Just as she reaches out, he turns around, slowly. His face is smooth as an egg, featureless. The Yokai freezes. He grabs the Yokai by the shoulders and brings his egg-face dangerously close to hers. He makes a muffled sound from where his mouth should be. "Rrrr!"

The Yokai stares at him, baffled. "Excuse me?"

"Rrrr!" he repeats.

"Never mind." This one is no help. She wrestles herself from his grip and continues on.

"Rrr!" he shouts after her. Disgusted, he bats his hands at her. "Ah, forget you. How rude."

The Yokai looks over her shoulder to rebuke him, then thinks better of it. Best not to get into an argument with someone without a face. He must have enough problems already. "Weirdo," she can't help muttering under her breath.

"I know, right? The people you run into around here."

"Tell me about it," says the Yokai, turning to look ahead of her to the source of the kind, feminine voice. "That guy had ... no face."

The Yokai finds herself face to face, for lack of a better term, with an old woman. At least, the Yokai presumes her to be an old woman. Her back is curved and bent, her hair is long and pale in the moonlight. Everything about her seems normal except for the absence of eyes, nose, and mouth. The faceless woman does not move.

"That's it? That's all you have to say?"

"Um ..." the Yokai says. "Yes?"

"Aren't you scared?"

The Yokai's stomach gurgles. She hopes the woman has not heard it. "Should I be? You can't help it if you have no face. Look, I'm just trying to ..."

"To what, dear? Where are you going?"

The Yokai shrugs half-heartedly. "I don't even know anymore."

"Well, how did you get here?"

"I don't know that, either. I'm not feeling all that well. And I'm *starving*. I just want to get out of here and go home."

"Home? Where is that? Oh, wait. I get it. You're the *yokai* everyone's been talking about. That explains it. Sorry. You've been at the *jinmenju*, I see." She points to the Yokai's feet, still covered in remnant streaks of peachy juice. "Yeah, better get them while they're still in season, eh? You're smart. Not like those other sheep teeming up the villages."

"The villages?"

"Yup. Can't get into a decent *onsen*, now. Gotta wait in lines like a bloody human until the fire festival's over. Pain in the ass. But what can you do? Come on. We'll get you home."

"'We'?" The Yokai turns around. The faceless man is behind her now, nodding. "Oh. Oh, thank you."

"That's the spirit, dear. This is not the best place to be alone ... in the dark ..."

Together, they watch an assortment of short creatures pass them on the path. A hoard of small lumpy creatures somersault and cartwheel past her; some run hand in hand with relatively normal-looking children. One of them is a wet-faced boy who stops to stare at the Yokai as if she is the scariest creature he has seen today. As one of the fleshy lumps extends an arm and pulls him along by the cuff of his pyjama sleeve, the boy lets out a wail and allows himself to get dragged along.

"See what I mean?" says the faceless woman. "Abnormal little creatures in these parts. They'll attract the *yamauba* for sure. Let's get out of here."

The Yokai presses on with the faceless ones. The scent of peach and the calls between the crows and crickets fade. The gentle breeze tugs at the Yokai's kimono, tickles her naked legs. She knows this place.

The faceless old woman interrupts the Yokai's thoughts. "What are you here for again, kid? You said you were lost or something?"

"Yes. I'm ..." the Yokai pauses. Suddenly, she cannot decide what is a more pressing matter. The lack of food, or her desire to go home. The last thing she wants to do is scare them off, as she did before with the other *yokai*. "I'm just looking for a place to eat," she decides to say.

"Ah. You can't be looking for the place I'm thinking of, then. There's only one in these parts. You do NOT want to go there." The woman shudders. "Disgusting place."

"Why not?" The Yokai asks, wary. "What's wrong with it?"

"It's made of sin," says the faceless man. "And eyes. Eyes everywhere. Watching, always watching."

"Hmm, yeah. Not my bag."

Deeper into the woods, on both sides of the path, the Yokai can hear more nocturnal creatures chattering, chirping. Something has them on edge. She stops to listen for a brief moment. She knows this road. Its twists and bends are familiar. The thick stench of blood and carrion that hit her like a punch in the nose are not.

"Ew!" The Yokai clamps her sticky sleeves over her face. She turns on her heel and runs away to catch up with the others. Behind her, four small shadows drag the remains of their evening meal across the path and head deeper into the bowels of the woods, past an arrangement of trees that do not match and are ever changing: thousand-year-old oak, majestic redwood, thick reedy bamboo, baby spruce, short fat pine, many others with no names.

The body they drag behind them leaves ten long fingernail marks of blood down the path; the trails curve where the road opens up onto a large abandoned garden. The body stains the dead grass as it lies in a crumpled heap of limbs, and is then slumped into a vacant hole under a skeletal bonsai tree. The shadows have no need to fret about their next meal tonight. Their work complete, they suck the last salty red globs from under their fingernails. Their heads turn in one swift motion; they are being watched. They recognize the young man, his cold grey eyes staring without judgment or emotion. *Oh, him. Who cares?* They do not even bother to hiss at him in warning. They leave the garden and leave Zaniel to his thoughts.

Zaniel stares up at the house he has come to hate. Same deep eaves, same worn-down wood-panelled walls, same faded *onigawara* tiles, same makeshift monument at the very top — a spherical structure stippled with an array of long spikes, all tarnished from wind, water, and the passage of time. It has held up quite well, Zaniel thinks, considering whichever ancestor of Akki's copied the original *Yumedono* roof decoration must have been a samurai, not an architect. Not that Zaniel can hear his thoughts above the voice yammering loudly from Akki's bedroom, repeating vocabulary she must have crammed before she went to sleep:

"Lutetium, carbon, iodine, darmstadtium —"

In the bedroom, a young woman gathers her clothes as she drills these words over and over in her mind. She has no idea where she is, but she is almost certain she is far from campus and therefore late for her big chemistry exam. Not that she is complaining. She had so much tension, so much steam to blow off. This exam will be a breeze … unless it has already started. Now, what could have happened to her bra? How strange; she is no longer sure that she came in wearing one.

"Silicon, iodine, nitrogen, sulphur, oxygen — tee-hee! No, wait! Sulphur, hydrogen, *then* iodine, nitrogen —" She smirks, and bursts into giggles. "Oxygen, nitrogen …" she trails off, studying her new-found lover as if she is seeing him for the first time. "Hey, what happened to you? Wow … you've changed! Your skin is, like … *glowing* … and I didn't see that dragon there before … oh, no! It's okay! I like it! Change is good! Change is important; otherwise, everything stays the same. So boring. Change, transformation … physical and chemical — consequent release of heat and sound — yes, that will be on the test for sure —" She giggles again. Yes, they definitely made quite a bit of sound, and heat, no question about that. "I've always preferred a man with muscles. Men are usually so skinny. You can't protect a woman with a body like your little friend. Oh! I'm sorry! Please don't look at me like that. I mean, he's okay, just … not as handsome and strong as *you*. I just didn't feel as much chemistry with him … yes, chemistry: enthalpy and entropy — basic thermodynamics," she continues nonsensically to herself. "Endothermic, exothermic transformations … oxygen, nitrogen —"

Akki grabs his black *yukata*, runs out, and slams the door behind him, practically flying down the stairs. He does not even bother to put on his sandals. He goes out the front door, desperate for a smoke. He can still *hear* her talking inside. He rubs his brow, right in the spot where he can feel pressure starting to bloom. "Zaniel," he curses. *One of these days I'm gonna eat this kid.*

He walks out into the garden and looks back at the house as he dons and tightens his robe. It is just the way he remembers it. Everything seems normal: an ancient, traditional Japanese home. This has been the only home he has ever known, and it was not until its mysterious disappearance that he began to appreciate it. Not that it stopped him from setting it ablaze when the mood took him. Like a loyal dog, it always returns to him, and listens only to his command. *Why can't everyone be so obedient?*

The front gardens remain as they are, as well. Zaniel is right where he should be, waiting on a cold stone bench, hunched with his hands in his pockets, staring at the rock gardens that have not been touched in a century. Hino has just arrived from wherever her night adventures had taken her. She is not alone. Several green-hued creatures, no taller than her knee, scuttle after her like children. A heavy-looking plastic shopping bag swings from her hand. Hino sits down on another bench, as if unaware that Zaniel, Akki, and the little creatures are around. She removes her blazer, lays it across her short skirt and exposed thighs, and dumps the contents of the bag onto her lap: cucumbers. The sight of them stirs the creatures into a frenzy. Their eyes glow bright red with a feverish excitement. They chirp with eagerness, nipping at Hino's pale-skinned knees. She slices the cucumbers by hand — literally.

Zaniel watches with a mix of fascination and horror as Hino saws her long, sharp fingernails through each cucumber until they are slicing into the palms of her left hand and then tosses the vegetables for the *kappa* to fight over. She draws no blood, for there is no blood to be drawn. The wound in Hino's left hand opens and closes in a steady cycle of self-repairing gashes. Zaniel has never seen this before. He is finally beginning to wrap his mind around what kind of *yokai* Hino truly is. He is so horribly fascinated that he does not notice Akki standing nearby until Hino has dealt out the last of her third cucumber.

"Yeah?" he asks without thinking. He then leaps to his feet with a deep bow at the recognition of his own apathy. "I mean, I'm sorry, Akki-*sama*. I must have kept you waiting. Were you looking for me?"

"Damn right I'm lookin' for you. What —" Akki points to a window on the upper floors, where they can hear the young woman's incessant chatter "— is THAT all about?"

"Barium, potassium, uranium ... Barium, potassium, uranium ..." floats down to them from the upper window.

Zaniel hesitates. "She is ... who you requested? The one you met at Yoshida campus? She did tell me she dreamed about you, and from what I saw in her mind, she *really* wanted to —"

"Oh no, she's the same chick — and she's a fuckin' bore! I wanted young, nubile, and excitin', and you bring some chemistry *otaku*? You're KILLIN' me, boy."

"I'm sorry, Akki-*sama*. I suppose ..." He is not sure what to say. If he were to tell the truth — that looks and deep-rooted desires rarely have any correlation with interests or even personality — Akki would destroy him on the spot. He knows too well the dangers of pointing out the mistakes of his superiors; however, he cannot think of a better argument. "I suppose," Zaniel says finally, "it is possible that my ability to read people isn't what it used to be."

"I'll say." Akki spits on the ground. Zaniel looks away, holding back his gag reflex as the large blob of saliva foams and sizzles the earth. "Fuck, man, I remember when we first met, you could get a dozen bitches in one place, one night to meet me. I had to be so fuckin' selective back then. Now, we're chattin' up, like, one chick a week? And that's on the nights when I fuckin' call *you* up. What's goin' on? You losin' your touch? Chicks don't dig the eyes anymore? No, wait, I know. The human realm gettin' on your ass again, is that it?"

"No, Akki-*sama*. Far from it. In fact, things in the waking world have never been better."

Akki flashes his teeth in a menacing smile. "You're lyin'," he sings.

"Uh, wait. I didn't mean to — I meant ..." He bows low. "I apologize. You're right, things *have* been better, but right now things are okay. They're stable. I'm ... managing." It is truthful enough for Akki to relax his smile: although Zaniel's boss and co-workers are horrible to him, his work situation is not his biggest concern. He had assumed Akki already knew that. "I have no cause for complaints."

"So, nobody's beatin' you up, buggin' ya for lunch money anymore, eh?"

"No, Akki-*sama*. That was years ago. I've long since graduated."

"Grad ... u ... a ... ted...?"

"Uh ... *sotsugyou*?"

Again, Akki turns over each syllable in his mouth. He shakes his head as though he does not much like the taste of the word. Zaniel is surprised. The word must not translate well into *yumego*. Then again, Akki has never been much of an eloquent *yokai*.

"Whatever. That's good. I guess. Means more beauty sleep for me." The *yokai* stretches and yawns as the chemistry major's monologue continues somewhere in the upper room, through a window:

"Lutetium, carbon, iodine, darmstadtium …"

Akki makes a disgusted noise. "Well, *I'm* done for the night. Go on, kid, get outta here."

"Yes, Akki-*sama*. My apologies, again." Zaniel bows a graceful ninety degrees and turns away while Akki begs Hino for a cigarette, trying to hide the excitement in his voice at her return. Zaniel does not bother to bid Hino farewell; she is too preoccupied with the two small green creatures fighting with fiendish delight over her slices of cucumber. Past Akki's gate the forest is now a dark void of dead trees, stripped bare of their autumn leaves, into which the young man disappears without a sound.

The obsidian beads on Akki's left wrist begin to glow. "Ah, shit. Seriously?"

"Wow, so soon?" Hino takes out a cigarette for herself. Akki does not answer. He is already on all fours, his fiery-green aura rippling into the shape of a boar. He charges toward the gate, headlong into the bramble.

"Where are ya, kid?" the boar growls. *He couldn't have gone far …*

"Son?"

Akki whirls around and lets out a squeal, ready for anything. He is not entirely prepared to see a ginger-haired foreigner with his pants about his ankles exposing his rear end at him, but neither is he surprised when a giant eyeball appears where his anus ought to be. Zaniel is cowering against the base of a tree. "A *shirime*? What the hell you doin' in this neck of the woods? This is *my* turf."

The eye swivels and focuses on the boar. "… Akki?" The man's eyeless head peeks between his legs. "Is that you? Damn. Then that means …"

"Exactly. The kid's mine. Beat it, asshole. Uh, that didn't come out right. Whatever. Just leave the kid alone."

"Crap. And I had this awesome *gaikokujin* disguise, too. Least I know it works."

The disgruntled *yokai* crawls off into the woods in search of another target for his prank. Akki morphs back to his humanoid form and offers a hand to pull Zaniel to his feet. "Relax, kid. It's gone."

"I'm sorry, Akki-*sama*. I …" Zaniel's blush is visible to Akki, even in the dark. "I panicked. I was too preoccupied with my thoughts, and when that *shirime* appeared, and called me 'son,' I forgot where I was — I didn't know what to do, so I —"

"Eh. No worries, kid. That's what the bracelets are for. Go on, get outta here before another one shows up."

Again, the young man bows a perfect ninety degrees before he curls back up against the tree. Akki waits patiently for Zaniel to fall asleep. It only takes a moment for him to disappear. With a disgusted shake of his head, Akki tromps back to the house. He is relieved to see Hino is still there doling out cucumbers, but his good mood is dashed when his latest conquest sticks her head out his bedroom window.

"Samurai-*sama*! Samurai-*sama*, where did you go?"

Akki rolls his head back with a hand on his immense forehead. "Ah, fuckin' hell … it never *ends*."

"She is looking for *you*, I believe." Hino cuts another slice of cucumber in her hand.

"Yeah, no shit." Akki tilts his head at her. "Say, how'd you get those, anyway? I thought *yokai* couldn't run around the human realm all people-like."

"You forget, I am not restricted by territory. I am completely different from you. I have my ways."

"Oh." The giant *yokai* rubs his temples. "You don't think I was too hard on the kid, do ya? Or maybe I wasn't hard enough?"

"He is your minion, not mine."

"Stop callin' him that! You're confusin' him with my nightmares. Zaniel's my wingman. He's my buddy, my *kouhai*. I look out for him, and he helps me with my chick game. The pact works out for both of us."

Hino's stoic voice and expression do not change in spite of her bewilderment at this declaration. "How can you call him your 'buddy' when you did not even know he was half-Japanese? How can you call him your *kouhai*? He is the one doing *you* the favour, navigating women with a samurai fetish through this realm for you. Such strange terms you choose, Akki."

"So what if I don't know the word for it? Can't expect me to keep up with all this bullshit human lingo."

"Why not? I thought you used to be one."

Akki snorts. "Prove it."

"Hmm …" Hino dangles a cucumber slice above the *kappas'* heads and relishes in their dance without smiling. "Well, if you ask me, I question whether he still needs your protection. He looks like a grown man to me."

"'A grown man'?" Perhaps. Try as he might, Akki cannot recall how much time has passed between this *shirime* attack and the first time he came to Zaniel's rescue in these woods. The boy's hair was not quite so long, of that he is certain. He shakes off his doubts. "Nice try, Hino," he rebuffs. "Always knew you had a thing for him. But like I told the *shirime,* you can't have him. He's *my* human."

Hino ignores him, more concerned with making her point than hearing about the demonic encounter. "He is a timid, insecure man to be fair, but a man, nonetheless. All I am trying to tell you is he is no longer the boy you followed into the wrong part of the woods. You heard him, he graduated years ago."

"Agh, this *word* again." Akki nurses his temples once more. "You *know* how I feel about learnin', Hino-*chan.*"

"He knows these mountains like the back of his hand, now," she goes on, slicing up her last cucumber. "And I am certain the *yokai* around here are familiar enough with *you* to leave him be — for the most part. From what I have overheard, there are fewer threats to him every passing year."

"*Please.* You saw how fast my wrist lit up. *Yokai* still mess with him, and he's scared shitless about it. If you'd seen him cryin' into that tree, you'd know what I'm talkin' about. Shit. If he were a real man, he'd fend 'em off like one, but what does he do? He calls *me.*" Akki holds up his left forearm, gesturing to his black bracelet. "So when the mood takes me, I call *him.*" He holds up the red one on his right. "And by the way, before you even ask, he always answers. Yup. Still comes around with these broads lookin' for a good time with a *real* man, so he must need me around for somethin'. Sure ain't to keep himself entertained at night."

Akki's latest conquest emerges from the house. She comes up to him and pulls at his *yukata* in a coy fashion, enticing him to come back to bed. Without turning to acknowledge her presence, Akki reaches out a large hand and plants it right on her face. He hoists her several feet off the ground, ignoring her fruitless kicks and muffled screams as he continues his conversation with Hino.

"To be real with you, I'm surprised he don't take none of these chicks we meet for himself. I wouldn't be bothered by it. I'd be impressed, to be honest. But hey, I ain't complainin', either."

"But are you not afraid the boy will take off on you one day? Ever worry he will lose his ability, or get inspired come springtime to KonMari his life, starting with us? Or, who knows, maybe he will just start ignoring you altogether one day ..."

"Yeah, *right.* It'll take more than spring cleanin' and the cold shoulder to get rid of me. I don't plan on removin' those bracelets no time soon. Believe that."

"Yes. I suppose I could believe that." Hino tosses the last of her cucumber slices on the ground. The *kappa* creatures tackle them like ravenous birds. "But what will you do until such a time comes to live without him? You must have some plans to prepare for this distant future without your 'buddy/*kouhai*'?"

"Pssh. Easy. I'll do what I always do: whatever I want."

Like a stovetop filament, Akki's hand glows. The young woman's screams grow higher, reaching a screeching cry. Her face bursts into flames.

"Whoops!" Akki drops her. "Almost forgot about these." He reaches down to pluck out her eyes. "Fuck. Overcooked 'em again. No wait, this one's still good." He flicks the burned eye into the air and catches it in his mouth like candy.

Hino narrows her gaze at him, at the remains of human soul sizzling in his hand. "And what, pray tell, do you plan to do with *that* one, Akki?"

Akki quickly shifts his enclosed fist behind his back. In his fervour it had not occurred to him that Hino might show concern. "What are you?" he says. "A cop? Ain't none of your business what I do with my eyes. I mean, *their* eyes — I mean … uh … Whatever, man, it's the only way I can sleep!" He backs away toward the house, his burning green eyes shifting. "You're not gonna tell the kid, are ya?"

"Tell the kid what?"

Akki relaxes. "That's my girl! … Or, whatever y'are. I'll see ya 'round, Hino-*chan*."

Hino watches him turn and head back into the house with a blank stare. "Yes," she shakes her head at the closing front door. "I suppose I will."

Elsewhere, on the other side of the forest, the Yokai wakes up. She looks around, bewildered. A sliver of moonlight reveals a large clearing again. Perhaps it is the same one as before; she cannot tell. She only knows that she is all alone. The faceless people are gone.

"What …?" the Yokai says out loud. She struggles to remember how she got here. Half-remembering, the Yokai sees, in her mind, a group of children that passed by, chasing one another. Or, being chased. A vague image of an old, gawking woman floats through her memories, as well. She remembers a child left behind, screaming, swallowed up by a wall of darkness. She does not remember walking about the woods after that, but here is where she must have ended up.

"I've gone in circles, I guess," she says, deciding it is best not to think about it too much. The Yokai figures it is better to preoccupy herself with how to get out of here.

Slowly, the clouds part above her, exposing a blanket of stars in a sea of violet darkness. One at a time, the stars descend on her; like fireflies, they blink as they approach. They come close, so close she can reach out and touch them. Twinkling like gold, they float down, down, down like falling leaves, then bounce along an invisible horizon above her head.

"How pretty," she whispers.

"Wish I could say the same for you!" Someone blows a raspberry in her ear.

"Hey!" The Yokai leaps to her feet. She finds herself surrounded by blinking lights, will-o'-the-wisps of gold that now float around her. She hears laughter, but not the kind that she would want to join. Mean, threatening laughter. "Who said that?! Who's there?!"

The laughter grows louder and more intense. "Well, well, look who it is? The freak everyone's so scared of. What's wrong, freak? You lost again?"

"Don't bother explaining, freak," one of the lights barks at her. "You ain't welcome here. You're the *futakuchi-onna* or whatever who ate Akki out of house and home. You better beat it!"

"You sure she's a *futakuchi*, brother?" says another light. "She sure don't look like one."

"Yeah. What in the hell are you supposed to be, anyway?"

"Maybe she's some sorta shadow *yokai*."

"Well, she's a pretty gnarly shadow, if you ask me. She just looks like a freak."

The Yokai whirls around at the sound of each chastising word. *Why do they keep calling me a freak?* The Yokai thinks about all the creatures she has seen tonight. The strangeness of them all, and yet she is the one everyone runs away from. It does not make sense. What makes her more monstrous than them? Her words are on the tip of her tongue, but for some reason she cannot bring herself to speak. Instead, she tries to smile. "I'm sorry, I —"

"Ew! What's wrong with her face? What's she doing?"

"Are you *smiling*? What is wrong with you?"

"She must be stupider than we thought."

"Or stupider than she looks!"

"And what the hell is that on her robe? Is that — ew, it is! It's blood! It's fucking *blood*!"

"No!" The Yokai waves her hands. "It's peach … I think …"

"You think?! Oh ho, look at that, guys. She 'thinks'! Could've fooled us, freak."

The Yokai feels her stomach lurch again. Not from hunger, but from fear. She stops smiling. "I'm sorry," the Yokai repeats. "I'm just lost."

"Yeah. We know *exactly* where you're trying to go. There ain't no way in hell we're letting ya, so don't even bother trying to play nice with us!"

One of the lights descends so close to her face that her vision is blurred. The Yokai squints through her fingers and sees that it is the brightness of the other lights that is also blinding her. They dance around her in a wide halo of light. They are singing:

"Lost little Yokai
Looking for a friend
Wandering in a wilderness
She cannot comprehend!
Looking for the others
That she cannot befriend
Posing as a human fool
Or tryin' to pass off as a ghoul

Dumb and stubborn like a mule
So she must meet her end!"

"Little? I'm not …!" The Yokai looks down at her body. She is about half the size of an average human. She can practically feel herself shrinking under her lengthening white robe. "Stop! *Stop it!*" she cries.

"Ha, ha, look at her now!" the voices cackle. The Yokai can sense them pointing invisible fingers at her. "She's shrinking! Let's make her shrink until she disappears!"

Without warning, they swarm her. She waves her too-long sleeves across her face, swatting fruitlessly, as they attack. Some fly past her ears, the chainsaw-buzzing startling her each time. Others sink invisible fangs into her robe and rip the clothing away. More lights come at her, attacking her exposed skin. Soon she is naked. She makes a hopeless attempt to cover her bare parts while pressing her hands against the missing chunks of flesh they take out of her. She collapses into the grass, crying, huddled into a ball for protection.

"That ought to get the message across," says one of the lights. "Only *real* demons can get past us. And even then, you gotta be ready to take us all on!"

Another voice laughs. "Yeah, stupid! No freak like you is going anywhere! We're like that new restaurant: '*oni* only!'"

"Oh, geez," says the first voice, the ringleader. "Do *not* mention that restaurant."

"Why not? The boss seems to like it. Says they got good eatin'."

"Shut up! We can't talk about that place in front of *her*. She's a wannabe. This ain't no place for creatures like *that!*"

Curled up in the grass, the Yokai weeps. The first light lowers itself down to the grass and nips at her toes, savouring the blood. She cries out again.

"Ha! I think she gets it now, chaps. Guess the freak speaks *yumego* after all. Come on; let's get out of here. The smell of her is making me sick."

"Yeah. Good."

The other lights dance over her head and drift away, still calling her every awful name they can think of. One light lingers behind, illuminating her vision in the darkness, for even the moonlight is gone. The Yokai watches the lights grow smaller and smaller. She sits up a little and looks down at her body, covered in bloody holes, blisters, and bites. Why did they do this to her? What had she done? Perhaps she should have stayed with the faceless *yokai,* for at least they were civil to her. Even the first group of *yokai* had not treated her like this. If only she knew the way home ...

The light hovering over her head makes a darting motion. It hits her square in her jaw, knocking out a tooth, then flies away to join the others. "Ha!" it shouts. "Guys! Guys, did you see that?! I got a tooth! A whole tooth!"

The Yokai can hear them all laughing at her in the distance, congratulating their comrade, over the sound of her own lamentation. She holds a hand to the burning spot on her face and feels blood oozing from the corner of her mouth, wet and thick like paint. When she tries to feel around her mouth with her tongue, she gags on something sharp. The Yokai coughs, and coughs, and with a cautious hand, she slowly guides a long, sharp sliver out of her mouth. There are more inside, a spiky network of pins and needles that seem to be growing as she removes another and another. She is afraid to speak, let alone swallow, whimpering as she takes out each one. She lets out a fresh sob once they are all gone, sitting in a pile in the grass at her knees.

Careful not to disturb the small mountain of spiky metal, she crawls away. Her hand plunges into something wet. Water. The moonlight returns. A small pond stretches out in front of her. She crawls into it, hoping the cold water will soothe her. It is not enough. Each gaping hole on her arms and legs still burns like acid. She sits in the water and hugs her knees to her chest. More than anything she tries not to look at her reflection in the water. The reflection of a monster, the monster that everyone else sees: skin dark as a shadow, grotesque bulging eyes, swollen lips encircling a mouth ready to devour and maul the innocent, and scars, scars everywhere. A patchwork of hate.

"I just wanted to go home," she whispers. She is grateful that this time there is no one around to reply.

five
POOLS OF TEARS

覆水盆に返らず
There is no use crying over spilled milk

"*Ima okina-EE-to, okurema-SOO, yo … Ima okina-EE-to, okurema-SOO, yo …*"

TGIS: Thank God it's Saturday — the longest time until I have to go back to Zozo. I just need to keep breathing until then.

As I put on my skirt suit and butter up a slice of Texas toast, I almost look forward to this networking party tonight. I'm in a good mood for once. It also occurs to me that I haven't been eating as much as I ought to, staring down the Kraft Dinner I just made for lunch. Zozo doesn't have a fridge or a microwave, but it'll keep warm in my bento box until twelve. After this, I'll make it a point to eat healthier.

I'm slowly riding past Yagi-*sama* and the post office when I hear my phone vibrate in my purse. The clock in the post office says it's not even quarter to ten yet, but my purse tingles a second time and once more as I ride past Tully's. What the hell is going on? It's not like I'm late. Maybe it's text spam … or maybe someone from home wants to get a hold of me. Maybe something's happened. Something serious. Or it's Lieko harassing me again … but for what? For running late? Late for what? I'm never late. Late, my ass. If anyone accuses me of being late for anything I will dragon-punch them in the throat. For crying out loud, they can't make me pedal any faster than I'm already going so get off my freaking phone and —

No. I stop myself. That's the "old" Cybelle losing her temper over meaningless premonitions. This Cybelle is polite, professional, and has not been late once in all the years she's lived in Japan. *There's no need to go into attitude mode. Don't be so paranoid. It's time to enjoy English!*

Just to be safe I decide to take a quick detour under the train tracks. I'll get to Zozo a little faster and maybe shut everyone up a little sooner.

The tunnel is a small pocket of darkness, as expected, occupied by only one passerby: an old woman, by the look of her unkempt grey hair and staggering gait. Nothing out of the ordinary — until I pass her. The silence of the tunnel is torn by a long, loud snort erupting from her nasal cavities.

"Nooo!"

I crush the brake levers on my handlebars and skid to a halt. She hocks a massive projectile that splats on the pavement. It misses me by inches. I can't help gasping in horror as I shut my eyes and turn my head away before I can see what is on the ground. My "nooo" echoes down the tunnel. The old woman turns and snarls: *"hrrrrnh …"* It's a guttural, gurgling, angry sound. I can feel her eyes on me in the dim light. I know that if I look down at the ground at what could be on my bike or on my clothes if I hadn't stopped, I will puke. Unsure of what else to do, I back up and walk my bike around her, to give her plenty of space. Once I'm out of the tunnel I can't help looking over my shoulder. She has stopped in her tracks. She watches me go with bloodshot eyes and dribble running down her chin.

Now I'm glad I might be late for work. It gives me the perfect excuse to pedal faster than I've ever pedalled in my life, because *that* is what I would call a premonition. I don't want any more nasty surprises projected at me. I should turn back, go home, and call in to use one of my sick days. Wait, how many sick days *do* I have?

And is it me, or have I seen that woman somewhere before?

Cybelle, you idiot. You're being paranoid. Let's enjoy English. Must enjoy English …

The elevator opens onto Zozo's floor and I come face to face with the cutest, chubby-cheeked boy I've ever seen, chewing on my foam sunset picture. His pants are billowy and white; his shirt is deep blue with a red bow tie and a white hood with a blue sailor's hat sewn on. It's a Donald Duck outfit for toddlers. His eyes widen, making them look quite puffy underneath. I've never seen a toddler's eyes go so wide. I smile, anyway, trying my damnedest to ignore my drool-soaked picture in his hands. I don't even want to know how he got it. It belongs to him, now.

"Oh, hello," I say. "Who might you be?"

He screams. He runs away and throws himself into a young woman's arms. He screams and screams some more. The woman stares at me like I just kicked him. *"Ohayou gozaimasu,"* I greet her with a bow. She doesn't respond. Whatever. That's fine.

I go to the other side of the entryway to change my shoes and prepare to sneak away. Lieko and Misaki are sitting on the lobby floor. They've already been playing with him for a while it seems, but now that I'm here I'm causing too much of a distraction. Misaki can't get the little boy to return his attention to that disgusting Anpanman toy gyrating on the floor. She picks up Anpanman and nuzzles it against the boy's back as he continues to scream like a banshee into his mother's small bosom. "Say, 'hell-o, Sheee-belle! Hello! Hello!' Aww … he is so shy!"

Yeah, shy, my ass. I turn to go to the staff room, not in the mood to deal with Misaki or Lieko's staring or any more strangeness today.

"Cybelle," Manager stands up behind the info desk. He smiles with tremendous effort. "This is Hitomu. He is your *trial lesson today?*"

My jaw twitches, like it's about to unhinge. I think long and hard before I speak. "I'm sorry, Manager. I don't remember you telling me about it."

His smile fades for about a second. So, I'm right; he never told me. His smile quickly returns to disguise his epiphany. "Ah ... it was Wednesday. As you can see, Hitomu has some troubles. So, *mama* takes Hitomu to doctor on Wednesday. Hitomu cancel, before dinner for Misaki-*sensei*. Hitomu rescheduled to this day. He called, last night. After Cybelle went home."

"I see. But why not text me?"

"Ah, Lieko say she text you and you don't reply. But now, it does not matter. You can do trial lesson today? Please?"

"Sure." I look back at the shrieking child. "Hi, Hitomu."

Didn't think it was possible, but yes, he can scream louder. Whatever, fine, let's get this over with. "Okay, fine, I'll get Room Five set up now —"

"Ah, Cybelle-*sensei*," Manager sucks air in through his teeth. "Ah, lesson is, not now. Hitomu will take your lesson at lunch. So, please take your time, but ... maybe, Hitomu will need some time to get ready. So, you must be ready for sometime between twelve and one o'clock."

"*What?*" I can't keep the edge out of my voice. "I'm sorry, but I thought trial lessons only take ten minutes. It's Saturday. When am I supposed to eat lunch?"

Manager's smile twitches. I'm pretty sure everyone sees it. "Ah ... Cybelle-*sensei* ... *jitsu wa* ... maybe, it is the only time that Hitomu can have a lesson, with you. So, maybe, you must do it between twelve and one o'clock. So, maybe, it is best to get ready for Miyu's lesson, and Honoki and Reiki's lesson, and Sakura and Ayuna now, otherwise …"

Is this happening? I mean, I'm fine in terms of lesson prep, but I wonder if I'm hearing things right. Is this guy really telling me I have twelve minutes to get ready for seven hours of back-to-back classes *without* a lunch break? "Ow," I rub my eyes. "Son of a — I mean, I see."

"Ah! Thank you for your understanding! Okay, Hitomu, please take your time and say, 'See you again, Cybelle!'"

Hitomu screams again, and clings harder to his mother.

"Uh, 'take your time' doing what?" I ask.

"Ah, well, Hitomu and *mama* are not sure what lesson they want to take. Hitomu and his mother want to watch some lessons first. You see, Hitomu is almost three years old, so maybe he is too old for Baby Two but maybe, he cannot do Zippo and Zappo. He has no experience without *mama*, so they would like to see *all* lessons, and then maybe they will choose. Maybe."

"Oh." I think for a moment. "So, they're going to stay here until twelve."

"Yes. And maybe, they will stay until Zozo closes at seven."

"Say what now?"

A horde of excited children streams out of the elevator and swarms around the reception desk before I can muster a scathing follow-up. I am not happy, but I can tell Manager is not happy either after Hitomu disrupts the first two hours of the day screaming in the lobby. Several parents ask who he is and what's wrong with him, and if his mother is really his mother or did his mother step out and leave him with a stranger, and so on and so on. I wish I had answers for them. I'm curious as to what the heck is going on myself, but it's fine. I can be professional. That's the Zozo policy: always be professional, polite, and playful. I can do all three, easy.

When noon comes around, I'm waiting with Manager in the lobby, which does not get any quieter. Manager spends about twenty minutes talking to Hitomu's mother about what my trial will be like as he makes attempts to pry Hitomu from her arms and drag him kicking and screaming into Room Five. He finally gives up and allows Hitomu's mother to accompany him inside. Had I known this would happen I would have wolfed down my mac and cheese fifteen minutes ago.

"How are you, Cybelle? Ready?"

"Hungry," I blurt out.

Manager cringes, hissing air through his teeth. "Ah yes, now Lieko and everyone are eating lunch. I am very sorry, Cybelle."

"Yeah, don't worry; I got this. It's for the company, right? Plus, it's not like I can't eat once it's over."

"Eh? I beg your pardon?"

"I mean, I understand."

"Ah. Yes. Thank you for your understanding. Our school, it is not very good. We need many students, maybe, or it will be troublesome."

"So I've heard."

"Eh?"

"I mean, yes, I understand."

"Yes, that's right, you are always understanding. Many foreigners are not. That reminds me, your re-contracting form … you signed it, yes?"

"YAAAAAAH!" Inside Room Five, Hitomu screams in his mother's arms and scratches at her. It's almost like he's answering Manager on my behalf.

"Ah, maybe, now is not the time. But, let's discuss it again? Because many students, maybe they will not stay if Cybelle leaves. It will be *mendokusai* — eh, I mean, troublesome. But maybe, for now, we can wait. Please do your best." Manager bows and bends down to reassure Hitomu and his mother for the thousandth time.

He closes the door as he murmurs aside, to me: "After your lesson is Lieko, who is eating now, so you only have to teach for maybe ten minutes. I think, maybe, Hitomu will cry even with *mama*, but please do your best. Okay, Hitomu! Time to enjoy English with Belle-*sensei*!"

And that's that. Manager closes the door, and I am trapped with a grim young woman and her violent child.

"Hello, Hitomu! How are you today? Okay, we'll just get started. Hitomu, do you know who this is? This is Jibanyan! Jibanyan, can you say hello to our new friend Hitomu? *Hello, Hitomu! Nice to meet you!* What's that, Jibanyan? You want to give Hitomu a high-five? No? Not happening? Okay! Let's sing Hitomu the 'Hello Song,' what do you say? *Hello, hello hello hello, hello hello hello, hello hello what's your name?*"

Hitomu screams for the whole lesson. The kid does not even stop to take a breath; in time, he starts to cough, his entire face turns beet red, and I'm pretty sure he's about to throw up. His mother has to hold him and rock him back and forth the whole lesson to keep him from scratching at her face and throwing himself against the door to escape. I've seen some shit in my time at Zozo, but this is by far the worst trial I could ever conceive. I try everything. I use my silly Jibanyan voice. I blast Raffi on the CD player (the volume of which can only go so high). "Frère Jacques" and "Baby Beluga" are no match for this kid's lung capacity. I throw my whole plan out the window and blow bubbles. I try every junior toy in my teacher kit. Hell, I even convince Manager to retrieve the sunset for him from the lobby to chew on again. Nothing helps. Not for a second. Over my shoulder Manager watches us through the window the way one watches a hospital operation go wrong. I have a feeling this trial lesson has gone way past the ten-minute mark.

After what feels like hours of ear-splitting hell, I notice Lieko in the window about to open the door. I give Hitomu — well, I give his mother — a star sticker. "Good job, Hitomu!" I say. I'm gathering all my crap back into my teacher box when I hear the door open and Lieko's voice stretch several octaves to greet him.

"*Otsukaresama desu!* Hello, Hitomu!"

Boom. Silence. Like someone hit pause on a video. The kid is quiet and still. What the hell? Did she slug him in the face or staple his mouth shut? I dare a peek over my shoulder as I slip out the door. Hitomu's eyes are wide open, his mouth closed; he sits sniffling in his mother's lap while Lieko kneels a foot away and makes weird gestures with her arms. Then they all get up and hold hands as she sings the Japanese Zozo welcome song.

That's when I hear his tiny little voice on the other side of the door: "*Oni baba, doko?*"

"It's okay!" Lieko sings. "She's *gone!*"

Oni baba? I can feel my stomach acid boil with rage. *Seriously?*

There's a small gathering of pity in the lobby. Yoshino and Yuri are nodding, looking pensive. "*Sugoi,*" they murmur to each other. They must have seen or at least heard it all. Manager has his arms folded and I can already hear him hissing through his teeth. No one says a word to me or looks my way. Guess I'm the only one who heard a toddler call me "old demon woman" and my co-worker *reaffirm him.*

Sneaking into the staff room with a giant box stuffed with toys and papers isn't as easy as I thought. "Here, Cyb, let me get that for you," Yoshino slides the door open for me. "Talk about the trial lesson from hell, huh? I've never heard anything like that. Whoa. Cybelle, are you okay?"

"I think …" I can't look her in the eye. "Never mind, it's nothing. I'll be in the staff room."

She nods. "Of course."

This is when Manager notices me and tries to intercept me at the staff room door; Yoshino is faster. She covers for me as Manager drills her for information on what I said to her. She's good at bullshitting our two-second interaction into a complete rundown of everything I did in my trial lesson.

Lesson. Ha.

"Shinjirarenai!" Misaki is at the bench with her back to the door. She shakes her head, muttering in Japanese to Seri, Yuki, and Jun: "He just kept screaming and screaming. Did you hear him? *Kyaaa, kyaaa!"* She waves her hands in the air, a vapid attempt at an impression of Hitomu. "Does she always scare the students that much?"

Seri's and Jun's heads are down over calculators and notebooks. They nod and make low humming sounds in pseudo-agreement. None of them say a word to me or look my way. I stand there, frozen in time as Misaki goes on about how our branch school is losing more and more money, and it doesn't help if teachers scare the students. I'm going to assume they don't realize I'm here. Every sentence makes me lose my appetite for my mac and cheese, which is great because there's no room for me to sit down, anyway. Screw this. I'm going out for some HORUS Bakery buns. Hopefully by the time I get back this horrible child will be gone.

I head back outside and hide my box of gear behind the reception desk. Manager and the others are watching the rest of Lieko's perfect fucking lesson. I put on my shoes and go down the elevator. The lunchtime rush is over, so the streets are relatively quiet. Hell, a rave would be quiet compared to what I just went through. My ears are still ringing. I decide to walk down to HORUS rather than take the bike, since I still have time to go on foot, come back, and eat lunch before my next class. If there still isn't enough space or peace and quiet in the staff room, at least I can squeeze in a couple of buns before my next class. All I want is space, peace, and quiet, anyway. Who needs food? *Not Cybelle.*

At HORUS, I try to immerse myself in the scent of cinnamon and the classical guitar music playing on a small radio. I take time to select half a dozen croissants and three Totoro cream-filled buns like it's the toughest job I'll have all day. Anything beats dwelling on what just happened. I thought Zozo and I were done with all the "scary *gaijin*" crap I dealt with when I first started. It's like everyone has forgotten about all the kids I won over, all the countless walk-ins and trial lessons that I got signed up after those initial moments of fear. I would have said I was doing pretty damn well. Up until now. Or, rather, up until Lieko joined us. That's when things at Zozo got awkward. Something about the way she stares at me and then avoids me completely whenever it suits her mood. The way she talks to me (on the rare occasion) doesn't help, either. I take my tray of goodies up to the counter, and rethink that. No, I'm being unfair. Lieko is just one factor of how crappy I feel right now. I can't blame it all on her.

The salesgirl rings me up without looking at me. "*Sen ni-hyaku san-juu ichi en desu.*"

And that's when I realize I have no money. I walked right out of Zozo without my purse. Ignoring the stares of the people in line behind me I check my pockets for even a coin or two so I can walk out of here with a shred of my dignity. Guess I left *that* back at Zozo, too. "*Sumimasen ...*" I begin.

"*Eh?! Okane nai no?!*"

"*Saifu wasurechatta,*" I clarify. I left my wallet. I'm not begging for handouts.

The young salesgirl winces with mock sympathy. When she asks if she should hold them for me, I shake my head. There isn't enough time to go and come back, and HORUS will be closed by seven. "*Gomen nasai, ne,*" she says with a grimace. I excuse myself and run out of there before more stuck-up customers can judge me any further. Now I remember why I don't shop at this bakery ever.

In my back pocket, my phone vibrates. Someone at Zozo must wonder where I am. This is turning into a nice, shitty Saturday.

It doesn't get any better when the doors slide open on the Zozo lobby and a sour-faced Manager is waiting for me at the desk, arms folded so tight he's created some substantial cleavage. "Ah, Cybelle," he hisses through his teeth. "You, ah, left Zozo."

"Yes ...?" Where is he going with this? Am I supposed to chain myself to the staff room bench when I have nothing else to do? "I went for a walk?"

"Ah! Okay, that's great. Sorry. I, ah, thought maybe Cybelle was sad and went home. Then, it's okay. You, ah, cry?"

My eye twitches. "No." I rub it. "I'm fine."

"That's great. Ah, but yes, if you must cry, please cry only in staff room. It is empty now. Hitomu and *mama* are still here. Maybe ..." He hisses again, bracing for the impact of his next words. "Maybe, Hitomu is afraid of strangers. So maybe, if you stay in staff room, Hitomu will not cry. So. Please, return to staff room?"

You've got to be fucking kidding me.

I hear Hitomu's mother talking to him down the hall, probably in the washroom. Whatever, it's fine. At this point I could care less about Hitomu or his mother, or Manager, or HORUS, or the planet. I want my lunch. Manager barely notices my half-assed shrug as I return my shoes to the shelf and head to the reception desk for my box. I take it to Room Two, ready to drop it as loud as I dare.

"Cybelle," a voice coos behind me. I almost drop my prop box in earnest. Like the silent, stalking banshee she is, Lieko poses in the doorway, baring all her teeth like a death's head grimace. "Hel-*lo*. There you *are*. You are *here,* getting ready for your students. Good job!"

"Uh-huh," I wipe my other eye. "I am *here*. And now, I'm going *there*." I gesture to the staff room around the corner. Lieko keeps grinning at me, hands braced against the doorway. Just past her shoulder I can see a small Donald Duck head bobbing up and down in Hitomu's mother's arms. She sees me too and moves out of my vision. Yup. Lieko is blocking my path.

"You cannot walk about until Hitomu leaves," Lieko drops her singing voice. "I told Manager it is best for Hitomu." *Oh, so you're the brainchild behind Manager's groundbreaking idea of the century. Why doesn't that surprise me?* "Yeah, but they're leaving soon ... aren't they?"

"Now, they are coming. You must wait."

"Wait for what?"

"Manager told them they can stay until seven to observe other lessons."

"This is a joke, right?" It takes every ounce of strength to keep my voice calm. "Sorry. It's just that my lunch is in the staff room, and I *do* have time before Miyu gets here, so ..." The staff room door is *right* around the corner; how will he see me if I move five feet *that* way? Does she really need me to explain it out loud?

"Zozo is not a place for jokes. This is a serious business, a serious company. You should understand. Zozo policy states we must all 'be professional, be polite, and be playful.'"

"Yeah, I know the policy —"

"As the only *gaijin*, you must be professional because Hitomu is very ... *shy*. But his mother wants to sign up for many lessons. So, we must all work very hard. Many Japanese staff miss their lunch hour, or they must work very late, so even though you are *gaijin*, you must also work very hard."

This woman is serious. But I don't have the chance to argue. Halfway through her insipid speech, I hear the elevator doors open and Miyu singing hello to everyone, adding something about cookies.

"Oh, look, Cybelle, your student Miyu is here! You should not leave her alone! That is not good. You ought to start early; your students will like that. They always enjoy your lessons. Okay, Miyu, let's enjoy English!"

She leaves me there. I try hard not to let my jaw drop open in front of Miyu and her mother, who are smiling bright with the prospect of English entertainment. Great. There goes my chance to eat — *and* the chance to pee before my six-hour stretch of classes. With a forced grin, I bow to them, then sit on the carpet and arrange my toys, cut-outs, and books on the floor. Miyu runs into the room after me and throws her baby backpack open on the floor. "*Sensei*, here you are! It is a cookie!" She holds up one to my mouth. I recognize it as a HORUS cookie. Well, at least I won't starve.

Somehow (my guess is by the awesome power of chocolate chips), I trudge through my classes and keep the million-watt smile going for all my students and their parents without a break. By four my bladder is about to burst. In the five minutes it takes to stop caring about Zozo company policies and go to the washroom, I pass Hitomu on my way to Room Five and spend the next twenty minutes telling my students that screech they hear is *not* a fire alarm or the emergency exit. By six, I realize my biggest mistake was not sneaking my lunch into the washroom with me when I had the chance. I run into the staff room to make photocopies for Naohiro (who forgot his Zone 2 textbook *again*) and I'm hit with a wave of stuffy heat.

"Is it just me, or is it warm in here?"

Misaki is the only one in the staff room. "Ah, Shibelle-*sensei*. Lieko-*sensei* turn on the heater. Staff room, very cold. But, maybe, you feel *kimazui*? Eh, unpleasant? Because you are American?"

"Canadian."

"Ah, yes, Canada is very cold." She goes back to her work. Oh sure, Canada's cold. About as cold as the look on my face as I hold back what I really want to say. The heater must have been on for hours. Too bad it couldn't heat up my lunch. Say, where is my lunch? I swear I left it on the bench this morning.

Yoshino gently elbows me with a smile as she squeezes behind me into the staff room. "Hey, lady. Ready for tonight?"

"Can't think of a better way to start the weekend. Just need to collect the garbage before I go home and change."

"That ... might be a good idea, except ... Lieko says we must stay together. All the girls want to come — Seri-*sensei* and Yuri-*sensei*, and Yuki-*sensei* and Jun-*sensei*, too!"

Well, isn't that just great. The Ice Queen gets to join us. Whoop-de-fucking-doo. I decide to ignore that part. "Well, I'm not really dressed for a club —"

"Oh, don't worry about it! Especially in your skirt; you look fine!"

"Thanks." I look down at my suit. I may look fine, but with all the running around I've done today, I doubt I smell fine. "But —"

"Besides, if you go home, we cannot go to the station together! Please stay. I really want you to join us! Please?"

"Oh, okay, I guess I can wait ... for a bit."

"Thanks for understanding, Cyb. One more hour and we'll be out of here."

"One more hour," I sigh wistfully. "This day already feels like it's been half a dozen years."

"Because of Hitomu?" Yoshino kisses her teeth. "I know. Weird, right? Don't worry about it. The kid's got issues. It's nothing to do with you."

"I don't know, Yoshino ... you heard him today. I mean, sure, I've had some bizarre reactions, but this was like I was some kind of monster."

"He doesn't think that! How can he? He's still a baby. He'll come around. All kids do. You don't need to care about him. Focus on having fun tonight!"

"That's good advice. Thanks." She's right. I need to stop thinking about this kid. And about Lieko's penchant for ruining social situations. This party will be fun if I make the effort. Isn't that what life in Japan is all about? And with Yoshino there, what's the worst that can happen?

"*An*-punch ... *an*-kick ..." something groans.

"What the hell?" I murmur. Yoshino doesn't hear me, she's too distracted by whatever it is she's photocopying after me. I know exactly what it is before I even see it. "Um, quick question. Why haven't we trashed this thing yet?"

"What thing?" Yoshino asks.

"*That* thing." I point with my slipper to the Anpanman toy. I wonder how long it's been hiding under the staff bench, peeking up at me from behind the trash containers. "It's got to be at least twenty years old. Why haven't we thrown in away?"

"We have," Yoshino says, still distracted as she organizes her papers and tidies up the bench. "Several times. Someone must keep taking him back out."

"Oh. Well, that's disturbing." I don't have the courage to pick it up, and besides, I'm in the middle of a lesson. It's someone else's problem now.

At seven, I do one last sneak-around to collect the garbage, grateful that Hitomu has managed to cry himself to sleep in his mother's arms. She gives me a slight nod as I pass her in the lobby, on my way to collect from the reception desk. I can't wait for them to go home. Hell, *I* can't wait to go home. But I did promise to check out this party ... with a tacit agreement with myself to make at least one new friend tonight.

"But, I think everyone there will be *gaijin*," I hear Misaki in the staff room. "I can't speak English! Can you?"

"*No*, no," Lieko's voice reaches that high pitch of hers. "That's impossible! I can't speak English, either."

"Well, neither can I! Maybe Seri-*sensei*, and Yuri-*sensei*, can they speak? Ah, *dou shi o?* What can we do?!"

Lieko replies with a hiccupping sound that I assume is laughter. Screw it, if I have to hang around here until everyone wraps up, I'm eating. I slide the staff room door open, stunning Lieko and Misaki into abrupt silence, and put the garbage bags away. No sign of Anpanman, thank goodness. But then I realize I really cannot locate my lunch. It's not on the bench, it's not on the shelves. What. The. Actual. Fuck. Did someone take it? Did someone *eat it*?

Ugh. I give up. I don't feel like eating anymore. It doesn't matter; Yoshino *did* say they'll have food at this party. I pull up a stool and take out my phone. Right on cue, Misaki and Lieko leave the room. Whatever. I'm still going to check the weather and play Snake and pretend I have things to do on here. I see three missed messages from phone numbers I don't recognize. Great. I brace myself for catching up on all the profanities from Lieko or Manager or whoever tried to reach me this morning.

Cybelle come home! Your family needs you! Your sister is to be married, did you hear? Congratulations!

Hi Cybelle may this message find you. I hear Bully is about to get married. Congratulations. Just checking in on you. Lots of love and God bless u

Cybele I hear your sister has been engaged. May the lord bless her and you in your far-off travels. I pray China takes care of you. Please call home, your mother must worry

Hey C-Note, if you find yourself the recipient of several strange text messages, sorry. Mom's been getting calls from all the relatives and I think she gave out your email to throw them off our scent. Brace yourself. Bully <3

PS you know there's no date for the wedding yet, right? ^__^"

Well. Only one message from a person I recognize — my sister. Not a single text from anyone who works here. Nothing from anyone about a trial lesson or a "where the hell are you?" text. Go figure. Well, I'm not in any mood to reply to any of them about this wedding that doesn't even have a date set.

I organize flash cards and write little reminders on Post-its and stick them onto their respective textbooks, mentally run through my schedule between next Tuesday and Saturday, and try to focus on how much more comfortable my regular students are with me. They don't scream or hide under tables. They don't cower behind their parents when I enter the room. And their parents, they're not bothered by me, either. They don't stare, or glare, or make mock sympathetic faces when I make a mistake. So I can't be all that bad. Next week everything will be back to normal; I'll never have to deal with this Hitomu kid ever again.

Maybe it's not Hitomu I'm upset with. It's my co-workers. Lieko and Manager are not Stratford actors: the whole foreigner-fear phenomenon may go over some people's heads, but not theirs. Not after working with me all this time. *Oh, Hitomu is shy,* I hear Lieko and Manager's voices lecturing in my head. *And Sotaro, he is shy. And that child you saw acting normally with a Japanese teacher up until the second they saw your face and morphed into a shrieking, volatile whirlwind of doom? They're shy, too! Do your best!*

"Arrrgh!" I push the books aside and hold my head in my hands. I can't think. I shake so hard that I curl up into a ball on my tiny chair with the intention of staying in the staff room forever. I give up trying to get anything done and rest my head on my arms.

Knock knock.

"Cybelle!" Lieko hisses. "Get out here!" The door slams.

Nope. Never mind. *No breaks for you, gaijin.* Whatever, it's fine. I can be professional for a little while longer. I can sacrifice a couple of hours to meet people and feel socially acceptable. Maybe even make at least one friend outside of work.

High-pitched voices congratulate one another on the other side of the wall, which means Seri and Yuri are finished with their students and Hitomu and his mother are getting ready to leave. I lift up my head and see 7:35 p.m. on the clock. Son of a bitch, it's been over half an hour. I'm pretty sure I could have biked home and changed out of my armpit-sweat-stained shirt. Maybe snagged an *onigiri* from the fridge and shoved it into my purse to eat before the thirty-minute train ride to Osaka. Little things to make one-self presentable for a single-and-mingle party at a fancy club and make a new friend. One will do.

Manager has pulled Hitomu's mother aside. He asks her what she thinks. I can hear him offering "a private lesson" and "Japanese teachers." I can see the little guy clinging to her leg. He doesn't know I'm out here, in the lobby. The mother cocks her head. She hums a little sound, then looks about the room. She catches my eye, pretends she didn't. After some time, she kneels down and mutters to Hitomu. Manager gets down to his level, too. I'm sure I will never know what he said. My imagination can only go so far. All I know is that Manager is jumping to his feet, shouting. He looks wildly around the lobby and catches sight of me. One would think he'd spotted wild game.

"Ah! Cybelle-*sensei*! Come here!"

This is it, isn't it? The moment I get fired. Oh well, guess that's Zozo for you; fired after however many years because people believe you scare business away. We've put up with you for too long, but no hard feelings. Maybe Manager will ask Head Office to let me go and save himself another three weeks of asking me about my re-contracting form. Well, might as well go home, pack my bags, head back to Toronto. It's all for the best. Mom's been worried and now that we have this wedding coming up, anyway ...

"Cybelle-*sensei*, please say something to Hitomu," he beams and points at the sniffling child. "He will join our school. Please do your best!"

I can hear every employee in the lobby gasp. The mother is still nodding at Manager. Manager is still bowing and humbly thanking her. Hitomu is still sniffling, his face buried against his mother's knee.

"Uh ... I ..."

"Yes. Hitomu is waiting. Maybe say, 'Good job'?" He is practically sweating enthusiasm as he nods with such pointed exaggeration that I can picture him stabbing me in the shower tonight if I don't comply. The mother's eyes dart between him and I with a puzzled look.

What else can I do?

"Good job today, big guy!" I kneel down on the floor and smile until it hurts. "I'm glad you had fun. Can't wait to see you again!"

Hitomu peeks out from behind his mother's leg, looks me right in the eye, opens his tiny mouth, and screams.

I was wrong. I can think of a bajillion better ways to start my weekend. Rearranging my socks. Steam cleaning my futon. Digging out that giant cicada corpse from under the radiator on my balcony. Fleeing for my life from a swarm of Japanese hornets. *Anything* would beat this waking nightmare.

This is no networking party. It's just a snack bar with a pall of second-hand smoke, jam-packed with people. It's hard not to look at all the tables behind me. They're still covered with empty plates and bowls with tortilla chip crumbs, blobs of salsa, platters streaked with ketchup and bits of overcooked cheese that have been here since we arrived. Telltale signs that we missed all the food. The music is so loud I can feel the beat pulsing in my veins. It's only been about half an hour since we arrived, but I'm exhausted, like I've been drunk dancing all night like the majority of people in here. And I'm so hungry I could cry.

My second rum and Coke is finished. I'm not in the mood to go back to the bar and get elbowed for a third. Nothing left to do but try and be social. I leave the so-called comfort of the empty snack table and look for the rest of the Zozo staff. Yoshino and Misaki are gone but there's still nowhere to sit with my co-workers. We're all fans of giant purses, and they have strategically arranged them on their seats to take up room. Lucky for me, a table nearby becomes available as the four men sitting there see me come closer, look me up and down, exchange glances, and vacate. A few feet away they burst out laughing, looking back at me. *Assholes.*

I sit down with a forced grin. "Pretty packed in here, eh? You'd never know it's Saturday night."

The girls look up at me, horrified. "Ah, Cybelle-*sensei, ne,*" Seri confirms in Japanese.

"Thank goodness," Yuki adds in Japanese. "That was so scary for a moment!"

Oh, for crap's sake — I stop and take a deep breath. *No, no, don't get upset. Don't get upset. Just laugh it off.*

"Scary? Why, am I wearing a Halloween costume or something?" I joke. They laugh nervously. I take a sip of the icy Coke water in my glass. *"Minna, genki?"* I try.

They nod but still murmur to each other in Japanese. Something along the lines of "Can she speak Japanese? Did you know that? No, I didn't. Amazing. Mmm." And then they retreat into awkward silence when they see I'm listening. Or, trying to listen. It's loud as balls in here. Hang on … didn't we all have dinner three days ago? What do they mean, 'Can she speak Japanese?' I'm really getting tired of this *Twilight Zone*–language thing going on with my co-workers.

"I've never been to this part of the Bay Area before," I say instead. "How about you?"

"Sorry, Cybelle-*sensei,*" Jun speaks in English this time. "We have never been to this part of Osaka before, either. But I am sure we are safe! We are in a group. Besides, it is not late at night."

"Of course, we're safe. We're all here together, right?"

Lieko gives me a dirty look, the first she's given me since we left the school. "Yoshino should have checked before bringing us here," Lieko scolds. "But I am sure nothing will happen as long as we are not separated." The others nod in agreement, even though they don't look too convinced.

"What's everyone drinking?" I ask. I'm desperate, now. They make little *kanpai* gestures with their glasses; even through all the smoke, I can tell it's all oolong tea. All right, one more attempt and I'm out of ideas.

"How have your lessons been going?"

"Um ... good ..."

They turn to Lieko. She concentrates hard on stirring the ice in her glass with a straw. "The oolong tea here is very good, isn't it?" she says in Japanese.

The others nod eagerly. "Oh, yes, very good! I agree." They start up a conversation in Japanese about how healthy oolong tea is for women. My co-workers believe in sticking together, all right — to themselves. Screw it. Why did I leave the snack table in the first place? Hell, why did I come *here* in the first place?

"Well," I stand up. "I think I better get another drink."

"But ..." Jun exchanges glances with the others. "Lieko says, we must not be separated."

Obviously, no one noticed that I was at the snack table without a place to sit up until now. "Um, well ... I won't take long. See you all later!" We wave to each other (except for Lieko, naturally) and I squeeze through the crowd. I'm getting the hell up out of here, with or without Yoshino. This sucks.

Luckily, I find her at the bar, lighting up a cigarette. "Yoshino, thank God I found you. Oh. Oops." I've just waded into a whole group of young men with dark- to pale-blond hair and a mix of British and Australian accents. They've all stopped dead in their conversations to stare at me.

"Hi, Cybelle!" Yoshino says. "Come, join us!"

The guy who has his arm around Yoshino's shoulders notices me for the first time. He recoils in horror. "AUGH! You're not American, are you?!"

"Cybelle is Canadian," Yoshino explains. "You getting another drink, Cybelle? Rum and Coke?"

"Sumimasen!" the guy yells at a bartender at the same time. "Two highballs!"

It's fine. I manage to order a rum and Coke as Yoshino and several of this loser's friends get drinks. "So, Yoshino-*chan*, what do you do again?" the guy asks.

"My friend and I are English teachers!" Yoshino gestures her cigarette at me.

"Oh, really? Hey, my buddies here are dying to get English lessons!" He yells out two names and scoops two sheepish-looking Japanese guys up with one arm. "This is …" Yoshino leans into the crook of his neck for a long time to relay our names. "Yoshino, and what? *What?!* Uh, o-*kay*, that over there is Civic."

"Eh?! Civic?! Honda Civic?" they yell. *"Nani o sore?!"*

"No, it's Cybelle," I say. "CYBELLE." They burst out laughing again and make shooing hand gestures to imply they don't understand.

My stomach growls loud enough to be heard in this smoky sardine can, and I'm pretty sure my smile looks more and more like a grimace. If someone hadn't hidden my lunch deep in the staff room cupboard, behind Lieko's purse (where Yoshino eventually found it), I could have eaten it before coming here. Hell, I could have gone home, eaten my weight in food, or grabbed something from the Family Mart by Nishibe Station. *Why didn't they just let me eat?!* On second thought, that's not a bad idea. Maybe there's a corner I can hide in and eat my lunch. It'll be cold and stale, but —

"Hey!" one particularly large man grabs my upper arm. "I know you from somewhere, don't I?"

"Uh, I don't think —"

"Yeah! I totally know you! You got some kinda weird name, I *know* it! Seatbelt! No wait — Cybelle, am I right? You don't remember me, do you? What the fuck, come on, you remember me!"

I squint. I think he just spat in my face a little. "Ummmm … Josh?"

"YEAH! I told you you remember me! You're not still working for that clown company, are you? Zozo?! Geez, you *are*, aren't you? Fuck, aren't you tired of that *eikaiwa* kids' bullshit yet?!"

"Um," I repeat. I guess I got it right. I don't recognize him, but he must know me. No wait, I do know him. He's heavier, and has lost a lot of hair, but he's the same obnoxious asshole trainer I met when I first came to Japan. Terrific. Of all the people I could have run into from my past, it has to be a jerk. "What are *you* up to?"

"Translation, baby. Sweetest gig if your Japanese is good enough to get it. I barely gotta do shit where I work now."

"That's fantastic. Excuse me, I gotta —"

"Hey, what happened with you and that guy you hooked up with?"

"Uh, who?"

"You know, that guy! You were both in the same training group. You were *obsessed* with him! Come *on*, you remember! Super tall, all the chicks wanted him ... you know who I'm talking about, right?"

Yup. He's definitely spitting in my face. "You know what? I think you have me confused with someone else."

"Nah, nah, it was you! Had to be, you were the only one with a weird name! Fuck, this is going to kill me, hang on." He pulls his smartphone out of his back pocket. "I'm still friends with the guy on LINE, I'm sure of it. Say, while we're on the subject, what's your number? Are you on LINE? What's your nickname?"

"Uh ... hey! I see a friend of mine! Excuse me."

I shove through the crowd and almost throw myself at Misaki when I see her. She gasps, scared to death. Then she relaxes. *"Ah, Shibelle-sensei! Bikkuri!"*

"Misaki-sensei, tasukarimashita!" I'm saved.

"Heeeey!" a Japanese salaryman with his arm around another man steps in front of me. "Can you speak Japanese?! *Nihongo sha-beru no?!"*

"Uh, not really, no. *Sumimasen* —" I try to walk around him. Misaki is already distracted by the group of guys that have ensnared Yoshino.

"*Sugoi!* You speak very good Japanese!"

"Thank you," I put on my serious teacher voice. "Could you take a step back, please?"

"Oh, sorry!" They jostle around a little but we are still stuck together. My glass still can't reach my lips. "How long you stay in Japan?"

"Wait, do you mean how long have I *stayed* in Japan, or how long *will* I stay in Japan?"

"Eh, difficult. English, difficult! One more, one more time!"

Fuck, I really don't want to do this.

"Oh, wow!" The other guy shouts, even though I haven't done anything special. "Ah, English teacher?"

"Yeah, I work for an *eikaiwa*. But it's kids only!" Who knows, maybe Lieko's cockblocking techniques will work on these two long enough for me to drink.

"*Eikaiwa? Sugoi! Sore ja*, please! Teach us English!"

"Ugh." I give up. "Misaki, how's it going?" I edge my way past the two drunks to return my attention to her. She jumps again, but her presence seems to repel the eager salarymen away to a more comfortable distance. However, they don't go away.

"Hey!" one of the salarymen asks me. "Together ... teachers?"

"Yeah. This is Misaki. Misaki, this is ... uh ..."

They don't need me. They introduce themselves to one another in Japanese and even exchange cards. In fact, they start a whole conversation about what companies they work for and how their card designs are so similar. That would be nice; to have the same small, perfect laminated Zozo business cards with my name and the stick-figure children holding hands on the front and the date and time of their trial lesson printed in tiny, neat kanji on the back. I wonder how Misaki got hers so fast. Oh, well. I can wallow in self-pity about it over this drink.

Cold liquid splashes over the rim of my glass and down my sleeve as someone pushes me from behind. Three other salarymen, a little shorter than me but way more intoxicated, shove each other and point at me, laughing. One raises his hands in apology once he notices me glaring at him. "Oh, so sorry," he says in English, then punches his friends in the arms. "*Nande ya nen! Gaijin abunai yo!*"

"*Ike!* You go! Go — speak — English!"

"Fuck you!" the first guy shouts back. They collapse over one another, laughing hard. It's fine. I can grab a napkin, wipe the sticky liquid off my fingers and the glass. No harm done, my little friend. Well, maybe it got my suit a little, but other than that —

WHAM.

Someone slams into me, hard. My drink slips from my grip. The music is at full volume, the bass is shaking the floorboards, but everyone can hear my glass crash onto the floor. Is it an unfortunate accident? One of those things that happen in a crowded bar? No. Several women glare at me, swearing. They wipe at their clothes and their legs, then stand upright with relieved sighs that they are completely dry. Makes sense — all of my drink has already soaked through my shirt and skirt. The guys are laughing even harder now, their voices lost in the music as they retreat. The last words I can hear are how the Coke stain on my shirt matches my face.

My co-workers seem to have made new friends, too: a small group of foreign guys, including Josh, flank their sides. Their faces light up as they raise their hands and clap: "Nice. Way to go. Brilliant."

"Brilliant?" asks Misaki. She turns her back on me and tilts her head. "Why? What do you mean, 'brilliant?'"

"It means 'smart,' Misaki-*chan*." Lieko appears behind her. "But, he means, that girl is *not* smart." She turns to Josh and tilts her head, too. "*Hiniku, ne?* Sarcasm. Is that right?"

"Yeah, that's right! Hey, I used to know that girl, like a decade ago! Check this out — I KNOW I can find an old photo of us on here somewhere! Thank God for Facebook, you know?!" He whips out his cellphone and invites Misaki and Lieko to lean in close. They both giggle behind their hands as they do so.

It wasn't a decade ago. It was six and a half years. I've been in Japan for six years and six months, and probably about six days, to be exact. It's fine. I'll let them figure that out on their own. I need to find a bathroom. Something's really going on with my eyes.

I stagger through the tide of people, following the signs to the washroom. They point toward a tiny nook where I see at least ten women lined up along the wall. It's fine. I just need to step out. Find a convenience store or a McDonald's or the like. They all have bathrooms.

I walk down the main street but all the stores are closed. The temperature has dropped, or maybe it's colder here because we're close to the bay. I can smell it in every deep, panic-reducing breath I muster. It smells like salt with a hint of onion.

There are no convenience stores or fast-food places between Kappa Garappa and the station. Nothing but love hotels, other snack bars, and clubs, none of which I'd dare enter on my own. I guess I can use the washroom at the station. According to the number of people on the streets it's getting pretty late. Okay, not really, but since it will take a while to get back to Osaka Station alone, I might as well get on a train.

It's fine.

I spend the first part of the train ride squished between the railing at the end of the seats and a salaryman who clubs my shoulder with his head because he's nodding off so hard. He gets off the same time as a staggering drunk man who's busting out of his button-down shirt gets on. The drunk mutters *"fakku gai-jin"* loudly, over and over, until I get off at my stop. I can feel the invisible camera waiting for me again, following me back to Zozo, where I unchain my bike. There's no way in hell I can ride it now, which is great because my feet are on fire. The walk to my apartment feels like a mile of hot, burning coals. I'm famished, but not enough to strike up a conversation with the 7-Eleven employees smelling like a smoky snack bar with a big brown stain on my shirt.

Halfway home, I have to stop to give my feet a rest, so I wheel my bike over to a bus stop and sit down on the bench. I can't stop dwelling on how horrible this whole week has been. I don't understand. Okay, so I'm not the prettiest girl to look at. Doesn't make me a monster. I'm not mean. I'm not loud. I smile when people look at me so they don't jump to the conclusion that I'm some snooty bitch. I try to strike up conversations when I can. It's never enough. There is something *wrong* with me. And everyone can see it except me. Maybe everyone's right: maybe I am a monster. It's been this way since long before Japan. It's been going on for years, and it's holding me back in … well, in life. What I wouldn't pay to have it ripped out of me and see it destroyed.

Over six years ago I had it good. I had my family, I had friends. Now I have nothing and no one. My only constant companion is this rusty, hand-me-down, decades-old bike.

It starts to rain. Then the wind blows, ever so gently, and my bike crashes to the ground.

My cellphone buzzes in my purse as I lock my apartment door behind me. I'm soaked and I can't stop my teeth from chattering. My clothes and hair reek of alcohol and second-hand smoke, reminding me of why I stopped going to bars and clubs ages ago. I read my newest message:

Just remembered you're not home now. I got your msg about you going out tonight. Good for u! The other day I was starting to think there was no one for you over there, but it's ok, miracles happen! I'll keep my fingers crossed you finally meet someone! Hurry up and come home, and bring back a husband, k? I want grandkids lol

Love you sweetie!

Mom

I sniffle. My eyes still itch. I'll do my best, Mom. I have to admit, though, it's a little hard to land a husband when I can't find someone who will talk to me once or twice before deciding I'm the most *kowai* creature he's ever laid eyes on.

Six and a half years. Six and a half years without business cards. Six and a half years without a welcome dinner. Six and a half years of "look, it's a scary foreigner." And, if I had actually hooked up with Josh's imaginary friend, it'd be six-and-a-half years since that happened, too. But I'm not supposed to complain. After all, this is my job. I'm a Native English Teacher. My duties: To be the bigger person. To ignore the fact that I shed forty-five hours' worth of blood, sweat, and tears in a house of lies. To smile throughout everything that this eat-or-be-eaten world throws at me. To show everyone, young and old alike, that I'm not some she-beast who blends into the darkness at night to steal your purse. To demonstrate that English is not the scariest language in the world, and it's impossible to contract some kind of skin-darkening disease by talking to me or giving me high-fives, and that I am not — repeat, am *not* — a horrible blood-thirsty creature from beyond the realm of human understanding.

But oh, Cybelle, you're so understanding ...

The burning sensation in my eyes is too much. Tears begin to trickle down my face. Then they gush. My throat closes up so fast I topple over. Lying slumped in my dark living room — Zozo's dark living room — I bawl my eyes out.

Back in Osaka, I wanted to go home. Here I am — and I still want to go home.

And once I'm there, I'll *still* want to go home.

Idiot.

"I hate you." The words drag themselves across the carpeted floor. "I hate you, I hate you, I hate you!" I can feel them slither up the paper-thin walls, writhe all over my ceiling. I let the words echo throughout the building and reverberate through my cold, shaking bones.

My eyes are wet, sticky, but I notice a glow in the corner. A big bright halo of light on the carpet. It can't be a stray light coming in through the window. The curtains are closed. I blink through the tears, and it's still there. I lie there, still as a statue for a long time, and try not to sniffle too loud.

It looks like a star. Perhaps it's a shooting star that has landed on my floor. I should make a wish.

But I can't string words together, even in my head. The sound of me cursing myself still rings in my ears. So, I watch it. I wait for it to reveal itself as an illusion — a mirror angled the wrong way, or a light from the street peeking through a coincidental crack in the curtains. I wait for it to disappear.

It stays right where it is. I struggle to keep my eyes open, to see what it will do next, but in time, I lose the staring contest.

six

THAT DELICIOUS DREAMY FEELING

仏の顔も三度まで

Even the Buddha, after three times

In a quiet forest upon a mountain, on a cold autumn night, a wide dirt path winds through an assortment of trees: thousand-year-old oak, majestic redwood, thick reedy bamboo, baby spruce, short fat pine, many others with no names. The sky is red, the grass is a tawny brown, and the moon is bleeding. There are no sounds except for the *tap-tap-tap* of a wooden stick on the dirt road. There are no living creatures, save one: a young man down the road, walking in silence, tapping a long stick before him.

It is the first time in many years that Zaniel is venturing into this part of the woods on his own. Heart beating in his throat, he looks back over his shoulder at the house of his protector. Occupied with another woman. He can still hear their grunts and moans from here. *Good*, he thinks to himself. He will not go far; he just wants to know if the Yokai is out here, in the woods. *Yokai* do not often venture close to the house. If Zaniel is to find her again, he is certain that he must seek her out. The stick is for his own safety. The largest he could find, with a sharp point at the end for defence, and a wide girth in the middle should a demon try to tackle and bite him. A trick he picked up when he first discovered these woods. Worst-case scenario, a heavy stick to the head will shock and return him to the safety of his own bed. He hopes the tricks of the trade when it comes to dealing with certain demons still work. He still remembers their weaknesses, their flaws. Ever since Akki gave him the bracelets, however, the *yokai* in these parts have mostly left him alone. All they need to see are the young man's wrists, or recognize his bright silvery eyes, and they often turn away and ignore him completely. Still, better safe than sorry. It is the new creatures that are dangerous. And, as the other day had proven, there are always new creatures about.

Zaniel finds himself heading toward a wall of darkness. Here, he cannot even see the trees on either side of the dirt path. He looks back over his shoulder once more; Akki's house is still visible, a shadow in a crimson backdrop beyond the trees. The blackness is only here, in front of him, blocking the way. Zaniel's face does not show fear or concern; in fact, this is what he has been preparing for. He takes the stick and sweeps it along the ground in front of him in long, slow movements.

"Stop that," says a deep voice.

Zaniel does not stop. He bows forward and sweeps again, making grander motions with his arm.

"Please stop that," says the voice again.

Ignoring the voice, Zaniel makes one more sweeping gesture.

"All right, that's enough," says the voice. High above, Zaniel sees a bulging wet eye appear. It opens, blinks a few times, then swivels round and round until it points back down at him. "If you won't stop, I'll just have to move."

"That's the idea," says Zaniel.

"Hmph," says the voice. "You could have just said 'excuse me,' you know."

The darkness is still grumbling to itself as it rises a few inches off the ground, exposing small, black, dainty-looking feet that shuffle the wall of darkness off the road. Zaniel continues down the path. *That's one,* he thinks to himself.

Zaniel walks and walks. The dirt path turns to cobblestone. Soon he hears the sound of tiny footsteps of wood on stone growing louder and closer. Zaniel sneaks a glance out of the corner of his eye and immediately turns away, pretending not to have seen. A boy and a girl, no older than two years in appearance, run up to him from behind and plant themselves in his path. Their hair and kimonos are completely soaked. Zaniel suppresses a sigh, knowing he can go no further.

"Whoa, buddy, you're a long way from home." The boy scowls up at him. "You lost?"

"No. Look at him, brother." The girl wipes a sticky tendril of hair from her cheek. "His eyes. See?"

Zaniel gives her a stern look, trying to appear tough. He cannot show fear, not in this place, lest his bracelet turn on again. "What about them?"

"You hide them. You hide their true colour. They're grey here. Like your grandfather's. But not *there.*" She grins. "In the real world, you disguise them. And there, see his bracelets? You must be that boy who works for that mean old pig. You must be! You must be!"

"Oh," the boy nods. "Sorry, kid. Didn't recognize you. What'cha doing here by yourself? Akki find someone new?"

Zaniel looks away again, tucking his hands deep into his pockets to obscure his wrists. "I'm taking a break."

"Yeah, well, that's what this place is here for, I guess," the boy shrugs. "Okay, if you're one of Akki's gang, we won't hassle you. You can have something from us on the house."

"I'm not his *gang*, I just ..." He shakes his head. "It's a long story."

"We're immortal, kid. We got plenty of time."

"No, thanks, just, uh ... I ... I'm not really in a talking mood tonight; I just want to get things over with."

"You want some flowers, then!" The girl kneels down. The boy removes a small sack from inside his sleeve, unties it, and takes out a handful of dirt. He gives it to her; she shapes it into a small hill and presses it into the stones. "There. It'll be a couple of minutes." She cups her hands over the mound. Droplets of water fall from her fingertips. It takes a few seconds to create a good steady shower.

"Good choice," the boy tells Zaniel. "Girls like flowers. They're so full of symbolism and deep meaning, they're bound to catch someone's eye. Make them red, sis. That should really get the message across, save him some time."

Zaniel prepares to say that no, he is in no need of flowers tonight, but in the end, he thinks better of it. After all, it is unwise to refuse a gift from any *yokai*. The three of them watch the flowers bud and bloom from the earth, under the girl's tiny rainfall. The boy collects the flowers in threes.

"What's it like, *hafu* boy?" the girl suddenly asks. "What's it like, going back and forth all the time, pretending for so long? Is it lonely?"

She is concentrating too hard on her rainfall to see the glint of anger in Zaniel's eyes or hear it in his voice. "Maybe in a hundred years you'll find out for yourself."

"Not likely. We have each other. Here you go." The boy obviously did not catch it, either. He hands Zaniel a full bouquet of red roses. The whole process only took a few minutes, as promised. "Good luck with these. Well, we'll let you get on with your break." He helps his sister to her feet and they stroll away, hand in hand. Zaniel watches their backs, listens to the *clop-clop* of their wooden *geta* get quieter and quieter. *That's two ... or is that three?*

Zaniel is cold all of a sudden. He tucks the flowers under one arm and folds his hands into the warmth of his armpits. The flowers will survive, of course, assuming he can keep his eyes open long enough to put them to use. He feels the impending danger of nodding off, so he continues his walk. "Idiot," he curses himself. *Who gets sleepy in a world where he's already asleep?*

He walks farther along the path, concentrating on the trees and the shadows they cast against the red sky behind them. They begin to normalize now, matching the deciduous trees that exist in the real world. The sky begins to darken to a deep, warm brown. He relaxes a little, but only a little, for he knows that *yokai* may still lurk here.

He is correct. It is not long after that another shadow appears. This one sits in the middle of the path, squatting as some humans like to do. Zaniel assumes he is meditating or sleeping. Were it not for the man's long red nose, Zaniel would skirt right around him. He knows that would be a most unwise choice. This creature is a *tengu*, and *tengu* deserve the proper respect.

"I apologize for disturbing you, *Tengu-sama*," Zaniel begins with a deep bow. "I merely want to pass through these woods unscathed. Please, let me by you without due harm."

"So formal. Oh, wait. You are Akki's boy. Why not say something, kid?" The *Tengu* rises to his feet, brushing itself down. "Do you not know how dangerous these parts are? Humans get devoured up here all the time."

"How do you know me, sir?"

The *Tengu* darts up to him and taps the black beads on Zaniel's left wrist, just visible past the cuff of his jacket sleeve. Zaniel clutches his bracelets, instinctively, as if to hide them. "Oh. I see. To be honest, I didn't think it would matter ..."

"You are Akki's," he repeats. "Of course it matters. Have you no idea how important you are to him?" The *Tengu* clicks his tongue. "Kids these days."

"With all due respect, sir, I'm not a kid. I'm actually almost —"

"A thousand years old? No? Then guess what." The *Tengu* rolls back his shoulders. A pair of thick black feathered wings expand from his back. "Walk with me, human."

Reluctant, Zaniel complies. He wonders what Akki would say at the sight of him walking alongside another *yokai*. He wonders if Akki would even allow it.

"I know what you are thinking. I will not take much of your time. I only want to share my thoughts with you: if you are not a child, as you claim, then perhaps the time has come to depart from your bodyguard's company. Perhaps the *yokai* of these woods have grown accustomed to your presence enough to leave you alone. Have you considered that?"

Zaniel shakes his head. "Not really. I guess … no, not really. There are so many new creatures about these days."

"Were I you, I would talk with your guard. He is clearly fond of you to have kept you all this time. Perhaps he can teach you ways to defend yourself. Or, perhaps, I can impart some of my wisdom upon thee. Do you accept?"

Aha. There's the catch. "With all due respect," Zaniel repeats. "I am not worthy of such wisdom. I am but human."

"Rumour has it you are *hafu*."

"Only in my ethnicity. I am half-Japanese, but fully human."

The *Tengu* stops walking, and sighs as if saddened by Zaniel's reply. "Suit thyself," he shrugs. "I only offer but once. Good night and good luck, human."

He lets Zaniel take a few steps more, then spreads his wings, flaps them twice, and takes flight high above the trees. *And that makes three. They always come in threes.*

Zaniel is not disappointed to see him go. *Tengu* are renowned for their wisdom in swordsmanship and martial arts but are even more famous for playing tricks on unsuspecting humans. He would never hear the end of it; Akki would call him all sorts of names and chastise him for being so gullible. And Zaniel has no idea if that would come before or after Akki's fiery rampage. It would all depend upon the fearsome *yokai*'s mood, untameable and ever changing as it is. Case in point, Akki had let him off easy the other night. On the other hand, perhaps the *Tengu* simply wanted to be helpful. It is Zaniel's nature to be suspicious, after all these years of wandering the woods. He will never know now, and that suits him fine.

Zaniel arrives at an opening in the forest, a crossroad in the path. One direction, he knows, will lead him deeper into the woods, farther away from the supposed safety of Akki's domain. The other will take him closer to the city. He makes a face. He does not really wish to choose either one. There is no telling what *yokai* he will encounter should he take the road on the left, and he has no indication that he may find the Yokai should he choose the road on the right. He does not suppose her to be much of a social creature. He sighs. His search was fruitless after all. All he wants now is to awaken. Perhaps he can try again another night — if he can gather the courage to do so all over again, that is. He lays his flowers at the intersection and heads down the path to the right. A place closer to the city will be safer to rest long enough to wake up.

If only he had waited a moment longer, for someone is running up from behind.

"Hello? HELLO?"

It is the Yokai. She comes running down the path, stopping at the crossroads. She is certain she saw someone heading this way, but which way could he have gone? "Damn." She is more than lost, now. Maybe it is for the best. There are so many strange noises and shapes in the dark, there is no telling if the one she has been following would have been any benefit to her. None of the others were. At least here she can see the stars up above, providing her with a little more vision and comfort than the forest.

She can see a city below the mountains, brimming with life and lights. She can see her hands before her face. Now if only she can determine which way to go.

The Yokai looks down at the ground, noticing the bouquet of roses. She approaches them and kneels. They look and smell heavenly, too unreal, too perfect to be true. The scent of them make her dizzy when she stands. If only they were pointing toward one direction or the other, she thinks to herself, they might give her a hint of which way to go. She looks up at the sky again. The stars give no suggestion of where to go, either. Not that she can read stars, she remarks with chagrin. "Too bad you can't talk," she mutters out loud.

"Says who?!"

Watching in bewilderment, the Yokai notices some of the stars glowing brighter and closer to her face. "Uh-oh," she says. This feels all too familiar.

One of several dozen glowing balls of light buzzes in her face, making a sound like an angry wasp. "That's right, freak," it says. "We're *back*. Now, go away. Don't make us teach you another lesson."

"Another lesson?" The Yokai makes a puzzled face. Something about these glowing stars, these lights, makes her feel wary but she cannot for the life of her remember why. "That doesn't sound right."

"Yeah, well, neither do you. Get lost."

The Yokai groans, impatient. "I *am* lost. That's the problem."

"We told you not to come around here. We thought you got the message."

"Okay … don't know what the heck you things are talking about, but I'm just trying to get … I'm supposed to be at a …" the Yokai trails off, noticing the patterns on the horizon have changed. The city is now on her left-hand side instead of her right. "Wait. The mountains were in front of me a minute ago. I have to go back that way. Or is it this way? For crying out loud, will you all just stop *moving* for one minute?!"

The nightmares' laughter is like the hissing of snakes. "Aw, poor Yokai can't keep her directions straight! Boo hoo hoo!"

The Yokai takes another deep breath. She believes it best to remain calm. "Listen, guys. I'm starving, I'm tired, and I'm really not in the mood to argue with anyone. I just *saw* someone go this way and none of you batted an eyelash, so unless you're getting paid to stand out here and be assholes, you have no right to bar me from anything. It's a free country."

"Uh, NO it isn't," says the first light. "Where do you think this is, the human realm? Idiot." The others back it up with jeers of their own.

"You can't stop me." The Yokai says, resolute. "You're just a ... what the heck are you, anyway? A will-o'-the-wisp?"

"What a dumb-ass. We're your worst nightmares."

"Oh no, a glowing ball of light. How terrifying. I think I just soiled myself. Give me a break."

"You loser," another light groans. "You think we're playing? We're NIGHTMARES, hello!"

Again, the others chime in. "Yeah! Don't underestimate us!"

"*Fine*," the Yokai groans. "Then point me back the way I came."

Another nightmare, fat and bright, buzzes in her face. "No! We changed our minds. We're fickle like that! You're gonna stay here and suffer! Ha! You want everyone to think you're human with that tacky disguise? Well, you've got your wish; now you can rot and die up here like all the humans who're too stupid to stay away from here — you know, where they *don't* belong."

The others watch and laugh, but there is an air of nervousness in their chuckles. They altogether find it strange that she does not remember their last encounter. One would think the trauma of it all would have scared her right from the beginning. But in the backs of their minds, they chalk it up to just more of her human-like behaviour. She is a strange creature indeed.

The Yokai huffs. Now she is upset. "You know what? Shut up. I don't want to hear it. You're just a bunch of glowing will-o'-the-wisps with no authority, and you can't stop me from — Ow! Son of a —!"

She was too caught up in the moment. By the time the one fat light had lowered itself to the height of her hand, it was too late to get away before it gnashed her fingers. She sucks at them, tasting blood.

The fat nightmare lets out an evil laugh. "Oh, *now* she's listening," it says. "Look at that. It speaks the language after all. Let's see if you can understand this, freak show. Take your ugly — hey! Let me go!"

"Ha! Not so tough now, are you?" The Yokai holds the large, bloodthirsty light, enjoying the warmth and electricity as it wriggles wildly in her fists. Its friends float in the air, helpless.

"You bitch! How DARE you mess with me!"

"Maybe if you apologize, I won't do something we'll regret. Now, what do we say?" the Yokai addresses the others. "Are you going to move aside, or do I have to get ugly?"

The nightmare in her hands makes another angry buzzing noise. "What do *I* say?! I say you can bite me! I say, you're *already* ugly! I say you're — nooo!"

With a couple of popping clicks her jaw unhinges and she brings the glowing sphere to her mouth. Its last cry for help disappears behind the Yokai's lips. A pair of snakelike fangs shimmer among her teeth as she sinks them into the nightmare. It screams as she pulls at it, tearing a large chunk of its substance off, sending a spray of golden liquid everywhere. Waves of hot sugary lemon flood over her tongue. A half-torn ball of radiance, the nightmare thrashes, spraying its fellow orbs with its golden blood. It almost escapes the Yokai's grip, but she is faster. Its cries are muffled as she crams the rest of the nightmare into her mouth and clamps her hands over it. She chews and chews and chews. The nightmare puts up a good fight but ultimately succumbs to its fate. The other lights watch in silent horror as the Yokai doubles over onto the ground, radiant blood dribbling from one corner of her lips. She makes a loud groaning noise as though she is about to be sick. Two single tears stream from her eyes.

"Oh my gosh. Oh. My. GOSH."

Slowly, she stands upright and swallows with a satisfied gasp. The other lights quiver in fear. She revels in their reaction. "Hmph," the Yokai poses in triumph. "Say something now, you little pieces of dandruff! How many humans d'you know who can do *that*? What's wrong? Run out of insults? No one else wants to be a hero?"

The lights detach themselves from their hedge-like barrier; as they float away the leaves tremble, the branches unravel, and everything separates like two doors sliding apart. They expose another world of darkness. But the Yokai cannot show fear now. She plunges forward, as if it was her intended destination all along.

"That's right," she waves without looking back. "Tell your friends about me."

The lights do not reply, but they do their best to make a sort of bowing motion of deep respect until she disappears into the dark.

One breaks the awkward silence. "Shit. And we thought that kid of Akki's was weird …"

"That's what we gotta do!" says another voice. "You heard her! We gotta tell Akki!" The nightmares zip away, screeching into the night, straight to Akki's lair, crying out his name on the wind like frightened children.

In the meantime, the Yokai strolls in the dark, more confident than ever. Even the pavement feels warmed by her recent meal. Wait … pavement? Yes, the road has changed somehow. It is colder, scratchy under her bare feet, more solid than the cobblestone path she had followed all this way. She can feel each rugged stone and pebble embedded in the cement under her toes and heels. Her senses must be heightened by the hallucinogenic effects of her nightmarish snack. She can feel it digesting in her stomach, warming neighbouring organs. It is harder to focus her vision on one focal point — not that there is anything to focus on in the darkness — and with every step she takes, she can feel every synapse vibrate in her muscles, from the soles of her naked feet all the way to her brain. She wishes she could have another to eat, right now.

The air around her begins to change, as well. It carries a pungent odour of stale cigarette butts and urine. The Yokai hopes she is stepping on neither. The darkness begins to lift; in the distance, the Yokai sees something bright orange. It is a small torii gate. An old man huddles next to it, holding his hands over a trash can fire. As the Yokai comes ever closer, she notices the torii is situated between two brick walls slathered in a colourful assortment of indecipherable graffiti. The hues blend together in a discombobulated, deconstructed rainbow. Squinting, she discerns four characters painted in crude white brush strokes:

自 分 自 身

She reaches out and touches the brick wall, outlining the white marks with a fingertip. She knows this place. It looks and smells very familiar, with the scent of salt and sensation of heat emanating from the dark space in the centre of the torii's entrance.

The old man jolts alive. *"Konbanwa, irasshai irasshai,"* he croaks with a toothless grin. *"Kin o motte iru ka?"*

"Pardon?" asks the Yokai.

"Kin. Gorudo, gorudo." He points down at the Yokai's hands. The Yokai notices for the first time that her palms are covered in a shiny gold dust. It must be from the nightmare. She rubs them. The dust does not feel like a soft powder. If anything, it feels like dried, once-sticky liquid. Dried blood, if she must give it a name.

"Yesss," the old man hisses. "Gold." He gestures to the fiery trash can.

"Oh. Okay." Hesitant, the Yokai dusts her hands a safe distance over the fire. The old man claps his own hands with glee at the sight of the gold cloud she creates. He scrambles up to the old torii gate and pulls back the barely visible tarp. It is pitch-dark underneath.

"No way. I'm not going in there."

"Yes, yesss! In! In!"

The Yokai sighs. "Damn it ..." She follows the old man's gestures and ducks under the tarp. It is a bit of a tight squeeze at her size, but at least here it is warmer.

A dim light comes into view through the darkness. A woman in a beautiful kimono materializes before the Yokai, candle in hand. "Welcome." She bows low. "Sorry to keep you waiting. Please, be yourself. This way ..."

She gestures for the Yokai to follow her. The Yokai does so through the darkness. Suddenly the panels of dark slide away, revealing a tiny courtyard with a giant cherry blossom tree illuminated from below. The Yokai cannot help but stop and stare up at the branches littering petals all over her. "Oh, wow ..."

The maître d' smiles. "Beautiful, isn't it? Please, this way. You've arrived at the best time. It is busy, but there are no humans around to bother you. They are not permitted entry for the remainder of the night. Please, feel free to shed your disguise and be yourself."

The Yokai follows the maître d' into the restaurant, barely acknowledging the restaurant's greeting, for she is distracted by two long buffet tables in the pit, groaning under the weight of a hundred dishes. Upon the stage, three massive iridescent squids with white *hachimaki* headbands bang fast steady rhythms on a dozen taiko drums. The Yokai takes it all in: the creatures, the waitresses' kimonos, the food, the mayhem. At the peak of "*oni* only" hours, Jibun Jishin is in high-spirited chaos.

The maître d' walks up to the table on the left, past a group of women in business suits eating pink sashimi slices and feeding *gari* to the lips hidden in the backs of their heads. Beside them, seal-like *yokai* toast Turban Shell sashimi with their flippers while tiny creatures crawl all over their bodies, licking salt off their fine hairs with tiny pink tongues. Across the table, red-eyed leopard-spotted monkeys nibble roasted spiders and smoking cedar chips. The maître d' stops between a large rooster sitting before a heap of flaming bamboo shoots and a one-legged *yokai* holding a freshly sucked crab shell. A stool pulls itself out for the Yokai as dishes form before her: steamy gyoza, sizzling lemon-ginger fried chicken, golden yellow corn drowning in butter and soy sauce, warm crunchy pumpkin sushi rolls, glistening lotus root chips, a giant bowl of *niku jaga*, matcha ice cream dusted with dark green powder sublimating a frosty incense-like smoke, freshly baked *taiyaki,* bubbling lava cheese tarts, and colossal stacks of alternating hamburger patties and sourdough buns layered with lettuce and slices of tomato, and dripping mayonnaise and ketchup.

The maître d' smiles. "As you can see, we strive to provide our guests with their innermost desires, whatever they may be. Now, which one would you like?"

The Yokai takes a deep breath. "All of it." She dives in: a gyoza here, a scoop of corn there, a *click-click-pop* of her jaw unhinging to take a bite of burger, and so on. The other *yokai* slowly return to their own meals but cannot help watching, overwhelmed with fascination at her spectacle of sustenance.

"Wow," the one-legged *yokai* says after staring for some time. "So ... you can use chopsticks, eh?"

"Oh, don't start with that. Of course, she can." The rooster clears its throat. "*Basan,* from Shikoku. How about you, kid? What are you? Where you from?"

"Um ..." the Yokai covers her mouth, still chewing.

"Never mind," the rooster says before she can speak. "It's not important, either. You really can eat, huh? Here, would you like to try some of this? It's good." It nuzzles a fiery bamboo shoot off its plate in her direction.

"Okay," says the Yokai with a mouthful. "Thanks."

"Amazing. She ate it! Um, how about some of mine? Would you like to …?" The one-legged *yokai* takes a chopstick serving of crab flesh and places it on her plate.

"Sure. Thank you. Mmm, I like it. It's salty."

In moments, other *yokai* surround her. They test her and offer her more and more of their food. Each one the Yokai politely accepts and lifts to her mouth. Now beginning to relax in her presence, the demons start asking her questions: Has she ever eaten this before, is this her first time at Jibun Jishin, how long has she been using chopsticks, does she like the food, where did she come from? She simply nods "yes" to everything, unable to speak with her mouth so full. No one asks many follow-up questions, to the Yokai's relief, because she is too immersed in the sensations each mouthful brings her: the tart, the crunchy, the sweet, the salty, the gooey, briny, buttery, sweet, firm, rich, decadent food all swim in her stomach and send quivers up her spine. Her voracious appetite shows no bounds. Everything placed in front of her disappears into her mouth. She feels like butter melting in warm sunlight.

The squids on the stage make their final bows, sticks in tentacles, and shuffle off the stage to make way for the *koto* musicians. By now, the Yokai is high as a kite. She staggers from her chair, following the *tanukis'* gestures toward a sake-dispensing machine in a corner of the pit (they highly recommend she try it). Next to the machine, the Yokai cannot help staring at a pile of velvety cushions where a massive red hornet sits in a cloud of smoke. It watches the Yokai with solid dark-red eyes like five garnet mirrors, fingering peach cigarillos in each of its six legs. The scent of them makes the room spin even more.

"*Suzumebachi,*" the hornet introduces itself with a lofty cloud of smoke breathed into her face. "Here to try the sake?"

"Oh. Yes. Sorry." The Yokai helps herself to a tiny cupful. The sake is piping hot, but not so hot it burns her tongue. She drinks it down easily and dispenses another refill. "Mmm, that's good."

"Yes. Not my thing, however. I much prefer mantis." The *suzumebachi* wiggles its stinger and takes another drag on one of its cigarillos. It wants to talk to her, but does not want to engage in insipid conversation, which is what it supposes the other demons have been doing with her all night. It is difficult, however, to know where to start. "You seem to enjoy all varieties of foods, I see."

"I guess I do."

"Is there anything you will not eat?"

"I don't know. I don't really like liver."

The hornet wiggles one of its scarlet antennae. "River?"

"Liver."

"Lever?"

The Yokai giggles. "*Li-ver.*"

"I see. So, you do not like to feed on the living."

"No," the Yokai says, not quite understanding.

"I see. Perhaps you just have a hungry *yokai* in your stomach. Or you are pregnant."

"Ha! Not bloody likely."

"No extra mouths to feed?"

The Yokai shakes her head, trying not to focus so hard on the *suzumebachi*'s mandibles as they open and close. "Nope, just the one."

"So, not one of the *futakuchi.*" The hornet points to where the group of young businesswomen sit. "Hmm. What about your shape? I hear you can grow as big as a house when it suits you."

"Can I?" That would be quite an ability to have, the Yokai thinks to herself. "How?"

"Don't ask me. I just hear these things." The *suzumebachi* takes a puff of the cigarillo and blows it in the Yokai's face, making her dizzy, but she does not wave the smoke away. She does not want to seem rude. "Hmm. You seem to have all your limbs, and you do not have any extra parts. I cannot place what kind of being you are."

"That makes two of us."

"Fear not, child. There are millions of us *yokai* these days. I am sure you will find your kind somewhere."

The Yokai looks down at her cup. "That's the dream," she says before knocking back more sake.

"What did you say? The dream … ah, yes. Now *there* is a possibility. Tell me, child, do you eat dreams?"

"How could I?"

"Now, now, don't take offence. It's only a question." Its wings bristle, then calm down. "Have you heard? They say there is more than one kind of dream. They come in all sizes, it seems. Some are tiny, so brief they pass by like *sakura* petals on the wind. And then there are the ones so vast you could sleep a hundred years and never see its end."

The Yokai snags a giant gyoza from a passing waitress's tray, stuffs it in her mouth, and says something. "Pardon?" asks the *suzumebachi*.

"Sorry." She swallows. "I said, 'Sounds deep.'"

"Yes, true. They can go deep as the ocean, too. Be careful not to drown in any of yours, child."

The Yokai wonders if that is possible. The *suzumebachi* seems to recognize the perplexed look on the Yokai's face. "I would not think on it too much, young one. Just be yourself. That is all any of us can do. Now, if you will excuse me, I have some mantis to find."

The hornet alights into the air, straight up, flapping its giant wings so that the cloud of smoke around the Yokai dissipates and makes her cough. By the time it all clears, the Yokai notices the waitresses removing the tables. They fold the second-to-last one up and carry it away, making room for creatures to dance, for the squids have returned for an encore performance. The Yokai, however, is still hungry. All that sake has only made her more desperate for food, something to sober her up and soak up all the alcohol in her stomach.

Everything seems to shimmer with light. Colours swim before the Yokai's eyes, bounce off *yokai* bodies, reflecting their scales and shells, dying their fur all the colours of the rainbow as they pump their fists, wriggle their shoulders, and stomp their feet to the music. The Yokai catches a gleam of gold between her fingers and licks it before she can think twice about doing so. She wishes she could have another one of those glowing lights from earlier. She does not see a waitress she can ask. No, it is not a nightmare she wants … she was looking for something before that … no, not something, someone …

"Hey!" A giant *tanuki* is shouting, pointing. "Who ordered the human?"

On the last remaining table, Zaniel sits upright. His bed is gone, replaced by a cold, silver platter scattered with lettuce and grapes for garnish. He cries out as a *futakuchi-onna* reaches for a grape with her chopsticks and snags his T-shirt. Scrambling off the platter, he nearly misses a black paw that almost scratches his naked leg. It takes him a moment to recognize where he is, and when he does, his panic doubles.

A waitress comes running up to the Yokai, dodging around the dancing demons. "Sorry, miss, last call for all-you-can-eat just ended, but I believe that one is part of your order just now?" She points at the young man scrambling away from *yokai* hands and claws.

"I didn't order anyone," the Yokai slurs.

"I see. All right, we'll take him to the kitchen. *Sumimasen, ningen-sama!*" She wades through the crowd and tries to grab Zaniel's wrist. He snatches his arm away too late. The waitress reels back in pain, cradling the fingers that she singed on his obsidian bracelet, now glowing with fierce heat. The other *yokai* back away in fear.

"Hey, hey," the Yokai leaps onto the table. "Leave him alone. He's not *food*. Come on, guys, I thought you were cool." She places a steady hand on Zaniel's shoulder. "You okay? They won't hurt you." The waitress tries to stop her, but the Yokai holds up a hand. "Relax, I'll take him."

"Hai, wakarimashita." The waitress bows.

The Yokai takes hold of Zaniel's left wrist and guides him down from the table. Zaniel allows himself to be guided. Feeling her hand enclosed around the bracelet on his wrist, sensations flow through him. Warmth, protection … safety. "Wait," he says. "It's you."

"Who?"

"It's you. You're …!" He is at a loss for words. What is she doing here? What is *he* doing here? He whirls around. Akki is nowhere in sight. *What is going on?*

"Well, the food's all gone. Will you dance with me?"

"Pardon?"

The Yokai does not wait for an affirmative answer. She is already guiding Zaniel's hands to her waist and putting her head on his shoulder. "I'm dizzy," she murmurs. But they are spinning together, slowly, out of time and sync with the drums. Zaniel looks around the restaurant. He sees other *yokai* point and giggle at them. Some of them even copy them, caressing and pirouetting around one another, then giving up and returning to their thrashing, hopping dance moves. Zaniel was unsure of how he could refuse, but now that he is holding the Yokai, he is grateful. The other demons have left them completely alone, ignoring them as if they are not even there. Zaniel turns his head to look at the stage, blinking in the process.

When he opens his eyes, he finds himself in a small living room, cozy and familiar. Snow falls outside the window. A low *kotatsu* table sits at his feet, covered with food he recognizes from his own childhood: kimchi *nabe* with pork and mushrooms, freshly baked *taiyaki*, and bowls of green tea ice cream with matcha powder sprinkled on top. He is warm and safe here, in this dream within a dream.

Zaniel blinks again. The surroundings of Jibun Jishin have returned. The Yokai is still in his arms. The only difference now is they are ascending higher and higher into the air, at least seven storeys up. The Yokai does not seem to have noticed. Zaniel is so afraid of falling into the mosh pit of demons below that he decides against pointing it out.

"Mmm," the Yokai snuggles against his shoulder. "You were so far away just now. Looked like you were daydreaming. Dreams come in all shapes and sizes, apparently. Tiny, big, deep ... Do you think it's the same with nightmares? I forgot to ask."

Good grief, I hope not, Zaniel thinks to himself. "Ask who?" he says instead.

"The *suzumebachi*. I once had a dream that I ate a s'more the size of a house. I don't know. I wouldn't mind a dream like that being deep as an ocean. What about you? What do you dream about?" Before Zaniel can answer, she places a hand on his chest. "'Being free?' What does that mean?"

Ever so gently, Zaniel removes her hand by her sleeve with his right hand. He notices for the first time that his ruby bracelet is glowing, but unlike every other time, it does not hurt him. "Are ... are you doing this? How?" he asks her. He finds himself asking two bewildered-looking Zaniels, two solid reflections in the pitch-dark of the Yokai's eyes that grow bigger and bigger. No, they are not growing; it is her, leaning forward, coming closer and closer. "What are you?" he whispers against her mouth.

"Gotcha!"

A hand reaches out and snatches Zaniel by the back of his shirt, ripping him from the Yokai's embrace. "Hang on, kid," says the gruff, familiar voice. "I gotcha."

Zaniel dangles precariously off the tenth floor until he is swung over the railing to safely stand on his own two feet. His saviour: a giant creature in gold samurai armour from forehead to foot. He recognizes the voice immediately. "Akki ... *sama?*"

"That's my name, don't wear it out." The *yokai* removes his facial armour and helmet and shakes his dark, angry-looking mane. "Geez, kid. What the hell're you wearin'?"

"This is what I sleep in. And I could ask you the same thing."

"I ..." Akki looks down at himself. "Huh. Well, ain't this new." Being honest with himself, he has no idea where any of this came from, but Akki does not dwell on it. He simply chuckles as he removes each piece of the golden suit. "How the hell'd you get here, anyway?"

Now it is Zaniel's turn to be at a loss for words. "I ..." Any semblance of an explanation he might have given is interrupted by a watery splash. He takes advantage of Akki's distracted process of undress to look over his shoulder down below. The pit on the first floor has transformed into a literal sea of demons. Even ten storeys up, Zaniel can read the mystified, puzzled looks on various *yokai* faces at how the floor suddenly turned into water. They do not think about it for too long, however. Once the aquatic species revel in the transition, other creatures start to paddle and wade, then dive and roll, and very quickly, the *yokai* are splashing each other playfully and spewing water from their mouths and trunks like cartoonish fountains.

"I don't know," Zaniel finally answers. It is not a complete lie. "What about you?"

"You summoned me, kid. Figured you needed rescuin' — *again.*"

Akki gestures to the young man's wrist. The light from the bracelets has dimmed now that the giant *yokai* has arrived, but they are still glowing. *How odd.* Zaniel blinks with confusion. *They've never glowed* together *like this.* When he raises his gaze again, Akki stands before him, completely naked save his black *fundoshi* underwear. The dragon on his chest stirs and opens its eyes into two narrow slits. It gives Zaniel a brief sneer before turning its back on him and curling up into a ball to return to its nap.

"So, who was that messing with you there, kid? Looked like someone took you up awful high."

"What? Oh. I don't know. It's okay, though. It was nothing."

Akki narrows his eyes. "You sure about that? Didn't look like nothing …"

"Yes." Zaniel bows. "I'm sorry, Akki-*sama*, for summoning you all this way. I apologize."

Akki sighs. "Whatever. Let's get you out of here. C'mon, follow me."

The giant man leads the way past private booths shrouded by shimmery silks and bamboo curtains to the nearest staircase that will take them back to the ground floor. Members of the wait staff step back to make room for him and his young companion, who feels much more self-conscious about walking around in his sleepwear.

"By the way, kid, I've been thinkin.' I've been a bit soft on you about your taste in chicks these days. So I came up with a plan. You got three more shots to redeem yourself, see. How much time would you like?"

"Time? I'm afraid I don't understand, Akki-*sama*. Are you giving me an … an ultimatum?" Akki glares at him. "I mean, *saigo tsuuchou?*"

"Yeah, that's it. Let's see …" Akki leaps down the last few steps, sending a boom that ripples through the floor and knocks a drink or two off nearby tables. "Let's make it three broads in four nights. Yeah. I'll make it easy on ya with an extra night."

"Three women in four nights!" Zaniel starts after the *yokai*, then holds his tongue. He looks down at the translucent-tiled floor. He has no idea what he is going to do. "Understood."

"And *don't* think about gettin' no creative ideas. I'll pick one out, you bring her up to the house, I take it from there. That's how our little routine's been workin', and that's how it's gonna *keep* workin'. If you can't deliver, you can find yourself a new body-guard. You got it?"

Zaniel is not listening. Rather than follow his protector, or worry about this new-found urgency, Zaniel has stopped in his tracks. Under the floor beneath him, he sees the Yokai, swimming after him. He holds in a gasp. She seems trapped, until she waves up at him. Zaniel snaps his head up. Akki is far away, already past the koi pond at the entrance. "Kid, you listenin'? I said, *you got it?*"

"Yes, Akki-*sama*."

"Well, come *on*, then! Let's get you outta here, before they put *you* on the menu."

Akki watches the young man reluctantly follow. He cannot put his finger on Zaniel. *The boy is actin' strange.* Stranger than usual, which coming from a *yokai* is saying something. What is he doing *here*, during "*oni* only" of all times? Another *yokai* could not have brought him. Who would be that foolish? He watches Zaniel now as the young man crosses the stone bridge, looking back over his shoulder as if pining for something. Perhaps Hino had the right notion — maybe Zaniel came here trying to prove something to himself. In the end, Akki decides not to drag out a lecture tonight. Whatever his reasoning, he believes Zaniel has learned his lesson. This new ultimatum will suffice.

Akki ducks his head through the sliding doors into the pitch darkness that will take him back out onto the streets of Osaka. He does not see Zaniel look over his shoulder one last time at the Yokai, now peeking above the surface of the koi pond. She watches him long-ingly, unable to follow, for the fish are tugging at her long white robe.

"Come, child," says one of the koi. "Let's go eat some more and dance until dawn!"

"You don't want to mess with that one, child," says another. "That boar god is dangerous. And that human will only draw his ire to you. You don't want that."

"Boar god?" the Yokai asks the fish.

"Yes, join *us*!" They ignore her query. "Show us what else you can eat, little one."

"I'm not little!" But the Yokai is laughing. She has already forgotten about the man with the grey eyes and his samurai protector. She wades neck-deep through the water, then lets the water close over her head as the demons dance above the surface, wading up to their knees from the restaurant shore. The demons dance and dance until the eventual arrival of the dawn. Meanwhile, the Yokai sleeps at the bottom of her ocean, underneath all their antics and mayhem, warm and satiated, content and complete.

PART II

seven

A VERY IMPORTANT DATE

七転び八起き

Fall down seven times, get up eight

It hurts to open my eyes. The curtains of my apartment are drawn, but it still feels like there's a flashlight on my face. It's boiling in here, and the room smells of … what the heck is that?

I jerk upright and bang my knee on the underside of my *kotatsu*. Good thing it's not on, unlike my living room light. As I try to stand, my hand crunches down on a pile of empty plastic containers coated with fragments of *okonomiyaki* sauce and soy with bits of gyoza chips and onions. My apartment is awash with food containers and empty cartons that still smell of Hokkaido milk and green tea ice creams, like they all swept up on a beach with the tide. That explains the smell.

I stretch on all fours like a cat as I contemplate the giant heap of laundry spilling out from the one basket covered with empty grocery bags. There's also a small mountain of blankets I had completely forgotten about. Together with the laundry they engulf the vacuum cleaner in the corner. I have my chores cut out for me this week. As disturbing as this whole scene is, I feel nice and warm and satisfied. I snuggle back under the *kotatsu* and feel something hard and plastic at my feet — the TV remote. The TV greets me with pleasant daytime talk show chatter, so soothing to my ears I consider going back to sleep. I can do with a nice cup of tea first. No one can say I don't have exciting weekends; by the look of this place, I enjoyed myself last night.

Something draws my eyes to the TV. It's set to a morning show on NHK, but it's not the weather forecast talking about Typhoon Lan that pulls me in. It's the time of day in the upper right corner. My blood runs cold: the clock says "10:59."

10:59.

I have one minute to get to work.

"Shit!" I pull off my pyjamas, trip over the *kotatsu*, and tumble to the floor. It's a sign. Forget getting dressed. The first thing I need to do is call Manager, beg for forgiveness, and lie that I'm a two-second bike ride away. "Shit, shit, shit ..." I scramble through the wreckage for my purse and find my phone way down at the bottom.

It's dead.

"SHIT."

I create more chaos by flinging clothes from the laundry basket, looking for pants and a shirt that don't reek from my Saturday night outfit. Everything smells. Fuck it. I throw on one of my best skirt suits, stick some lip gloss in my pocket, wrap a toothbrush in my handkerchief, shove that into my purse, and stuff a mint tea bag in my mouth knowing full well that I don't own any mints or gum. Bad idea. It tastes so awful I spit it back out. There's no time to bother with my hair. Zozo and the rest of Japan will just have to deal with it.

In hindsight, I should have opted for a taxi instead of the most death-defying bike ride in the history of *gaijin* lateness. It's raining buckets, and everyone insists on stepping in my path. I'm a sopping mess by the time I get to the Zozo building. Something tells me to pass on the seven flights of stairs and succumb to the whim of the elevator, where I mop my forehead and prepare any and all excuses to Manager. My limbs shake with adrenalin. My eyes sting. Good. Maybe tears will make him take pity on me.

"I'm so sorry, everyone, Manager! I — hello?"

The doors slide open to near-complete darkness. There's no one here. If I didn't recognize the eclectic mascot on the wall illuminated by the neon-red exit sign and the light from the elevator, I'd say this is the set of a Japanese horror movie. Apparently, Zozo is closed. There's nothing that shows signs of anyone being here ... except maybe the Anpanman toy on the reception desk. Which I don't remember anyone putting there. It faces the elevator, faces me, grinning at me with its beady little black eyes. It almost looks like it's about to say something. But why would it?

Then again, I did say, "hello."

I step back into the elevator and mash the button for the ground floor. Oh, well. It's not like anyone is around to see what an idiot I am. Outside, everything looks the same, except the rain has stopped (what wonderful timing). A couple walking by me gesture and whisper, *"Kowai, ne ..."* A woman holding a child's hand pulls harder when he stops and stares at me. All the shops and stores around me are busy. I squint down the street. People are coming in and out of the bank, and a worker is standing outside the City of Nishibe Post Office, handing stuff to passersby. Why the hell is Zozo closed? What's going on? Everything looks like a typical, normal —

Oh, my gosh. I bite my lip. Today isn't Tuesday, and I'm not late; it's Monday. "Shit," I mutter to myself. My calves ache, but there's nowhere to sit except on my bike. Fine. I just want to stand here for a moment and feel sorry for myself. How could I be so stupid? And why did I say "hello" in a scary, deserted place? That's what idiots in horror movies do.

As I curse every force of nature that brought me into this nonsensical situation, I notice something else. Among the coffee shop propaganda and baristas handing out free pumpkin spice latte samples is a silver-haired man. He leans against a small *kei* truck advertising udon and puffs away on a cigarette like he has all the time in the world to stare at me. Nothing out of the ordinary about that, in my position ... but something else about him bugs me. Something about his face. I cross the road to HORUS and pretend to admire the buns in the window. I watch his reflection in the glass. His head turns to follow me. *Who is this jerk?* I turn around and our eyes meet. His mouth stretches wider.

He's smiling. That's what's bothering me. Fuck this. I kiss my teeth, take my bike and my business back home. Might as well while I can beat the next batch of rain.

In my apartment I plop down on the small patch of floor that isn't covered in garbage, relieved I didn't get fired, but still pissed off at myself. Through the windows and thin walls, I can hear everyone down below on the street chattering away, happily: the sounds of happy families with their happy children in their happy strollers. Behind the closed curtains I can tell the sun is shining, too. *How could I be so stupid?* I mentally kick myself one more time for not buying breakfast on the way home. Something tells me my fridge is empty except for a few bottles of condiments, and I'm going to need strength to get this place cleaned up.

My intestines gurgle as I survey the relics of a food orgy I cannot remember. My head is swimming, which is perfect because I feel like I've been walking along the bottom of the ocean. What did I get up to yesterday? Hazy memories of binge-watching *xxxHolic* and eating everything in my kitchen surface. How did I wake up, forget a whole twenty-four hours, wipe a home buffet from memory, and mistake today for a Tuesday? And now that I think of it, Zozo's security is really lax. If the place is really closed, I shouldn't have been able to access our floor. Anyone off the street could just walk in and take ... well, I'm sure there are many things of value in our school. And what the *hell* was up with Anpanman sitting at the reception desk? Maybe someone found it in the elevator again and popped it there out of convenience. Still, I don't get how the school's oldest toy keeps making its way around. Something fishy is going on.

I take one more look around at the mess on the floor. Then the events of Saturday seep in. That child, that fucking awful night out with the Zozo teachers, the embarrassing trip home through the rain ... and something on my carpet. Now there is only one thought on my mind.

"I am *so* hungry."

Might as well find something around here to eat.

"Ima okina-EE-to, okurema-SOO, yo ... Ima okina-EE-to, okurema-SOO, yo ..."

I open my eyes. It's Tuesday. For sure, this time. It has to be. And this time, I'm taking my fucking umbrella.

I eat some *tamagoyaki* with my toast today and pop on one of my child-friendly cotton shirts and dress pants, fresh from the laundry. Yesterday I felt pretty warm, so it isn't time to break out the long sleeves yet (I don't care what anyone says). For lunch, what starts out as Kraft Dinner becomes a hefty portion of baked macaroni and cheese with sautéed *shiitake* mushrooms, some leftover broccoli from one of my 7-Eleven bentos, and a *panko* crust that I mixed with black pepper and nutmeg. Outside, there's a light drizzle, and the air is cooler today. Maybe a little too cold for most people this morning, so the streets are emptier than usual. How I wish I could join the people presumably cooped up in their cozy little homes. After yesterday, I'm not too eager to go to Zozo. Hell, I'm not too eager to even be awake right now.

"Good morning!" says a cheerful voice behind me as I snap my giant plastic umbrella into the bike holder. It's the old shrine worker. *"Ogenki desu ka?"*

"Hai, genki desu. Um …" I try my luck. *"Ojisan wa?"*

"Hai, hai, meccha genki ne! Welcome!" His eyes are friendly. "Welcome … to Japan!"

I laugh. *"Arigatou gozaimasu. Ittekimasu."*

"Itterasshai! Ganbatte ne!"

"Hai, ganbarimasu!" I give him a genuine smile. He continues down the street, clacking his wooden blocks in a steady rhythm. What a nice man. He must walk by here around this time every Tuesday. Why couldn't all my Tuesdays start out like this? No … why *shouldn't* they?

I muse over this idea as I cruise down the streets on my rusty, trusty bike. That's been my problem. I've been starting my days off on the wrong feet. Yesterday was not only a fluke but also a sign. Being late and not getting caught must have been the universe's way of telling me that things in my life need to change. I need to up my *genki* back to what it used to be. I wasn't always this grumpy spinster with no friends and nothing to look forward to in the drudgery of a thankless job. *Meccha ganbarimasu*: I will do my *freaking* best.

My determination channels into my biking speed all the way to the Zozo building. According to my watch, I have another fifteen minutes to get upstairs and sign in. Smelling the warm, pumpkin-scented breeze coming from the HORUS bakery, I question what better way to start the work week than with some treats to fuel my big toothy *gaikokujin* smile?

I take my time to select the best-looking, plumpest Totoro buns, some lemon Baumkuchen cakes, matcha-and-white-chocolate bagels, and an extra melon *pan*. The salesgirl from Saturday seems happy to see me again, and I'm happy to tell her that I have my freaking wallet this time. Outside, I lean against my bike as I wolf down my bread. No sign of any students to hide from, no sign of that rando with the *kei* truck, no sign of the old spitting lady. I don't even see too many people staring me up and down today. My day is off to a great start already.

My phone buzzes in my purse. *Cybelle it's your MOTHER, we need to talk about this wedding! Not now, of course, you're probably at work. Give me a shout when you can …* scrolls across the external display. No backlash about not calling home again. Score.

"*Sumimasen!*" A Starbucks employee with a tray beckons me. "Pumpkin spice, *ikaga desu ka?*" I graciously accept one of the little espresso cups on her tray. Warm, creamy, and delicious. Hello, caffeine; I've missed you. I thank the girl and head in to buy a tall size for myself. Double score.

My sweet latte elixir is finished by the time I'm in the elevator. I feel pumped and more than ready to do some freaking English teaching. Today is going to be great. This week is going to be great. *Good morning, everyone*, I prepare to sing as the elevator bell dings. *Let's enjoy —*

"Cybelle." Manager rushes me the second the doors open. "Come-with-me-quickly-please-NOW," he says in one breath.

Am I in trouble? Oh shit. I *am* in trouble. I'm about to get fired. Manager must have seen the security tape from yesterday morning and now he's going to fire me. I'll be going home super early for my sister's wedding after all. Hang on; do we even *have* security tapes?

There's no time to ask him. He ushers me through the empty lobby into the nearest classroom, Room Two, and shuts the door behind us. "Cybelle, I have something I must tell you." Halfway through his sentence there's a knock on the door. "*Shimatta,*" Manager hisses under his breath. "I will explain later."

He opens the door. A grey-haired woman in a pressed suit and fancy scarf beams at me. I recognize her from the Head Office newsletters — Miss Saito, our *bucho*, a.k.a. the regional manager.

Guess she's here to fire me in person. Wouldn't it have been easier to send a fax?

"Hello," she says to me. "Excuse me. 'Shibere'-*sensei, ne?*"

"Um," I raise my eyebrows. "Yes?" I think?

"I am Bucho. Nice to meet you."

"Nice to meet you, too."

She tells Manager in Japanese to call several students for something as soon as he's finished telling me whatever he scooted me in here for. Her tone isn't as kind when she switches languages. "Thank you, 'Shibere'-*sensei*! *Mata ne!*" She closes the door behind her.

"I am sorry, Cybelle," Manager whines. "I wanted to warn you before you saw Bucho. She is Bucho from Head Office. Ah, she will be here this week, and she is very hard-working. Very strict. She will ask you if you are re-contracting, maybe many times. Have you decided? About *imouto-san*'s wedding?"

I feel something in my eye. "Sorry, not yet."

"Ah, I see. Please decide very soon. You must send the form in less than three weeks, so, please, decide soon. Oh, wait. Ah, Bucho must use computer, maybe for a long time, so please do not use computer if Bucho is in the staff room. Which is, maybe, all the time."

"So how am I supposed to sign in?"

"I will sign you in when Bucho is not using computer. Please, do not worry. Please, go to lessons, as normal. I will change the times later. Also, she is very afraid of internet virus, so we cannot use internet, so maybe, no printing for you this week. So sorry."

I nod. "It's okay." Good thing I did all that last week.

"Thank you. And, also, today, we must clean very hard. Today I label towels in washroom, so if you see 'WB,' please clean only whiteboard, and if you see '*mado*,' please clean only windows, and ..."

He swears. "Ah, sorry, Cybelle! I write labels in Japanese. So, later, I will write translation for you. In staff room."

"That's okay, I'll figure it out."

"No. I must. It is very important. If you use wrong towel, it will be very troublesome. So, please, do not clean until I write translation. Ah, and, tonight, after cleaning, we must wait for Bucho to tell us when everything is clean. So please, do not go home until Bucho says. Please wait in lobby with other teachers. Is it okay?"

"Okay."

"Thank you, Cybelle."

We hear the elevator chimes. The sound of Akiko greeting everyone with flowers she collected outside fills the lobby. Manager lets me out of the room to get ready. He's so anxious he doesn't even comment on the drink cup I have behind my back. After I toss it into the staff room garbage, I can't help but make a face. So, the Zozo staff is going to get more anal over things that don't matter. Wonderful. If I wasn't so full, this would totally kill my *ganbarimasu* epiphany. But it's okay. The time to enjoy English has begun.

I make a quick dash to use the washroom before any of the students can get to it. Sure enough, one towel under the sink now has "WB" written on the washing instructions label. Another says "トイレ" for the toilet, a third says "窓" for the windows. The rest are all in kanji I vaguely recognize. On a normal day I'd add this to my list of reasons not to re-contract. Good thing I'm still too buzzed with caffeine and sugar to care.

Still hungry, though.

Bucho almost bumps into me as I come out of the washroom and she tries to go in. "Oh! So sorry! Eh, 'Shibere'-*sensei*, yes?"

"Cybelle," I correct her.

"Eh? She ... She-bera? Shiberia? That's a strange name for a foreigner," she says to herself in Japanese. "What kind of a name is that? Why would your parents name you after Siberia?" Good grief, lady.

"There's no H. And it's 'bell' … like a bell."

"*Ja* … Seh-beru …" She pauses, then claps her hands to her face. "*Eh, muzukashii!*" She wonders why I can't just have an easier name, and other things that I don't need or care to hear. She also teases me, asking if I understand her, because I should by now. I hope my face looks as blank as I'm trying to keep it. Wasn't this woman in a mad rush to go to the washroom a moment ago?

"So, how long will you be at our school?" I ask.

"Eh? Ron-gu? How wrong … ah! How long! Eh …" She counts in her head. "Yes, one week. *Yoroshiku, ne?*"

"*Douzo yoroshiku onegai itashimasu.*" I bow, ignoring her applause and praise about my Japanese pronunciation. "I have to go."

"Okay! See you again, Shibera!"

I turn my attention to getting ready for my new Moms' class. I start by nodding my way through the cluster of parents and children in the lobby to the peaceful quietude of the staff room. Yoshino is already there, on a stool, shoving a giant box onto the highest shelf. "Hey, Cyb!" There's a hint of a smirk in her smile.

"*Oha*, Yoshino-*chan,*" I greet her.

"Oh, stop, you!" she hops down and playfully slaps my shoulder. "You're one to talk! Who'd *you* disappear with the other night? Heh heh."

"Meh, no one special. I just went home. Sorry I didn't see you before I left." Rather than disappoint her, I decide to convince her that I had a decent time. "How about you? How was your Saturday night? *Fun?* Did you 'stick together' with anyone?"

"*Well* …" A wistful look comes over her face. "Yeah. I did kinda ditch the others. I ended up talking with this guy Matt — that first guy we met, remember him? — and we decided that place was way too rowdy, so we took off. Sorry we lost track of each other." She lets out a theatrical sigh. "It's okay, though, if you don't want to tell me about whatever sexy man whisked *you* away. I won't ask questions. But if you're interested, I'm going back there the day after tomorrow. Matt said he'd be there again. His company goes there every Thursday."

Oh, *hell* no. "Uh ..."

A pleading look comes to her eyes. All the humour goes out of her voice. "Aw, please? I don't want to go on my own, but I don't want to ask the others. They were such sticks in the mud! But you, I know you're fun. What do you say?"

"Eh ... I don't know. I was pretty exhausted after work. Plus, Friday I start early *and* it's one of my busiest days. I'll be wiped."

"No problem! If you want to go home first, I can wait here. I'm sure I'll have tons of paperwork to do after the last students, anyway. You can get changed, rest, have dinner. I don't mind waiting for you!"

I clear my throat. Maybe I should pretend I'm coming down with something. But I don't want to lie. "I don't know. To be honest, I didn't have the best time. These guys, they —"

"Oh, don't care about guys there. Most men at drinking establishments are a waste of humanity. Who gives a rat's ass, we'll have fun just with each other!"

I laugh, but I'm still ready to refuse. "I *really* don't —"

"Please? We can get food this time, I promise! And your first drinks are on me. Pleeeease?" She grabs my hands and whimpers until I have to close my eyes and turn away.

"Argh, no, not puppy-dog eyes! Okay, okay, I'll think about it."

"Yay! Pinky promise?"

"Ugh." I roll my eyes and meet her crooked finger with my own. "Pinky promise I'll *think* about it."

"Fair enough. Thanks, Cyb!" Outside in the lobby Manager bellows her name. "*Hai, hai!* We'll talk later," she whispers, and runs out of the room. I cozy myself up on one of the stools and get to work. The first thing I do is write at the top of my lesson plan in pencil: *put off this week's prep so you don't have to go back to that awful bar.*

Time plods on slowly. With my planning done, I have time to kill until lunch. Maybe I'll sit with a cup of tea and text Mom back. That'll save me the trouble of Skyping her tonight. Multitasking for the win, right? Plus, my throat hurts. Tea will help me get through the next few hours of talking and singing.

I stick my head under the countertop to look under the computer. I see nothing. No sign of Mr. Kettle anywhere under the bench. I decide to find a bag of tea first, before I venture out to find someone who may know where the kettle is. I cross the staff room to the cupboards before I realize the tea, instant coffee, dry creamer, honey, and sugar cubes have been replaced with my kindergarteners' construction paper and playdough. What the hell is going on *now*?

Lieko slides the staff room door open on the other side, coming in to make a photocopy. I take a deep breath. Might as well ask her. "Hey, Lieko, have you seen the kettle? I was hoping to make some tea."

Lieko sighs, never looking up from the photocopier once. "Bucho took the kettle away. Zozo is not permitted to have kettles for the staff room in the first place. So, she confiscated it."

What?! "Since when? We've had that kettle for years. Why take it away now?"

"I do not speak for Bucho, but she is Bucho and she knows the rules. It is against company policy to have kettles in the staff room. Kettles may spill and destroy many teachers' important works. You should know this."

I should? "But —"

"Please do not ask Bucho about the kettle. She will think it was you who wanted the kettle, and she will think we are giving you special treatment."

"But I never — Wait, what are you doing?"

Lieko has just picked up the remote for the air-con above the computer and turned it on. "Cool biz ends this month?" she says, like she's talking to an unintelligent child. Then she picks up her photocopies and leaves the room.

Great. No more kettle, and by the blazing yet stale air coming from the unit, I'm supposed to sit here and deal. I can't help sticking my tongue out at the staff room door. Like the kettle was *my* idea. That ancient kettle has been here long before I came to Zozo. It's been the only consistent thing here besides me. I didn't even get to say goodbye. Oh, well. I'm left with nothing to do but eat my lunch now. It's fine. I grab my bento bag and sit down, but not before picking up the remote to turn the heat off. Cool biz ain't over yet.

My lunch is delicious. Each morsel of the thick, creamy, spiralled pasta dabbled with the speckles of browned mushrooms and still-crunchy broccoli all layered with spicy golden crust is better than the last. I devour it in minutes, then get to planning. After thirty minutes of cutting pumpkins out of orange construction paper, my stomach growls again. Guess I didn't make enough mac and cheese after all; I quickly venture out to Family Mart for more food and some dessert. No one at Zozo sees me; no one at Zozo stops me. Let my Tuesday *genki* continue.

Yoshino comes in with Yuki and Misaki for a while. I can't quite make out what they're saying at first, but I hear snippets of "Bucho," "open house," and *"saikoukimitsu,"* which I know for sure means "top secret." I try not to eavesdrop, but I can't help it unless I get up and leave the room, and I'm not about to do that. My second lunch is just too good. I've already wolfed down my *wakame* salad and chugged my miso soup, and now I tackle the grilled salmon, hamburger patties, and rice, eyeing the small heap of Ghana chocolate bars that wait for dessert. The last thing I want is for someone to come along while I'm away and stick my lunch somewhere strange again.

Yuki and Misaki leave when Manager calls their names out in the lobby. Yoshino quickly types something into the computer. "Manager hasn't signed you in it, Cybelle-*sensei*, want me to do it for you?"

"Yes, please."

"*Uwaa*, such a smorgasbord! Looks delicious!" Yoshino takes the stool next to me. "Did you eat well this weekend? I know you didn't get to eat much on Saturday."

"*Oh*, yeah," I reply. "Ate my weight in food, apparently. And then this morning I went and bought these." I run to the cupboard and pull my hefty HORUS bag from the shelf. "Don't know what's going on with my appetite lately."

"Ooh, that Totoro looks good."

"It's chestnut cream!"

"Mmm," Yoshino rubs her belly. "Sounds much better than what I had for breakfast. I woke up late, so I only had time for an *onigiri* and a melon *pan* on the train."

"You ate them on the train?"

Yoshino nods. "Wolfed them down in one gulp. They do *not* go well together, in case you're wondering."

"They don't sound very filling, either. Here."

I offer her a Totoro. She's polite at first, but with prodding she takes it. Manager walks in as she's cradling it in her arms. "Ooh, *oishi-sou*," he says, several times until I give in and offer him one. As he accepts, Lieko walks in and makes cooing noises.

"Ooh, lemon cake! And *Totoro!* They look so delicious."

"They're from Cybelle-*sensei*!" Manager and Yoshino say in unison.

My hands reflexively squeeze the neck of the plastic bag. Maybe if I hold it tight enough, I can protect my last bun from her sharp, carnivorous fangs.

"Oh." Her voice is curt. She walks right out of the staff room. I breathe a sigh of relief. My last Totoro is spared. Note to self: only go to HORUS on the way home.

Yoshino and I finish our lunches, then go out into the lobby. Bucho is nowhere to be found, so I take a seat at the reception desk computer while Yoshino flips through one of her big files next to me. She waves a hand when I offer her my seat. "It's all right, I don't need," she says.

I swivel back and forth for a minute, letting her work in silence. Then I break it. "Yoshino, may I ask you a question? About last week's open house?"

"Sure. I'm just pulling student files. What's up?"

I whisper, just in case. "Does Bucho not know about it?"

Yoshino looks up. She shakes her head. "You heard, huh? Sorry, I should have included you in the loop when I told Yuki."

"No, no! I get it. I apologize for eavesdropping, but I wanted to make sure."

"Oh, no! It's okay. Yeah, Bucho doesn't know a thing about it. It's not that we're not *allowed* to have it, but I don't think she'll take kindly to Manager inviting strangers to the school without her being here. It'll look extra-bad because we didn't get any clients out of it. So, Manager is asking the staff not to let her know we even had one."

Geez. "What exactly do we need to do? Is there anything I can do?"

"Not unless you know any new people who'd be willing to drop a few hundred thousand yen to bring us up to quota for October. Do you?"

"Sorry."

Yoshino laughs. "It's okay, me, neither. It seems like everyone is going to this new branch in Osaka. It's the same Zozo, but from what I hear, their manager is more thorough. She actually cares about the students and their progress. Imagine that." She makes a face. "If you ask me, if Manager wasn't such a misogynist, they'd all come back."

"I'm afraid to bring this up, but ..." I brace myself. "Do you think there's a chance of us getting a different manager?"

"That's what *one* of us would like, but Manager isn't willing to give up without a fight. You didn't hear any of that from me, of course."

"Terrific," I mutter under my breath. I don't need to ask who that 'one of us' would be. The idea of Lieko being manager fills me with dread, as I'm sure it does Yoshino. "Well, I'm not going to let it get to me. I guess for now, my best is the best I can do."

Yoshino tilts her head in thought. "That's such a good outlook," she nods. "I like it! Maybe *that* should be Zozo's motto! You're such a great role model, Cybelle."

"Thank you, Yoshino," I laugh. I know how cheesy that sounded, but it's true. I'm not going to let Lieko, Manager, Bucho, or the school's fate bring me down. I've got students to be *genki* for. I get up from the receptionist's chair and strike a pose. "You know what? I'm ready. Bring on the students! It's time to enjoy —"

"YADAAAAA!"

No. NO. It can't be.

But it is.

"Oh!" Yoshino's smile cannot disguise her shock at the elevator opening to Hitomu and his mother, who is now struggling to peel him from the bar that runs along its perimeter. "*Hello*, Hitomu! Good to see you again! *Okaasan, konnichiwa! Ogenki desu ka?*"

Hitomu's mother nods in reply as she carries the scrambling, scratching child in her arms down the hall, I presume to the washroom. I turn back to the elevator and see Sotaro is also here, holding his mother's hand, both of their jaws hanging open.

"Ah, yes! Cybelle-*sensei*," Yoshino says. "I don't know if Manager told you, but ..."

"Oh, no."

"No, no! Not Hitomu!" She waves her hands. "He has a private lesson with Lieko. You have a private lesson with Sotaro. You can use Room Three. It's just forty-five minutes. Is it okay?"

My smile returns. "It's more than okay. Hi, Sotaro! How are you today?"

Sotaro's mother shakes him to his senses. "Sotaro-*kun, sensei ni aisatsu shite,*" she reprimands him. To my complete shock, Sotaro bows low to me. When his mother tells him to follow me to the classroom, he does so without hesitation. Lieko tries to block Hitomu from seeing me as I head to Room Three. I close the door behind me and turn to see Sotaro sitting in the middle of the room in perfect *seiza*, hands in his lap. The whole time we have our lesson, we hear Hitomu's screams down the hall. Despite the fact that he's with Lieko he must know I'm nearby, because he doesn't stop for the entire forty-five minutes. Sotaro, meanwhile, is a perfect angel. Maybe Hitomu is scaring him into behaving. I give him two stickers for not giving me a hard time. He sticks them on his cheeks and sprints out the door to show them off to his mother.

It must be raining cats and dogs again when my mom students and their kids stumble from the elevator. Their arms are laden with drenched umbrellas, raincoats, and bookbags. I let them take their time to dry off with their dozen and one hand towels while I set up our table for a quick round of Jenga before our lesson. Our textbook is pretty horrible, so all we can do is walk through the questions together, then read a paragraph. We talk a bit more about Dr. Martin Luther King Jr., but my students seem more interested in literal dreams, which is great for me because it means less talk about America's current political climate.

"*Ne, sensei.* Textbook says to write our dream," Mami says. "For homework. Is it homework?"

"Sure, let's make it homework. If that is okay with everyone?" My students nod. "Okay, we will skip the lesson on REM sleep and next week we can talk about our dreams. Write a sentence to answer this question." I get up and write on the whiteboard: *What do (did) you dream about?* Underneath, I write: *I dream(ed) about ...* and explain a little bit about past tenses and American versus British

English, all of which my students jot down furiously in their notebooks. I try to think of how to finish my example and stop. Wow, I really can't remember things I dream about. I don't even think I *do* dream these days. I leave it blank.

"Oh!" Fumiko exclaims. "Last last night, I had a dream!" She furrows her eyebrows, pausing between rapidly typed translations on her electronic dictionary. "I dream ... the day before yesterday, I dreamed I take test. In English. I don't know answers because I can't read test. When I ask teacher for help, I can't speak. It's very scary."

I smile at her. "I think that means you were worried about this class, maybe."

She laughs. "Maybe. But in my dream, I was in school. Maybe ..." She types again. "High school, or ... junior high."

"Was English class difficult for you in school?"

"Yes, very difficult." Everyone nods in agreement.

Miyoko is the next to volunteer. "A few days ago, I dreamed that I was still in Kyoto with my husband, but I don't remember ... anything except Kyoto."

I nod, holding back on my thoughts this time. Oh, who I wouldn't slap in the face for a weekend in Kyoto right now. It's been ages since I've been back there, but my first year in Japan I went every chance I could get, to the point of shocking all my old co-workers and students who still hadn't been there. I went to all the big festivals: Gion Matsuri, Jidai Matsuri, Kurama *no Hi* ... Now that the weather is bearable, October is a perfect time to go. But I get so bogged down with work and chores I don't have time and energy during the week. That's what happens with a Tuesday to Saturday schedule and all the national holidays falling on Mondays. We get scammed out of the little free time we actually have.

Mami looks left out. "I never remember what I dream."

"That's okay," I tell her. "I don't, either. Actually, I used to write down my dreams. Not anymore though, I'm too busy. I just come to work and go home, so my imagination isn't what it used to be. I don't think I've had a single dream this whole year …"

I trail off as I realize that what I'm saying isn't BS at all. It's completely true. That, and no one has any idea what I'm saying.

"*Sumimasen, sensei,*" Miyoko raises her hand. "I don't understand."

"That's okay," I repeat. "Um, let's see … I don't remember what I dream, but when I was young, I used to dream a lot."

My students nod. "What do you dream, when you were child?" Mami asks.

"Well, I guess I'd dream about usual things, like flying, or falling, or monsters, or babies, or —"

"*Sensei*, I have question," Miyoko raises her hand again. "About Halloween monster. In Canada, do many people dress as monsters? For Halloween? Like America?"

"Oh yeah, tons of people."

"And, will you dress up for Halloween?"

"Yes. I have my costume all ready. But I won't be a monster. I will be a scary Tinker Bell for Halloween."

"Ah, *kawaii* — how cute!"

"*Ne, sensei*, what is 'monster'? Is it like, '*pocketto monsutaa*'?" asks Fumiko.

"Monster is like *oni*. Or *yokai*." Miyoko turns to me. "Do you know *yokai*?"

"Ah, yes!" Fumiko says. "Like Ghibli?"

"And *Yo-kai Watch*!" Mami pipes in. "Taiga *loves* Yo-kai Watch! Do you know?"

"Yes," I tell her. "I have a Jibanyan hand puppet!"

"Ah, *kawaii*! *Sugoi*, you know many things, Cybelle-*sensei*!"

"Thanks! Well, there's one thing I've always wondered. Er, one thing I don't know. What's the difference between *yokai* and *oni*?"

"Eh …" the moms all look away, deep in thought, nodding to themselves. "Maybe," says Miyoko. "Only '*oni*' at Setsubun? Do you know?"

"Yes!" Mami smiles. "Setsubun … at Nishibe *Jinja?*" She checks her dictionary. "Ah! Nishibe Shrine! We throw beans at *oni!*"

I nod, smiling wider. "Yup, I know it. I've gone to the Setsubun festival there — just once, though." I keep my mouth shut that it was four years ago, the one time I didn't have work the morning after, and how I learned the hard way that festivals aren't a lot of fun when you're a *gaijin* on her own. Nope, not going to get into that. "Okay, we have five minutes left!" I pick up my box of playing cards from the table and start to shuffle them. "Who wants to play cards?"

"Oh, *toranpu! Yatta!*"

We play Slap Jack for the rest of the class. Mami is the ultimate winner. We hear the room next door open and release the flash flood of seven-year-olds, which cues the four-year-olds' class down the hall to also let loose. I bid the moms farewell and get ready for the next stream of classes.

"Ah, Cybelle-*sensei!* Look!" Mami walks past me and grabs one of the kids in the lobby by his backpack (I assume it's her son). She points to the characters on it. "See? Taiga, *sensei ni kaban o misete* — please show *Sensei* your backpack!"

I grin. "That's the one! Hi, Taiga, I see you like *Yo-kai Watch.* Which one's your favourite?"

Taiga wrenches himself away from his mother. *"Oobaketto!"* He punches me in the crotch.

"Taiga!" Mami smacks him in the back of his head, not too hard but enough to give him something to think about. "Oh, my *goddo,* I'm so sorry, Cybelle-*sensei!* Are you all right?!"

"I'm fine," I laugh weakly. I don't add that I think I just skipped my next period.

Thankfully, the pain wears off after a few minutes and I get through the rest of my classes unscathed. My kindergarteners have decided to become obsessed with tea parties. They insist on having another one after we read a couple of fairy tales from my big book of stories and force me to make more desserts out of playdough like I did last week.

"*Sensei, nani shiten no?*" Momoko asks me.

"I'm making you a cupcake."

She tilts her head. "Pupcake?"

"Cupcake."

"Pupcake?"

"*Cupcake!*" Motoka yells, reducing Momoko to tears. I let her sit in my lap for the rest of the lesson.

Next, I have Zone VI, where we do some listening activities out of the *Sesame Street* textbook. Reiji and Riko get into a heated argument about whether or not Mr. Snuffleupagus is a boy or a girl and they both go home in tears. After that I have my private lesson with Kennichi, who suddenly wants to learn anything and everything there is to know about "ice" hockey. Minus the crotch punch, another typical Tuesday afternoon.

Since the teachers must line up at the end of the night, I end up getting ahead on all my lesson planning while I wait, sabotaging my plans to not hang out with Yoshino Thursday night. The only interruption is Manager, who (after asking me why I haven't left yet and remembering his own instructions to me earlier today) tells me I'll have a teacher interview Thursday at four. Not sure why, when we're losing students, but instead of asking, I nod and smile.

Because the weather outside is relatively good, when we finally are released from Zozo, I take my gurgling tummy grocery shopping: the usual fare from my three local supermarkets plus some Attack laundry detergent, Halloween Pudding Kit Kat, instant coffee, and a jumbo pack of Mentos (not that I'll repeat yesterday's antics ever again). I buy as much as I can carry without dislocating my shoulders, drop everything off at home, then head to 7-Eleven. There's a small shelf next to the cold food section displaying new items. I can't read the box, but they look like graham crackers for about eight hundred yen. Graham crackers again, eh? Hmm, maybe I'll give it another week.

The only cash open is in front of a new employee, glaring at me with all his might. I take the three remaining futomaki and inari zushi bento boxes to the counter and add a bunch of bananas and a handful of Black Thunders. His co-workers are still helping people. I take out my wallet; I'm not waiting in the long lineups to get served by someone nice. I'm hungry, now bordering on hangry. When he nudges each chocolate bar with his barcode reader until they flip over instead of picking them up individually, I take out my giant personal shopping bag and lay it on the counter. *"Fukuro iranai,"* I mutter, just as he tries to wiggle my bananas into a plastic bag without touching them.

The new guy gasps. *"H-hai,"* he stutters, taking the bag away. *"Anou* ... chopsticks, okay?"

"Uchi ni arimasu," I refuse.

"Ah, sou ka ..." He is now grinning from ear to ear. "Eh ... can you ... use ... chopsticks?"

"Um ... yes?"

"Ah! And, do you ... like ... sushi?"

Out of the corner of my eye, I notice every other staff member I usually chat with peeking from the back room, snickering. "I do."

"Ah! Me, too! I like sushi the best!"

Good grief.

"See you again!" shouts the new guy. I wave back, walking past the sliding doors just as he whispers something to his co-workers about how amazing it is that there are *"kurojin"* in Nishibe. I'd rather not hang around to hear their responses. I return home, lock my apartment door, sit right down in front of it, and rip the plastic off the top bento, devouring the first few rolls by hand like some ravenous sushi-predator. As I eat, I turn on the TV and watch the tail end of a kids' show where they sing about taking a bath, letters of the Japanese alphabet, then do the goodbye song and shower the kids dancing on stage with balloons. After that is a commercial showing three aliens balanced on top of one another in a long trench coat disguised as a human being so they can sneak into a *kaitenzushi* restaurant. I'm still hungry. There goes bento number two.

I shut off the TV, sigh out loud in my big empty apartment chock full of grocery bags. Might as well see if Mom is online.

As my old laptop boots up, I change out of my work clothes, put all my groceries away, gather all my stuff from work from my purse, and grab art supplies from my plastic dresser. Once Skype loads, I click on my mom's profile. I take photocopies of cookies, apples, and ice creams I made from my textbooks weeks ago and prepare to spend the next hour colouring them with markers, cutting them out, and wrapping each picture with parcel tape.

"Hello?" says my laptop.

"Mother?"

"Who is this?"

"Your first-born?"

"Hi, sweetie! How are you?!"

"I'm good. You?"

"What time is it over there? Did you just wake up or something? You sound so far away! Why isn't your video on? How are your students?"

I chuckle, since technically, I *am* far away. "They're … um, they're the same. How is everyone?"

"Oh! They're *wonderful*," she says. My webcam kicks in while she gives me a thorough rundown of how wonderful everyone is, doing what they love, hoping I'm doing the same, being in the most exotic country in the world and all. She asks how my weekend was, hoping I didn't just do chores the whole time. No way am I telling her how my Saturday night really went.

"I *did* go out with some co-workers, but they were kinda —"

"So, go without them! You don't need a babysitter." Mom has this thing about giving me advice long after the event in question has passed. "You need to *socialize*, Cybelle! You can't stay home every weekend for seven years and —"

"Six and a half, Mom."

"Don't interrupt, Cybelle. My point is, you need a real life, sweetie. You don't want to end up old and bitter. I'm sure your school wouldn't want that, either. Doesn't your school understand that you need a life? If you're enjoying teaching so much you can just do that here. *And* you'd actually have time to yourself. Please tell me you're not signing up for another year there."

Now seems like a good time to busy myself. I put groceries away, pour rice into the automatic rice cooker and let it do its thing. My apartment is massive by Japanese standards but small enough that I can move around and Mom can still see me on the webcam while she rants and raves about scandalous English conversation companies going under and how I should go home and work at a *real* school.

"I know there's nothing exciting for you to do anymore," Mom continues. "I warned you not to do everything your first year. Now you're bored. Why do you insist on staying?"

Oh, that is *such* a lie! She's the one who insisted I do everything adventurous my first year. "I don't have much of a reason not to," I say instead. "The money is good, my location is decent, I don't pay rent, and the students and parents have finally gotten used to me. Well … most of them." I refuse to bring up Hitomu.

"I know you'd rather just stay there and keep making lots of money, but are you *really* happy doing just that? That's something you need to think about, too, you know. Money can't buy happiness. Oh, and speaking of happiness! Did you get my message?"

"Yup."

"About your sister? Your youngest sister?"

"Yee-up."

She giggles. "What did it say?"

"That she shaved the rest of her head?"

"*No*, Cybelle. Very funny. No, I said that she has finally set a date! So now you *have* to come home as soon as possible!"

I make a buzzer sound. "WRONG. You said she was getting married. Which I kinda figured would happen, eventually."

"Well, now it's official. She's getting married once she graduates next year. In June."

"You mean, she's getting married in June or she's graduating in June?"

"She's graduating, Cybelle. *Duh*. I don't know if she wants a June wedding. I think it would be perfect, but that close to graduation? I don't think it's a good idea."

"I thought you just said she set a … You know what, never mind. If she's not getting married until after graduation, there's really no rush to come home, is there? If I stay another year, I can always take time off for the wedding."

"Cybelle, enough. Just come home, okay? Start mentally preparing. You'll need a couple of months to adjust, find a place to live, get a job, maybe find a boyfriend you can move in with …"

Here it is. The part of the phone call I've been dreading. I add a few "mm-hmms" and "uh-huhs" in the right places while I sort my laundry, start the machine, and iron out a pantsuit for tomorrow, just in case more Head Office honchos decide to pay us a surprise visit and shut down the school. Once I finish making a few more pumpkin cut-outs, I pack up my purse and hang it up, just in time for Mom to come back to her previous point:

"And I don't know where you're going to live. Toronto is *so* expensive now. I'm too busy getting ready to retire and sell the house, and I've already started making travelling plans, so living here is out of the question, and you know your sisters, you can't really count on them to put you up for long. But don't think of it as coming back to 'nothing.' You just need to be positive about it! Just think about it, okay? It's not like you're moving up in the company. After seven years, *you* should be running the place."

"Six and a half."

"Same thing. My point is you don't sound excited to be living there these days. Remember when you first got there? You were so active back then with your travelling, and all those cooking and karate classes. I knew you were doing all right, but now ... well, I'm more than worried. I just want you to be happy. You *are* happy, right?"

"Eh ..."

"'Eh'?! What is *that* supposed to mean?!"

Somewhere in the kitchen I hear Canon in D Major. Mom hears it, too. "That sounds like your rice cooker. Are you making dinner?"

"Beef curry and rice. And I might make some stir-fry for the week, too."

"Stir-fry *again*? After all those cooking courses you insisted on? Hurry up and come home."

I hate it when she says that. What does she mean by 'hurry up'? Work around the clock or six days a week to end my contract sooner? Neither is an option under Zozo's current business hours. Speed up time? Who am I, Superman? I shrink Skype to a corner so I can put in my Flying Pig order and browse worksheets online.

"Mom," I say. "Even if I do go home, what am I going to do there?"

"You can figure that out when you get here! Anyway, we'll discuss this later. You go have dinner. Glad I finally *caught* you, sweetie! We'll talk again soon. Love you!"

"Love you, too, Mom."

"And *please* look into getting a smartphone, will you? Then we can just WhatsApp each other. Or LINE, I hear LINE is a good app, too."

I narrow my eyes.

"I'm so sick of Skype! Aren't you sick of that giant computer yet? You're not tired of texting on that little flip phone of yours?"

"Nope."

"Ugh. FINE. Love you, sweetie!"

She hangs up. I let out a huge sigh. My left eye is itchy as hell for some reason. Probably just stress, as usual. Good thing I didn't joke that our school is going under; she would have kept me up all night with interrogations. I return to the kitchen to heat up and sample the beef curry. Last "unhealthy" meal, I swear to myself. It's nice and spicy, just the way I like it. But it could use a little something more. I'm digging around in the cupboard to see if I have any more potatoes left when I hear my phone vibrate. Mom must have forgotten to tell me something. I hope it has nothing to do with what she already chewed me out about. I don't complain too much, considering all the crap I have chucked at me. Especially in the past month, with Hitomu, with Lieko. I think I'm doing pretty darn well.

It's a text from an unknown number. *You did not wear a skirt today. Again.*

Okay, so maybe I complain a little.

運は勇者を助く

Fortune favours the brave

The Kurama Fire Festival in Kyoto is over. The torches and pyres have been returned to the shrine for another year. And yet, the village of Henba is in flames. Clouds of thick smoke rise up to the pale, twinkling stars, while down below villagers in their underwear flee from never-before-seen horrors that split the earth open. Scores of immense centipedes — *mukade*, to be precise — loom above the burning rooftops and come crashing down. Each centipede is the length of five cars. They slither after the villagers with rapid peach-coloured claws and sickle-sharp pincers. More cauldron-black bodies lie invisible in the shadows where the fire has yet to lay waste, lazily spreading their mandibles apart, ready to welcome the surging crowd getting closer and closer.

The human-sized Yokai could hear the thrum of their circulatory systems were it not for the blood-curdling human screams.

The crackle of fire is equally deafening. Thick flames lick the sky as they sweep from house to house like crashing waves. Hot embers float in the air, singeing everything they touch. If this is indeed what the end of the world looks like, the Yokai thinks to herself, it is not very exciting. In fact, it stinks. Literally. The air smells horrible, not unlike burned hair. She lifts one hand to squeeze her nose closed as she manoeuvres what was once the siding of a house in the other hand and takes a bite. It melts in her mouth and tastes like fresh gingerbread baked to perfection. Not burned and crumbling like the other houses. Another bonus, this house was empty. Again she makes sure by sifting through the rubble a third and fourth time. *So far, so good.* And yet, there is something missing …

I should be bigger. Why am I not getting bigger?

The Yokai's questioning is interrupted by a villager in no hurry to escape the carnage. She totters down the street at a turtle's pace, arms stretched out in front of her. *"So tasty, so tender. I want to eat."* Her voice is a raspy snarl, her words drip like the drool that runs from her mouth. She stops to glare at the Yokai, then starts wobbling toward her, pointing at the gingerbread in her hands. The Yokai crams what is left in her hands into her monstrous mouth and glares back until the old woman hisses at her and continues on her way. "Hmph," says the Yokai, taking another handful of the brown rubble. *I showed her.*

A man calmly emerges from the neighbouring house. He too is unfazed by the giant *mukade* and villagers scrambling past him; he raises a cup of tea to his lips as he saunters by the Yokai. He slows down long enough to make eye contact. He appears to be staring not at her, but at the house sandwiched in her hands. The Yokai narrows her eyes at him, taking in his bulbous-shaped head and monk-like attire. His grin is crooked but kind; however, she is still not willing to share. She simply stares back until the man raises his cup to her. "Welcome!" he says, then continues down the road at his own leisurely pace to the next house. The Yokai is relieved. She takes another bite.

Now why does all this feel so familiar? She closes her eyes against the bright orange flames and smoke, tries to shut out the sounds of her own chewing against the background of humans pleading for their lives, the pounding and drumming of human feet like taiko. A silhouette forms in her mind. She can remember him now, but only a little. The man at the restaurant. That is what she is trying to remember. What was it called again? What was *he* called again? She cannot remember, nor can she think with all the commotion around her.

She opens her eyes again. There is a tingle creeping up her spine; someone is watching her. She looks around. The only people not running from the flames or the giant insects are the ones standing across the road. Four gorgeous red-faced, red-haired women in matching red kimono stare back at her. They are not at all bothered by the chaos unfolding around them. It seems they have been watching her for some time and have now decided to make their move.

The first woman bows. "Hello."

"Hello," the Yokai says. "Let me guess; you want some?"

"Can it be true?" the first woman says, ignoring the Yokai's question. "Are you the one?"

"The one what?"

"I believe it is, sister," says another woman. "It must be."

The third woman nods. "Look at her, chomping away on another house. It can't be any other."

"Well, colour us pleased," says the fourth. "Ah, yes ... we've heard about you. Quite the appetite you have on you. Still hungry?"

"I'm always hungry."

"Then why not have a villager or two?"

The Yokai shakes her head, furious. "Ew! No! I don't eat people. Why does everyone keep asking me that?"

"Oh, no, dear, it's quite all right! We all have our own ... *tastes* ..." The other women giggle behind their red sleeves.

"Listen. This isn't at all where I meant to end up. But then I got hungry." The Yokai lowers her head, feeling sheepish as she speaks. "There wasn't anyone inside, I swear."

"We don't mind, child," says the first woman. "In fact, we have a surprise for *you*. We have a mutual friend who is very interested in meeting you. Come on, come with us. We promise we won't bite ..." Her voice trails off, as if another word should follow.

The Yokai shrugs. "What the hell. Sure. Watching a bunch of *mukade* crawl around isn't my idea of fun, anyway."

Two of the women cross the road and take her by the hands. Up into the eastern hills they all retreat together into the dark, cold sanctuary of the ancient forest, farther and farther away from the violent unrest of Henba. As they ascend the mountain path the Yokai gulps at the sweet mountain air, grateful to be away from the choking smog and the stench of sulphur.

"By the way," says the fourth woman, "the word you're looking for is 'massacre,' dear. A group of *mukade* is called a massacre."

The climb is long and steep. The women head up a dark path with only moonlight to guide their way. The Yokai is grateful that two of them are holding her hands, because there is no way she would be able to see on her own. It is a mystery that they themselves can see where they are going.

The trees clear, exposing the grounds of an old, modest house. Its front door slides open and shuts behind the group. The inside is lit with lanterns and filled with the scent of burning incense. The corridors are a labyrinth of balsam wood and tatami floors, and there is a display of ancient samurai armour in every corner and swords above the rice-paper doors, which have gorgeous silk screens with landscapes sewn into them.

"Wow," the Yokai says. "What is this, a museum?"

The women laugh. "You could call it that!" the first replies with a kimono sleeve over her mouth. "It's been around long enough."

"Not much of a museum, though," says the second, the one holding the Yokai's right hand. "Look! Everything's covered in dust. Neglected. Like he finally got sick of pining over all these lost relics of his old life and if he ignores them long enough, they'll get so dusty they'll disappear from sight."

"Hey, now, don't talk like that. At the time, he was only *human!*" the third woman spits the word out, as if it leaves a wretched taste in her mouth.

The fourth one pretends to pout. "Dear me. Are you really going to slight the one allowing us a chance to dine on such a rare, exotic dish in his home tonight?"

"Hmm." If the Yokai had a hand free, she would stroke her chin in thought. She is not quite sure about whom they are talking, but they are so friendly she does not want to say anything that will offend them or spoil their good mood. "Well, whoever he is, he doesn't sound like such a bad guy."

Her comment makes the women laugh even louder and harder. "Once upon a time," the third one begins to sing, "there was an evil, sadistic *rounin* who dedicated his life to warring, wine, and women, rather than die with honour and keep his teacher's legacy alive. Rumour has it he was even the one responsible for his teacher's death. Can you imagine that! Anyway, eventually his awful, wanton ways caught up with him. He was tried and executed, but, story of all our lives, it didn't take. What a way to go. Oh, relax, dear. He has come to terms with his new existence — for the most part."

The second woman cuts in. "Protecting a human? Partnering up with it to sleep with *other* humans? You call *that* coming to terms?"

"Can you blame him, dear? We all need to satiate our demonic needs somehow."

"Well, I suppose you are right."

"And don't forget," says the third woman, "he's allowing us this private party here tonight. He may be a fledgling asshole of a *yokai*, but when you think about it, he's really come a long way in the last one hundred and fifty–odd years." The others nod.

"That's right," says the first. "It was that long ago. Why, he must have been younger than *you* when he turned, dear! Times were different — samurai were considered men at fifteen back then." The others nod again in agreement. The Yokai does not know how to feel about that statement.

"It sounds like you have yet to run into him. Would you —" the fourth woman's eyebrows dance "— like to?"

"Not really. No."

The first woman snickers. "Well, we suppose only time will tell. Here we are!"

A long flight of steps has taken them up to another hall-way, into a large room with a small *butsudan* altar in the corner. The walls are lined with hundreds of candles. Underneath a large red lantern in the ceiling sits a low, long table that stretches the length of the room. The Yokai's eyes light up. Every inch of the table is covered with food: plates and platters longer than her arms laden with pink and orange sashimi, bright yellow flowers, sushi arranged to look like planets, and mint-green blossoms of wasabi. Cornucopia of autumnal fruit — short, fat persimmons and giant Fuji apples — are surrounded by enormous bowls of ice creams and puddings, and tiny plates of herbs and spices are scattered in between. In the centre of it all sits one large, silver covered dish.

"Well, ladies? Let's dig in!"

"Itadakimasu!" the women cry and take their seats together, on the other side. The Yokai sits alone on her side. She does not mind. More elbow room for her, she thinks to herself. What she does not notice is how the women watch, unmoving, as she piles up her

plate and devours everything she takes. Every time she brings a roll of sushi or a sliver of sashimi to her lips with her black lacquered chopsticks, they make little gasping sounds as if every morsel may cause the Yokai to explode.

"What?" she asks them. "It's not dynamite."

The first woman purses her lips. "No. We suppose not."

When the Yokai takes a break from chewing with a cup of green tea, the women exchange glances between themselves and the large, covered dish. The first woman cocks her head. "You are full?"

"Mm-mmm," says the Yokai.

"Good! We have a rare delicacy tonight. We caught it fresh, up in the mountains!" The other women clap. "We were going to eat it ourselves, but … we thought to share with you. To officially welcome you to the fold. We have seen you so many times now, we thought it would be nice to get to know each other … to become friends?"

"Okay. Sure! Nothing wrong with that."

"In that case, please." The first woman reaches forth and removes the lid. "Dig in!"

The Yokai looks down, expecting a delicacy. A scream chokes her. Arranged in a ring of green leaves with a carrot flower on its belly is the biggest baby the Yokai has ever seen. It is fast asleep but wheezing, twitching, as if sick. The harsh transition of light makes it squeeze its eyes, then blink and stir.

The second woman sighs. "Uh-oh, now look what you've done. You've woke it up."

The first shakes her head. Long wisps of her red hair litter the table. "No, no! This is good! Now it will thrash and scream in her mouth. A much better dining experience."

"All that chasing after it will be worth it, then. Ooh, tell us how it tastes! Go on, tell us!" The fourth woman's dress sleeves wriggle as if her arms are boneless. The others follow suit.

Suppressing the icy shudder that runs down her spine, the Yokai clears her throat. "There's clearly been some kind of miscommunication here. Once again, I find myself having to explain that I *don't* eat people. Especially not babies."

"Oh, come now, you silly thing. You eat *everything*! What are you waiting for? Don't you want to be big and strong again? And besides, this isn't 'people'! He's barely a century old."

"I don't eat people," the Yokai snaps.

"Now, now, sister, you must explain it to her," the third woman raises her sleeves toward the Yokai. "It's not like it's a human child! That's bona fide *Konaki Jiji*. Aged, but well-preserved. It must be the fresh water up around the lake. Nice and healthy." The women all nod.

The fourth woman reaches across the table and pokes the baby's inner thigh. "This one's good and plump, too! That's a rarity these days. Go on, better start before it goes back to sleep. Oh! We should ask, do you know how use *chopsticks* on this one?" They all laugh at an inside joke the Yokai does not understand. "Ah, just teasing! You wear such a … *unique* disguise. I just had to throw that in there. Now, start with the toes and work your way up. It takes a while for the endorphins to run through the whole body, but you should begin to taste it by the time you reach the thighs."

"Oh, that's just an old wives' tale! Don't you listen to her, dear. You dive straight into the organs, hear me?" The third woman flicks the carrot flower away with her too-long sleeve. "This is just empty calories. There you go. You have to drive your chopsticks into the belly button and —"

The Yokai grips her chopsticks hard enough to hurt. "I am NOT eating a baby."

"Uh-oh …" The women mock her. "Poor widdle *yokai* can't eat even a widdle *Konaki Jiji* toenail … boo hoo! Akki-*san* will be so disappointed to hear the new demon is just like her disguise — sad and pathetic as a human. Too bad!"

"Right up his alley, then." The first woman crosses her arms. They flop around each other like raw dough. "That scumbag. Laying with human trash like they're better than us. Who the hell does he think he is?"

The second woman shudders. "Ew, please. Would *you* sleep with him? I wouldn't touch him with a ten-foot *shinai*!"

"Well, neither would I. But it's the principle of the thing."

"Oh stop, you two," says the third woman. "We can stand here all century arguing; we'd never figure out what that awful Akki's deal is."

"Agreed," the fourth woman sniffs.

"Can I go now?" asks the Yokai.

"Silence." The first woman points a sleeve at the Yokai's nose. "I say we save him the trouble of wasting time meeting you."

"Yes. I must admit, I did wonder what *you* might taste like. What do you say, ladies? Anyone mind if I call dibs on her toes?"

"Fine by me. I call dibs on her hair. It's so ... so *fluffy* ... like fairy floss."

"I hear the best meat is in the rump!"

The women laugh. They are amused and giddy at the prospect of her warm succulent flesh melting on their long forked tongues, now wagging in the air and dripping saliva down their clothes. The Yokai staggers back from the table. The women crawl over the long table on all fours like stalking animals toward the dish — toward her. Their lips pull back to expose rows of shark-like teeth, grinding and gnashing.

The baby is live and kicking now. "Help me," it croaks.

"I ... I don't know what to do ..." The Yokai's breath quickens with panic. She needs a weapon. She needs multiple weapons. But the only thing on the table are the empty plates and dishes, used chopsticks, and leftover spices.

The Yokai hopes the baby's eyes are still closed.

She grabs a dish of bright orange *togarashi* spice and blows it right in the women's faces. A blast of hot, spraying sand, the spices burn their way into their eyes and up their nostrils. They clutch their faces, writhing in such pain that their red wigs fall, exposing perfectly bald, egg-shaped heads. The Yokai sprints atop the table, kicking at whoever gets in her way, scoops the baby into her arms, and runs out the door.

"After her!" comes the women's collective shrieks. "She's got our dinner!"

As careful as anyone could hold a baby under the circumstances, the Yokai runs down hallway after hallway, a labyrinth of intricately designed walls, in sheer panic. There are no signs of any doors or windows, nothing that can serve as an escape. The sound of claws on tatami flooring is not far behind her. If only she knew her own power, if only she knew how big imagination can stretch the house, and if only she knew her way through its maze-like halls, she could have found her way to the other side, to find Akki lying in a vast bedroom with his most recent guest. Not that he would have any inclination to help anyone at the moment.

"Aaaah," the young woman beside him sighs. "That was *just* what I needed." She stretches under the silk ivory sheets like a cat. "This new job is so stressful. I can't believe it! Who knew that kids had so much energy? And you have to smile all day and get them to speak, and they don't understand a word of what you're saying so they just keep talking and ..." Interrupted by the flicker of flame, she turns to the man next to her. "Ugh, you smoke? That's so unhealthy! Can you open a window or something? I don't want to get sick. I just started this job, you see, and it would look really bad if I'm ill my first week. Anyway, the other day all the girls took me to this restaurant, and the food was so good! But you had to use all these forks and knives, and it was so confusing! I don't know how foreigners do it. If I were to live in a foreign country, I don't think I could survive. I was lucky though, when I visited

Australia, I didn't go to any fancy restaurants. Oh, there was this one time, when we went to this teacher's house for a barbecue, and we had all this meat but we had to eat it with our hands, it was so funny! And then we — hey ... what happened to your skin? So bright! You've changed!"

Akki grumbles and pulls the sheets over his head. He just wants to sleep. *No chance of that happenin'.* He rips the sheets away and gets up.

"It's okay! Change is good! I wish I could change my body like that, whenever I wanted. I would change myself all the time! My hair, my breasts, my legs, my eyes — what a fortune I'd save if I could just *snap!* Wouldn't that be wonderful? It would be like having superpowers!"

Akki slams the door on her words with a great swing of his arm. Downstairs he slips his feet into his giant pair of *waraji* and steps outside. It is nighttime. *As it should be.* He really needs to get over this new-found paranoia. "Ah —" he flinches as pain jets through his lower back. As he mentally curses Zaniel, something in the air makes him pause. He sniffs. Smoke. Smoke and immortal blood. *Yes!* Wading through the darkness with pristine night vision he heads around to the back of the house. Wisps of cigarette smoke float up from the giant koi pond in Akki's backyard. Who else could it be?

"Shit, girl, don't you ever put that thing *down*?!" he jokes in place of an excited greeting. Hino has a cigarette in her mouth and is engrossed in typing a text message on a keychain-laden *keitai* with both thumbs. "Huh. You actually get a signal on that thing up here?" Hino rolls her eyes. "Who are you textin', anyway?" She does not answer. "Forget you, then. Where is that scrawny son of a bitch?"

Hino takes a long time to answer. "Why? This one was not what you were looking for, either?"

"Are you kiddin' me? I threw my back out on this one." He rubs his hip dramatically and pouts when Hino still does not look up. "That's the second one to disappoint me this week. Two out of three. Come on, let's get out of here. I need a massage."

Akki's eyes catch a slight bulge in the front pocket of Hino's blazer. He pulls out the cigarette box without so much as a brush against her breast, lights one up with the lighter inside, which, to his chagrin, lights up with pink sparkles and plays a very loud electronic rendition of "Butterfly." *"Ai, yai, yai,"* the lighter squeals over and over again.

"What the *fuck*?" Akki exclaims. "How do you turn this off?"

"You do not. It plays the whole thing."

"The hell it does." He winds up his arm and lobs the singing lighter through his bedroom window. Flames lick the air. "I hate that song."

"Hey!" Hino yells indignantly. "That lighter's as old as your human years! Where am I supposed to find another?!"

"So? Come on. She can go on about her superpowers and bum-fuck *gaikoku* on her own time. I ain't no shrink."

"I suppose. There is something you should know, Akki. I think your human has …" She trails off with a fed-up sigh. She is still thinking about her lighter. "Honestly, Akki, was that necessary?"

"What?" He shrugs, not understanding. "She runs around after little ankle-biters all day. She can run fast enough to get out of a burnin' building. It's not like it'll *actually* kill her."

Hino watches him strut on ahead through the dark woods, oblivious to the roaring flames and the sounds of crumbling infrastructure behind them. There are not many things in either of these worlds that Hino would say she likes, but she *really* liked that lighter. She is no longer sure she wants to be conversational anymore; sadly, her options are limited. "I think that human of yours has an infatuation with someone."

Akki stops dead in his tracks. "A what?! With who? Since when? And who?!" He sinks to his knees, ready to transform on the spot. "Doesn't matter. Bring 'em on. I've been *dyin'* to fight for a long time."

"An infatuation, Akki. A crush. He likes someone. You know what I mean, do you not?"

He thinks for a beat, then bursts out laughing. "You've got to be fuckin' kiddin' me," Akki gasps, holding his sides.

Hino passes him now, heading deeper into the darkness. Her deep voice floats through the air. "I do not know. He ran out of Jibun Jishin the other night trying to chase someone down. Mistook it for a human at first. Have you not seen it? The *yokai* often posing as a human?"

"Uh, *no*," Akki retorts. The glow of his cigarette falls to the ground and disappears. "How would anyone notice somethin' like that?"

Only someone as thick as you would miss something like that, you obtuse fool, Hino thinks to herself. "Well, the rest of us have noticed it hanging around. Zaniel does not understand, of course. He can think whatever makes him comfortable, I suppose. I cannot blame him; it is quite lonely to think you are the only one who can do what you do." She vaguely remembered what that felt like, centuries ago, when she first stumbled on the shores of Ryukyu in her new form. It was so much easier to get away with murder back then. Before forensics. Good times.

"So, what makes *you* so sure it ain't human? I mean, Zaniel ain't the sharpest egg in the box but maybe he just wandered into some chick's dream of bein' a superhero or somethin'. Ever think of that? Not that chicks dream about that kind of thing … do they?"

Hino resists the urge to claw his jugular. Not that it would do him any harm. It would just make her feel better. "Have you ever heard of a human bending this world to its thoughts and wishes, even if it means cancelling out yours, Akki? Ring any bells?"

"Uh … what?"

"Oh hell, Akki. Your *house*. She's the one who ate your house, for cripes' sakes! Did *you* suddenly decide to make it all disappear and leave you out in the woods, alone? Isn't that why you flew into a fiery rage and scorched half this forest down? This ... *thing* ... has the same power of manipulation that you do. Maybe even more!" She steadies herself with a deep calming breath. "She changed things here, on your territory, where everything is supposed to bend to *your* will. When is the last time you ran into a human who could do *that*?"

The shapes of gnarled trees return to their eyes as the sky swells red with the impending approach of dawn. They follow the path as it climbs uphill and comes to a high cliff overlooking the ancient town where their fellow *yokai* reside. It is difficult to determine whether the town is waking up for the day or winding down after a long night. It is too quiet, too still.

"Where would he be?" Akki says in a quiet, dangerous voice. "Right now, where could I find him?"

"In the human realm, naturally. It must be five, five thirty in the morning by now. You got lucky you ran into an eager woman sleeping on a train."

"Oh, yeah. But ... I thought he worked nights. People don't dig graves during the day."

Hino throws up her hands. "You fool. Zaniel does not work in a graveyard. You're thinking of 'graveyard shifts,' and that was when he worked at Family Mart. Akki, I know it's been years, but we *have* talked about this."

"Argh, it's too hard to remember all this bullshit human lingo! I've got to find him. Make him explain what the hell is goin' on. I'm goin' down there; you comin'?"

"No. I have to show up at my school."

Akki's anger dissipates into scathing laughter again. "What for?! Hasn't your school figured you out yet? You never do homework, you never study ... Don't you just nod off at the back of the room? Can't they put two and two together? Fuck, even *I* can do that!"

"Akki ..." Hino sighs like she is explaining herself for the hundredth time. Come to think of it, she is sure she has reached four digits by now. "We cannot all threaten humans to do our dirty work for us. It is as I said the other day: the old ways are just that. Old ways. Zaniel cannot keep escorting women here for you forever, you know. Eventually someone will corner him into a loveless marriage with children and he will not have time or energy to walk through a dozen dreams for you. Do think about it."

Hino leaves Akki standing there, looking out over the mountains. He squats down over the earth, his eyebrows furrowed in his strenuous attempt to grasp his situation. Is it time to let Zaniel go? Why should he?

"What kind of an idiot would go and screw with somethin' that's always worked for him?" Akki asks himself. "Take this valley. What would it be if it gave in to change? If it tried to fit in with the rest of the country?" No one answers. "It would disappear, that's what. Everythin' that made it interestin' would die along with it. Where would the old ones go then? Where would *I* go then?"

Although he can feel he is being watched, again no voices respond to his queries. He suppresses a deep shudder. It is something he has always wondered but dreads to think about. He clambers up to a standing position and, still facing the valley, relieves himself in the underbrush. Hino was right about one thing: it *has* been a few years.

Akki walks back through the woods toward his home in time to hear a gut-wrenching scream. *It can't be. Bitch should've been gone long ago.* He prays his most recent visitor is not dreaming about being able to walk through fire, or he is in for another earful.

"Where is it?!" a high-pitched shriek echoes through the night. "What have you done with it?!"

"Talk, demon child!" screams a second voice.

It is followed by a third, sharper and more distinct than the others. "She let it go, you fools, can't you tell?!"

"Maybe she didn't," a voice of reason interjects. "She can't be that stupid. Maybe she ate it herself!"

"Then let's get it out of her!" snarls the first voice. "Quickly, before she digests! Get her robe off!" Her next words are cut off by another high-pitched scream.

Akki finds himself intrigued. He follows the sounds of scuffling and struggle to a house he barely recognizes. It is his own home, but larger, labyrinth-like. Down one particularly wide hall, he recognizes four squid demons in the guise of bald women wrestling something in their arms. It is a human. *What happened to the* yokai *they wanted to bring?* Curious, Akki positions himself behind a large display of samurai armour he does not recall ever owning (but somehow, here it is). He cannot help but marvel at how they could entice a human all the way here, up into these mountains. They are not exactly what Akki would call hypnotists. *No*, he pauses. *That is no human. The skin, it's all wrong.* It is a creature he has never seen before.

"Help!" the Yokai screams. Her eyes are aimed right at Akki. "Help me!" She can see him.

One of the squid demon's tentacles shoots out like a whip and wrenches the Yokai's head back. The demons have not noticed Akki, or they are too hungry and angry to bother making up excuses for their intent to spill blood on his tatami floor. He can say something, intervene, rescue this human-looking thing in the nick of time, and if he plays his cards right, give the creature a chance to make it up to him. But he has already sent Zaniel on his way, and the boy never takes long to return. Akki leans against the armour display with an amused grin. *Let's see how this plays out*, he tells himself. Perhaps luck will be on his side and he will have two individuals to give him company tonight.

The Yokai lets out another scream, a strange sound that makes everything still — the squid monsters in confusion, Akki in anticipation. It is completely unlike any sound they have ever heard: half rage, half determination, not a hint of fear. No one is sure what is happening to her until she twists her upper body and sinks her sharp teeth into the tentacle wrapped around her right wrist. Its owner reels back in pain. Something glistens in the Yokai's hand: two small, shiny slivers of black lacquer. She stabs the tentacle pinning down her left arm; once free, she lunges at the third demon, springing up from the floor like a crazed cat and puncturing the ink gland in its head. A thick, heady black liquid sprays all over the Yokai and leaves an outline of her figure on the wall behind her. The fourth, uninjured demon lunges at her, tackling her into the wall. Facing the demon, the Yokai jerks one arm free and brings her weapons down into the fleshiest part of its back. The fourth demon releases a strangled cry and topples over with the Yokai landing on top of it. Akki watches, rapt with fascination. The Yokai wrenches herself from its slimy clutches, poises her weapons over her head, and drives them deep into the squid demon's eye. The squid tries to push her away. Its attempts to escape only infuriate her. She stabs it in the face, over and over and over again.

Akki looks on, licking his lips, savouring every moment.

Outside, Zaniel has emerged from the woods with many names and no names at all to enter Akki's garden. He is not alone. A young woman follows, giggling to herself. "I hope we're almost there. This samurai ... I can't wait to see how big his sword *really* is."

They have barely set foot in the garden when that demonic scream rips through the air. Both cover their ears at the sheer volume of it.

"What was that?!" the young woman inquires.

"No idea. Wait here."

"But what about your friend? He's supposed to be here." She wrinkles her nose at Zaniel. He does not need to hold her hand to know she would rather be in the handsome, muscular samurai's company than in his. "Take me to him, already!"

Zaniel does not respond. Ignoring the invisible eyes watching him, he guides the young woman to one of the stone benches and heads toward the house. On the other side of the garden he hears *yokai* voices in the woods, their conversation turning from amusement at the night's *mukade* celebration to confusion and caution. He approaches the front door, wary of entering; the last thing he wants to do is encounter Akki and learn he has disappointed the demon yet again. However, some inexplicable force pulls him to the door, draws his hand to the knob, and urges him to enter the house.

Three squid demons in the form of bald women collide with Zaniel on the stairs as they bump along the walls, groping their way to the exit. They hold themselves in various places, crying in pain, dripping thick black ink in place of blood all over the floor. One of them hisses and pushes him aside. "Damn humans! Out of the way, freak!" it spits from the leaking, black wound where its mouth should be.

Humans?

Cautious, Zaniel enters the house, goes up the stairs, and is startled by the wide black pool snaking along the tatami floor of a long, vast hall he has never seen before. Several feet down the hall, a strange lumpy figure is heaped in the middle of the black mess. It groans softly. Akki is over there, too. He is not alone. The Yokai is there, and she has not relaxed her offensive stance. Crouching on the floor, she is brandishing a pair of chopsticks in her clenched fist, pointing them up from her chest as if to strike Akki with them.

Nothing diverts her attention — not Zaniel down the hall, not even the black ink that has splashed her from brow to waist, soaking her white kimono. Not when Akki could have helped her.

Akki still makes no move toward her. He simply stares at her with a wicked, almost lecherous grin, savouring the scent of her. Neither breaks their gaze as she takes a step back, then another and another, until she is a safe distance to turn and escape down the hall.

"Oh, well," the giant *yokai* shrugs to himself. He sniffs and whirls around himself abruptly. It is difficult with all the ink-blood in the air, but he could have sworn he smelled the boy.

Zaniel, however, is able to slip back down the stairs before Akki can spot him. Something in his gut guides him through the darkness on the lower level. His hands steady him along a singular twisting, turning hallway. It leads outside to another garden area, in worse condition than the front. Zaniel has never seen this side of the house before. There must have been plants and flowers here, a long time ago, but now there are only patches of earth and several dead brambles. The ground is higher on this side, overlooking a cliff with a sharp, winding path that leads into another part of the woods. Were it winter he would be able to see the cable car station and temple past the trees, and in clearer weather, the rest of Kyoto City and the dream world farther down the mountain. But for now, there is just darkness and moonlight, and someone naked kneeling in the dirt, smothering her face with her hands.

Zaniel forgoes all notions of reuniting with the young woman waiting out front. He approaches, careful but sure. "Hey," he whispers.

The Yokai whirls around, still sniffling, but chopsticks armed and ready. Zaniel holds up his hands in defence. "It's okay. I'm not going to hurt you. It *is* you. I thought so."

"Me?"

"Yeah. It's me — Zaniel — from the restaurant. Don't you recognize me?"

"I have never seen you before. Ever."

"Yes, you have. We ran into each other the other night."

"We met the other night?"

"Well, we'd met before, too. Don't you remember?"

The Yokai blinks wet tears at him.

"I begged you not to eat me?"

"Why the hell would I do that? What is with everyone today?" The Yokai throws her hands up in disgust. "First, those horrible, awful women. Now you. Who are you all, anyway?"

"Whoa, hold on. I'm nothing like those women — er, well, I guess they're not exactly women."

"You can say that again. Look at me." The Yokai gestures to the black ink that sprayed all over her. Zaniel blushes. She does not seem to notice, let alone mind, that she is naked. "How am I ever going to get this stuff off?"

"There's a pond. Behind you."

The Yokai reaches into the pond, cupping murky water to wash the ink-blood off. Looking away, Zaniel sees a strip of white cloth on the dark ground. It is her robe, albeit with a big tear down the side. When he hands it to her, his long fingers accidentally caress hers. He does not mean to, but his eyes flutter before he can stop them.

Zaniel falls into another dream. He is back in Akki's house, or somewhere just like it, standing in a corridor. The sound of running feet crescendos into a crash against the wall. A ghostly figure hurtles toward him, cradling a bundle of something in its arms. The figure looks left and right, not seeing him. With a panicked look it reaches out, long fingers brushing the wall. A window appears where one did not exist before. The figure lifts the bundle — a baby — to the window. Zaniel hears the Yokai's voice as her figure takes shape.

"Go on, kid, get out of here!"

Without hesitation, the baby scrambles up to the window and flings itself over the side. A split second later the Yokai is snatched and dragged away by a teeming mass of tentacles. They, too, slowly

take shape. The four demons have her. The fight continues to play
out as it did before.

"Hey," says the Yokai, now standing behind Zaniel. "That's
me."

"Yeah." Zaniel turns to her. He clears his throat, ignoring her
confused look. This is, after all, finally his chance to talk to her.
"I'm glad you're here, you know. I owe you for what you did for me
the other night. I never got the chance to thank you. No one has
ever stood up for me in front of other *yokai* except for … well …"
Now that he thinks about it, he does not really know what to call
Akki. They are not friends, but he feels silly admitting he needs a
protector — at least, to her. "Anyway. I'm glad I found you here. I
never know when I'll see you again."

The Yokai looks taken aback. "Oh. You're welcome. I guess."
She looks down, uncomfortable. "This is so weird …"

"Is it?" Now that is something Zaniel has never heard a *yokai*
utter before. He looks down, noticing for the first time that he is
still touching her, sharing her robe between them. His blush deep-
ens. He snatches his hand away. "Sorry. I don't usually … I mean,
I didn't mean to … I'm sorry."

The gardens and the violet-red sky return. It is as if Zaniel
has stumbled into another terrible dream. A hundred pairs of eyes
stare back at him, most of them sharply shaped, glowing with the
fading moon's reflection. He is safe here, on the hill still within
Akki's domain, but the shock of their number and assortment
makes beads of sweat form on his forehead.

"What happened here, boy?" A *tanuki* waves its paws in the
air. "What did the boar god do to those squids?"

"It wasn't him. It was …" The Yokai is nowhere to be seen. Not
a single pair of eyes belong to the Yokai. *Where did she go?* On the
other side of the crowd a dirt path lines the woods and stretches
into the distance. He can see her now, at the forest edge, clinging
to a tree branch and shaking it for all it is worth. Something drops

to the ground, giggling. She bends to retrieve it. Even from here, Zaniel can tell she is eating it.

From the ground up, she swells and grows. With a pleased chuckle she takes another fruit from the trees and brings it to her mouth, and another, and another, growing more and more each time. *This* is what she has been missing, she thinks to herself. She moans with pleasure, a sound so loud it makes *yokai* heads turn.

"What's that?"

"Oh, no, it's that creature! The one that ate Akki's house! She's growing again!"

"What? How?!"

"The *jinmenju*! Look, she's eating its fruit!"

"What do we do?!"

"Run, stupid!"

"Yes, run! Before she eats us, too!"

"No, wait!" Zaniel steels himself, then leaps down from the hill. Not the wisest choice: he bumps into a *tanuki* and finds himself flying over the rooftops of Arashiyama. He rouses himself from that dream and continues his pursuit. He brushes against a *tenome's* arm, then dreams he has eyeballs in the palms of his hands. Again, he fights through the illusion to return to this realm, and runs toward the now-giant Yokai, who continues to devour and grow. At her size, it is impossible for Zaniel to keep up with her. She disappears over the side of the mountains, off into the glowing horizon. He squats down, hands braced against his quaking knees, struggling to catch his breath. His eyes shut on their own accord. Without intending to, he wakes up.

"Damn."

Zaniel lies in his bed, the light of dawn seeping through the curtains that shut off his tiny, cluttered apartment from the rest of the world. He concentrates on the ceiling as his heartbeat decreases and his breathing slows. He lets the last vestiges of the dream wash past his eyes, recalling as much detail as he can. It is a calming technique, an old habit, to contemplate how those images are now just memories, and they can no longer hurt him. However, he realizes, there is little need to calm himself. It is not fear that fills his mind, but ease.

Ease, and perhaps a taste of exhilaration, that after all this time, at long last, he may have found the answer to his prayers.

Now, he only has two nights left to find her.

nine

CURIOUS CREATURES

良薬は口に苦し

The best advice is the hardest to take

"Ima okina-EE-to, okurema-SOO, yo!"

"Ack! Son of a …"

I'm in the middle of eating breakfast when my alarm clock goes off. It startles me, running over my outstretched hand on the floor as I'm engrossed in a children's show on the TV. I have to get out from under my *kotatsu*, warm but switched off, and crawl after it on my hands and knees.

"Ima okina-EE —"

"Enough, you little monster." I wonder why it's going off again. Maybe it has a snooze setting I haven't figured out yet. I go back to devouring my stack of Texas French toast drowning in real maple syrup and topped with expensive but delicious strawberries. Worth every yen. I clean up my dishes, get dressed for work, turn off the TV, and pick up my purse … which is oddly heavy. Oh; it's the coffee I bought the other night. Then it hits me that Bucho got rid of our beloved electric kettle. Crap.

My doorbell rings. It turns out to be my Flying Pig delivery, way earlier than I expected. The guy freezes when I open the door, but he's polite and hands me everything nice and quick. *"Nihongo jouzu desu ne,"* he adds before he goes. I leave everything in the *genkan* except for the pumpkin and jack-o'-lantern tools. Not even the dark stormy weather waiting outside dampens my excitement about getting my kinders nice and messy.

Biking to Zozo and passing more and more stores with Halloween and autumn decorations, I see more than one person with face masks on. Half of my Zippo and Zappo students were mysteriously absent yesterday. I hope there isn't something going around. I myself haven't been feeling great. That Hitomu-related headache never fully went away, but I know how Zozo feels about sick days. Basically, they don't exist. I'd have to pass out in full view of Manager for him to even think about letting me stay home. I'll have some *kitsune* udon for dinner, then I should be fine. For now, I'm looking forward to my lessons with Asako and the Gotou twins. They're different levels, but both of their books are getting into Halloween.

The lobby is empty, but when I enter the staff room Bucho is sitting at the computer. So much for signing in. *"Ohayou gozaimasu,"* I greet her. She gives me a strange smile and stares as I take off my jacket, pull half a dozen jack-o'-lantern tools from my purse, assemble them in my teacher's box, squeeze my pumpkin into my purse space in the cupboard, and sit down at the bench. I hope it doesn't have something to do with my three-quarter sleeved maroon shirt. It is not cold outside. If anything, it's quite warm in here.

"Shibere-*sensei, ohayou!"* she says. "Very bad weather, today, *ne?"*

"Oh, it's not so bad. Just a little cloudy."

"Eh? But ... short sleeves."

Oh, my crap. This again. "Yes, well, I feel very warm these days. Especially in here," I end up saying. I don't feel like getting into an argument about this.

"Eh? Warm? Ah, yes. Warm. It is warm biz soon. So why short sleeves?" She mutters something under her breath about whether or not Manager and Lieko taught me about warm biz and having a word with them about this.

The elevator dings. "Yay! Students!" Oh, thank God. I go out to greet them. "Good mor—"

"*YADAAAAA!*"

Shit.

Hitomu scrambles up his mother's legs as the two Zippo and Zappo students I didn't see yesterday step out of the elevator. They move slowly, watching the spectacle this small child creates as his mother stumbles with him and tries to put him down on the floor.

"Ah*, anata wa* Hitomu-*kun deshou?*" Bucho steps out of the staff room. She goes up to the boy and kneels, reaching for him. *"Ogenki desu ka,* Hitomu-*kun?"*

Hitomu's screams reach a keening pitch and he sprints through the lobby in terror, scrambling for safety under the reception desk. *"Oni baba! Oni baba! Oni baba!"*

"Ah! Hitomu-*kun, ohayou!*" says Manager, coming down the hall. "And Cybelle! Eh, Cybelle-*sensei*, can we talk?"

"Sure." I know it's Manager's way of shooing me into the staff room, but I don't care. I'm grateful for the excuse to get farther away from this child.

As Manager slides the door behind me, Bucho calls after him, saying something about a meeting later. Manager turns to me. "What is Cybelle doing in staff room?"

I blink. "You just told me to come in here."

"But, why are you not ready for Zippo and Zappo? In Room Five?"

"Uh, because that was yesterday?"

"Ah! So sorry! Now, you have two Zippo and Zappo; only Hanae and Shizuko on Wednesday, and Yuta and Toshiro are today. New class today, at eleven o'clock, from now on. Sorry."

"Oh. So, in like … five minutes." Oh, brother.

Manager walks with me as I carry my box to Room Five and set up. "Yes, Yuta and Toshiro will have Zippo and Zappo with Cybelle on Thursdays. And today, I have unfortunate news. Two classes today are cancelled. Asako and the Gotou twins. So, no Zone V lesson, and no Zone IV lesson today."

"Oh. That's okay. They'll be back next week, right?"

"Eh? No. They, ah, transfer to Osaka Zozo. So, no more lessons. So sorry. But! Good news! Interview at four today is cancelled, so good news is that Cybelle has long lunch, and more time for planning lessons." He grins at me as if he expects me to jump up and down. "Also, we have staff meeting today."

"Really?" A staff meeting — with me? After six and a half years? About time. Maybe now I can finally find out what is going on with our school and feel like a crucial cog in the *eikaiwa* machine again.

"Yes! But you don't have. Only Japanese teacher, and Bucho. So, when you have lunch, please take your time."

"Really?" My voice is dejected this time. I finished all my prep work for the week on Tuesday. What am I supposed to do for three hours? Take a nap?

I escort the boys down the hall toward Room Five. Yuta shows off his new Squirtle rain poncho and Toshiro demands stickers for the two pages he coloured in for homework. We head into the classroom and do a few preliminary bubbles. Then I hear Lieko's high-pitched voice.

"Hitomu-*kun*! Let's enjoy English!"

"Yada! Yada yada YADAAAAAAAAA!"

Yuta and Toshiro turn toward each other, letting the last of the bubbles fall to the carpet. *"Are wa nandarou?"* they wonder.

"Cybelle!" Lieko glides into the room. "Hitomu is here for your lesson! Say, 'Hello,' Hitomu!" Hitomu does not appear. All I can hear past the door is the sound of him struggling in someone's arms to escape and his horrified, diaphragmatic screams. "Yuta, Toshiro, meet Hitomu! He will have this class with you. Please help him in Cybelle's lesson, okay?"

"Wait — I have all *three* of them?"

"Yes, Cybelle! And we will enjoy English very much!" she sings. "You may start the lesson. I will bring Hitomu-*kun*! And please, when he comes in, please do not talk to him. I will help him."

"But —"

"You just teach Yuta and Toshiro. Hitomu is too afraid of you. If you talk to him, you will only make things worse. Just keep doing the lesson. Hitomu is my job." She bounds out the door singing words of English encouragement.

This is bullshit. This is bullshit on a stick. Again, I wonder who the hell orchestrated this recipe for disaster. But for Yuta and Toshiro's sakes, I will get through the lesson bright and cheery. I made a promise to myself, and I plan on sticking to it no matter how many xenophobic children this company throws at me.

We hold hands for the greeting songs and do a few rounds of "Ring Around the Rosy" while Hitomu thrashes and cries in Lieko's arms in one corner of the room. His screaming, combined with our dancing round in a circle, starts to make the room spin, so I direct everyone to sit on the floor. We learn a few new animal words with giant flash cards, and then we practise counting.

When I high-five Toshiro he catches and holds my hand. He whispers in Japanese: "Belle-teacher, what's wrong with Hitomu?" Yuta suggests Hitomu wants his mother. *"Mama ni aitai?"*

"It's okay!" Lieko shouts in English over the screams. "Hitomu is just shy! I will take him outside for a quick walk. Say, 'See you again,' Hitomu!" I hop up to open the door for them, at which point his screams reach a frenzied pitch. "It's okay, Hitomu, now we're outside! We are safe!"

Safe? I grit my teeth and count to three in my head. The boys watch me, wondering what's next. I take a deep breath. I can't lose focus. "Who wants 'Head, Shoulders, Knees, and Toes'?!"

The boys jump up and down. *"Yossha!"*

Lieko re-enters the room holding Hitomu's hand just as Yuta, Toshiro, and I are about to go through the super-fast version of the song. His face is dry, his sobbing reduced to frequent hiccups. Without a word, she closes the door behind him. When he turns and realizes she is on the other side of the viewing glass, he bursts into fresh tears and runs to the door. Lieko holds the doorknob on the other side to keep him from escaping. Trying to finish the song is a bust. Yuta and Toshiro refuse to put their hands over any body parts other than their ears. Hitomu gives up with the doorknob and collapses in a corner. I congratulate everyone on a job well done and put magnetic stars on the board beside their names, even Hitomu's. I really don't feel good.

"Sensei, mou ikkai!" Yuta and Toshiro beg. "One more. One more time!"

"You know what, guys, let's take a break from 'Head and Shoulders.' Please get your colouring books!"

"Yossha!" the two boys repeat, pumping their little fists. We all sit down on the carpet and break out our crayons. Lieko's figure bobs back and forth between the door and the window. She's talking to someone, maybe Bucho. I sneak over to dig out Hitomu's colouring book and crayons and discretely arrange them next to his shivering figure. I obeyed Lieko's ridiculous request by not saying a word to him. I did my best. *Ganbarimashita.*

"Sensei, sensei," Yuta smacks me on my thigh for attention. *"Hitomu ga naiteru no."* Hitomu is crying.

"I know, sweetie, but I'm contractually obligated not to talk to him."

"*Eh? Nani?*" he asks Toshiro. Toshiro shrugs, continuing to colour. "*Eigo wakaranai.*" They colour for another minute, then suddenly Toshiro claps his hands over his ears. "Damn, I can't stand it anymore!" he curses in Japanese. "HITOMU! SHUT UP!" "Toshiro!" I snap. He pouts. "*Gomen ne, sensei ...*" he begins. "Don't apologize to me. Say it to Hitomu." I point to the small child now scratching at the carpet. "We don't yell at each other like that ... no matter much we might want to," I add to myself as Toshiro drags his heels to the other side of the room.

Toshiro speaks softly to Hitomu and even pats his shoulder. "We must do our best together, okay?" I hear him say in Japanese. Hitomu rises to his feet, either nodding or about to bang his head against the wall. I'm relieved to see it's the former.

"Thank you, Cybelle-*sensei*!" I hear a voice on the other side of the wall. Manager opens the classroom door. "Hitomu, time to go home!"

"Noooooooooo!" Hitomu curls up into a ball again, muffling his screams. He wraps his arms over his head like a bomb is about to go off. I notice Yuta's and Toshiro's mothers behind Manager as he kneels down to tap Hitomu on the back. They look more than eager to collect their children. I, however, stand stock-still. Did Hitomu just say what I think I heard?

"Cybelle-*sensei*, please sing the 'Goodbye Song' with Toshiro-*kun* and Yuta-*kun*! Their mothers are waiting!"

"What? Oh ... right. Sorry." Okay, sure, let's end this shit show with a bang. I take the boys' hands in mine and we all swing our arms back and forth in a circle. "*English school is over ...*" we sing.

"NOOOOOOOoooo ..." Hitomu wails again.

"*We are going home ...*"

"Someone heeeeeelllp!"

I stop singing. Now I *know* I'm coming down with something because I'm sure I heard Hitomu say ...

"Sensei," Toshiro asks. *"Hitomu wa nihonjin?"*

"Of course, he is."

"Demo, kare no koto zenzen wakaranai!"

I give Toshiro a dramatic shrug. I can't really say much with Manager and the parents standing watch. We should just get this over with. *"Goodbye, goodbye!"* I wave to the boys. They wave back.

"Get away from meeee ..."

I freeze while Yuta and Toshiro twirl around themselves without me. "We are going home! Goodbye! *Sensei*, bye-bye!" They fly out the door into the warm, welcoming arms of their parents. After what seems like a lifetime Hitomu's mother comes in to peel her son off the floor. I follow Manager and the parents outside for a quick lobby talk with my biggest professional smile plastered on my face. What the hell did I just hear?

"Eh, they were worried about Yuta and Toshiro," Manager explains. "But now, they are glad to see they enjoyed Cybelle's lesson. Thank you for your lesson, Cybelle-*sensei*!"

"Not a problem." Normally I'd stand here, nodding and smiling until I saw a politer window of opportunity to take off, but my head is *killing* me right now. "Do they have any questions for me?"

"Eh, no, I do not think so. So, please, go to staff room?"

"I'm way ahead of you."

"Eh? 'A head'?"

"I mean, yes, I understand. But can I ask you something, Manager? Did you hear Hitomu?"

"Ah, I think, maybe, *everyone* hear Hitomu ..."

"No, I mean, when we were singing the 'Goodbye Song.' You didn't hear anything?" Manager blinks at me. "You know what, never mind." Hitomu and his mother have already left so there's no way to follow up and ask, anyway. Not that Manager would believe me. I wonder if I have any Advil in my purse.

In the staff room, Yoshino, Misaki, Seri, and Yuri are frantic as they prepare for their lessons and I assume for this special staff meeting. "Has anyone seen the footstool?" Yoshino asks. "I need to put these things back on the top shelf."

"Allow me." I take the binders in her hands and put them on the shelf by standing on my tiptoes. It turns out I don't need to strain as much as I anticipate. Maybe I've grown a couple of inches lately?

"Thanks, my tall friend," Yoshino says. "Don't want to leave these lying around, there's hardly enough space on the bench as it is."

"No worries. So ... what's this meeting all about, anyway?"

"Oh, the usual," Yoshino rolls her eyes. "Except now we have Bucho to rake us over the coals for losing students to this new branch in Osaka. You're lucky not to be part of it, trust me."

"I guess. I'll be so *bored,* though."

"Sorry," Yoshino apologizes for no particular reason. "On the other hand, it gives us more to look forward to when the day is over!"

"Oh ... yeah!" I had completely forgotten about hanging out with her tonight. So much for nursing this headache with soup and rest. "Can't wait! Um, what's the name of the bar again? Parappa the Rapper?"

"Kappa Garappa. And don't worry about me staying late tonight. With this meeting, I don't think that'll happen. She's going to have two hours to chew us out, and then it'll be up to Manager what needs to be done next."

"Ugh. Suddenly I'm not so jealous about this meeting."

"I don't blame you."

Outside, we hear Bucho snapping at Manager, who sticks his head into the staff room with a quick *"Minna-san, kaigi ga hajimarimasu!"* Even before he finishes his sentence everyone makes a rush to grab their things and head out. I sit down at the bench and toy with my phone, waiting to hear them all reply to Bucho's *"Yoroshiku onegaishimasu"* that starts their meeting before digging into the Cambodian-style fried rice I made last night. Twelve minutes later and I'm still hungry. I search the mountains of papers and binders left behind, hopeful for another box of leftover cakes or some untouched *omiyage* snacks. No such luck. I write a note on a little Gudetama Post-it (*Cybelle will be right back!*) and pray that I don't return to an earful about the dangers of leaving Zozo unattended or unsupervised while Bucho is here.

I stick my head out of the staff room to peek down the hall. I can hear Bucho's voice in Room Three. Perfect. I can simply walk out without anyone seeing me, but I still tiptoe just to be safe. No one comes running when the elevator bell dings, and I let the doors close with a satisfied sigh. How to kill the next three hours is a complete mystery to me. Almost as mysterious as whatever the heck Hitomu said during our class. I swear it was English ... but no one else seemed to hear it. Maybe I'm hearing things. Maybe I've been working too hard, stressing too much. Wouldn't be the first time. Probably won't be the last.

"Whatever," I say to the empty elevator. "I'm hungry."

Outside the Zozo building the happy weather from my bike ride this morning is gone. The dark Halloween clouds and the cold autumn chill have returned. And apparently, so has the weirdo with the udon *kei* truck. "Pssst!" is the first thing I hear when I walk past the bike racks. At first I mistake it for a snake. Turning around, I inadvertently make eye contact. The man giggles and beckons me like a mechanical *maneki neko* cat. Weird. I can't help smiling awkwardly as I shake my head no. He beckons me again, more forcefully this time.

"Uh ..." I break into a run. His laughter follows me into the HORUS bakery. I take my sweet time choosing which buns to take, and when I line up, I pray for the *obaachans* in front of me to have lots of small change to pay with. No such luck, but on the plus side, it's the manager of the store who rings me up today. She takes two of the fresh garlic buns on the counter behind her and adds them to my bag, telling me in Japanese that she wants everyone to try them, so it's my lucky day. Even better, the creepster and his *kei* truck are gone when I look out HORUS's window. Thank goodness. I spend another twenty minutes or so wandering around the shops and the mall, then head back to Zozo, arms laden with goodies. Riding up the elevator, I check my phone again. 12:54. Son of a ...

The doors slide open to the empty lobby. Bucho is still audible from Room Three. I slip off my shoes, grab my Tinker Bell slippers, and ninja-run to the staff room, all before I hear the door open, someone go *"Are? Dare mo inai na,"* and the door close again. Yes! The perfect crime.

Speaking of crime, now seems like a good time to print everything I need for the next couple of days off the internet. I successfully do so without downloading any viruses or whatever it is Bucho worries about. After clearing the browser history and shutting things down, I take out a few kids' books as I stuff my face with two cinnamon rolls and the garlic buns. By the time I pick up my *Treasury of Japanese Folktales* and flip through "Momotaro" the sleepiness kicks in. I set my phone alarm to go off before my kinders might show up, then fold my arms on the bench and rest my head on them. I don't even feel all that sleepy. Just bored.

Bucho's lecturing fades. All of Zozo is quiet now, except for the hum of fluorescent lights. Time passes. A delicate arrhythmic ticking sound is audible through the wood of the bench. Something with several legs, crawling ... getting closer. I lift up my head, let what I presume is a giant *mukade* crawl on by, and lower my head back down on my arms. On my shoulders, I feel cloth settling. Someone putting a jacket — I'm guessing my jacket — over me, like a small blanket. It feels nice.

"Thank you," I yawn, opening one eye a little. There is someone sitting at the computer. She holds an abnormally long black cigarette holder between her fingers. She has the same face as Fumiko, with Mami's hair colour, and Miyoko's voice when she finally speaks, after staring at my face for a long time.

"You look unhappy, child. What is wrong?"

"Nothing. I just had the weirdest class with a student. And I have this snack bar to go to tonight. What should I do?"

"That sounds like fun. Where?"

"Osakako Station."

"Oh. That is quite a trip. Well, if you want my advice —" she takes a long drag and exhales a cloud of blue in my face "— just go and be yourself."

"What does that mean?"

She doesn't answer. Outside the staff room we hear the ding of the elevator doors. It's louder than normal, almost like a fire alarm. The mom's head turns sharply toward the sound. She gasps. "A student is here. Get up, 獏."

"What'd you call me?"

"I said, GET UP."

I sit upright, eyes wide. The room is empty, except for me. No jacket over my shoulders, no other people. I almost believe I'm alone in Zozo until I hear Manager's quiet whine and Bucho snapping at him. Just as I'm about to pick up my phone, the alarm goes off. It is exactly 2:40.

"Hai, kaigi o owarimasu. Yoroshiku onegaishimasu," Bucho sings from Room Three. Manager and teachers sing back to her, and I hear the shuffle of chairs and the flipping of tables. The staff meeting is over. Right on cue the elevator bell dings, and I hear my kinder students shouting for me and Lieko. I love it when good timing happens.

I waddle over to the shelves (my legs are still asleep and full of pins and needles), take the pumpkin and wrap my jacket around it, then exit the staff room holding it against my abdomen. "Hi, ladies," I greet my students. "Guess what I got?"

"Eh?!" Momoko points at my stomach. *"Mama, mite mite! Sensei ninshin shiteru!"*

"Now how do you know that word?" I laugh. Momoko's mother grabs her extended finger, trying to shush her, but I wave my hands to let her know it's okay. I pretend the pumpkin is part of my stomach and giggle like the girls are tickling me when they poke it and knock on the clothed surface.

Behind me I hear Manager come out with a couple of other teachers. Lieko is one of them. "What is *that*?" She says pointedly at me. "Is that your *stomach*?"

"Of course, it is," I say with heavy sarcasm. "It's the aftermath of my lunch. I swallowed a baby. Must have been, oh, seven kilograms?"

Lieko's eyes widen in horror.

Motoka, rubbing my so-called belly, exposes a bit of orange under a jacket sleeve. "Lieko-*sensei*, it's pumpkin! Not baby!"

"Dekkai kabocha! Onaka ja nai!" Momoko giggles.

Lieko purses her lips, still staring at me. "Hmph."

Momoko and Motoka have a hold of my wrists and are pulling me into Room Two to have a better look at our afternoon project. Lieko watches us through the open door for a few seconds, then goes about her business. I leave the kids with the pumpkin to get my teacher's box from Room Five. My guess is Lieko retreated to the staff room or something because I don't see her on the way. Good.

"Do you like my squiggles?" Motoka points to the black lines she drew all over the pumpkin.

"I love them," I reply. "What are they?"

"It's the hair."

With lots of cheering from the kids I cut open the top and encourage them to dive in. We practise the word "slimy" together a few times, then the girls start yelling at me to cut out the face. They watch me hack away at it for about a minute, then demand to make more playdough desserts. So much for the jack-o'-lantern. After class, the girls put on their backpacks and take their delicate confections straight to Lieko in Room Three. She doesn't look pleased, and I can feel her evil gaze on me all the way to Room One, where I work until my next lesson.

Around quarter to five, I leave to use the washroom. When I come back, my fourteen-year-old bilingual student Yukina has magically appeared. She's already sitting across from my seat with her notebook and pens arranged neatly next to a strange-looking box. She stands up when I come in.

"Good afternoon, Cybelle-*sensei*! I brought you something. White peach cakes, from Okayama. Have you tried them before?"

"I don't think so. Thank you!"

The box is beautiful, a golden peach with pink cherry blossoms and pastel-green leaves drawn all over it. I offer a cake to Yukina. We eat a couple more as she talks about how school is going and how she misses her life in L.A. We even get into a long conversation about the Me Too movement. I don't have time to hide the box of cakes before my Zozo Junior class, so I endure Takeshi, Ren, and Hayato's endless pepper of, "*Sensei, ke-ki choudai,*" throughout the lesson. As they get up and leave for the night, I make a grand show of sneaking them each a cake. "Thank you, Cybelle-*sensei*! *Uwaa, umai!* Cybelle-*sensei* is *da besto!*" they salute me with deep bows. They can be the sweetest boys when they're not sleeping or cracking jokes about my hair.

After the boys leave, through a very well-laid-out plan of action, I'm stealthy enough to wipe down all the viewing windows in every classroom (yes, with the "窓" towel, because contrary to Manager's beliefs, I'm not stupid). Now I can kick back for my final hour and relax with some playdough for tomorrow's kindergarten class and my Okayama souvenirs. I finish half the box of my white-peachy cakes in the staff room before anyone comes in, at which point I hide them. I'm not sharing these; I'm too hungry, and they're too delicious.

"*Anou*, Shiberu-*sensei*, can I ask favour?" Bucho sings as she sits down next to me and sees my finished playdough desserts. "Oh! *Oishi-sou!* You make?"

"For my kindergarten students. I might use it for some of my Zone VI lessons, too. They're learning how to order food next week."

"*Sugoi!* Like *sampuru*. You have such talent! Where you learn?"

"Nowhere, really. I just kinda made them on my own one day."

"*Sugoi,*" Bucho repeats. "Do you know *Kiyomizu-yaki?* From Kyoto?"

I can't tell if she's stroking my ego or actually trying to make conversation. Either way, it's a nice change from our first encounter. "I do. I've been to the Pottery Complex a dozen times."

"Eh?! You know *Kiyomizu-yaki?! Sugoi!*" She pauses. "*Anou,* Shibere-*sensei*, can I ask you for favour? Tonight, we must do interview. It is very important, because many students from *higashi* school will come here. We need more teachers, therefore, ah, we will have interview. Tonight."

"Sure."

"Eh — *ima.* Now."

"*Oh.* Okay, let me put these away and I'll get my jacket."

"And then, you may go home." Bucho beams so hard I fear her face might split in two. "Manager says you work very hard! So, after interview, and cleaning, go home."

This sounds too good to be true, but I get all excited, anyway. "Does that mean I don't have to line up?"

"No, no lineup!" Bucho waves her hands. "Reward for hard work." She pats my shoulder. "Now, Yoshino-*sensei* will finish interview soon. Let's go enjoy English!"

Yoshino is very happy to hear Bucho's news as she steps out of Room One. I make a grand gesture for Bucho to enter the room first. As she informs the young lady who I am and why I'm here, Yoshino winks at me. "Good stuff! Now you can go home and have a nice dinner and get some rest first, yeah?"

Yeah, she's got me there. "In that case, I'll see you back here at, let's say, eight o'clock?"

"What?! No! If you come back here, they'll *never* let you leave early again, goody two-shoes! I can meet you at the station, at Tully's." She struggles to make a gang sign with her arms full of papers. "West side!"

I laugh. "West side. Got it."

Inside Room One, Bucho squeezes herself around the one table taking up the room to close the door behind me. "Shiberu-*sensei*, this is Miss Ari Sato. Sato-*san*, this is our native teacher, Shiberu."

Ari Sato stands, gives my hand a weak shake, then tilts her head. "Nice to meet you ... eh, Shiberu?"

"Cybelle. Nice to meet you."

"Oh! Shi-belle. Nice to meet you, too —"

No time to correct anyone today. "Please, have a seat! Tell me a little about yourself."

"Ah, myself?" She starts to pant. "I am Sato, and I enjoy English?"

"Awesome. Why do you want to work for Zozo?"

"*Eh?!*" she exclaims. She looks all around the room in a panic. Her head hangs low to avoid Bucho's stern gaze and pretend not to notice Bucho's cheeks and neck turning red. I let a minute of thinking time pass. Then I reword the phrase, twice.

"I enjoy English?" Sato finally offers.

"Fantastic. Now, tell me three things you'd like to do in the future that you've never done before."

Sato wrings her fingers, nervous. "Well, I travel — no, I *want to* travel to Europe. I really enjoy sightseeing! Maybe, London, or Paris? Hmm, I want to see Big Ben, or *Efferutou?*"

"Both very cool. Continue."

"Ah, second thing is, I want to marry — no, I want to *be* married — ah! Sorry! I want to *get* married. I like weddings. I want a big wedding!"

"Weddings, nice. Good food. Continue."

"Ah, third thing is, I want to go surfing. Because, I have never been surfing before."

"Excellent! Have you been to Okinawa? Great surfing scene there."

"No, I have never been to Okinawa."

"Well, I highly recommend it." I can end the interview here with a record of one minute, but to look like an enthusiastic professional, I throw in one bonus and pray it doesn't take her twenty minutes to answer. "All righty, last one: If you were an animal, what animal would you be and why?"

"*Eh?! Anou, eeto ...*" She struggles through her answer. "Eh, I would be a dog. Because, dogs are very energetic and happy, and I am very energetic and happy."

"Fantastic! Thanks, Sato-*san*, it was really nice talking to you! Do you have any questions for me?"

"*Anou ... eeto ...* you are from America?"

"Canada."

"Ah, Canada! *Sugoi! Anou*, do you like Japan?"

"Yes, I do. Do you have questions, Bucho?"

Bucho has been nodding the whole time, watching our reactions but not taking notes. She turns to Sato and thanks her, saying the English part of the interview is over. "Thank you, Shiberu-*sensei*! Please leave interview paper in staff room before home?"

"Okay. Thanks again, really look forward to working with you." We shake hands and bow; Bucho shoos me out the door. I look at the clock above the reception desk: 7:44. My cleaning duties are done, so according to Bucho, I'm done, too. I plop the papers next to the computer, sign out, scoop my jacket and purse under my arms, throw my Tinker Bell slippers onto the shelf, and step into my sneakers. I am free.

"Ah, Cybelle-*sensei*, just a moment!"

Son of a —

Manager comes running down the hall and catches the elevator doors just before they close. All of a sudden, he's the Terminator. "Ah! Cybelle ... you are going home. You must be tired. Lieko says you had a good nap today."

"What?" Why the hell would she say that? And why would she say it to Manager, of all people? I'm not in the mood to engage in any Lieko-related nonsense right now. "Yeah, I'm off. Bucho said I could go now."

"Ah, yes! She said, very good, hard work. But, this week, you have window duty for cleaning, so before you go home, I must show you the towel and you must —"

"Already did it. And yes, I used the correct towel."

Manager pauses, and mutters to himself that yes, that explains why the windows are all so clean. "But, before you go, very important. Tomorrow. Please come to school at nine, not eleven. For trial lesson. Three boys, same family. They want private lessons. This would be very good for our school, so please ... work VERY hard. It's very important this time."

"Yes, sir." I salute him. He seems entertained by the gesture, but not convinced to get his hands away from the doors.

"So ... I think you should prepare for trial lesson. Please."

"I will. Good night, Manager."

"Now. Before you go home."

I look him firmly in the eye. "How old are these boys?"

"They are kindergarten now. Eh, maybe."

"So, they're about three to four years old? They'll have their own group-slash-private lesson? And they'll either be doing Kinder-Zozo or Zone 1?"

"Yes! Very good! Wow, you know Zozo programs very —"

"If that's the case, I have all the materials for their age group ready to go. But now, *I* have to go. See you tomorrow, okay?"

Manager freezes, stunned. He reluctantly pulls away from the elevator. "Yes, I see. Maybe. Okay. See you again. *Otsukaresama deshita.*"

"*Otsukare!*" I keep waving until the elevator doors slide closed. *Thank you, God.* I close my eyes, relieved. I don't bother putting my coat on, even when I get outside. I stuff it right on top of my purse in my bike basket and put the pedal to the metal. I'm starving (again) and for some reason, I feel ready to freak out some squares in the name of co-worker camaraderie. Maybe it's the sugar rush from all those delicious cakes.

I bike home and sadly have to choose between eating a real meal and changing into something I don't mind reeking of smoke later. I go for changing into a fresh black button-down and black jeans, taking only my wallet and my phone. I'm not dressing to impress anyone tonight. Yoshino lets me park my bike in front of the Zozo building so it won't get stolen. Kappa Garappa isn't packed like last Saturday, nor is it as chock full of smoke. We grab a table and polish off two small bowls of edamame and some slices of daikon with a couple of rounds of highballs. Yoshino's guy still hasn't shown up, but we are having a great time without him.

"You want the last edamame?" I ask Yoshino.

"No way, I've already had, like, ten. You have it."

I laugh. "Only ten?! I've had *way* more than that!" We argue for a minute before I finally snatch it up with my chopsticks. "We're like Mr. and Mrs. Sprat," I say around a mouthful of soybeans.

"Who?" Yoshino chuckles, taking out yet another cigarette from her purse.

"Jack Sprat. And his wife. Have you heard of that poem? *Jack Sprat could eat no fat, his wife could eat no lean?* You're Jack, and I'm your wife."

She bursts out laughing with a gust of smoke she quickly tries to wave out of my face. "Sorry! That's kinda cool that you can remember poetry like that. Nursery rhymes, right? Geez, I can barely remember what I had for breakfast with the shit show Zozo has become."

"I feel you on that one." I chase my last bite of daikon with a swig of highball. "But I'm not going to complain about it anymore.

I said I was going to do my best, and I meant it. Can't let things like Hitomu-tantrums and co-worker side-eye get me down; otherwise, I'd never be able to leave the house. Just got to keep being myself!"

"You know what?" Yoshino takes a long, thoughtful drag on her cigarette. "I've been thinking. That boy Hitomu has issues. Hell, his mother has issues. You should hear some of the things she says to him in Japanese! And she thought *eikaiwa* lessons would fix him? Please. More like she wants a couple of hours a week to have some peace and quiet."

"Well, something is definitely going on between Hitomu and me. I just wish I knew what it was."

"It's not just you!" says Yoshino. "I saw him point and scream at Aoi's Jibanyan backpack, and Aiko's Pikachu raincoat. Geez ... what's he going to do come Halloween?"

"Explode?"

Yoshino bursts out laughing. "That's awful! But I wouldn't be surprised. I don't know. Maybe he's scared of quality anime."

I laugh. "*I'm* not an anime!"

"No, no! You're a quality teacher! I meant for that to be a compliment."

"It was. I was kidding." I polish off the rest of my highball.

"How was it? You want another one? Or, time for rum and Coke?"

"Hmm, let's see ..." I pick up the laminated menu. "Ooh, Fuzzy Navel. Haven't had one of those in a minute." My voice drops as I read the *katakana* one more time. It'll be peachy, and delicious, and won't leave a giant stain on my shirt if some punk starts a shoving war again.

"Okay." She walks over to the bar and talks to the *mama-san* behind it. She returns with our drinks. Behind her, the *mama-san* gives me a cute wave, which I return. "Thanks a lot for coming here with me, again. I owe you big time. Sorry, I don't know what's taking Matt so long."

"No worries. Thank YOU for letting me change first! Sorry I can't stay much longer. But I won't go anywhere until you see what's his face and you feel comfortable enough." I may hate this place but I'm not about to leave Yoshino here with some weirdo.

"Thank you! And remember: anything you want to drink is on me."

"Oh, I remember. Tee hee hee."

We have ourselves a little chugging contest. I lose, but Yoshino applauds my effort. Then, three young-looking salary-men surround Yoshino and ask her ... eh, I don't know, I can't hear them over the music, which has increased in volume with the most recent upsurge of customers. She points to me as she leans toward them to be heard. They exchange worried glances and squirm.

"They're from some company with an office nearby," Yoshino yells. "I didn't catch the rest ... or their names. They want to know if we have boyfriends."

"If *we* have boyfriends, or if *you* have a boyfriend?"

"Um, well ..." Yoshino blushes. "Sorry. I don't really want to talk to them. Pretend you don't see them."

"Why don't you just tell them to piss off?"

She wrinkles her nose, shy. "Mmm, it's okay." I shrug and let Yoshino rant a little more about work. Her three new admirers still hover behind her, tapping her on the shoulder and asking her more personal questions. "Ugh! Can they not take a hint?!"

"Let's find out." I ease Yoshino to one side so I can lean toward them. "PISS OFF."

The three young men reel away, jostling each other for a few seconds, asking what I could possibly mean and who among the three of them has the guts to find out. They decide it's not worth it to gain closure and head to the bar, leaving us alone.

"*Sugee na!* Cybelle, you are one brave chick."

"Not really. I didn't think that would work!"

Someone jabs me in the shoulder. "It looks like you've met a
few of our co-workers!" a female voice shouts English against my
neck. "Now you know how *we* feel."

Two young women about our age take the empty seats beside
us. "We know those guys. Don't worry, they hit on all the cute
girls. I'm Ailsie and this is Lacie." They look wasted out of their
minds.

"Hi! I'm Yoshino and this is Cybelle, my partner in crime."

"What?! You guys are *partners*? Like …" the first girl, Ailsie,
makes some kind of gesture with her hand that's hard to see in the
dim light. I'm pretty sure it's an offensive one.

"We work together," Yoshino answers.

"*Oh*. That was like, weird for a second! I was about to say,
whoa, *Japanese* lesbians, really?! Not that I have a problem with
that sort of thing! It's just, you know, weird. I mean, this culture is
so repressed … and to meet a Japanese lesbian who dates outside
of her race, that's got to be like, *what*?! Not that there's anything
wrong with that! Anyway, what are you, English teachers?"

We nod. I wish I had more edamame.

"That's gotta suck. I guess if we hadn't majored in East Asian
Studies, that's what we'd probably be doing, too. I mean, the
hours are so horrible, and you don't have, like, *any* say in who
you teach!"

"That's true," Yoshino replies with a congenial tone. "We were
just talking about that. Cybelle has a young student who screams
every time he comes to our school, and —"

"Well, that makes sense. I mean, he's probably never seen a —
you know, person like *you* before. So yeah, I understand that can
be pretty terrifying! But no, I'm talking about when you have to
teach, like, the really crazy, *sketchy* people. I would die if I had to
teach English here."

"Oh …" Yoshino looks crestfallen. "It's not that bad … is it?"
She turns to me, like I've been hiding some dire secret of hating

my job from her all these years. Like I'd step over an unconscious body to work with shitheads like this girl.

"It isn't," I tell them firmly. "I mean, yeah, it's hard. Long hours, back-to-back classes with kids who *never* get tired. But it's fun. And at the end of the day I don't regret it. I'm fucking exhausted, but I don't regret it." I smile as the words pour out and I realize it's all true. I've been rolling with all the crap that happens. If it were really all that awful, I'd have left years ago.

But Ailsie has other things on her tiny mind. "So, you're probably into Japanese guys," she points to Yoshino. "But what about you?" she asks me. "Because those guys, they're freaks. Tell them, Lacie."

Her friend Lacie, who has been flirting with a salaryman all this time, reacts to her friend's elbow in her rib cage. "Oh my gosh, those pervs? Get this: every Monday, the short one, Matsubara, harasses me about my weekend. Where I went, who I was with, if it was a guy, is he your boyfriend, 'do you go to love hotel?' *Every weekend.* And then they spend every lunch hour looking at porn on their computers, and they sit, like, *right* next to my cubicle!"

"Oh!" Yoshino says. "That's horrible. Can't you tell your boss?"

"Our boss is just as disgusting," Ailsie cuts in. "Geez, it took, like, three months when I first started for him to stop putting his hands up my skirt."

"Let me get this straight," I interject. "You work with jerks who goof off with porn, you get harassed every week, and you can't take up any of this with your boss, who is clearly a sex offender ... but you'd rather die than have *our* jobs?"

"Uh ..." The sound leaps from her throat, something between a forced laugh and regurgitation. "Hey, where'd Tillie go? We should find her." They go away. That's all I wanted.

"Well," Yoshino gives me a look. "That was enlightening."

"That's one word for it."

She breaks into a grin. "One good thing came out of it, though. I'm glad to hear you enjoy Zozo. With all that's been going on I was worried you might leave. You know, with your family, and now Hitomu ..."

"Ha! Don't worry, my friend. It'll take a lot more than a wedding and a screaming child to send me home for good." In the opposite corner of the room I notice heads bobbing up and down. "Hey, you feel like dancing?"

"Yes! Absolutely. Let's do it!" We finish our drinks and head on over.

I don't know what song is playing. I've been out of the loop on music since GReeeeN. All I know is I'm moving more body parts than "Head, Shoulders, Knees, and Toes" could squeeze into one song. I've never felt so limber. The tipsy sensation I had back at our table is gone. I can spin 360-degree circles and not feel the least bit dizzy. The floor gets crowded as more and more bodies press up against one another. I keep my balance. My feet don't stop. I can't lower my arms. It's too dark to see anything so I let my eyes close and let the music course through me. Yoshino yells when her guy finds her with an army of his friends. They keep their greetings short; they fall in step with the song. I don't have to stop to shake hands. I can't stop if I wanted to.

A woman tugs on the hem of my shirt in between the song change. "You are good dancer!" she yells at me.

"*Ashi nagai!*" another voice shouts in my ear.

"Where are you from?!"

I have no idea who I'm even talking to. I have no clue where Yoshino went. I don't even know where I am. I'm floating outside of myself, over the crowd, unable to pick myself out in the smoky haze. I can't formulate responses in time, even if I wanted to. I can feel my mouth contorting into a stupid grin as I raise my hands again and feel the groove. Several female-shaped shadows join me. They're way too close for me to move around as much, but I do not stop dancing. The music is a tidal wave of sound. It sweeps me under. I'm a slave to the rhythm.

Something vibrates against my butt. My hands reach behind me and — oh, it's the alarm on my cellphone, vibrating. Time to catch a train if I'm to get to work earlier than usual tomorrow. Yoshino is on the other side of the room at the bar with her gentleman caller and his entourage.

"There she is!" Everyone applauds as I approach. Yoshino punches me on the shoulder. "I didn't know you could move like that! Look at you. Full of surprises, girl!"

"I'm no expert. I just know the basics."

"Liar! You were twirling like a freaking ballroom dancer. You got a double life the rest of Zozo don't know about?"

"Nah, the trick is to go limp."

A blond man leans over, crushing Yoshino from behind; she cringes at his beer breath and pulls away. "That's what *she* said!" he guffaws.

"I'm sorry, were any of us talking to you?" I ask. He stops laughing with a crestfallen look, like I just stole his puppy and kicked it across the snack bar. "That's what I thought. Hey, Yoshino —"

"Listen," she says. "They all want to go for food, then come back for karaoke. Would you mind coming with us? We won't be long!"

She's already locked her arm with mine and is smiling up at me with a pitiful puppy whining sound. *Damn it.* "I can stay for one or two songs. Manager wants me at Zozo super early tomorrow."

"Ah, yes, your trial lesson! Don't worry. Thanks, Cyb."

"Your friend coming with us, Yosh?" Matt asks, turning to me. "We're going to Mickey D's. You're not, like, vegan or anything, are you?" What kind of stupid question is that?

Outside, the crowd of us herd down a few side streets and into a bright *shoutengai*. The fresh air is heavy with the scent of rain and cinnamon gum. It takes forever to locate a McDonald's, walking past several Lotterias, KFCs, and *conbinis* before we find one. I let Yoshino's powerful arm guide me. The lights and lit-up signs make my senses throb so hard I can feel them like my own pulse. It's like the music from Kappa Garappa has followed me, the rhythms of the music having seeped into my veins, still pumping a beat. I wonder if this is what a migraine feels like.

"You okay, Cyb?" Yoshino asks me.

"Hungry."

"Aw, don't worry, baby," says Matt's blond friend. "Whatever you ladies want is on me!"

"No, it's okay," I reach into my back pocket for my wallet, wishing I'd brought my purse, which I'm pretty sure had a whole bottle of Advil. My headache is coming back. "I got it."

Without warning, he pulls the arm now holding my wallet in hand and drags me up to the counter. "Go ahead. Order anything you want." It almost sounds like a dare. He barely notices my glare as he smirks at the man behind the counter with a *"Chotto matte ne?"* and a side note in Japanese that women sure do like to take their time to order.

I look the McDonald's employee right in the eye. "I want two large fries," I say, deadpan.

"Hai —" the blond guy reels back. "Wait, *what*?!"

"And twenty chicken nuggets."

"... are you fucking serious?"

"Make it happen."

He makes good on his promise. I share my fries with Yoshino as we wait for the others to order their food, but everything is almost gone on the walk back to Kappa Garappa. The guy who bought my food watches me eat with his mouth wide open.

"Cybelle should put a song on first," Yoshino tells Matt. "She has to go soon ..."

McDonald's Man takes his chance to fall in step with me and reach a giant finger to poke my last nugget as I'm about to eat it. I jerk my face away, swallowing it down. If this guy isn't careful, he's going to lose that finger.

"I still can't believe you ate all that food," he shouts. "Where'd you put it all?"

I pretend not to have heard him. Back inside the snack bar, Matt actually lets me have the first song choice. Everyone goes nuts for "Thong Song." The English-speakers all sing along, and the Japanese-speakers wave their arms in unison to the beat. Impressed by my high note, McDonald's Man jumps up and joins me on the mic. There's no point in shaking him off since the song is pretty much over; at least he's not hugging me.

"Girl, you made my night!" He leans in toward me. I wriggle away in the nick of time. I don't do hugs. One of the Japanese salarymen gets up and takes the mic from me, bowing, as the first lines of *"Kiseki"* begin.

"Good song choice, Cyb," Yoshino pats my shoulder. "That was awesome!"

Now's my chance. I murmur against her ear: "Yoshino, I gotta bounce. Are you good here?"

"Yes, I'm good! See you tomorrow — and thanks again! Get home in one piece!" she adds in a whisper.

"No problem! I'm good at getting home!" I give her and what's his name a quick wave and throw a few high-fives to his co-workers' outstretched hands. I'm so glad to be leaving in a good mood this time. Now for part two of my good day: a hot bowl of soup and that Advil I've been pining for.

"Hey!" The blond guy is grabbing my arm again. "Are you leaving?!"

"Uh … I'm going to the washroom," I say, choosing my words carefully.

"You sure? How do I know you're not sneaking off? The night is still young, you know!"

Hmm, how do I get out of this without pulling out a karate

move on this dickbag? "If I was leaving," I begin to smirk, "I wouldn't leave my purse behind, now would I?"

"Huh." He looks me over. No purse in sight. He lets go. "I guess so. You BETTER come back, girl."

"Yeah, whatever." I sneak a glance at Yoshino, who winks back at me, and head to the washroom. It's not a bad idea, going before the long train ride home.

Just as I walk out Kappa Garappa's door, McDonald's Man walks right into me. His face is bright red, his necktie is inches from sliding off his neck, and he stinks. I think he just finished throwing up outside. "And where do you think *you're* going?!" he pretends to pout.

"Yeah, well, I kinda need food and rest to stay alive, so ..."

"Aw, come on," he repeats himself. "You ain't going nowhere. Your night's just getting started."

"It's a free country, pal."

He lets out a barking laugh right in my face. The smell of vomit is strong enough to choke my good mood. "Since when?" he scoffs. "You're not in Kansas anymore, Dorothy. This is Japan, not America!"

He wraps a strong, meaty arm around my waist and begins steering me back inside. That's it. No one gets in my way when it comes to my bed and a hot meal. I swing my arm around and lock it against his so that the slightest twist of my body will pop his arm out of the socket. He laughs for a second, then cries out when I demonstrate that I'm fucking serious.

"And YOU," I emphasize the word with a jerking motion, "are not in a position to tell me what to do, let alone put your freaking paws on me. And I'm *Canadian*, you drunk swot. Maple syrup, poutine, rainbow money, not to be trifled with. Got it?"

"OW! Okay, okay, I'm sorry!"

"I knew we could work this out." I release him. He apologizes again, stumbling away. "You and your friends have a lovely, decadent evening."

"Thanks ... I think?"

Outside, I revel in the salty sea air. "Ha, ha!" I pose in triumph. No one's around to see the wild *gaijin* girl laughing into the night. Not that I feel the least bit self-conscious right now. I'm just hungry.

Adventures befall me on the way to the station. A host falls in step with me. I keep my gaze down on his pointy ostrich-leather boots. *"Ii desu ka? Ikaga desu ka? Ii desu ka?"* he asks me in rapid-fire Japanese, then abruptly turns and walks away. A woman grabs my wrist, asks me to take a photo of her and her family. When I try to take her camera, she self-corrects and pushes me toward her family so that I can take a picture *with* them. She bows and thanks me in what I believe is Thai. On the walk home from the Zozo building with my bike, I can taste autumn on the wind. I can already taste the piping hot bowl of udon waiting for me at home, too. I take a quick look around. No cops. *Chansu.* I swing one leg over my bike and ride like hell, cackling loud as I speed down the street like greased lightning. Like the Wicked Witch of the West. The only time I might look a little past wasted to anyone is when I drop my keys outside my door. I giggle and shush myself. Oh, what a day. I flick on the lights and rip off my smelly clothes.

"All righty," I sigh out loud. "Make some *kitsune* real quick, hop in the shower, and then it's off to bed, young lady! Time to enjoy ..."

I yawn. I'm running out of steam to keep being this weird. I kick my futon to roll it out and flop down. I'll lie here for a few seconds, just to let the giggles run their course.

I'm not sleepy, not really. It's just been such a long day. I'll be fine once I rest my eyes a little and then —

ten

THE OWL AND THE PANTHER

合縁奇縁

Uncanny relationship(s) caused by a quirk of fate

Ah, the familiarities of morning: the screech of an electronic alarm clock, the official toll of the bell to cue the passing of night, the sweet moment of silence as the clock sails through the air, the splintering of plastic against the wall, and the clatter of batteries on the floor. Morning.

The process of getting out of bed, showering, inserting contact lenses, donning a suit, and excavating keys and wallet from a pile of empty chip bags and Pocky boxes are all clockwork. No need for a handbag, for there is nothing else to carry. No umbrella, there are plenty of spare ones at work for emergencies. Breakfast is an egg sandwich and coffee at the McDonald's by the station. Lunch will be a Cup Noodle and a can of Boss Rainbow purchased from the nearby Family Mart. The three bentos for this weekend's dinner can wait until after work. The train is packed, as always, like sardines in a tin can two sizes too small. All of the commuters' heads are bent at the same odd angle and illuminated by smart-phone screens. All but one.

Zaniel gets off the train at his usual stop and heads toward his office building. He finds himself surrounded by several shorter, stockier men who laugh and poke at him as if they are adolescents. He enters the lobby, gets into the cramped elevator, and pretends not to hear the voices berating him in Japanese:

"Well, what are you waiting for, Banana Boy?!"

"Press the button already, *hafu!*"

Other voices chime in. "Twenty-two! Twenty-two!" they jeer in English until Zaniel complies.

The ride up is speedy and the windows provide a near-pan-oramic view of the city as the elevator ascends. Zaniel pretends to enjoy the view, ignoring the jostles and jibes from his hostile co-workers. After several years of living in Japan he is accustomed to this manner of morning greetings, if he receives any morning greeting at all. When the doors slide open, Zaniel walks past the receptionist, who bows and greets the employees stepping off the elevator: *"Ohayou gozaimasu,* Matsubara-*san. Ohayou gozaimasu,* Maruyama-*san. Ohay—"* She stares at Zaniel briefly, then returns to her work.

Someone speeds past Zaniel to catch up with Matsubara and Maruyama and clips him hard with his shoulder. It hurts. *"Doke,* Banana-*kun."* Out of the way, Banana Boy.

Zaniel says nothing. He slogs through a large office with dozens of small cubicles where everyone is busy. They are typing away or barking into phones, or snoring like buzz saws, or sipping tea with very loud, satisfied gasps. The room is abuzz with noise: businesslike propositions and instructions, electronic clicks and dings, hissing gossip, boiling water, and the *ka-chak, ka-chak* of staplers attaching endless amounts of paperwork.

"Attention, everyone," says a voice on an invisible intercom. "Please gather in Room Three for a very important meeting. *Now.*"

The room is void of cubicles now. It is much smaller, and all of Zaniel's co-workers are seated on the floor in a circle. He recognizes faces from the elevator ride — Matsubara-*san*, Maruyama-*san* — glaring at him. There is a woman in the middle of the circle of male co-workers. She, too, sits on her knees to account for her tight skirt. Large sheets of cardstock are perched on her lap. Her back is turned to Zaniel, but he can see when she lifts one of the cards for his co-workers to see.

"This is a pen!" the woman sings. She lifts another card. "This is a ball!" She repeats her actions. "It's a cat! Now you try!"

The men shout in gleeful unison. "This is a pen! This is a ball! It's 'catto'!"

"Good!" The woman puts the last card down and claps her hands as though nothing can please her more. She turns a few degrees to her left and repeats the phrases for the next round of co-workers. Then, she turns to Zaniel and the men sitting in front of him. She gasps. She glares at him. Zaniel does not respond, merely waiting for her to make a move. It takes her a moment to gain her composure again. "This is a pen!" she says shrilly, holding up the first card. Her smile is a clenched row of sharp teeth.

Zaniel shrugs and mouths the words with his co-workers' enthusiastic cries. There is not much he can do. "This is a pen!"

"Good! This is a ball!"

"This is a ball!"

"It's a cat!"

"It's 'catto'!"

"It's a cat," Zaniel mutters at the same time.

The men turn to him with fierce glares. *"Ehhh."* They exchange glances with each other. "Fucking little show-off, just because he's a *hafu* …"

"Hey, Banana Boy!" Matsubara shouts across the room. "Go back to America if your English is so good. We're trying to learn!"

"Machinasai!" Another woman suddenly appears. She is older, bigger than the first, and she is heading straight for Zaniel. She picks him gruffly by the arm. She tells him in a jumble of words that he should be ashamed for showing off. It makes the other students feel bad. Maybe a few minutes of standing out in the hallway to think about his actions will show him the error of his ways. She shouts for the English teacher to resume, closing the door behind him on her words.

Zaniel now finds himself standing in a tiny hallway. He stares at the bright green door with a giant "3" shut against him. He does not recognize it at all. Nor does the orange door beside it look familiar. This is not his office. He follows the hallway around the corner. He almost walks straight into a reception desk in an equally small, empty lobby. More bright colours leap at him off the walls, painted shocking shades of neon orange, yellow, and green patterns. He squints at them: the walls are covered in sheets of paper with animated, unintelligible writing. The words move. He steps back and exhales.

A dream. "I knew it." No wonder his co-workers were taking it easy on him.

Around the corner, a door slams. Someone rushes out and almost walks right into Zaniel. It is the woman with the flash cards. Their eyes meet once again. She lets the flash cards fall at her feet. "I'm dreaming," she shakes her head, talking as if to herself. "I'm dreaming, I'm dreaming, I'm dreaming ..." she chants. Zaniel can still hear her as she speed-walks down another hallway in a huff. He watches her go before he finally decides to take the elevator down and out of the building. He can do as he pleases now, and nothing would please him more than to leave this strange place that reminds him of work.

The elevator doors slide open onto the street, which is devoid of human existence. The air is grey and foggy, though not so dense that Zaniel misses the signs pointing in the direction of the train station. It is close, apparently. Just around the corner of the lone elevator in the middle of the street. Nishibe Station, a sign briefly reads in kanji, 50 m.

"Hmmm," Zaniel frowns at the words as they mutate into squiggly, contorted characters. Strange that he ended up so far from home, and farther still from the mountains. But it does not matter. Getting to familiar territory is easy.

At the station, Zaniel hops over the turnstile in one agile leap and practically flies up the three flights of stairs with single strides. A train is already there, waiting for him. He has his choice of seats, for the train car is completely empty. He feels the jolt of electricity under his feet before he can even choose where to sit. Not that he wants to. He would much rather find Akki and get this dream over with. He walks to the next car. No one is here, either. *This is useless.* Akki is not on this train. Why should he be? If anything, he is waiting for Zaniel at home. But then, would his bracelets not tell him so? Neither one is glowing. Zaniel's eyebrows furrow. Something is wrong with this dream.

He walks to the next car, slides the door open and lets it shut behind him. He closes his eyes and counts to three, trying to calm himself despite the rumbling of train around him. He counts slowly, letting his body sense the solidity of his pillow underneath his head to block out the bouncing sensation of the train and the feel of metal and gears under his feet. He opens his eyes. He is lying on the ground now, trees looming above his prostrate body: in the foreground of a violet sky, there they are. Thousand-year-old oak, majestic redwood, thick reedy bamboo, baby spruce, short fat pine, many others with no names ...

Zaniel closes his eyes, relieved. *Much better. Never thought I'd actually be happy to be back here.*

Someone nearby lets out a sob. Zaniel bolts upright. "Who's there?" he calls out. The crying stops.

"Dream Eater," a high, tiny voice sniffles. "Is that you?"

"Uh ..." It is a voice he does not recognize. *A yokai?* It must be ... but what kind?

"Do not be afraid! Here — follow my voice!"

"I'm, uh, not sure if I want to." Zaniel scrambles to his feet, preparing to run. Dead leaves rustle from behind a nearby tree. A hiccupping sound accompanies it.

"This way."

Damn. Zaniel picks up a fallen twig that looks sharp enough to stab, or at the very least keep any fanged creature at bay. He follows the sniffling sounds to a tall patch of underbrush. Swallowing hard, he moves some of the foliage with one end of his stick.

It is a baby.

No — it is *the* baby. Zaniel recognizes him immediately. The one from his vision, the one in which the Yokai was running around Akki's house. He looks like a typical toddler, sitting as peaceful as a Buddhist statue, except he bears the face of an old, old man. "I know you."

"And I know you, child," says the baby. "You are Akki's. Yes?"

"Yes." Zaniel lowers his stick. "And you're the *Konaki Jiji* that ... that demon rescued the other day."

"Correct, child. I am looking for that very creature. Have you seen her?"

"No. The truth is, I've been wondering where she is myself."

"Hmm." The baby — the *Konaki Jiji* — closes his eyes, nodding. Zaniel half expects him to fall asleep, but his small lips continue to move. "Interesting. Walk with me, child."

Zaniel supresses a groan of reluctance as the baby rolls onto his hands and knees and pushes himself to a standing position. *Well, as long as I don't have to carry him,* Zaniel supposes. He follows the small demon as it toddles through the bush to the ever-familiar winding path of the woods.

"The creature you search for," the *Konaki Jiji* tells him, "is a Dream Eater. A very rare specimen in these parts, but a genuine *yokai* nonetheless. Rumour has it she manipulated and consumed the boar god's home, then ate one of his fattest nightmares, and gained access to Jibun Jishin with its blood. She has been pining for the restaurant ever since. Yes. Akki and the Dream Eater. Their names are now oft-mentioned in the same breath in these woods."

"That's nice and disturbing," Zaniel says in a dry tone.

"Disturbing. Yes. What a pair they would make, would you not say?"

Zaniel stops and looks down at the *Konaki Jiji* with a sharp look. "What do you mean? They'd be enemies ... wouldn't they?"

"Who knows?" The *Konaki Jiji* pauses. "Maybe you," he answers his own question. "Yes. You know the nightmare demon best. He who shuts himself away from most *yokai*, leading a solitary afterlife ... and yet, once upon a time, he made himself available to you and your entreaties for protection. Yes ... you may know better than anyone. But I digress. I search for the Dream Eater to thank and reward her. Are you sure you do not know where to find her?"

"Wish I could help you."

"As do I. In which case, this is where we part."

The *Konaki Jiji* points a chubby finger in the air. Zaniel can see the roof of the old house beyond the trees. "Good luck in your search, child. Should you find that creature before I, please relay my message to her, will you not?"

The *Konaki Jiji* does not wait for a response; instead, he waddles right back into the bush as he speaks, and the sound of his little feet disappear instantly. Zaniel is alone again, left at the invisible border that separates Akki's territory from the rest of the *yokai* domain. He sighs. He feels somewhat disheartened that perhaps the *Konaki Jiji* would have walked with him farther and divulged more information about the Yokai. *Dream Eater*, the demon called her. Zaniel allows himself a small grin. At least now he has a name to give to a face. His grin fades. "Damn," he says aloud. He had no intention of coming this way. Not without a companion for his protector to meet. He turns away from the house and closes his eyes. *Okay ... think ... you still have a bit of time. You've got to find somewhere with a lot of people, and fast.*

He recalls to memory the sounds of the city. It is often said that sometimes, in the World, one can hear the city all the way up in the mountains, past the din of car horns and traffic. He tries to imagine those sounds now. All he hears is the mysterious echo of laughter in the distance. *Tengu-warai*, people call it. Zaniel presses his hands over his ears. Now is not the time to be thinking of *tengu*, and he knows it. It is humans he needs, women. His legs start to wobble with the sensation of jelly. He takes a blind step forward, and feels as if he is moving against water, as if he is on the bottom of the ocean. He is falling, falling forward, in increments of time. *Yes. There.* Now all he has to do is imagine, just a little more, a city — any city — a place where he can find someone ... someone for Akki ... someone suitable, if not perfect.

"Hello," the Yokai says.

"What?" Zaniel looks around, confused, and rightfully so. He is lying in the classroom where his co-workers once sat. They are gone; so is their teacher. Only the Yokai sits here now, on her knees in polite *seiza*, hands on her lap, looking down at him with a hungry grin.

"You," the Yokai lightly taps his nose, "fell asleep."

"I did? No, wait a minute. I saw them. The trees. I was in the woods ..." He trails off. How on earth did he end up back here?

"The woods? You must have been having some dream. Well, come on." The Yokai urges Zaniel to his feet. "Let's go find Mommy and Daddy. I have a party to get to."

"What? Who?"

The Yokai is already pushing him toward the door. "No, wait …
I need to talk to you." Zaniel's mind reels. He does not know where
to even begin.

Just before they reach the door he feels the cold sensation of
pain snaking from his wrists up along his arms. His black bracelet
burns with cold light, his red bracelet with a sharp heat. *They're
both glowing again … but why?* He closes his eyes. If he concentrates hard enough, he will return to the forest. Akki must already
be there. But the Yokai is *here*. If he goes, what will happen to her?
"Please, listen to me. I need to —"

A door opens. "There you are, sweetie!" a woman's voice cries,
along with the high-pitched chirping of what must be a dozen
other mothers. He feels the Yokai's hands slip from his shoulders.
Then his head is submerged in a sea of fingers running along his
face and neck.

"Oh, isn't he adorable! How old must you be, eighteen, nine-
teen months?"

"Looks about 323 months if I'm not mistaken!"

"How CUTE!"

"Ew! Stop!" Zaniel refuses to open his eyes, but that does not
stop him from swinging his hands around to combat the searching
fingers that now pinch his arms and cheeks. He is surrounded, and
he knows it. He feels the swarming hands wriggle down his arms
like long-legged spiders.

That's it … spiders.

Zaniel's eyes fly open. He throws up his arms, exposing his
bracelets. The light from them is blinding. "Get off me!"

"Oops. Sorry, kid. Yeesh. Must have been some dream *you*
were having. Get off him, ladies, that's Akki's kid."

A collective "aw" rings in Zaniel's ears as dozens of spiders
scuttle down his body and off in different directions. A heavy
appendage lands on his shoulder. Zaniel looks up into the feverish-
orange eyes of a *Tsuchigumo*, a spider in every sense of the word

except for it being the size of a horse. "Again, sorry there, kid. Don't hold it against 'em, eh? Please don't tell your boss. I'm not in the mood to deal with him."

The spider lumbers off, down a dark hall, still scolding his scores of minions. Zaniel looks around him. He is not in the forest anymore. The room in which he stands is vast, dark, and hectic with *yokai*. Something tugs at the cuff of his pants. "You looking for your friend, kid?" Zaniel locates the voice to a Brazilian spider, not nearly as large as the *Tsuchigumo* but still about the size of his foot. "Check that way." The spider extends a leg past Zaniel and scampers away.

"But I don't have any —" Zaniel sighs — *friends*, he finishes to himself. He takes stock of his new surroundings. There are dim lights that allow him to see tables arranged around the room. Scores of *yokai* sit around him, shouting and singing to each other as they shovel heaps of food into their mouths while human-looking women in feathers and glitter dance among the tables. Somewhere a samba band plays a loud rhythm that makes everyone gyrate in their chairs. Zaniel stumbles past several fountains oozing hot liquid cheese and frothing chocolate, toward the centre of the room. He can make out a dais where a large gathering of *tanuki* play upon various instruments. Someone pushes past him and apologizes — a conga line of dark-green demons with spiky fringes, beaks, and scissor-like hands, waving sheaths of hair to and fro over their heads to the beat of the music. Everything is reminiscent of Jibun Jishin; however, this is undoubtedly not Jibun Jishin. "What is all this?"

"Hey, kid! You sumo?"

He feels another tug at his pant leg. A *Kappa* is there, pinching the fabric with a gleeful look in its shining, wet eyes. "Oh. You Akki's boy."

"Yeah," Zaniel says, still looking about the room. "But I'm looking for someone."

"Ah, you looking. Sumo with me, win against me, and maybe I'll tell you." The *Kappa* grins its sharp fangs up at him.

Zaniel's wrists burn. *I don't have time for this.* He turns and bows low as he dares to the *Kappa*. When the *Kappa* bows in return, the water from its dish-like head drips onto the floor, then spills entirely. The *Kappa* lets out a scream. "My WATER!" it cries woefully.

Zaniel leaves the small demon to its efforts to scoop the water back into himself. *She must be around here somewhere.* Somewhere among the mechanical stuffed toys playing *Karuta* at one table, and the *shamisen* demons playing themselves at another, strumming the strings taut across their faces as they jam to the music. A few *yokai* regard Zaniel as he passes: "The *rounin*'s assistant," they call him, wondering what he is doing here alone, but are too busy enjoying the music to pay him much attention. Over the sound of the samba beats, he hears a crow of voices:

"Takenoko takenoko nyoki ki!"

Zaniel wades through the array of round tables spread about the room, letting his eyes gloss over the multitude of strange faces. Then, he sees her. The Yokai, smiling. Arms in the air like a bamboo shoot sprouting out of the earth, sitting between a white rabbit and a grey mouse making the same gestures. A corpulent badger across from her shouts something that makes everyone at the table all scream and jeer. The badger gives a happy shrug, picks up the bottle marked "焼酎" before it and takes several gulps. *"Nonde, nonde, nonde!"* the creatures at the table chant until the badger can drink no more. Zaniel curbs around the bystanders watching the game around the table, approaching the Yokai's side. The badger slams the bottle down on the table, dribbling alcohol from the corners of its mouth. The demons applaud, and the drinking game begins anew.

"Takenoko takenoko nyoki ki!"

"*Ichi!*" says the rabbit, hoisting its paws into the air.

"*Ni!*" the mouse squeaks.

"*Sssan?*" a giant serpent raises its tail, unsure.

"*SHI,*" says the Yokai in a playfully malevolent voice. Everyone titters.

"*Go!*" cry a black bear and a deer together.

"OH," everyone points at them. The bear and the deer each take a drink.

"Hello again," the Yokai looks up at Zaniel. "Want to play?"

"He can't play with us," the rabbit puts simply.

"Aw, don't be like that," the Yokai chides. "Sit down, honey."

Zaniel blushes at the pet name. "Thank you, but I'll just watch." *One more round*, he decides as he takes the seat next to her, the pain in his wrists subsiding with the glow of his bracelets.

"*Takenoko takenoko nyoki ki!*"

The demons watch each other with sharp, eager eyes. Some giggle, some keep their faces and features stern. "*Ichi,*" booms the bear, firing its arms into the air.

"*Ni,*" the mouse squeaks, doing the same.

The Yokai and a dog with a human face make the gesture at the same time. "*San!*" they shout.

"OH!" everyone points at them both. The Yokai throws her head back, laughing, as the human-faced dog hands her the *shochu* bottle with a grandiose gesture. She takes a pull, to the delight of everyone at the table, and hands it back to the dog.

"Ugh!" he says. "That's it. No more for me. I'm drunk."

The Yokai fakes a gasp. "Are you bowing out? That's not like you."

"You're nuts, girl. This *shochu* is hard stuff! I still don't get how you can keep knocking it back. Tastes like *tanuki* piss."

"Hey!" someone shouts from the dais. "If I'd pissed in that bottle, *Jinmenken-san*, you'd know it!" Everyone laughs.

"Waiter!" the Yokai raises a hand. Something shorter than the table whom Zaniel cannot see comes bobbing through the surrounding crowd. "Got any *umeshu*? Some of us can't feel our taste buds anymore."

"One bottle of *umeshu* for the honoured guests, coming up!" A pair of gremlin-like fingers rise above the table and snap. In a *poof* of smoke, a giant cask appears on the table.

The rabbit and mouse dive at it, but the Yokai is faster. She snatches it. "Now, now, children. Behave yourselves. Everyone will get a turn. *Tanuki-san, Shika-san*, put the *shochu* down before you spill it, please. You know what happens when you fight over things. Thank you."

They play another round, counting all the way to a suspenseful *"roku"* before the Yokai and the old tortoise three seats over shout *"nana"* at the same time, and in so doing, lose.

"Well, that was interesting," Zaniel forces a grin. He inches his chair closer to the Yokai. This is his chance. "Um, can we talk somewhere? Just for a minute? There's something I want to ask you."

"You sure you don't want to play?"

"He *can't*," the rabbit insists.

"Takenoko takenoko nyoki ki!" the others sing.

"Ichi!" the Yokai shouts, distracted.

"Ichi!" the deer shouts a second after.

"OH!" Everyone at the table throws up their arms and points at the deer. "You lose!"

Zaniel hears a loud gurgling sound. "Is anyone else hungry?" the Yokai inquires. "Where's the waiter? Can we get some food?"

"No food!" the animals shout. "We finish the *umeshu* first!"

"Aw," the Yokai folds her arms and pouts. "Sorry, what were you saying?"

Zaniel clears his throat. "I was just saying —"

"Ooh," the deer bats its long eyelashes at him. "Is this a *private* conversation? Can I join, too?"

"No," Zaniel says.

"Hey, wait a minute," the mouse points at the Yokai. "Is it just me, or have you gotten bigger?"

"Maybe," she replies. "So? What of it? And isn't everything big to you?"

"Good point. Hmm, too much *umeshu*, maybe. How about we switch it up?"

The human-faced dog kisses its teeth. "You just don't want to get the runs, *Nezumi-san*."

"Well, yes, that's true. But come on, who does?"

"Touché."

"*Takenoko takenoko nyoki ki!*" the serpent and badger sing.

The Yokai joins in on the game. *Damn it*, Zaniel swears to himself. *This is harder than he thought it would be. He gets an idea. Okay. Plan B.*

The chaos continues. The band takes a pause to *yokai* applause, and the *tanuki* conductor cues up another round of music, louder and twice as fast as the previous song. The *kamikiri* resume their conga line with swaying arms and kicking feet. On the other side of the vast room, a door kicks open. Light breaks through the mild darkness. Many creatures remain oblivious to the entrance of another *yokai*, but the ones closest to the door shield their eyes and hiss. In the doorway stands a giant in a black house robe, his thick hair loose around his shoulders. He rubs the sleep out of his eyes. "The fuck are y'all doin' here?"

"Akki-*san*!" A flock of *kappa* run to him. "Hino — where?" they chitter.

"How should I know?" he snaps. "We ain't joined at the fuckin' hip. What are you *doin'* here? What the hell is all this?" He raises a beefy hand before the *kappa* can answer. "Wait. I smell human." He storms off to the middle of the room, straight for the Yokai's table. The scent of human blood mingles with fresh peach as he gets closer. *It's the boy ...* and something else that he cannot put his finger on. Something just as delicious. Savoury, though. Not as sweet. But still tasty ... familiar.

Aha.

Akki sees the long dark hair and pale skin in the distance, the shocking contrast of Zaniel's grey eyes against them both. The boy is sticking out his tongue for the demons' amusement; they marvel as he touches the tip of his chin with it. They applaud when he rolls it in the middle. It seems they have never seen a human perform such tricks. They hold one another in gleeful horror when he puts his hands together and separates his thumb at the joint and beg him to do it again and again.

What the fuck is he doin'?

"I still don't understand!" The mouse darts back and forth across the table, examining Zaniel's outstretched fingers. "All the joints are still intact! What human trickery is this?"

The Yokai waves a finger. "If you keep analyzing how things are possible, *Nezumi-san*, your hair will turn grey ... or greyer." She winks at Zaniel, a signal of a promise to keep his secret.

"Fassscinating," says the serpent. "I don't remember humans being so versatile. You've taught us a great deal, er ... Akki's boy."

Zaniel bows. "You can just call me Zaniel. That's my name."

"Zaniel ..." the *yokai* repeat in chorus.

"Wait, I know that name ..." the Yokai says, making Zaniel blush.

The bear leans over to her. "I didn't even know he *had* a name!"

"Me, neither!" says the deer.

The badger burps. "You know, Akki's bo— er, Zaniel — for a human, you're all right."

Zaniel turns to the Yokai. "Okay, now it's your turn. What's your hidden talent?" He is about to extend a hand to her when he notices the table is trembling. He turns and sees a haze of green *yokai* energy barrelling through the crowd. He freezes. "Akki! ... *sama* ... what are you doing here?"

Chest heaving with puffs of anger, the giant manlike creature gives Zaniel a bewildered look. "I LIVE HERE."

Half the demons at the table flee, looking about the room for an exit as they realize that yes, this house does have a boar-like smell, and they must be in the wrong place. A few of them even give Zaniel an apologetic nod as they depart. *Sorry, kid; you're on your own.*

"What are *you* doin' here?" Akki demands. "Where's my woman at?"

"Uh ..." Zaniel gulps, at a loss for words.

The Yokai takes a polite sip from the *umeshu* bottle. "We were playing a game."

"Oh." Akki sniffs. That strange scent is stronger on this side of the room. "Can I play, too?"

Another fraction of the demons at the table also get up, saying something about how late it is getting and that they ought to get home before the wife gets upset. The Yokai, now sensing that something is off, tries to follow suit and get up from her seat, but Akki's sharp voice stops her in her tracks. "Hold on. I know you. You're that chick those squids were tryin' to kill."

"Uh ... who?"

"*You* know. You're that — say, what are you supposed to be, anyway?"

The Yokai ponders the question. "Well ... I'm supposed to be a lot of things, I guess. I don't really know where you'd like me to start —"

"Never mind." Akki approaches Zaniel's chair. "Well, boy? Where's my woman?"

"Uh, well ..."

"Time's up, you know that, right?"

"Well ... yes ... but I ..."

"And that last chick sucked. Why'd you leave her outside, anyway? What I tell you 'bout gettin' creative?"

"That wasn't … I …"

The Yokai's eyes light up. "Yes! Food's here!"

Akki and Zaniel turn their attention back to her. She now has a giant bowl of floating soup in front of her, jacked with thick udon noodles, fluorescent pink slices of fish cake, and a glowing *aburage* in the form of an oddly shaped sphere. Several *yokai* stop and stare as the Yokai, without hesitation or empathy, plucks the sphere from the bowl with her bare fingers. "Help me, Akki *nii-chan!*" it cries before it disappears behind the Yokai's suckling lips. The *yokai* watching her gasp. Those that were still lingering at the table hopeful for another round of their game get up and leave, muttering something about having to be somewhere important. Even Zaniel stares, shocked.

A *"dream eater."* The Konaki Jiji *was right.*

"So. The rumours are true, then." Akki straightens up, his voice disturbingly quiet and smooth. "We have a *baku* in our midst."

"Name-calling will get you nowhere," the Yokai folds her arms, equally cool. "But if you're going to get weird, fine. You can have it." She pushes the bowl of soup toward him and leans back in her chair. "I'm waiting for the garlic sirloin, anyway."

"Garlic sirloin for the honoured guest, coming up!" The well-timed waiter bobs behind the table and snaps its fingers in the air. In a poof of smoke appears a handsome man with an olive complexion holding a sword slathered in meat. He winks at the Yokai as he slices steaming portions onto a massive plate that has also appeared out of nowhere. It is piled with slices of cranberry coconut bread, salads of corn and beans, and cassava frites. The man bows and disappears in another cloud of smoke.

Akki is too stunned to unleash his usual ball of fiery rage upon the creature tucking into a plate of what looks absolutely delicious. Probably for the best, considering what she did to those squids. He takes another look around at the varieties of *yokai* cavorting and capering about, all blissfully unaware he is in the room with them. He cannot even place what room this is within his own house. Who could have brought them all here and changed everything, right under his nose as he slept down the hall? He turns back to the Yokai.

"Wait a minute. It's you. The one who's been changin' up my house!"

"*Your* house?" The Yokai swallows a mouthful of steak. "What are you talking about?"

The *yokai* at a nearby table who are too intoxicated to recognize Akki laugh. "Your house ... yeah, right. We would know if this was someone's house!" Zaniel, too, cannot help feeling puzzled. He, too, would know ... would he not?

"It *is* you. Say, what's the big idea?! You've got some kinda beef with Akki?!"

"How could I? I don't even *know* Akki."

Another wave of laughter erupts from the nearby *yokai*. "Akki! The boar god with a bad case of mortal worship? Okay, we'd *definitely know* if we were in that scummy scumbag's house!"

Akki ignores them all and eyes the Yokai, suspicious. Then, without warning, he stoops down and takes a deep inhalation through his nostrils, right up against her neck. She recoils and leaps out of her chair, which only seems to entertain him more.

"Bwa ha ha, so that's where that smell's been comin' from! I know that scent ..." He wafts the air and grins. "It's human! Not sure why it smells so ... sweet, but it's definitely part human! Zaniel! Way to think outside the box, kid!"

"What? Part human?" Zaniel repeats. *Like a half-yokai?* "But ... that's impossible. She can't be —"

"Well, she's gotta be. Unless there's another human-lookin' *yokai* runnin' around eatin' nightmares. Oh, my. You *have* been searchin' high and low, haven't you? Well done, boy, well done!" He ruffles the young man's hair. "I take back all the nasty things I said about you. You haven't lost your touch after all!" Akki clears his throat, straightens up a little, and smooths any potential wrinkles in his *yukata*. He would have preferred a little warning, a little more time to look more presentable and tone down his fiery aura, but since it is another *yokai* he hopes it will not matter.

"Akki-*sama*, wait, I ..."

"What? This *is* the girl you brought me to meet, isn't it?"

"Well, no ..." Zaniel's cheeks flush as he smooths his hair. "You see, I didn't bring her here at all. I think she brought *me*."

Akki bursts out laughing. "That's fuckin' impossible, boy. Come on, now. I thought you were smarter than that."

"No. It makes sense, because the bracelets ..."

Akki sniffs at the young man's wrists. Indeed, Zaniel's bracelets have been activated recently. He puts his hands on his hips. "Oh, ho ho ... I see what's goin' on here." He gives the Yokai a nod of admiration. "Listen, babe, if you wanted to meet me so bad, all you had to do was ask. The kid would've brought you straight to me. There's no need to show off. You got my attention, and you've earned my respect; let's do it. Gotta warn you, I've never done it with a half-human before, but I'm sure I can figure it out. I mean, really, how hard can it be?"

"What?!" The Yokai recoils at Akki's extended hand. "Ew, no! I'm not 'doing' *anything* with you, you reprobate. Get away from me."

The *yokai* around him cannot help laughing and cheering her on. "Ha, ha! That's telling him! Take *that,* boar god. No *yokai* in their right mind wants to sleep with *you!*" A passing octopus reaches out for a congratulatory high-eight. Zaniel suppresses his relieved smile, but his stomach drops at the look of embarrassment on Akki's face. He does not know what to say or do.

Akki's lower lip trembles. "Then ... why are you here?"

The Yokai gestures to the room. "Duh. I'm here to eat."

Akki glowers at her. "Okay, fuckin' with the house is one thing, eatin' my nightmares is another, but now you invitin' all this riff-raff with you, messin' with *my human,* and turnin' ME down?! I don't think so, bitch. Time for you to go. You and everybody else. Don't know how y'all got up in here in the first place. Go on, shoo." He flits at the flesh-coloured blobs dancing in his path and reaches over to grab the Yokai.

"Let go of me!" she wriggles out from his grip. "Where do you think you are, the 1800s?!"

"Ha! I fuckin' WISH."

He lunges at her again. She sidesteps him, looking to Zaniel with angry black eyes. "What is this guy's deal?"

"Yeah, Zaniel-*kun,* what's my deal?" Akki says in a high-pitched voice, a mockingly feminine whine. "What could I *possibly* be so pissed off about? I mean, it's not like anyone's been fuckin' with my territory and *then* tellin' me it was all for nothin'!"

"Akki-*sama* …"

"Tell her, Zaniel. Tell her who she's dealin' with … Unless there's somethin' you ain't tellin' me."

Zaniel's face turns red.

"Oh, shit. Don't tell me you're *into* this thing." Akki smirks, recalling Hino's words. "So … you *are.*"

Zaniel's eyes dart back and forth between the two demons. He is being forced to choose. It has been years since he felt this afraid. Nor does he know which frightens him more: Akki's wrath or the notion of life without that wrath to protect him. In all the years he has traversed this realm there was never a choice between Akki and another demon. Akki has always been his protector, and, over time, has slowly become his master. It did not occur to Zaniel when he first decided to approach the Yokai that he would have to do so in Akki's presence. This is not how he had planned things to go. A part of him prays to wake up from this nightmare, but the rest knows he cannot, not without consequence.

"I …" he repeats dumbly. He looks to the Yokai and, seeing her, forgets all the words he considered using to placate Akki.

She is now well over six feet tall.

"I think you've worn out your welcome," the Yokai says firmly.

"Ha," says Akki. There is no humour in his laugh this time. "Who do you think you are, growin' like that and talkin' 'bout who's welcome? You're in *my* house. And don't even *think* of tryin' to take the kid with ya; he's mine. Everybody knows that. Don't know what you want him for, anyway." He folds his arms. Perhaps, he thinks, he can sway her mind. "He ain't gonna do nothin' for you; what could you possibly want with him? He's a spineless pissant of a human who can't walk the streets without *me* to take care of him."

"Now that's *quite* a thing to say —" The Yokai begins, but the giant demon cuts her off with a pointed finger.

"And YOU." Akki points at Zaniel, who cannot bring himself to look anyone in the eye. "Who you think you are, developin' FEELINGS and shit? You wanna go back to bein' chased down by bloodthirsty *yokai* every time you close your eyes? 'Cause we can go back to that anytime you want. Until then, you do as I say and nobody gets hurt. Not you, not any of these ... *intruders* ... and not your *girl*, if that's what you wanna call her."

"Hey!" the Yokai glares.

"Fine, your 'Dream Eater,' *whatever*." Akki rolls his eyes. "You're the one with the crappy human disguise. Now, come on."

The Yokai clenches her fists. "Ugh, enough!" She growls. "Everyone's always telling me to 'come on' around here. Why can't I just stay in one place and *eat* something, for once?!"

Akki is out of patience. "Shut up, bi—"

"Oh, YOU shut up. I'm finally somewhere I want to be and I'm staying." The Yokai steps closer to Zaniel, standing beside him defensively. "And so is he."

"Very funny."

Akki reaches clean over Zaniel's head to grab the Yokai's shoulder. She shakes him off. He reaches for her again, but she sidesteps him. Stumbling, the Yokai recoils from the giant *yokai* as he takes slow, deliberate steps toward her. Zaniel watches helplessly as she backs into the empty tables behind her. Then everything happens all at once, in a blur of arms and legs: the Yokai's elongating limbs get caught in a chair, and as she tumbles to the floor, the drunken conga line of *kamikiri* draws near. The dancing *yokai* swerve behind Akki, oblivious to his presence until the Yokai accidentally kicks him into the conga line. A pair of hairy limbs latch onto Akki's hips and sweep him away to the rhythm of samba drums.

Zaniel hurries over to the fallen Yokai and helps her up. She is heavy and must be at least eight feet tall. "Hey. You *are* getting bigger."

The Yokai looks down at herself. "I can't help it!" is her ultimate reply.

"Zaniel!" Akki shouts from somewhere in the room. "Get over here — *now*! Get off me, you fuckin' freaks!" The room erupts into chaos as the *kamikiri* disperse.

"Oh no! The boar god is here!"

"Run!"

Yokai scatter left, right, up, and down to get away. The *tanuki* band on the dais drop their instruments at the word "boar," creating one final percussive chord, and take to the air, using their testicles as hot air balloons to make a lofty getaway. The mechanical stuffed toys throw their cards, sending them flying in the air, blinding the *shamisens*, who overturn tables and run into one another in the commotion. The *kappa*, confused but not ones to be left out, give up their sumo wrestling and skip around the room to add to the chaos. Zaniel does not let any of this faze him. He runs straight through the crowd, pulling the Yokai's sleeved arm behind him. His shoulder is clipped by a large *nuri-kabe*, a strong cuboid-like creature that plows through the crowd, straight into the dark wall at one end of the room, and crashes through it, exposing the blinding skyline, streaked red with the imminent sunrise. All the other creatures use this hole as their escape, taking running leaps, except for the *tanuki*, who glide out and let the gentle wind carry them to whatever relative safety lies nearby. One of the mechanical toys stops to turn around and bid the Yokai farewell. "*An*-punch! *An*-kick! *Mata ne!*" he waves, and leaps through the hole.

Wrenching herself away, the Yokai runs for the gaping hole. "Well?" she yells at Zaniel.

Zaniel approaches the hole, cautious and scared. "Is it morning already?" is all he can think to say to her. He feels that he only just got here.

"Who cares? Let's get out of here!"

Before he can fathom a more rational response, Zaniel is jerked backward by the scruff of his shirt. "Oh, no you don't," a deep voice growls in his ear. Spun off his feet, his body is whirled around. He now faces Akki up-close, but Akki is not talking to him. "He's not goin' anywhere with you," he says to the Yokai. "He stays right the fuck here, and he's gonna explain himself."

The Yokai does not respond, but Zaniel feels when she grabs his free hand and pulls. He is now caught in a tug-of-war: the Yokai has his arm, Akki has his shirt. He feels like he is going to be pulled apart between them. "Let go!" Zaniel shouts. Without thinking, Akki complies. Something about the shock of the volume of his voice, perhaps, makes the giant demon relinquish his grip. It is all the Yokai needs to win the battle.

"Heh." Akki glares at the two of them, standing together. "Okay, chickie. So you've won. What're *you* gonna do now? Eat him in front of me? I dare you."

"Didn't your friend tell you? We're going on a trip. See you next fall."

"Next fall? I don't get it." Akki searches the ceiling for meaning. Did he hear that right? Are they going away for a year? Is he missing something? Then he notices the angle of their bodies and the sensation of mountain winds against his cheek. Akki lunges forward to grab Zaniel's jacket again, or the Yokai's arm — but he is a split second too late. Akki watches in paralyzed shock as the two hurtle to the ground, a skyscraper's distance away.

Zaniel screams for dear life. He can feel the air being sucked out of his lungs as the wind rips past his ears. He can only manage one good yell before the adrenalin chokes his throat. "What the hell is wrong with you?!"

"We got out of there, didn't we?! Hang on, don't let go of me!"

"What?!"

What Zaniel sees when he tilts his head in the direction of their descent kills any further screams that might be brewing in his chest. A pool of water swells up from the earth underneath them like someone has dug deep enough to hit a spring. The water rises fast. In seconds, waves lap up against the walls of the house, drowning it.

A moat?

"Deep breath!"

They hit the water, cold as the Arctic. Zaniel's vision blurs with blue and foam. He holds his breath, but the surge of panic is too great. Just as he gasps for air, he feels fingers scratching at his chest, grabbing him by his shirt, and pulling him above the water's surface. The Yokai is choking on lake, too. They swim to the water's edge and take turns dragging one another up the wet, muddy banks.

"Whoo!" The Yokai collapses onto her side, her robe streaked with mud. "That was an adventure. Never again."

"'We got out of there, didn't we?'" Zaniel teases between coughs. "Wait — what am I saying?!" The lack of oxygen in his brain must be causing some kind of delirium. He is in trouble. They both are.

"ZANIEL."

The sound of his name echoes like thunder. He wipes the sting of out his eyes and looks up; the sky is growing dark again but Zaniel would recognize those two nocturnal glowing eyes from any distance. He looks back down at the Yokai, wet and shivering. There is no going back to Akki now. He takes her by the arm. "He's faster than he looks. Let's get the hell out of here."

"You don't have to tell me twice."

Helpless, Akki watches them as they take off into the dark, two little shapes heading for the woods. He is fast but will never catch up with them in time. Akki takes his time heading back downstairs and out his front door, his feet drag with every step. This time he does not bother looking back to verify the state of his house. He can feel everything revert to normal. The short, simple flight of stairs, the simple, narrow hallways, the *shouji* doors — they have all returned. The house is his own again.

Hino is in the garden playing tug-of-war with a *kappa* over a slice of cucumber. The poor creature goes flying through the trees when Hino absent-mindedly loosens her grip, awestruck by a look she has never seen on Akki's face. "What happened to you?" she inquires. "And were you having some kind of party or something? It was like watching a clown car, the number of creatures coming out of your house … And where did this moat come from?"

"Hino," he plunks down on the bench next to her, "tell more about that 'fatuation' you spoke of. 'Cause you won't believe what just happened."

Meanwhile, Zaniel and the Yokai do not stop running. Despite the water that drenches and weighs down their clothes, they slog through the mist-laden woods, pulling one another when one starts to lag behind, until they reach the cliff, where one world seems to end and another begins. The clouds at the cliff face are bleached pink with the arrival of morning sun, but the peaceful scene does not calm either of them. Zaniel collapses to his knees, clutching his chest.

"You owe me some answers," he gasps. "Who are you?"

"I'm someone who's just been to the *stupidest* party she's ever been to." She wrings out the hem of her robe. "And what do you mean, I owe you some answers?!"

"I just ran away from the scariest creature in these woods. Don't you understand? I can't go back to him. He'll never take me back, now. I'm …" Zaniel pauses. "I'm free. I'm free of him." He whirls around, searching high and low. The Yokai watches him looking for someone that is not there. He is not being pursued. His bracelets do not glow. It is as though nothing happened at all. He is just a man, standing alone at the edge of the cliff. He lets out a sharp breath that could be a brief laugh. Even the *yokai* did not harass him. In fact … they had *liked* him. Especially when he did all those tricks. "You," he whispers to the Yokai. "You … you saved me. Again. But from *him*."

The Yokai's brows furrow. "Him who?"

"I have to know what you are." Zaniel points an accusatory finger at her. "You have to tell me."

The Yokai peers at him. "You have nice eyes."

"Thank you. Now tell me. Please."

"That dude — the giant one — called me 'Dream Eater.'" Her voice is soft, dreamy. She yawns. "But I don't know what he meant. I just eat whatever tastes good …"

He sets his hands on her shoulders. Piercing silver glares back at him in the reflection of the Yokai's dark eyes. "Please. Tell me what you are. Are you a *baku*? Can you really eat his nightmares?" As he speaks, he realizes his questions are rhetorical. He already knows the answers.

"I don't understand a word of what you're saying." The Yokai shakes her head slowly. "What's a *baku*? And what nightmares? What are we talking about here?"

Zaniel wanders off again. He is still searching the woods, expecting Akki to pounce at him from the shadows, from behind a tree, descend from the blood-red sky above.

"You don't get it," he mutters. He runs nervous hands through his longish hair. "If you're not what they say you are ... we're dead." It will only be a matter of time before Akki catches up with them, and then what? Perhaps he can feign ignorance, placate to what little benevolence the demon possessed, the benevolence that spurred him to look after Zaniel for all these years. After all, Zaniel is a mere human. He is in no position to challenge the *yokai* that may come at him; that is what Akki's protection is and has always been for. No. It is too late for any of that.

"What they say I am? Who's 'they'? You say weird things." She pulls the hood of her kimono over her head. "And all I did was get us out of there. It's not like anyone else was going to come to the rescue."

The direness of the situation grows heavier and heavier in Zaniel's heart. He understands now, why she did it. *She thought she was rescuing me. Why did she do that? What made her think she could?*

"I guess the party wasn't *that* bad," the Yokai says now to cut the awkward silence. "It just wasn't the same as the other place."

Zaniel thinks. "You mean Jibun Jishin?"

"Yeah. They had everything I could possibly think of. Now *that* place was a dream come true." She looks away, shy. "Kinda like you."

The answer hits Zaniel like lightning. It is simple. There was never a moment she thought she could not do that. She had not stopped to think about it because there is nothing for her to contemplate. No consequences to weigh in her mind. This is a dream. It is all a dream to her. None of it is real for her. She was going through the motions of someone dreaming impossible things. What would any normal person do in her place?

"Too cheesy? Yeah, sorry. I'm not really good at ... Dude, why are you looking at me like that?"

Zaniel is gaping at her. *That's it. A normal person.* His mind races to the past. Akki had said something along those lines himself. He had smelled her. *Human-looking* ... Perhaps he was not far off. After all, she had grabbed that nightmare from the bowl with her bare hands and — and *eaten* it.

A human-looking yokai. There is only one way to be sure of any of this.

He walks back over to the Yokai and kisses her.

A dream within a dream in which a dark room awaits. It would be pitch-black were it not for the large patch of sunlight inching its way in through the hole in one wall. Most of the tables in the room are flipped over, chairs thrown helter-skelter here and there. One table remains upright, its top covered in empty dishes, bottles, and casks. And somewhere in the disorder of it all, the bowl of *kitsune* udon the Yokai left uneaten, save for the one tofu pocket nightmare she managed to gulp down.

That is her singular desire.

I can read her. She is *part human.*

He pulls away but keeps his hands pressed against her hooded face. "Wake up. Do you understand me? You're dreaming. You need to *wake up.*"

The Yokai opens her eyes. Fear glosses over her face. Then a slow, steady smile spreads across her lips. She laughs. "What are you, an alarm clock? We're fine. I don't think that dude is coming back. And get your hands off my face, they're freezing."

She gently pulls at his hands. Her skin is warmer than anything he has ever felt. He can feel himself seeping into another dream, so he wrenches his hands away. The Yokai steps back, startled. "Geez, you *are* scared. It's okay. I'm not going to let anything happen to you."

"You don't have that choice, here." Zaniel stares at her, hard. He must make her understand, somehow. "You have to listen to me. For *once.* I want you to focus. Focus on what I'm telling you, now."

"Ugh. Fine. Okay."

"Close your eyes." He does his best to keep his voice steady when she obeys. The fear inside him makes his body tremble, or perhaps it is the cold chill of the lake water pooling at their feet. "Now, feel around yourself. No, don't move your hands. *Feel* where you are. Your bed. Your pillow. The horizontality of your body. You can feel it all, can't you?"

"I do feel something."

"Then you know what I'm telling you is true. You're asleep. You're dreaming, right now. And if you don't wake up, that man you just saved me from will come and get you. We need to wake up before that happens."

The Yokai inhales, her eyes still closed. She taps her bare feet in her own little puddle of water, her head bobs from side to side. "Wait. I hear something, too. Don't you?"

"What?" Zaniel whips around, his eyes searching the trees, the sky. Nothing but sunshine and peace all around. "What do you hear?"

The Yokai's eyes squeeze closed tighter and tighter. "'If you don't wake up now, you'll be late.'"

"Huh?"

"There! You hear that? It's singing to me. You don't hear it? 'If you don't wake up now, you'll be late. If you don't wake up now, you'll be late ...'"

Zaniel's heart quickens. He *can* hear it. Ringing through the air like birds calling to one another from the trees. It starts quietly at first, a gentle, almost mechanical chirp that picks up in tempo and volume. It reaches a shriek so loud that Zaniel has to press his hands over his ears. He cowers on the ground as the Yokai stands over him, eyes closed and lips curved upward as if she is wading in serenity itself. She sings along, repeating the words over and over again until her voice and the noise are one and the same source.

"If you don't wake up now, if you don't wake up now, if you don't wake up now ..."

"Wait! Who are you? What do you call yourself? You have to tell me! Please!"

"If you don't wake up now, if you don't wake up now, if you don't wake up now ..."

There is nothing for it. Zaniel leaps up and wraps his arms around the Yokai, who is still singing, and squeezes his eyes shut. He does everything in his power to steel his mind against the sounds drowning out his own thoughts. He can still escape this forest, this world, Akki's impending wrath ... he just needs to concentrate. He himself needs to wake up.

But not before he knows who she is.

"Ima okinai — Ima okinai — Ima okinai —"

I open my eyes, warm and snuggly in my futon. The first thing I notice is my alarm clock, which I must have snatched up in my sleep, held tight in my own kung fu grip. It's singing its little phrase, and the screen flashes a number: 8:57.

8:57.

8:57.

I have to be at Zozo in three minutes. No — I should be at Zozo *right now.*

"Son of a —!"

I get dressed, chew three Mentos from my purse, and bike faster than ever before. My stomach growls angrily as I chain my bike — I *think* I've chained my bike — shit. I make a mental note to double-check as soon as these trial students leave. If I don't get fired before then.

I run into the building and catch the elevator just before it closes, scaring the daylights out of some sour-looking *obaachan* who can't decide whether to get on or not. *"Hrrngh … gaijin, kuso —"* The doors shut on her cursing. Whatever. She looked familiar but I'm too freaked out to worry about it. She isn't a Zozo client; that's all that matters.

It's been a while since I've been this pissed off with myself. How the hell did I sleep through my alarm clock? More than that, how did I manage to grab it in my sleep and not wake up from it at all? I only have a few seconds in the elevator to dab the sweat from my forehead with my sleeve and pray my makeup isn't running all over my shirt. Droplets continue to stream down my face. I must look awful. My lungs still burn when the doors open. I prepare to apologize on all fours … with Bucho around, it's what I have to do in this kind of situation, right?

The lights are on, but the lobby is empty. No parents, no children, not even a staff member at the reception desk. For a brief second, I wonder if Zozo is open. "Uh … hello?" I call out, taking off my shoes. *"Sumimasen? Anybody home?"*

I hear *"Ah, shibaraku omachi itadakemasu ka?"* then Manager sticks his head out of the staff room door. "Eh?!" His eyes are wide, like he wasn't expecting me. "Oh! Cybelle? Why so early?"

"My trial lesson," I try not to pant. "Manager, I'm so sorry. My alarm clock … I don't know what happened …"

Manager gives me a blank stare.

"Yesterday. Just before I left. Remember? Trial lesson, three boys, kindergarten age?" Dude, come on; don't do this to me. Not today. Not *now*. "Manager, you said … *your exact words* were —"

"Trial? Ah!" he smacks his forehead and swears. "So sorry! Trial lesson, cancelled yesterday. Ah … no trial."

"Oh, you've *got* to be kidding me!" My purse, along with my dignity, hits the floor with a dull thud. "Are you serious?"

"Ah, yes, very serious. They do not trial lesson at this school anymore. They go to other school, in Osaka — ah! Wait! Don't leave. Just a moment, please!"

He ducks back into the staff room and unleashes a muted string of super-polite Japanese to someone, presumably on the phone. Meanwhile, there are a thousand bad words running through my head all at once, all fighting to get through my mouth at the same time. This is the last straw. The only trick is to move forward without violence. When Manager steps back out into the open, my bag and shoes are already back on.

"Ah!" Manager runs toward me. "No, wait! You — ah, can't leave."

"It's fine, Manager." I'll go home, eat breakfast, clean myself up, and *mentally regroup*, I hope. *We can just pretend you haven't jerked me around so many times.* "See you at eleven."

"No! No leave! Ah … no trial lesson, but, interview?" He stumbles over his words. "Ah … how can I say … we have interview. Very soon. So, we need native speaker. So, it is good that you are here. So, you stay and do interview."

Other staff members emerge from the staff room, slinking behind Manager. *So, the gang's all here, eh? Everybody arrived nice and early and the token is the one who drops the ball.* They now watch our conversation with horrified looks. Even Yoshino looks a little pallid. It doesn't matter. I'm going to stand my ground, even if I look like I spent the night in a rain gutter. "No."

Manager stiffens like he's just been shot with a poison-tipped dart. His head drops in deep thought. He folds his arms, sucks air through his teeth, then looks back up at me. "Please?" he whines. "This teacher, I really want. Ah, I mean, *we* really need."

"Cybelle-*sensei*," Yoshino steps forward, her voice gentle. Too gentle. "I think what Manager means to say is that … he is very sorry, but we need you. I can explain. Bucho just called and said we have a pretty amazeballs candidate — not her exact words — but she mentioned something about the highest TOEIC score she's seen in years. Lieko *was* going to do the English interview, but now that you're here, you can ..."

Behind her, Lieko is shooting daggers at both of us. No one needs to explain that officially she is not allowed to do such a thing.

Yoshino blushes as she continues. "Anyway, you'd really be doing us a solid because, well ..." she braces herself. "Manager just got off the phone with Bucho and said you would do it. She's on her way here now. She and the candidate are on the same train. I'm sorry, Cyb. Please don't kill me. Er, I mean, us."

On cue, Manager bows very low. *"Onegaishimasu."* The other staff members say the same, all except Yoshino, who mouths "I'm so sorry" to me, and Lieko, who storms back into the staff room and slams the door. I could say no. Hell, I *should* say no. I'm starving, and I'm pretty sure I look and smell like someone who hasn't showered since Sunday. Then again, this whole debacle stinks of seriousness. Maybe this interviewee is the president's daughter or something. This is not normal behaviour. I've never seen Manager bow this low, not even five years ago to the mother and baby who waited three hours downstairs on a freak typhoon day when the school was closed and no one notified her.

"If I start now," I say slowly, "it means I can come in an hour late another day. Or leave early tonight...?"

"Yes!" Manager snaps upright. "Of course! This is fair. And ..." He looks me up and down. "Do you have bento today?" I shake my head. "Ah! Okay, that's great; don't worry. I buy you lunch. And something from HORUS! More Totoro? Okay?"

Shit. He's onto my new weakness. "What time is she supposed to be here?"

"Bucho called from her station," Yoshino says. "They should be here soon. Is that right, Manager?"

"Yes, very soon. Because, Bucho comes from Osaka. So maybe, in fifteen or twenty minutes." Manager offers to take my coat and bag. "Please. Get ready, in Room One, and I ..." He gestures to imply he'll put away my stuff as he disappears into the staff room. Behind the sliding door, he yells in Japanese: "Lieko! Move this bag! What do you carry in here, your first-born child?!"

Huh. This interview *is* important.

Fifteen and twenty minutes come and go without any sign of Bucho. The short hand on the clock above the door inches along until it points at the number ten. My Baby Zero class doesn't start for another hour, so I really have nothing else to do but wait for her and this mystery teacher candidate. As I sit with my list of questions and a pencil in the tiny classroom, my co-workers run up and down the hall like the Queen of England is on her way. Despite all the cleaning we do around here, heads bob back and forth past the window, along with giant yellow gloves and our white rag towels. I feel like I'm in a madhouse. Then I hear the elevator doors chime as Manager yells, *"Urusai! Shizuka ni shiro!"* before his voice goes up three octaves to greet Bucho. A chorus of high-pitched voices echoes him. Voices continue, muffled.

Shit, now *I'm* nervous. I duck my head so it looks like I'm reviewing my questions. My stomach growls again, louder and more impatient. I want this interview over with so I can grab something quick, like a sandwich from Family Mart. A sandwich … *multiple sandwiches. Tuna, egg,* tonkatsu *with lots of sauce on soft, pillowy bread.* I'm so hungry.

"Cybelle!" Manager sticks his head through the door. "Ready?"

"Ready as I'll ever be." He stares at me until I clarify, "Yes, I'm ready."

"Okay! Thank you for your patience." He disappears down the hall. I hear him ask the interview candidate in Japanese if they're all right, or if they need another minute to get ready. "Great!" Manager continues in English. "Please, right this way …"

I can see Yoshino now, and another co-worker blocked by the wall. They bow energetically, raising their *keigo* two more octaves. Bucho stops at the window and looks in. She waves at me with a deceptive smile. I know that if I weren't sitting here, waving back, she'd be busting heads. I hear Manager off to the side explain that I am the resident English teacher who will do the interview, please do not be nervous, her English is perfect, but she is very nice, not like other foreigners … Oh, what's that? Yes, that is her, but she is Tinker Bell for Halloween, it is only costume, please don't worry, she is from Canada, not America, ha, ha, ha.

The new candidate does not pay attention to him. He is staring, through the window, at me. He looks me right in the eye, smiling so intensely that Manager has to gesture wildly to enter long after he has opened the door for him. Oh goody, a creepster. Just what I need to spice up this roller coaster of a career.

"Nice to meet you, my name is Cybelle." I stand up and reach out my hand. "And you are?"

My interviewee's fingers are long and warm, his grip is strong. Our hands bob up and down for a long time until, confused, he turns to Manager and double-checks in Japanese if this is his cue to introduce himself. Strangely, Manager is not disappointed; he's so desperate to have another Y chromosome in the school that he's willing to laugh it off and translate. No need to be embarrassed, yes, she *does* talk fast, ha, ha, ha. Just tell her your name.

"*Ah, naru hodo.*" His face lights up. "Pleased to meet you. My name is Zaniel. *Yoroshiku?*"

eleven

BEAUTIFUL SOUP

武士は食わねど高楊枝

One must put on a brave display, even in adversity

"Da-ni-e-ru?" Manager draws out each syllable. "Oh! Really? You have American name? May I ask, why? Daniel, is *hafu*?"

"No, not Daniel. It's Zaniel. Zaniel Kamisawa. I know, it's a strange name." He blushes. "Long story. But now that you mention it, my father is American."

"Oh, really?! You are *hafu*! *Ehhh!* So, you must be very good at English!"

"I like to think so," he flashes me a smile that reminds me of a shark. A shark with perfect teeth. "But I guess *she* will be the judge of that."

"Ah, Cybelle! I will get another chair … to watch you interview … but, please start without me! Please!"

He doesn't wait for me to respond; he's already out the door and down the hall. The man and I are left there, alone in our tiny toilet-sized room, gazes locked, frozen in time. His eyes are a little too light brown for my liking, like he's wearing hazel contacts. No, that's a horrible thing to say. If he's half-Japanese, it makes sense he might not have dark brown eyes. *Don't be so judgmental, Cybelle. Just do this interview and then you can eat.*

I muster a smile, trying to swallow down whatever might be coming up. "Kamisawa-*san*, I'm going to need my hand back."

"Ha, ha, sorry." He lets go and glides into his chair, still pinning me with his gaze. I'm grateful to sit down; I don't feel good. It must be dizziness from hunger.

"Well," I begin, "it's very nice to meet you, Kamisawa-*san*. Thank you for coming today."

"Thank you for having me. I'm glad to finally meet you. I hope you don't mind me saying this, but you're taller than I thought you'd be."

"Uh. Right." Without Manager, I don't have much to do. I pretend to shuffle some papers around in my hands. What the hell is that supposed to mean? Well, at least I don't have to talk like a tape recorder this time. "Manager mentioned you're from the Osaka area. You've travelled far."

"Not really. The express train only takes thirty minutes. Today was my first time getting off here, though. Nice town. Quiet." He looks me over again, taking me in. His grin widens. "Pretty."

"Um ..." Where the hell is Manager? This stupid school is *full* of chairs. Wait. Something outside the room catches my attention. "The hell is that?" I mutter.

Zaniel cocks his head. "Ah, I know this. Boccherini's Minuet. It must be playing on your loudspeaker."

We don't have a loudspeaker. Something fishy is going on here.

"Ah, Shibere-*sensei*!" Bucho sticks her head through the door, excusing herself to our candidate. Manager is right behind her. "May I join?"

Like I'm allowed to say no. "Sure, come on in."

Everyone makes a big scene about ushering her in, making room for her chair. The three of us all squish on one side of the table together while this Zaniel dude sits comfortably on the other.

"Now, please, just answer as though Bucho and Manager are not here," Manager says to Zaniel. "And, good luck!"

The man across the table rubs his hands sheepishly, blushing. "I'm sorry, I'm very nervous. I don't get to speak English very often," he says with perfect pronunciation. He bows in Manager and Bucho's direction. *"Douzo yoroshiku onegai itashimasu,"* he mutters. His cheeks flush in a way that's kind of cute. Both Manager and Bucho bow back with *"kochira koso,"* etc., etc. This goes on until finally Manager remembers I am there.

"Ah, yes! Cybelle, go ahead. She has very easy questions, don't worry! Cybelle, *douzo.*"

The hell I do. Not when I can finally have a decent conversation with a candidate. "What did you say your first name was again?"

"Zaniel."

"'Zaniel.' That's a pretty cool name. What does it mean?"

"Hmmm …" There's a mischievous twinkle in his eye. "What do *you* think it means?"

Crap, my face is getting so warm. I try to make sense of my interview papers and almost drop them all. "I, uh … okay, never mind. I have a few questions for you. Just answer them as best as you can."

"Love to."

"Why did you choose to apply to this company?"

Zaniel inhales softly, gazing up at the ceiling. The fluorescent lights catch on his long eyelashes. "Well, the truth is, right now I do translation work for this big company. I'm just a salaryman. I work in Osaka, way downtown, where it's super crowded and dirty. The job pays well, sure, but I've been doing it for years and it's killing me. It's boring, it's tedious, and as much as I hate to admit it, the atmosphere is pretty soul-sucking. I'd rather work *with* people, you know? Do something that lets me talk to people, have a real conversation. And I think my English is still pretty good, so I thought why not make a change?" He pauses, then gives a short bow to end his sentence.

Manager nods several times like he understood all of that and is now about to say something, but he turns to me instead. He leans so close to read my interview paper that I can count the dandruff flakes on his scalp. Wait. Something isn't right about all this ... and it isn't Manager's brand of shampoo.

"So, when exactly did you apply to this company?" I ask.

"Uh, just a moment," Manager sits upright and flips through his notes. He's holding what looks like the typical interview candidate profile, complete with a stern-looking photo in the top right-hand corner. The photo looks nothing like Zaniel. "Ah! Two weeks ago. And you passed the English exam at one hundred percent. *Sugoi*, Kamisawa-*san*! Thank you for your hard work!"

Two weeks ago? I can't help but give Zaniel a suspicious look. If Head Office knew about this guy two weeks ago, why take so long to interview him? Where was he all the Misakis and Ari Satos ago? And more than that, why wait until the last minute to tell me I'm interviewing him? Something about this guy stinks, and it isn't his peachy cologne.

"Oh, it was nothing. If you know what I mean." His eyebrow arches at me, ever so slightly. How could I understand what he means? I shake my head a little, not knowing what else to do.

"So," I start again, "why do you want to teach English?"

"*Ne*, Cybelle-*sensei*," Manager interrupts. "Maybe, ask another question? I think Kamisawa-*san* already answer."

I turn to Bucho, who sits stock-still like she's the one being interviewed. It's time to get her involved. "Do you agree, Bucho?" She blinks at me.

"Oh, that's okay —" Zaniel starts in, but I interrupt him. I've got plenty of questions for this candidate, this time.

"Fine, I'll rephrase: What makes you think you would make a good English teacher for young children?"

"Ah, Cybelle, hmm ..." Manager interrupts. "That is ... hmm, a difficult question. Maybe ..." He invades my personal space again to lean over my interview sheet. He beams and taps question #3: *Do you like children?* "Ah, maybe, ask this question?"

Interview Commando at a time like this? Seriously? "It's a valid question. I'm sure he can answer it."

"Valid?" he struggles with the word. He half-turns to Bucho for clarification but the look on her face is so stern he knows it's the worst time to let it show that he doesn't understand. "Eh ... 'balid'?"

"Yes," I reply tersely. "Valid."

"Ballad? Eh, music ballad? Eh? Hmm ..." he mutters to himself; eventually, he sucks air through his teeth. "I think, maybe, it's too difficult. You must be very tired, Kamisawa-*san*. Is it okay if Cybelle-*sensei* asks one or, maybe, two more questions? Maybe, *easy* question?"

"FINE." I realize I'm being a huge bitch but I want this interview over. "What are three things you would like to do in the future that you've never done before?"

"Ooh, good one. Let's see. I'd like to ..." Zaniel trails off, absent-mindedly stroking his lower lip in deep thought. "I need to learn how to swim. To be honest, I'm terrified of water. I don't think I even know how to float. So, learning to swim would be first on the list. Second, hmm, I don't want to say travel the world, everybody says that. I guess it'd be neat to see what Southeast Asia is like. I definitely want to check out Thailand and Cambodia someday. And, for the third ... let me think ... I've never really explored Japan much, so I guess I'd like to take a road trip somewhere. My grandma has this scooter she's always bugging me to put to use."

Bucho and Manager marvel at his *"sugoi"* answers. I can tell Bucho is restraining herself not to clap for him. I have to admit, even I'm feeling flabbergasted. I must look it, too.

"Is that a good sign?" he asks me.

"Oh, yes! Very good, very good," Manager nods several more times. "Okay, let's ask question number three, Cybelle-*sensei*!"

"All right. Do you —"

"Ah — Cybelle, you are, not taking notes?"

"Am I supposed to be?"

Across the table, Zaniel coughs. I think he's trying not to laugh. Underneath my jacket, the armpits of my shirt feel like sponges soaked in brine. I hope this is all a nightmare, but it's too real to be. I skip down to question five and look him dead in the eyes. They must be coloured contacts. "If you could be any kind of fruit, what would you be and why?"

"Ha, ha. Well, my boss would tell you I'm a banana," he grins again, "but I like to think I'm more like a pomegranate. A little baffling when you encounter it for the first time, but once you figure out how to get inside, you find it's sweet, charming, and really not so bad."

I bite the inside of my cheek. That was a damn good answer. "What would you do if one of your students wet himself your first day on the job?"

His smile grows wider. "I think I'd come to *you* for help, so the real question is, what would *you* do?"

I push any possible answer back down my throat. I'm not the one being interviewed here. I already got this job. "What are your thoughts on corporal punishment?"

"I've never been a fan, and it definitely doesn't belong in schools."

"How would you describe yourself in one word?"

He searches the room. "Resilient."

He's good. *Too* good. I narrow my eyes at him. "What gets wetter as it dries?"

"Um … a towel?"

"WOW! Very good!" Manager breaks into applause. "You can do conversation with native speaker! *Sugoi!* Okay, thank you so much, Cybelle. Now, we will do Japanese interview. Please —" he flaps his hands at me toward the door. It's fine. Without his insipid reminder I might have forgotten there was a door and hurled myself through the viewing window.

"Wait," Zaniel says. "May I ask you something before you go?"

Manager's and Bucho's jaws drop. "Sure." I sit back down. This ought to be interesting.

"I've just been wondering." Zaniel leans forward, squinting a little. "Two things: May I ask where you're from?"

"Oh. Canada."

He looks surprised. "You're *Canadian?*"

"Yeah?"

"Wow. That's cool. And, um, can you tell me … hmm … what made you decide to teach English in Japan?"

It's a good question. "I've always liked kids," I say, "so it seemed like as good a job as any. As for coming here to do it … I don't know, I've just always been drawn to the culture here. I especially love the fact that you're not expected to grow up here the way you are in the west. I love the stamp rallies, the mascots, the point cards for *everything* … and, more than anything, I love how no one tells me to grow out of any of it."

"And how has your perspective changed since you came to Japan?"

I snort. "My attitude toward people has definitely changed. You can't get attached to anyone you meet here. They're always coming and going, so nothing is set in stone like it would be back home. You kinda have to cherish every moment you have with people …"

Zaniel nods. *"Ichigo ichie …"*

"Exactly. But at the same time, my choices in friends are limited by being 'foreign' due to language barriers and *gaijin* fear. At

first, I wasn't picky about who I hung out with. That led to a lot
of bad experiences. It took a long time to understand that I wasn't
permanently stuck with them. Eventually, they left. Whether it
was to go back home or relocate to Tokyo. Everybody leaves."

"Interesting. So, you might say you have an *ichigo ichie* attitude toward relationships."

I give him a sideways glance. I think I'm smiling, too. "Are
you interviewing me?"

"Well, kinda," he grins back. "Not sure if you're up to the job,
though. It's not an easy one."

"Hey, as long as I earn enough to eat, I'm happy."

He leans back with a smile, then blushes under Manager's and
Bucho's shocked stares. "That's all I wanted to know. Thank you."

"Thank *you*." I have no idea what the hell that was about,
but it was a nice end to our interview. Maybe this won't be such a
shitty day after all.

I get up to reach for the handle. Zaniel reaches it first. "Please,
allow me." He's so close, I can smell him; he smells less like cologne
and more like real peach. It makes me so hungry I can't even thank
him. He seems to read my mind. "If anything, I should thank you.
For interviewing me. I know a hard worker when I see one."

Now I know I'm smiling, no matter how hard I'm trying to
hide it. "Good luck."

"Thank you. I hope I get to work with you someday."

I stumble my way to the staff room where the other teachers,
minus Lieko, have sequestered themselves to gossip; they swarm
me before I can collapse onto one of the stools. It's hard to understand any of them when my head is swimming this bad. I can
understand Yoshino, however, loud and clear.

"Ho-ly *shit*," she grabs me by the shoulders. "Could he *be*
any sexier?! What was he like? How good is his English? Tell us
everything."

"Well ... I ..." I got nothing.

"Eh, maybe, Shibelle-*sensei*," Misaki holds up her pinky. "*Rabu-rabu?*"

"No." I don't bother trying not to make a face. "I'm just hungry. I need food to be civil, no pun intended."

"Here. They're from Bucho." Yoshino starts to slide a half-eaten box of *shioaji manjuu* toward me. "No, wait! I want details first, woman. No, wait, forget it. Don't tell me anything, it'll break my heart if Manager doesn't hire him. *Please* Manager give us a break and *hire him.*"

"But I think it's Bucho who will hire him, no?" Seri pipes up. "Because I know Manager really wants male teachers."

"Yeah, good point. She better." Yoshino crosses her arms and pouts. "He reminds me of someone ... What's his name? You know, that guy ... Shoot, it's on the tip of my tongue ..."

Yuki asks, "Cybelle-*sensei*, was he kind? He looks so kind."

Seri agrees. "And I could hear him speak a little when I came in! His English sounds really good!"

"Yes! His English, so good! He can teach *us* English! Cybelle-*sensei*, are you sure he's Japanese?"

"I heard Bucho say he's half-Japanese."

"*Ehhh*, I'm so *exciting*!" Misaki claps her hands. "Maybe, he is ... eh, *dokushin?*"

Yoshino scoffs. "No way is anyone that hot single. They better bloody hire him; this place is bone-dry in the guy department, right, Cyb? Cyb, you awake?"

"Huh? Wha?"

"Girl, are you okay?" Yoshino edges the *manjuu* back toward me. I take a couple, but I don't eat any. I'm too wrapped up in my own conversation with myself. Who *is* this guy?

"You know what, Yoshino? I have a feeling I've seen him somewhere before, too. Do you think —"

"AH!" Yoshino snaps her fingers. "I got it!"

"You know him?!"

"Haruma Miura! Now I can sleep tonight."

"Eh, chigau yo!" Misaki teases, saying he looks nothing like him.

Well, that was a bust. I was *not* thinking of anyone remotely famous. Maybe he just looks like someone I used to know. Which is impossible, because I haven't had any friends around here for years, let alone spent time with any Japanese guys. But in the end, I nod and force a smile as my co-workers go on about how great a fit this guy would be at our school. He'd bring in clients, that's for sure. Every woman would step over her own husband to have Zaniel teach her children.

"Hai, otsukaresama!" Manager sings as a door opens.

"He's on the move!" Yoshino squeals. The girls bodycheck one another to get out of the staff room. They stop and behave when Bucho comes in with her interview notes.

"Excuse me, Shiberu-*sensei.*" She smiles at me. "Would you please come outside? Mr. Kamisawa-*san* is going out."

Ugh.

I've never smiled this hard in my life. The farewell is not as bad as I thought it would be. A lot of bowing with the other teachers behind the reception desk. I feel less self-conscious now. Not sure why, when all this paranoia is clearly in my head. Maybe it's because Lieko is mysteriously absent from all this excitement. In any case, I'm sure I don't know this dude. He, Bucho, and Manager exchange the usual pleasantries about going to Head Office for training, staying in their creepy dorms for one month, taking another test, yadda, yadda, yadda, all information he's heard before. He gives one final bow as the elevator arrives and the doors close on him. He doesn't look in my direction. Not once. And like that, he's gone. Good. More time to sit in the staff room and wait for the world to stop spinning.

"Well?!" Manager turns to me. "What do you think about the interview? *Kanpeki deshou?* Good fit, *ne?*"

"His English is good, all right," I admit. "But I don't know about him being a good fit. It doesn't sound like he has a whole lot of experience with kids, and we need someone who —"

"Yes, yes, but what about his English? It's perfect, yes?"

Bucho mentions in discrete Japanese that his English scores are off the chart. He could teach *her* English. Manager nods. "But, Cybelle-*sensei*, do you mean you don't like him? He likes you. At the end of Japanese interview, he said you are a true dream."

"A what now?"

Manager flinches. "Ah, I'm sorry ... he said to tell you ... true dream? Sorry, he said this in English; I did not understand. Is it a kind of American joke?"

"I don't know." I don't care.

"I hope he comes back ..." Misaki says behind me in a dreamy voice.

"Of course, you do," I blurt out. "Manager, can I go out and grab something to eat? Before my Baby students get here?"

"Ah! But ... Baby students will be here soon, so please, maybe, you should stay at Zozo. *Soshite*, as promised, I will buy you lunch. So please, be patient. In staff room. Do not buy, *ne*? My treat, today!"

"No, no, I remember. I just need some air. I'll be right back, I promise."

Manager doesn't look pleased, but he lets me grab my coin purse and swap my Tinker Bell slippers for my shoes without any further protest. I press the button for the elevator, but when it arrives, I turn to him. "Hey, Manager," I swirl my finger in the air. "What's with the music?"

"Ah, *yokatta*, you heard it! We play on your stereo in Room Four. Good impression for new teacher!"

"We're playing classical music to impress the new guy?"

"Yes! Do you think it works? I hope it works. Kamisawa-*sensei* would make good fit, *ne*?"

One of my eyes twitches sharply. "Be right back."

"Hai, itterasshai!"

"Ittekimasu."

The gentle motion of the elevator does not help my looming migraine one bit. Maybe if I just buy a little cake from HORUS, I'll still have an appetite for this free lunch I have coming to me without passing out from hunger. HORUS is closed. Shoot. It doesn't open for another hour, right when my Baby class starts. I settle for a handful of Black Thunders from Family Mart and wolf them all down in front of the station. Oh my gosh, the crunchy rice-puff base, the sweet but subtle chocolate coating ... these little bars have never tasted this good.

"Pssst!" I hear behind me. *No. Not again. No more weirdness today.* I hear it a second time, louder. "PSSST."

Trying not to turn my head too much, pretending to look for a garbage can for my Black Thunder wrappers, I peek over my left shoulder. The *kei* truck is back. I wander around as if desperate to find a trash can (which I kind of am). Like a jack-in-the-box, a face pops out from the red *noren* of the truck as I walk by. The face is smiling at me. It takes me a second to realize it belongs to a human being — the strange man's eyes and smile are so frozen his face looks like a mask. He snickers. "Pssssssssst! *Oide, oide!*" He waves a hand to say *come here.* Weird. I fake a smile and walk straight back into Family Mart. Guess I'll kill a few more minutes by pretending to buy something else. The man's face is still jutting out of the curtains when I walk out of the *conbini* empty-handed. (I *did* promise not to buy lunch, and who am I to shun Manager's free meal?) The man is still beckoning me. *So weird.* I guess there's no better time to head back to Zozo. As much as I might want udon, I don't have the time for it right now. I wave in polite refusal, then bolt. This whole day is shaping up to be one big ball of weird.

There's a sea of people waiting for the elevator. They're all Zozo students and parents, some of whom are in my Baby class. We all greet each other, I high-five the babies, and we pile in. I make faces at Mai, the baby closest to me, who giggles in her father's arms. I'm so busy crossing my eyes it barely registers when someone shouts for us to hold the door and leaps in.

It's Zaniel.

"Oh!" he says. "Fancy seeing you out here."

I work here, I almost say. "Did you leave something behind?"

"No. Didn't your manager tell you? I'm going to observe a few classes." He bows as best as one can in a crowded elevator. "*Douzo yoroshiku onegaishimasu.*"

"Oh. Um … *kochira koso,*" I reply. The parents around me burst into applause and praise. "Cybelle-*sensei*, you speak Japanese? Oh! *Sugoi! Jouzu!*" No one questions who this guy is.

Manager corners me when we all spill out into the Zozo lobby. "Cybelle-*sensei*! You are back! Please, Cybelle-*sensei*, take a rest. Don't worry, I will go out and get your lunch. Eh, soon."

"Yeah. That sounds like good advice."

"And, Kamisawa-*sensei, okaerinasai!*" Manager bows to him. He tells Zaniel in Japanese to have a seat and wait in Room Two. I'm in the middle of changing into my shoes when it hits me that that's *my* room.

"Wait. What's going on?"

"Ah, Cybelle, Kamisawa-*sensei* is going to watch your Baby Zero lesson today. Is it okay?"

"Um …" Well, I can't think of a good enough reason to say no, other than the fact that he makes me nervous. "Sure, I guess."

"Ah, great! Thank you for understanding, Cybelle!"

I pretend that he's just another observing parent staring me down from the window as my Baby Zero students and parents arrive and assemble in the room. Every now and then, as the babies waddle around the room and bob around to the music from the

CD player, the mothers turn to look back at Zaniel and maybe share a giggle or two with one another. They share their ideas about who he could be as the babies colour in their books — he looks a little foreign, maybe he's a new English teacher, or maybe he's a parent observing lessons, but he looks way too young and so on and so on. Azusa's mother proposes he's my boyfriend, but when the others gesture to ask me, she clams up and blushes. As much as I love my baby students, I feel like doing a backflip when our lesson comes to an end. Manager is talking to Zaniel so his attention is finally turned away from me. I see Zaniel bow and get his shoes, and, still bowing, he gets into the elevator. *Finally, I'm free.* It's bad enough getting stared at outside of Zozo; I don't see why I should have to deal with it here, too.

Manager bids the mothers farewell and thanks the babies for their hard work before turning to me. "Cybelle-*sensei, otsukaresama desu!* Thank you for your lesson! Now, about new male teacher, Kamisawa-*sensei* …"

I stop Manager right there. "Whoa. He's *not* a teacher. We haven't hired him yet. He hasn't even been approved for *training* yet. Can't we just call him Kamisawa-*san*?"

"Yes, hmm, this is true. But, about new teacher — maybe, when Bucho processes interview, maybe, she will hire Kamisawa-*sensei* right away. This is good news, *ne*?"

I sigh. This guy is not listening to a word I say. "Maybe," I try using Manager's favourite word. "I mean, sure, he's fluent in English, but that doesn't mean he's good with kids. And what about —"

"*YADAAAAAAAA!*"

I close my eyes. "Oh, for the love of —"

Manager turns on the charm. "Hello, Hitomu-*kun*! *Okaasan, ohayou gozaimasu!* Cybelle-*sensei*, please, staff room. Let us finish talking later. And, anyway, I think many mothers will like Kamisawa-*sensei*. Children, too; he is *hafu*, but, he is *genki*. Ah! The children can call him 'Zany Zaniel'!"

'I squeeze my eyes shut to keep from rolling them. "Excuse me."

"Certainly, Cybelle-*sensei*! Please, enjoy your lunch! It's *in staff room*!"

I duck into the staff room, careful not to slam the sliding door behind me. There's a large plastic bag on the bench with "セベール (Cybele)" scrawled on it. Sweet mercy, we haven't even hired this guy and we're giving him fucking nicknames already? What have they been calling *me*? "Psycho Cybelle"? On second thought, that wouldn't come out so bad in Japanese. Still. I have reasons to be pissed off. He doesn't work here yet and they already love him. I've been here for years and they still flinch when I step off the elevator. I wonder if this a preview of how they'll treat the new *gaijin* if I don't re-contract. I stomp over to the bench and grab a seat, slamming it into the floor as I adjust myself. This isn't *fair* —

I stop mid-rant. I'm being a baby. I take a deep breath and count to three. How am I getting jealous of a guy who hasn't been hired yet? On the other hand, a part of me doesn't care. I don't think I'd be so immature if I weren't so fucking hungry. There isn't anything I can do about it right now. Except maybe eat, and forget about him.

There is a *lot* of food here. I can't tell if Manager bought me food to choose from. Maybe he bought something for himself today. Nope, there's his bento cloth bag right next to all these *conbini* bags. I open them up and create a spread on the bench: there's meat sauce spaghetti, *oyako-don*, and a telltale 7-Eleven bento with egg on rice, plain pasta, and spicy barbecue chicken, all heated up. I start with the first, and over the course of an hour, end up eating them all. *Yum.*

There's also a massive box of assorted goodies from the Mister Donut in the mall. I help myself to three *pon de ringu* donuts in time for Misaki to come in and sit down with her lunch. From the corner of her eye she watches me hoover down the last one but doesn't engage with me at all. Good. Feeling more at ease, I put all the plastic containers and used chopsticks in the garbage, leaving the extra *ohashi* in a small baggie next to the computer, and sneak out of the staff room praying none of that food belonged to anyone else.

My Baby One students are already in Room Three, settling in. Two of the babies are fast asleep in their mother's arms. Baby Yukino is barely holding on. Aira is the only one awake. I assure the moms that it's okay, they don't have to wake them up, and pop in my lullaby CD to teach the moms a couple of songs.

"*Eh? Cybelle-sensei, dare?*" Takuya's mother points with a free hand. "*Boyfriend-o?*"

"What?" I turn. Oh, *no*. Zaniel waves from the window in the door, grinning from ear to ear. "No," I say through a clenched smile. "He isn't."

"*Sore ja* ... new teacher?" Aira's mother asks.

"No — er, not yet. He is interviewing."

"*Ah, naru hodo ...*" The parents all nod.

We end our class with the quietest rendition of the "Goodbye Song" so that all the babies can sleep. Even the kids running around in the lobby don't stir them awake, which is perfect because Manager, Bucho, and Hitomu's mother are all pitching in to drag the poor child into Room Two for "Cybelle-*sensei*'s exciting lesson." I don't bother to pull Manager aside and tell him I wasn't made aware of any freaking lesson. It's too late, anyway. Bucho already has him in her arms as Hitomu's mother dips out of the room.

"Come on, Hitomu-*kun*! Let's enjoy English! Cybelle-*sensei*, Hitomu is ready for lesson!"

Damn it. I take a deep breath as I retreat back to Room Three to get my teacher box. I can do this. I can *freaking* do this. After picking up all my books and toys, I pick up the box and look down at the CD player, which I also need to transport to Room Two. Shit. I can't do this.

"Need a hand?" says a calm, tenor voice.

Oh, no. Zaniel is already next to me, unplugging the CD player. "I thought you left," I try to smile. "I did. Your manager said I could run out to get something to eat."

"Oh. I see. Thanks," I mumble. He smells so good. "Yeah, if you can just … follow me."

"Sure. You okay?"

"Yeah, I'm fine. I just … well …"

Hitomu's screams pierce the air.

"Is that *your* student?"

I nod. "It's not my easiest lesson today," is all I can say. I'm not sure how else to explain Hitomu to this guy. This guy, who I feel like I know, but have obviously never met before, and, for all I know, may not even get a position here. As soon as we turn the corner and enter Room Two, Hitomu locks eyes with Zaniel. He stops screaming. Bucho continues to bounce him on her knee, but it's completely unnecessary. Hitomu watches Zaniel as he bows to Bucho with a *"shitsureishimasu"* and plugs in the CD player for me. It gives me an idea. Perhaps not the greatest idea, but if it works, the payoff will be worth it.

"Bucho," I ask in my sweetest voice. "Is it all right if Kamisawa-*san* stays in the room? To watch my lesson? Instead of outside?"

"Really?!" Zaniel turns in shock. Then he clears his throat. "I mean, yes, if that's all right, I would love to stay."

"Yes, *zehi, zehi!*" Bucho says. She seems more than happy to plop Hitomu on the carpet and get up off her knees. "Please, watch Shibelle-*sensei*'s lesson inside! Ask her any questions, *ne?*" She walks out the door, giving me a quick thumbs-up — "Thank you, Shibelle-*sensei*! *Yoroshiku ne!*" — and closes the door.

I take a moment to deep breathe again. The room is still quiet. I turn. Zaniel is kneeling next to Hitomu, whispering to him. Hitomu is staring up at me with tear-stained cheeks, even as I circle around them to get my Jibanyan puppet from my box and sit down in front of him. Zaniel tells him something in Japanese like, "now, let's listen to the teacher," and looks up at me. "He's ready for you."

I can't help but stare back at the boy. "He's never been this quiet," I finally say.

"Really?"

"Yeah." Holding my breath again, I bring the puppet as close to him as I dare. Hitomu looks down and reaches out for Jibanyan, strokes the top of his head. I make Jibanyan bow and shake Hitomu's outstretched hand. I pray Bucho is not lingering outside the door. *"Konnichiwa,* Hitomu-*kun,"* I whisper. *"Genki?"* Hitomu nods. So far, so good. I still don't dare to speak at a normal volume. "Kamisawa-*san,* would you mind turning on the CD player?"

"Sure."

"Head, Shoulders, Knees, and Toes" starts to play. I gesture for Hitomu to stand and follow along, and he does so; very slowly, but at least he's complying. Zaniel kneels at the CD player, watching all the while. We all clap at the end. I let the CD player continue with "Baby Shark" and a few more songs. Hitomu doesn't make a peep. So far, very good. I put Jibanyan away and blow a few bubbles. Hitomu watches them float through the air, reaching up with his hands to pop one or two. Mostly he just observes them hovering over his head. After a few minutes, he seems to get tired of them, and goes back to staring at me, wide-eyed. I feel like an animal expert working with a dangerous creature. Every move and gesture I make is slow, reassuring: I put the bubbles down, cross the room to his backpack, retrieve his colouring book and crayons, and place them in front of him with caution. He doesn't move a muscle until I flip to a blank page for him. In time, he picks up his orange and brown crayons and starts drawing wild circles all over the page of Zozo the Clown having a tea party with a rabbit, a mouse, and various other animals.

"You're really good with him," Zaniel murmurs.

"Thanks." *If only you'd seen him the other day,* I think to myself. I watch Hitomu continue to scribble all over Zozo's face. "What are you drawing there, big guy?"

"Akumu," Hitomu whispers.

"Akumu?" I turn to Zaniel.

"Nightmares."

"Oh." I tilt my head, trying to think of something to break the even-more-awkward silence. "They look like donuts."

Zaniel translates for me in a quiet murmur. *"Arigatou,"* Hitomu whispers.

We continue to watch him for another minute or two. Then Zaniel gets up and kneels beside me. "So, as I was saying before. I'm glad we finally have a chance to talk because —"

Bucho walks in. "Oh, hello, everyone!" she sings at the top of her lungs. Hitomu bursts into tears and screams. In one fell swoop he jumps and lands on my lap, burying his wet face into my shoulder, squeezing me with every one of his fingers in ten tiny kung fu grips.

"Don't let her eat me," he sobs. "Please, don't let her eat me!"

"What's this? A picture! Oh, this is a monkey. Ah! Hitomu-*kun*, are you a monkey? Oh ho, Cybelle-*sensei*! I think Hitomu is starting to like you. This is good! *Mama* will be so happy!"

"Won't that be something?" I fake-laugh.

Bucho pats my knee and exits the room, leaving the door wide open (Hitomu's mother will want to see, she warns whoever is listening outside).

"He seems to really like you," Zaniel says.

"Are you kidding? He's been calling me *'oni baba'* since he started here."

"Oni baba? You're way too young for that."

I sigh. Hitomu is heavy, and his fingers are still digging into my back. I can feel the moon-cuts they will leave behind already, but I can't bear to pry him off. He'd probably rip a few chunks out of my jacket. *I wish I knew how to help you.*

A tap at the viewing window makes all our heads turn. Manager is there, pointing to Hitomu's mother, who stands in the doorway. Hitomu is off my lap like a bolt of lightning and runs out. Manager pops his head in.

"Cybelle-*sensei*, thank you for your lesson! I think that's enough for today. Maybe we don't need 'Goodbye Song' today?"

Obviously not. But before I can answer, the staff room door behind the reception desk slides open: Yoshino and Lieko step out. Perfect timing. "You're very welcome! But I need to talk to Hitomu's mother before she leaves."

"Ah, I see ..." Manager looks over at the young woman yanking the world's biggest rain poncho over her son's head. Manager sucks a bit of air in through clenched teeth. "But, as you know, Hitomu's mother, she does not speak English, so maybe it will be very difficult for you to translate —"

"That's okay! Yoshino-*sensei*, if you're not too busy, could you ...?" I flag her down. Yoshino steps out from behind the reception desk with an eager look. She immediately explains to Hitomu's mother in Japanese that I would like to talk to her if she has time to spare. She confirms she does.

"Great. Um ..." Where do I even start? "Okay, here's the thing. First, I just want to let her know that I understand Hitomu is very young, and I fully understand why he can feel afraid being around a foreigner. So, please tell her not to worry, I will do my best to make lessons enjoyable for him."

Yoshino translates. Hitomu's mother bows, very apologetic about Hitomu's reactions. She tells Yoshino that, to tell the truth, there is something wrong with Hitomu, and not just when it comes to foreigners. Apparently, he cries whenever they have to leave the house, and for whatever reason has a more vicious reaction around foreigners, the elderly, and giant mascot costumes. She goes on to explain to Yoshino that she and her husband thought putting him through *eikaiwa* might help him integrate with others and force this habit out of him. Hitomu's mother says she is very sorry he cried in class today, too. She is embarrassed.

"No, no, it's okay, I understand," I say. "Yes, he was pretty upset today, but I'm sure over time, things will get better!" Yoshino and I exchange weak smiles. "But it's not his crying I wanted to ask about. You see ... Hitomu said something very interesting in class today. The other day, too."

"Oh, really?" Yoshino asks.

"Yeah. He's said a couple of things. 'Get away from me,' and 'Don't eat me.'"

"What?! He said this to *you*?!"

"Well, no. He kinda just said them out loud. But the interesting part was I'm pretty sure he said them in English."

Yoshino's eyes widen. Hitomu's mother looks at us in panic until Yoshino remembers to translate. Then Hitomu's mother's eyes widen. She says it's impossible; Hitomu doesn't speak any English.

"Does anyone in your house speak English? Maybe your husband, or another relative?" Yoshino translates; Hitomu's mother shakes her head. "Weird. Do you watch English TV shows or ... anything?"

Hitomu's mother shakes her head again, baffled. Then, she groans and hits her forehead. She says to Yoshino that sometimes, Hitomu talks to himself. Not in Japanese. It's some weird language, nonsense words, something he must have made up. After all, he's an only child. No one ever understands a word of what he says. It's even more embarrassing than his crying; she is so sorry. She will talk to Hitomu later about not speaking his made-up language in school. Yoshino explains all of this to me in English; even though she knows I understood it all, we have to keep up the charade. Company policy.

"But," Yoshino adds, "I think Hitomu is starting to come around. Look how quietly he's waiting for *mama*."

Hitomu has seated himself on the lobby couch next to Zaniel, who is showing him one of the picture books. His head is slumped down into his chest, giving him a chubby-cheeked pouty look, but no tears, no screaming. Hitomu's mother bows again and again, thanking us for our patience. She tells Hitomu to say goodbye to us. He just stares.

"It's okay!" I assure her. "One day at a time. Baby steps."

"Sorry, sorry," Hitomu's mother laughs awkwardly. She sits down next to her son to help him put on his backpack. Bucho comes over and tells Zaniel that Lieko and her students are ready in Room Five for observation, so Zaniel bids him farewell. "*Arigatou* bye-bye," Hitomu waves to him. Aw, he's so cute when he's not a screaming mess.

I go back into Room Two, leaving the door open so my kinder students can come straight in when they arrive. As I busy myself with organizing my books and toys, I overhear Hitomu's mother just outside the room. "Hitomu-*kun*, what is going on with you?!" she scolds him in Japanese. "You must also say thank you to your teacher. I'll bet you were crying and screaming at her all day, weren't you? Do you know how shameful that is? She's not going to teach you English if you keep embarrassing her. Next time I hear you've called her a monster, I'm telling Daddy."

"*CHIGAIMASU!*" he screams. I'm not sure what he means. I know it means "wrong," but what exactly is "wrong," I don't know.

"Shut up! You're not going to embarrass me anymore! You stop this behaviour and *never do it again*, or else! Understand?!"

Screw company policy, I can't take this anymore. "*Sumimasen,*" I say, sticking my head out the door. Hitomu's mother starts to bow and apologize in Japanese for yelling, but I come over and tell her no, it's okay. I ask her to wait for one moment and run to Room

Five. Zaniel is there, sitting alone with his phone. I pray what I'm about to do works out.

"Zaniel, may I borrow you for a moment?"

"Yeah!" He looks more than pleased to get up. "Listen, I know this isn't ideal, but I can explain —"

"Oh, I just … need you help me translate for a second."

"Oh." He looks crestfallen but follows me, anyway.

I bring him to Hitomu's mother to let her know I understand what Hitomu's going through. My youngest sister was the same — seeing monsters everywhere, drawing them. "In English we call it a 'boogeyman' phase. Hitomu will outgrow it. He just needs time and patience." Zaniel translates this last part. She thanks us over and over again. We bow as Hitomu and his mother bid us farewell.

"You didn't need me," Zaniel remarks. "You were doing fine on your own."

"Thanks. We're technically not allowed to speak Japanese — the Native English Teachers, I mean."

"Hmm, that's understandable."

Hitomu waves at Zaniel as the elevator doors close. "He seems to have calmed down. He even said goodbye."

"He said goodbye to *you*. He doesn't scream when you're around. It's almost like —" I turn around. I had no idea Lieko had been at the reception desk this whole time. She does not look happy. Not that this is a dramatic change from her usual stone-faced glare.

"Don't worry," she coos. "I'm not going to tell Manager you spoke some Japanese. He is in enough trouble with Bucho; he doesn't need to know. It will make things worse. But Hitomu's mother may call the school to complain about you. I will have to tell him what you said about Hitomu."

"Seriously? You make it sound like I told her he's going straight to hell. It's a boogeyman phase. My sister went through the same thing. Heck, *all* kids go through the same thing. How is that *your* problem?"

"Everything that happens at this school is my problem." Her lips curl in an angry smile. "Bucho wants me to be headteacher after January, did you know? She sees I work hard, so it's natural she wants to promote me. That means I am almost like manager, so I can stop you being a bad influence to *our* students. Not just yours. All students here are everyone's students. Your attitude hurts all of them."

She directs her stern gaze to Zaniel. Zaniel says nothing, hanging his head down like he's the one being reprimanded. The energy between them is strange, but I'm more focused on something else. Inside I'm boiling. For the first time since I've worked alongside Lieko, I'm pissed enough to say something. I've always taken her snide comments, her stink-eyes, and her cold shoulders without letting my rage show. Now I can feel it about to overflow.

"Are you on crack? *I'm* a bad influence? Why, because I smile and show compassion to students?"

"*Of course* that's why! You are too soft on students! You don't know anything about teaching them! Maybe in Canada it's okay to coddle, but that is not our way in Japan. That is not how we grow up to be strong. Hitomu is not a baby anymore; he is a student. He has to stop making excuses."

"Excuses? Aren't you the one saying he's 'shy' all the time? And who's the one who 'forbid' me to talk to him because he's afraid of foreigners? What do you call that, a *suggestion*?"

Lieko stiffens. She steps out from behind the desk to stand right in front of me. I think she's about to hit me. Bring it on, bitch. The staff room door slides open and Bucho announces to everyone that she is stepping out for a couple of hours. Just in time for Lieko to compose herself. "Maybe," she says in a low voice, "when you become a *real* teacher, you will understand. But that will not be for a long time, I think. And I don't think you can work in this country much longer. You are too different. You will never fit in, and you will never be happy here." She gives Zaniel the same look again. He bows and takes his leave, giving me one last look over his shoulder, as if to say "sorry." It's fine. He doesn't need to get involved in this mess. This is between her and I.

"I see. You're a fortune teller now. In that case, maybe you should ask Bucho to buy you a lottery ticket when she goes out. Then you can put your superpowers to good use for once. Now if you'll excuse me, 'our' students will be here any second."

I leave her standing there, staring at me with the lower half of her face pulled down by the weight of Bucho's sudden appearance. She smacks Lieko on the shoulder to ask her what I just said, translate, translate now. I strut to Room Two feeling more powerful than I've felt in a long time. It's hard not to throw or break the things I remove from my teacher box with the adrenalin rush in my veins, but I'm able to calm down by the time my kinders arrive.

Halfway through the class, I notice someone watching from the window. The girls notice him, too, and giggle. *"Sensei no danna-san?"* they ask me. I shake my head and go back to reading *The Princess and the Frog*, ignoring their snickers, ignoring Zaniel. They don't stop giggling until I put the book down and take out our playdough for yet another tea party. Zaniel ends up spending the rest of the day at Zozo, hovering by the windows of my classes, reappearing and disappearing, getting my hopes up, spurring questions from parents about our new mysterious guest who is yes, *hafu*, and no, not a Zozo teacher yet. At the end of the night, my Senior students give up on Jenga altogether — *"hazukashii!"* they giggle — and spend the rest of class on their phones looking up pictures of J-pop stars, trying to figure out my "type." So much for getting through the present perfect tense with them. I have half a mind to tell off Manager and Bucho for this whole observing-the-day thing, but when I go out with my students, Zaniel is gone.

"You just missed," Manager tells me without my even asking. "Why? You want to say goodbye to Kamisawa-*sensei?*"

"Sachina and Meruna sure did," I mutter, waving to them as they leave. They ignore me, showing Yoshino their phones and pointing at me. "Cybelle-*sensei no type-u wa?*" they ask her. She chides them to get out of here in a playful way.

"Wait a minute," I say to Manager. "What made you think I wanted to say goodbye to him?"

"*Eeto* ... Kamisawa-*sensei* say you are best teacher. He say he enjoyed your lessons. But I did not see, he did not talk to Cybelle very much. Maybe, he is shy."

Again with this *shy* crap. Rather than saying something that could get me in trouble, I bow and head to the staff room. Yoshino steps in behind me.

"Cybelle-*sensei, otsukaresama desu,*" she sings to me. "Damn, girl, you look zonked. Why are you still working? Go home, have a giant meal, get some sleep."

"Oh man, sleep. Can't wait for that."

"Are you okay, by the way? I heard what went down this afternoon. Between you and Lieko?"

"I'm fine. We just ... it's fine. We agreed to disagreed. I think. I don't know. Whatever. This whole day has been weird. I think I'm going to stop somewhere for dinner. I'm not ready to go home and cook anything."

Yoshino frowns. "You're letting her get to you like that? You shouldn't."

"No. I just don't feel like doing anything tonight. I need to start taking it easy."

"Tell me about it. Culture Day can't get here fast enough. Hope you feel better." Her lips spread into a wide smirk. "Hey, maybe next week we'll have a cute new co-worker to cheer you up? Heh, heh."

"Meh ... maybe."

"He's pretty sexy," Yoshino continues, following me out of the staff room and down the hall to Room Five. "What was he like, in the interview? I mean, honestly? You can tell me."

I shrug. "Perfect English?"

"You don't sound too happy about that. Don't tell me he's a total jerk. Just what we need: a tall, hot version of Manager." She shudders at the thought. "Is it true that he's half-Japanese? Manager said he was raised in America or something."

"He didn't say … wait, he said his father is American, though. I don't know. His interview wasn't too bad, I guess. And he did get my towel question."

"Really?! I thought *no one* ever gets to your towel question!"

I put down my teacher box and lean on it. "Just you and him."

"And *I* didn't get the answer until you told me!" Yoshino puts a hand to her chest. "He *is* good. Cybelle, we should be excited! He sounds like the best interview we ever had!"

"I guess …"

"Well, cheer up. If he can survive Head Office boot camp, you'll have plenty of time to get to know him! If you decide to re-contract, I mean."

"Ugh. Yeah. Another headache and a half I have to worry about."

"Well, leave it for another day. Get some rest, hear me? Hole yourself up in an *onsen* or something. Get a full *esute* session. Let them treat you like a queen." She spreads out her arms like she's dancing, then stops. "Blech. Now *I've* been working too hard."

I laugh. "Haven't we all?"

Yoshino leaves to get the garbage while I wipe down all the tables, then I get my things to go home. Outside, the pavement is slick with rainwater; too slippery for me to safely ride this old bike with its non-seasonal tires. My stomach is rumbling so hard I don't have the energy to ride, anyway. I'm dizzy. I need food, and I need it *now*. Maybe that's why, when I see the *kei* truck, the beckoning hand, and the sinister smile, I think *what the hell* and see where this bizarre-AF day takes me. The udon man's smile seems to get bigger as I wheel my bike over to him. *Please don't be a perv, please don't be a perv.*

"*Irasshai, irasshai!*" He bows and ushers me under the curtain. "Come, come!" He thanks me, saying he thought I'd walk right by him. Under the short little curtain it's warm from all the steam inside the truck's tiny kitchen. The man gestures to the four tiny stools arranged below the counter. "Ah, *jitensha*, please ..." He takes my giant umbrella and my bike, which he parks behind the truck to shield it from any potential rain. He also offers to take my raincoat and purse — there's a special little nook with hooks for guests' belongings. A little radio on the counter ledge plays an old-time blues song about beans and cornbread, which I've never tried but sounds delicious. I wonder what kind of beans ...

The man climbs into the truck and appears behind the inside counter, clapping his hands on his arms to warm up. "*Uwaa, samu,*" he hisses. "*Ocha?* Tea? Do you like?"

"Yes, please."

It's too hot to drink right away, but the warmth is a balm for my wet, shivering fingers.

"Ah, *suman na,*" the man apologizes. "*Atsu sugiru ka?* Too hot?"

"*Neko jita,*" I explain.

"Ohhh ..." He reels back with a grin. "I know! 'Cat tongue,' yes? *Sugoi!* You speak Japanese, very good! Eh ... your mother? Father? Japanese?"

I laugh. "You're too nice."

"How long, eh ... Japan ..." He scrunches his face, thinking hard. "How long?"

"Six and a half years — ah, *roku nen han.*"

"Eh, long time. *Ja*, where are you from?"

"Canada."

"Canada? *Hehhh* ..." He leans over the counter with a sly look. He *really* looks like a wise old fox. I can almost see whiskers and pointy ears sprouting from his face. I feel incredibly mean, but I can't shake the image out of my mind. I'm so hungry for this udon I can't stop associating him with foxes, that's all. "Canada. Really?"

I nod. He is not convinced.

"*Really* Canada? *Only* Canada?" There's an excited twinkle in his eye. It's hard to tell where he's going with this.

"Yes. Only Canada."

"And your parents? Also … from Canada? Not Japan? You … not *hafu*?"

Okay, I think he's asking more about cultural background. Let's go with that. "No, I'm not half-Japanese."

"Ahhh," the man stands upright, nodding slowly. "I understand. You — not Japan. Parents — not Japan. *Ja*, parents' parents?" He makes a rolling gesture with his hands like he's turning back time. "Not Japan?"

"Sorry, no." This isn't the first time this has happened. Something about being able to speak fluently confuses people now and then. I can never tell if it's a compliment or a microaggression, but I always treat it as the former.

"But your Japanese … so good! How? And how you can eat —"

"*Konbanwa,*" a bass voice gurgles behind me. The air suddenly reeks of seaweed.

"Oh, another customer!" The man switches to a dialect I've never heard before. It's no variation of Kansai-*ben* that I know of, but I can still understand. "Welcome, welcome! Have a seat, please."

The whole space fills up with the man's girth and smell. He's gigantic. He squeezes himself onto two of the four stools with a heaving grunt. His suit stretches like Lycra as he settles his elbows onto the counter. From the corner of my eye I see two spherical cheeks — cheeks so huge they reduce his eyes to two tiny black pearls — stippled with tiny black spikes of hair. He reminds me of a threatened pufferfish. Even his voice sounds like he's talking under water.

"Beer me," he gurgles in the same dialect.

"Of course! Here you are!"

"Ah," he gulps it down with a satisfied hissing gasp. "You got any *karaage* to go with this?"

"Sorry, no chicken, sir. Only udon."

"Unagi?"

"Did you not see the *noren*? Just udon."

"Edamame? Calamari? *Anything?* What kinda place you running here?!"

The fox man sighs and turns back to me. "Sorry to make you wait. You like *kitsune* udon, yes?"

My favourite dish. "I don't like it. I *love* it."

"Ha, ha! Good joke, good joke!" he laughs. *"Sore ja*, I make you 'deluxe' *kitsune* udon. Very rare, very delicious! Just a moment, please!"

"Thank you, sir."

The man turns his back on me, humming to himself. It sounds like the crosswalk music near my place. It can't be anything else. I hum the last few bars of "Comin' Thro' the Rye" along with him. He looks over his shoulder and winks at me. I think the man on two stools is cringing. "Aw, cheer up, sir!" he teases in his dialect. "You scared of something?"

"I am scared … of *her*."

"You coward. She's harmless!"

A part of me wants to argue that, but the rest of me — the hungry part — just wants to eat. I relax with my now-perfect cup of warm green tea and pour myself a fresh cup just in time for the man to set a steaming bowl down in front of me.

"Here you are. One VERY special *kitsune* udon!" It looks so delicious it glows, like there's a halo over the bowl. Hang on. There's something glowing all right. Inside the bowl. It looks all too familiar. Wait, no. I think it's a reflection of the lights overhead. Didn't this same phenomenon happen in my apartment the other day?

I'm tripping. I think.

The other man stares at my food in horror. "How did you …?" he begins.

"Tut, tut. A good chef never reveals his secrets." The fox man beams. "Eat up, my dear! Eat up!"

All of a sudden I've just hoovered the glowing *aburage* pocket down, wolfing down this giant bowl of soup and noodles with a hunger I've never experienced. I'm lost in a wash of sweet-and-sour flavour, slurping up every thick chewy noodle, alternating between the udon and bites of sweet *aburage*. The hardest part is not moaning in pleasure with every delectable bite.

"*Umai ka?*" the man asks.

Of course, it is. "*Meccha umai!*"

"*Ja!*" The man slips another *aburage* into my bowl at the last minute, just as I'm on my last bite. A little bit of soup drips down my chin. I giggle, embarrassed. The man chuckles, too. "*Daijoubu! Shinpai shinaide yo!* Eat, eat!"

The whole time I can tell the fish man is watching me. He's hardly taken another sip of his beer. Who can blame him? He must think I'm a ravenous demon. He signals the fox man and asks again, "How did you …?"

The fox man wags his finger with a mischievous snicker. "Ah, ah, ah, be careful. She can understand you! You should hear her Japanese! *So* good! I was surprised, too."

"Fine." The fish man clicks his tongue and tries again: "So. How did you catch one of those …?"

I giggle again. Not my best moment, drinking the broth from a giant bowl I could barely lift in the first place and breathing laugh bubbles into it. I have to manoeuvre the noodles and tofu around to one side of my mouth to talk without looking like more of a pig. "I can still understand you, sorry," I say in Japanese. The fish man gasps. "What? I'm not deaf."

The fox man laughs harder than ever. "She's got you, fat man! Look at her food — what did you expect? She's one of us, all right.

Another hard worker, trying to make it in the World, eh? Can't
judge books by their covers anymore!"

"Well —" the man sputters, angry now. "Well — my point is,
why does *she* get a special dish?!"

The fox man shakes his head at him, laughing. Anyone can
tell that was not the fishy man's real question. "*Baku* dish for *baku*
customer!" I hear him say, puffing up his chest proudly. "Can't be
helped! *Ne?*" He winks at me again. "You want more, don't you?
No need to ask, it's coming right up!"

I grin. Turns out this guy is pretty cool; I can see myself dining at this little truck every day after work. The radio changes
from a chorus of men to two girls, singing about dreams. This
place is so cozy, and the food is great. I may never have to worry
about feeding myself again. Hang on, I find myself mulling over
his words. Special dish, special customer ... special? No, that's not
what he said.

"Excuse me, uncle," I ask in Japanese. "What does '*baku*'
mean?"

"Eh?" he drops my chopsticks on their way to a tiny sink.
"What's that?"

"What does '*baku*' mean?" I repeat. "Is it like '*tokubetsu*'?"

"Uh, yeah! Special! You ..." he spreads his arms wide. "Are special! Here!" He rummages with something in a hidden fridge below
the counter, grabs a tiny plate from somewhere else. A few quick
movements and there's a gorgeous cherry blossom cake on a lacquered plate in front of me. "Special dessert, too. *Muryou.* Free, free!"

"Oh, come on, now you're just sucking up to her! That's not
FAIR," the fish man bangs his fist on the counter.

"Calm down, fugu man," says a familiar voice behind me.
"You're just jealous."

"Ah!" the fox man lights up at the arrival of a third person.
"Another 'special' customer! Welcome, welcome!" He gestures to
the remaining stool next to me.

The fish man slumps back onto his two stools, jowls quaking with fear. I find myself shivering a little, too, and it's not from the temperature dropping outside our little space. The scent of peach hits me.

"You!" he gurgles. "I know you! You're the one who works for …"

"Yes?" Zaniel silences him with an icy glare. The fish man's fear is contagious. My hand is shaking on my teacup, making it rattle against the counter. The sound startles me and the fish man into staring straight ahead.

"Please, *okyaku-sama*, have a seat! *Suwatte kudasai! Kitsune* udon?" asks the fox man. "Your friend enjoyed!"

"I'm okay, thank you," Zaniel says in Japanese. He stands behind me and gently puts his hands on my shoulders. How can his hands be so warm when it's getting so freaking cold out?

"I'm okay, too, actually —" I say. I want to pay the bill and go.

"Oh, don't worry about being polite! You must be starving after such a long day. You're a hard worker, I can tell! *Hai, okawari douzo!*" The fox man winks at me again as he places a fresh serving of udon before me. I don't know how I ate that giant bowl so fast, but I worry about exploding with another bite. *Under the circumstances*, I think as Zaniel slides in next to me like a slippery eel, *I'll risk it.*

Zaniel accepts a hot mug of green tea from the fox man with both hands. He takes his sweet-ass time, sipping it like he was starring in a commercial for the most relaxing tea, brewed by monks in the mountains under waterfalls. I want to throw it in his face — scorch off that sexy smirk of his.

"You're looking better," he says to me, switching to English. "Happier, I mean. That place must stress you out. They always keep you this late?"

I shrug. What do I do first? Wait for my udon to cool down, so I don't have to slurp the noodles and look like a gluttonous freak?

Stuff my mouth with noodles so I don't have to talk? Knock the bowl into his lap and run like hell? Okay, that one is not happening. My appetite is coming back and I'm not wasting good food on this weirdo.

He grins as if he's read my mind. "No need to be polite around me. You go ahead and eat. It'll give me time to explain myself."

As I continue to devour my food, he starts to lay out his story, starting with his parents. His father worked at the Yokosuka naval base. His mother wanted him to be registered in Japan, so she "fled" to Ota-ku to have him. They moved to some landlocked part of California, where he grew up with a resentful extended family. Then his story starts to get interesting. Around the age of ten he started dream-walking, using it to get "revenge" on people. Nothing too malicious, just enough to unnerve them when racial epithets were uttered in his presence. When his parents split up, his mother sent him to his grandparents in Osaka. The bullying didn't stop there. He had nightmares every night, and for years barely slept at all. He grew up without friends, girlfriends, or school clubs. "Akki came along right after my grandpa died," he says wistfully. "Without Akki, I wouldn't have made it to university. But I won't get into that, now."

He glosses over whatever "Akki" is, and I'm far too engrossed in his story (and my food) to interrupt him. He goes on about majoring in translation, and his current Osaka company. His Japanese co-workers hate him; the non-Japanese employees avoid him. "I don't blame them. Besides, there's no point in getting close to someone who's going to freak out when they learn what I can do."

Wait, now I'm lost; what is it he can do again? Right, his "dream-walking." He seems really hung up on that. I think I get why he's telling me all this. Maybe if I know his story, I can put in a good word for him. If only he knew the truth — that I have no say in what Zozo does. With my udon finished, I have no reason to stay and listen anymore. Then Zaniel says something that makes me pause.

"... but you, you're different. I found myself wishing I could be just like you. You have this ability, and yet you enjoy life the way you are. I saw you, the way you were with those kids, and even with the parents! You were being yourself."

"Huh? What do you mean?" What ability are we talking about here?

"You *know* what I mean. You don't hide any part of yourself. You're not afraid. You're just you. I didn't know someone like us could be that free."

Like us? What does that mean? "Oh. Um. I don't know. I don't really do anything like that. I just, you know ..."

"No, I do know! I get it! And I love it! I mean, I admire it. I wish I could enjoy being with other people, the way you do. It's wonderful to see it in real life. Seeing you today ... it makes me think there's hope for people like us. Like, there's hope for *me*. Do you know what I mean?"

"I ..." I pause. Maybe I do get what he means. Teaching doesn't come naturally to everybody and working with kids doesn't gel with everyone. How many people would recoil at a child like Hitomu leaping on top of them and burying their wet faces in their chests? Maybe this guy's just paying me a genuine compliment. And let's be fair, this isn't the first time a total stranger has laid out their life story to me. But I still can't help repressing a shudder when I think about how his face, even his name, has been plaguing me all day. It scares me. It scares me more that he's still hanging around me. What possible interest can this super-cute guy have in someone like me?

I have to get out of here. It's time.

"*Gochisousama deshita,*" I thank the fox man, and reach for my jacket and purse. When he sees me take out my wallet, the fox man waves his hands. I break out the English. "No, please! I had *two* bowls! I have to give you something!"

"No, no!" He replies in English and gestures to Zaniel. "Friend already pay. His treat! So kind, yes? Ah, wait! Maybe … not friend?" He holds up his pinky finger and gives us a sly wink. "Whoo!"

I can feel my face burning as I smile and bow my appreciation again. The fox man tells me to come back anytime.

Zaniel looks up at me from his stool. I can't even look him in the eye. "Thanks for the food," I blurt out.

Then I make a run for it. It's raining now, not so hard that I have to stop and dig out my portable umbrella, but I don't get very far.

"Hey, lady!" Someone yells in perfect English. "You forgot something!"

"I'm okay, thanks," I shout back.

A bell rings right behind me. Zaniel is there, on my bike. There's a white box in a tiny plastic bag sitting in the basket, along with my big umbrella. "You sure? This looks pretty important. You might want it back someday."

"Give it back."

His eyebrow lifts. "Ah, so it *is* important. How could you forget your bike, silly?"

"*Get off* and give it back."

"Man, talk about ancient." His long thin fingers fiddle with the bicycle bell. Everyone passing us gives him a dirty look for making so much unnecessary noise. "I'm surprised it hasn't taken on a life of its own yet."

"You know what? Fine. Keep the bike. It's a thousand years old, anyway!"

I snatch the umbrella and take off. The guy's good. Weaving through all the people, still able to keep a steady pace with me, slowly riding the bike without so much as a wobble. Shit, is he going to follow me all the way home now?

"Hey, wait a sec! Aren't you going to tell me how I did? My interview. How was I?"

"Go *away*, please."

"Your manager seemed to dig me. How much do you earn a month, by the way?"

"GET. AWAY. FROM ME." I don't care about the dirty looks anymore; we've already created a scene.

"Whoa, whoa. Calm down." He looks concerned but he's still freaking smiling. "Take it easy. We're the same, remember?"

"The same what? I don't *know* you."

"Cybelle." Zaniel swings the bike sharply and blocks my way. He's serious now. "It's Cybelle, right? Please, just ... look, I'm sorry. You've been on your feet all day, chasing after little kids for who knows how many hours. I thought you could use a laugh. And a hearty meal. And another fellow *gaijin* to keep you company."

Nope. He's not cute enough to wipe the teacher glare off my face right now. I want my fucking bike back.

"No? Okay. Sorry. I thought that would be funny. I'm sorry. I know you think I'm the world's creepiest dude right now, but if you give me a little more time, I can explain everything."

"What? You mean there's *more* to this lucid nightmare?"

"I'm going to ignore that." He gets down from the bike with a smirk and hands me the plastic bag. "Here. Your dessert. A peace offering — the first of many."

I'm very careful not to make physical contact as I take it from him. "Thank you." He's still holding onto my bike, though. I entertain the idea of pushing him to the ground and pedalling like the devil is after me, but I'm super full. I wonder if that was part of his plan, too. We stand there in the drizzle, awkward and out of things to say. Then some jackass walks right into me from behind, pushing me right into Zaniel. He catches me as I stumble into him. He blushes instantly. I pull away.

"Man, it's really starting to pour. Come on. Let me take you somewhere special."

"Yeah, no offence, but it's getting late and I think I've had enough of *special* this week." I look down, past my food baby at my dessert package. It's a small, adorable box with wire handles and a tiny fox-faced character hand-drawn on the front and a speech bubble saying, "Thank you, come again!" in English.

"Well, we can't stand here making googly eyes at each other in the rain all night."

"Uh, *who's* making googly eyes at who now?" I ask defensively.

Zaniel ignores my question. "Come on. Let's get a cup of coffee — uh, not from Tully's though, I think they were getting ready to call the police on me for sitting there so long. A man can only drink so many swirkles."

"I'm full, thanks."

"Then let's go for a walk. Give you plenty of time to let your stomach settle. If you liked this udon guy, I know a place in Osaka that you will *love*. It's real close to where Festivalgate used to be —"

"Osaka? At *this* time of night? With *you?*"

"Yeah! Don't worry, you'll be perfectly safe. Think of me as your 'bodyguard.'" He pauses a beat. "I heard they make this huge *ohagi* platter that you've gotta see to believe."

"Oh man, I love *ohagi*," I blurt before I can stop myself. Who am I kidding, I was doomed to give in to any of this strange man's requests as soon as my ass hit that stool. "I guess my *betsu bara* can shift around a little in the next hour. But I'm warning you, if you try anything, I will take a chunk out of your jugular and make it look like an accident."

"Fair enough, my lady." He bows and leads the way. He takes my bike with him.

twelve
A VERY CURIOUS SENSATION

虎穴に入らずんば虎子を得ず
Nothing ventured, nothing gained

Zaniel can't sing. That's not to say I'm chastising him for it, because he did warn me. I just find it funny that everyone at Zozo thinks he's Mr. Perfect, but when it comes to carrying a tune, he can't do it. He can, however, keep up with rap lyrics, so our rendition of the Fugees' "Ready or Not" starts out rocky and ends with a clean finish. The crowd below the stage goes wild. Most people are eating or on their cellphones, but they are all cheering. One elderly salaryman in the pit below us is bowing *Wayne's World*–style, and the ones around him make scooping motions with their arms and shout *"Motto, motto!"* But we're only allowed to sing one song at a time, so we bow and jog backstage.

"Whew! I didn't think I was going to survive that!" Zaniel gasps. "You were right, though, it wasn't that fast, so … Cybelle?"

"Yeah …" I trail off, distracted. There's another set of stairs back here, leading down into darkness. There's a cold chill coming from it, which is weird because it wasn't cold outside at all. "Hey. What do you think is down there?"

Zaniel shrugs. "I don't know. Come on. We still have to pick our next song."

"Right. Um, how do you feel about 'Gangsta's Paradise'?"

He chuckles as I list off an assortment of rap songs we both might know as we head back to our table. I'm glad for the subject change. Thoughts of secret basement dungeons and torture chambers wash from my mind with the tide of people we wade through in this giant restaurant Zaniel has brought me to. On the speakers and on the stage, someone is now singing the *Sailor Moon* theme song. "I know this! 'Moonlight *Dentetsu*,' right?"

Zaniel bursts out laughing. "'*Densetsu'!*" he corrects me.

"All right, all right. *Sorry.*" I make a face at him, but I'm smiling. "You're not perfect, either, you know!" I hum along, leaning back against the soft leather cushion of our booth. I'm so full and tipsy I can't sit upright anymore. The ceiling glistens with its star lights, people continue to shout above the restaurant commotion while servers run back and forth with trays of food and drinks. Up on the stage, a drunk salaryman has the mic and is surrounded by rambunctious co-workers. The crowd below the stage sings along. And here in the middle of all this mayhem is me, sitting across from this attractive young man I just met this morning. If he had told me this is where we'd end up tonight, I would have laughed in his pretty, doe-eyed face. But he's a nice guy — too nice to be sick of my gaping and squeeing by now. He just smiles and refills my sake cup.

"There you go. The rest is all yours. Give it a good home."

"It's finished, already? How are you going through them so fast?"

"Stop *nursing* it. If this were a drinking contest, we'd have to sew you a special 'LOSER' sash."

I empty the last of our second bottle of hot sake into my mouth and pretend to splash him with my cup. Our waitress offers to bring us a third bottle and takes away a giant plate that once held a lavish display of *ohagi* arranged around a bowl of *adzuki* and vanilla ice cream. I tell her we're still working through it. She nods and takes away the dishes that once held our "fall *futomaki*" sushi, lemon-ginger fried chicken, *wara-yaki* salmon, and banana tempura drizzled with jasmine honey. She also offers to take away the box I got from the *kitsune* guy, but I still have one bite of lemon *manjuu* left inside. I pop it into my mouth and give her the box.

"So. Lady Cybelle," Zaniel stretches like a cat, "how happy are you that you took me up on my offer?"

I finish chewing to speak. I did consider changing my mind when we had to go through all those dark, weird alleys. And the old man at the gate who shouted when he saw me didn't help, but by then it was too late to stab Zaniel with my keys and make a run for it. I had already been spotted by the gorgeous maître d', who looked safe enough for me to come in. So, I tell him the truth:

"I *love* this place. Didn't think anything could replace Christon Café as my favourite restaurant. I mean, that *tree* in the courtyard! And the food! And the fact that they have stage karaoke …!" I throw up my arms at a loss for words. "This place is *amazing*! I'm so glad I didn't stab you."

He laughs as he looks down at his cup. "Me, too."

"Shit. I'm sorry," I sit upright. "I've creeped you out now, haven't I? I tend to do that to people."

"After all we've been through? Besides," Zaniel lifts his ice cream spoon to his perfect, rosy smirk, "dark humour just happens to be one of my biggest turn-ons."

Well, that shuts me up. I look away, as if it will hide my big-ass grin. Our waitress with great timing brings our sake. We fill each other's cups, clink them together, and drink.

"Damn, Kamisawa-*san*," I giggle. "You can really knock 'em back."

He points to his nose. "Salaryman. It's a job requirement." We laugh as I pour him another and he drains it in one go. "Pick another song." He hands me the menu tablet. I know just the tune for us. While I punch words into the search bar, he continues with our conversation. "So, as I was saying, we all dream the same dream. It just depends on how you look at dreams in general."

"Yeah, you said that. So, you're a lucid dreamer …"

"A dream walker. But, yes. You can call it that."

"Right. You can walk into other people's dreams and communicate with them … or so you claim."

"Yup. But that's not —"

"But that's not the same as lucid dreaming."

"Exactly. Being lucid means you know you're dreaming. What I do is —"

"Different. Don't worry, I got that part. But I still don't get how this works. Okay, let me ask you a question. Let's say, you *can* walk into my dream when I go to bed tonight …"

He grins shyly. "Mm-hmm …"

"But what if I go back to Canada? If you're in Osaka, and I'm in Toronto —"

"I could still do it, if I had the time. I've been dream-walking for years, so I'm pretty good at it. Sure, it would be extremely difficult to find you, and we'd have to be asleep at the same time, so I'd have to figure out your time zone and plan around that — and then I'd have to sleep *long* enough to find you because there's going to be millions of people between here and your city — but I'm pretty confident, yeah, I could do it."

"I see. Damn, they don't have 'Sandstorm.' And I'm still hungry. Hey, do we still want that 'Potato Mountain'?"

"Sure. Order a couple of beers, too. And see if they have 'Dream On' by Aerosmith."

"Okay. Now, what if I wanted you to … walk into one of my sisters' dreams. Could you do that?"

"Yup," he says without missing a beat.

"How? You've never met her."

"I don't have to meet her. It'd be harder because I'd have to approach a lot of people and say 'Hey, are you Cybelle's sister?' and odds are I might *never* meet her, what with the odds of finding one person in seven billion who all sleep at an inestimable number of times in a twenty-four-hour period. But if you're asking if I have the ability to find her without meeting her in person, then yeah. Absolutely." He winks at me. "How else do you think I found *you?*"

"Yeah, right." I bite my lip as I find "Dream On" and queue it up. "What if I wanted you to find my great-grandmother in Timbuktu, who doesn't speak a word of English?"

"You have a great-grandmother in Timbuktu?"

"No. But if I did?"

"Still doable."

"Even if she doesn't speak English?"

"She doesn't have to. We could still communicate. My grandpa called it '*yumego.*' It's like a universal language. One person speaks, the other understands. Language in dreams doesn't matter as much as you'd think." Zaniel reads the look on my face. "Don't ask me how. It just works that way."

"I thought you were the expert on all this!"

"So did I, until I met you."

I shift around in my seat. This guy really knows how to flirt, doesn't he? "Wait, hang on. That doesn't make any sense! Couldn't I just show you a picture of someone and you say, 'Okay, I'm going to dream about this person' and you go into your dream state, *thinking* you're in that person's dream?"

"We don't go into other people's dreams. We just run into each other." He pauses to hand me one of the beer mugs our server has just brought us. "*Ookini.* Anyway, here's the way my grandfather explained it to me. He was way more poetic than I am, and I'm drunk right now, so bear with me.

"Just like when we're awake, we all share the same plane of existence: I'm sitting here, you're sitting there, that man is standing way over there by the door, those people who just left are, I don't know, going to their families who live an hour away, over 'there,' halfway around the world, your family is 'there.' We might be close, or far, but basically, we're all in one wide expansive place — this city, Japan, Earth — and it's the same when we dream. It's all one big place, we're just in different parts of it, at different times, but ninety-nine percent of people don't know it. We think that we're asleep, in our beds, not going anywhere. Okay, so maybe physically, yes, our bodies are still there — but 'us,' when we dream, we go far, far away, and we all go to the same place. But since we forget most of our dreams, or we don't even realize we're dreaming, when we come to it's like we never left our beds. You with me so far?"

I nod. In my head, my sober voice tells me *this man is deluded*, but Drunk Cybelle finds this to be an interesting conversation. "Go on."

"Okay. Ninety-nine percent, that's what I said, right? Well, then you have that one percent. Or maybe more, or less — whatever — and they *know* they're dreaming. They realize it all of a sudden, like, 'Whoa, shit, I'm dreaming!' But it's not something they can hold onto. They still get sucked back into thinking it's all real, and they just keep going along with it. It's just a fleeting moment and poof. That's it. Back to slaying dragons and showing up to work naked."

"That's another thing I wanted to ask you. Do dragons and monsters and stuff exist in this 'other' world, too?"

"That would make sense, wouldn't it? Think about all the scary things that show up in your nightmares — and hell, even the good things that show up in your dreams — sure, they don't exist here, but it doesn't mean they don't exist at all." Zaniel pauses to take a swig of beer. "My grandfather had this theory, that all the mystical creatures we know and love lived here for thousands of years, but now that all this modernization and globalization has kicked in, they have no place here anymore. They had to move on, go somewhere else. We can convince ourselves we hunted all unicorns to extinction and destroyed mermaid habitats, or bulldozed all the faerie mounds to build condos —"

"If you're willing to admit you believe in those sorts of things?" I can't help but tease him a little.

"Exactly." He lets out a dry laugh. "But we've also convinced ourselves that so many of those creatures were immortal. So, the whole extinction thing doesn't really work. I guess we could say that some of those things can move between the two worlds."

"Yeah, I guess it's like a weird zone in time or space or whatever where all the supernatural stuff people've stopped believing in exist. Then, when sleeping humans wander into their world, the creatures get all excited and go running after 'em. We wake up thinking it was all in our heads; never give them a second thought." I take another sip of beer and rest my head on the table. "And the world is so big, odds are … these things that chase after us … we never see them again. Not their exact likenesses. People say recurring dreams are rare, so —"

"They just don't remember. The World is big. The dream world — or, what my grandpa called 'Yume'— is even bigger. What are the odds you'll run into the same monsters over and over again? Well, there's truth in that. Usually, you don't. Not if they aren't looking for you. Not if they don't know where to find you. But not everyone is so lucky. Not the one percent."

"Damn." I gaze at him, resting my chin on one hand. "I feel so sorry for you, now."

"Meh," he shrugs. "I'm starting to see it's not so bad. Sorry, that turned into a long explanation. I wish I knew how to explain it better. More poetic-like. My mom can. She'd like you. My mother." He gives me a sleepy, silly grin. "You're pretty, and sweet. Anyway. Forget everything I said. Let's just enjoy each other's company right now. If we sit down to analyze how all this is possible, it's going to turn our hair grey."

I look down at the table, trying to be covert about smothering my hand over my ever-widening grin. "Sounds like a good idea to me."

"It should. That was *your* advice, lady."

That *does* sound like something I would say, although I don't remember saying it today. "So now you're just going to repeat me to stay on my good side?"

"If I did, would you fall for it? Nah, I forgot; you're smart, too."

I try not to bite my hand off. *Dude. He thinks you're pretty and smart. And he hasn't mentioned you being "kowai" once! Say something cool.*

"I gotta pee."

He shrugs. "Washrooms are one more floor up."

The bathroom appears to be hooked up with the same speakers that make up the restaurant's karaoke system. I wonder if Zaniel has slipped me something, because no way in hell would Sober Cybelle listen to anyone prattle on about how he can walk through dreams, no matter how hot he is. But to Drunk Cybelle, it all just sounds super trippy. I try to imagine it. It isn't hard. This restaurant itself is a dream come true.

"Jibun Jishin," I whisper out loud. "Hey, wait; I know this song!"

I quietly rap along as I wash my hands. Luckily no one else in here pays much attention to *Samurai Champloo*'s theme as it fills the ladies' room with the strong scent of peach soap. Just as I dry my hands my phone vibrates in my pocket; as *Mom* scrolls by on the external display, I see how late it's getting. It's going to be one hell of an adventure getting to work tomorrow. *Saturday.* I have to call it a night. I hope Zaniel won't care. This doesn't feel like a real date. Not that I'd know.

Hi Cybelle sweetie, I read, *how is Japan? How are ur students? Any new adventures lately? I've been talking to your sisters and I truly believe in my heart that you need to come home next year by April,* etc., etc. "Oy." I click my phone shut. Calling her will make this an adventurous weekend indeed.

There are more people wandering around the restaurant than before I went to the washroom. That looks like our table, over there. Everyone stumbles so much it's like walking through a nightclub. I wonder if the owner ever worries that someone might get knocked into these bamboo railings and tumble right over. A lawsuit waiting to happen. That's when I notice each floor is staggered; if you fell over, you'd land on the next floor below instead of plummeting seven stories down. Good to know. Someone could get themselves killed up here.

Someone squeezes my shoulder, hard. A deep voice breathes nicotine and sour beer into my ear. *"Sumimasen —"*

Without turning I tell him it's not a problem. *"Iie."* I shrug him off, just as hard. Then I pick up the pace and assertively worm my way back to my table. Drunk-ass weirdo.

Zaniel has definitely reached his limit, too. His whole face is bright pink. He looks like he's sleeping, probably dreaming about something wonderful. A part of me wishes to curl up next to him and pass out; together, we could just wait here until morning, safe in the arms of a warm, deep, unconscious world. Dreaming together. On second thought, no, I need to go home.

I sneak into Zaniel's side of the booth and flop down on the seat as hard as I can. Zaniel flails to life. "Oh, I'm sorry," I joke. "Did I ruin your nap?"

"No," he closes his eyes again and rests his head against the back of the seat with a lazy Cheshire grin, like he couldn't care less that he was caught dozing in public. "Just my dream … Ah. There. Right back where I left off."

"Do I want to know what you're dreaming about? 'Cause I could see that drunk smile on your face all the way across the room."

He blushes a little more, but his eyes stay closed. He suppresses a chuckle as he imperceptibly shakes his head.

"Oh, it's that good, eh? Never mind then, I don't want to know." He sits silently with his eyes closed for a long time. I pick up his chopsticks and aim for his nose. He catches me by the wrist so fast I let out a startled scream, which turns into a laugh. "I'm sorry. I couldn't resist!"

He doesn't let go. "Tsk, tsk. I knew there had to be a catch with you. Now I have to learn how to sleep with one eye open."

"Don't do that. You stress out too much, your hair *will* turn grey."

"You've heard what I do for a living. I'm already turning my hair grey."

"Maybe it's time to quit."

He guides my wrist back down to the table, but instead of pulling away, his hand slips underneath mine. I marvel at his long black eyelashes while he watches as his thumb caresses my knuckles. "Maybe."

Maybe. Manager's favourite word. Maybe he's thinking of something deep and dark in his past, something that gives him this perfectly angelic look as his eyes focus on my hand. My gosh. He's so beautiful I could kiss him. No ... maybe I *should* kiss him. After all, I do have to leave. Maybe ...

"Rise and shine, *lovers*," says a deep voice. Something smashes down on the table so close to my other hand I can feel the air from it. Zaniel is looking at something above my head with terror in his eyes. There's a man standing at our table, big as a house, dressed in a black *haori* and *hakama*, with a giant fist tight around the neck of the four-litre *shochu* bottle he slammed in front of me.

"Oh! I'm sorry. Did I scare ya?" There's no sympathy in his raspy voice; he laughs. "See, Hino? What'd I tell ya? Nothin' to be afraid of." He speaks with an accent I've never heard before but it's also like heavy *katakana* English. I correct myself — I *have* heard it before. The fox man and the fish man spoke it, too. Where are all these guys from? Apparently, he's addressing someone behind him, whose image I can barely see past him because he takes up so much room. And I recognize his voice. He's the guy who grabbed my shoulder. Who exactly is this fucker?

"A-Akki … *sama* …" Zaniel finally speaks. "W-what are you doing here?"

"You lose track of time, dummy?" The giant man laughs again. "Jibun Jishin's open to *everyone* this time of night. Trains'll stop any minute, so I should be askin' *you* what you're doin' here." He's talking to Zaniel, but he's looking right at me. There's a glint of green in his eyes, and I've never seen a dude with so many teeth. But maybe that's all the alcohol talking (I've had a lot). "Relax, Zaniel-*kun*. No need to freak out. I went through the trouble to get *this* for ya! C'mon, we'll all have some."

"But —"

"Geez, kid. You in some kinda rush? Didn't look like it a second ago. Guess you were right, Hino. He don't like us no more."

The giant man steps to one side, exposing a girl behind him, hands in her school uniform jacket. For whatever reason, she's wearing sunglasses. "Probably too busy with *real* life," the girl says in an equally deep voice. "Give him the bottle and let us go."

The giant man ignores her. "How *is* life, Zaniel-*kun*?" Geez, why the fuck is he *still* staring at me?

Zaniel swallows. "Fine."

The man's smile stretches further than the human face should logically go; it almost looks like something unravelling. He reminds me of the Grinch. It's hard not to stare, but harder to look away. "Ain't you gonna *properly* introduce us to your new friend?" he asks, leaning on the table so hard I expect it to break. He smells like a mixture of pine forest and sake strong enough to disinfect a toilet. I drop my gaze. Maybe I'll just stare at my lap until this awkward-ass conversation is over and I can go home.

"No. Come on, let's get out of here."

Zaniel takes my hand and gestures for me to get out of the booth. I'm so grateful I could kiss him. Hell, I would have, if it weren't for the giant man blocking my path with his crotch.

"Aw, what's your hurry?!" the big man shouts and stamps the table with his bottle again. "Sit down. We're gonna have a drink. *Oi, omae!*" He grabs a passing waitress by the arm and even bumps her against our table. "We need four glasses — and bring us a plate of fugu liver. I ain't waitin' for these *people* to clear out. I paid good money to dine here, too, y'know!"

Shit. Cornered by a drunk samurai wannabe the size of a Gundam. Talk about timing. Zaniel pulls me back into the booth, shaking his head. What have I gotten myself into? Time to do the only thing I know how: smile, nod, and make the best of things until I get myself back to my apartment, alive and physically unscathed.

The giant man makes a grandiose gesture to the schoolgirl, who bows with a polite *"shitsureishimasu"* before sliding into the seat as far as she can. I'm a little offended until the giant squeezes himself in and plops down on the cushion hard enough to make it pop. He still has one massive tree-trunk leg sticking out of the booth. "We weren't properly introduced. I'm Akki. I have a feelin' Zaniel-*kun* still hasn't told you about me."

Something tells me not to confirm this fact, nor offer my hand. I give him my best Zozo smile. "I'm Cybelle. Nice to meet you."

"Cybelle?" he snorts. "That's what you call yourself? Heh. Never heard that one before. You ever hear that one, Hino? 'Cause *I've* never heard of it. Weird, huh?" Akki can't seem to get over this new combination of sounds he's discovered. "Cybelle. What kinda name is that, anyway? Cybelle ... Cyb ... elle. That's a new one. Never heard of it."

"Relax, dude," I mutter. "Didn't ask if you had."

Zaniel looks like someone just jabbed him with a fork. He looks at Akki and seems relieved to see the giant laughing that loud barking laugh of his. "Oh, ho, ho, still cheeky, I see. I like that. Anyway. This is Hino."

"Nice to meet you, too." I nod at her. It doesn't make sense to fuel this conversation any further. Not that Hino looks interested in talking. She just sits there and stares in my general direction through her shades. "Sorry to cut this short, Zaniel, but I have to —"

"Sumimasen, okyaku-sama," two waitresses sing in harmony as they carry a giant platter of fries between them and set it on the table. "'Potato Mountain' *degozaimasu! Jibun rashiku ite kudasai!"* They bow and leave. Shoot, I forgot we ordered this. But judging by the disgusted look on this Akki guy's face, I don't have to share.

"Don't mind Hino, *Sigh*-belle, she's a bit of a bitch around strangers. No manners whatsoever, right? Not that —"

"Excuse me, Cybelle-*sama*," Hino cuts him off, clearly not listening to a word her friend is saying. "May I ask you … what are you doing here in Japan?"

"Uh, well … I work for an *eikaiwa*, about twenty minutes west of here."

"No. I mean, where did you come from? How did you come to be here?"

"I …" I'm temporarily distracted by the plate of quivering fish flesh a waitress sets down in front of the giant man, along with his four glasses. He slurps it down with one hand before the waitress has even finished bowing. "I came from Canada?" I want to add *by plane,* but something about this girl scares the sarcasm out of me.

Hino asks patiently, "But is that where you are *really* from?"

"Yeah, that's a damn good question." Akki squints at me. "How the fuck did you end up all the way out *there*?"

"I don't …" I trail off, helpless. What the hell are they asking me?

"Forgive me," Hino relaxes. "I understand; some of our kind are more concerned with privacy than others. I will not push further. May I ask instead, what brought you to our land?"

Our kind? Our *land*? "The food?"

When Hino smiles, I understand why she scares me. The movements of her face are just as frightening as Akki's but for different reasons. She looks like a perfectly normal teenage girl, but at the same time I can tell what her incisors would feel like if she were to sink them into my skin. They'd pierce through human flesh like a knife through soft butter. "Ah, now I see."

"What the *hell* is goin' on with you tonight?" Akki chuckles at her.

"Like you will ever understand. It was nice to finally meet you, Cybelle-*sama*. I hope Japan is to your satisfaction. We should all be honoured to have your kind here." She bows as low as she can despite the Formica table in her face, then turns to Akki. "I am leaving now. Excuse me."

"But we just got here —"

"Move."

With the agility of a startled spider, Akki scoots out of the booth for her to leave. At the last second, I get the bright idea to say I'd like to go with her, something about girls going to the restroom in groups. But I'm too slow. Akki blocks me a second time as she disappears into the crowd. He watches the girl almost forlorn before he finally sits back down.

"My, my, the effect you have on others, *Sigh*-belle," the man snickers. He seems to be the only one amused by all this. "Anyway, I think we got off on the wrong foot — least, that's what Hino thinks. She thinks we ought to be friends. Makes sense, 'cuz I ain't got any, 'cept for maybe Zaniel-*kun* here. So, I thought, let's get drunk and get to know each other! Ain't never met one of your kind before. Thought it'd be interestin'."

"Sorry, but I gotta leave. Zaniel, how much do I …?" Zaniel gives me a sad puppy-dog look. Shit. Not the puppy eyes. I want to go *home*. Or at least far away from this rando.

"Ah, don't worry about the tab, kids! It's on me." The giant man yanks a golden ring off his finger and flings it onto the table.

"I'll even cover the *gaijin* crap. I'm that nice. But like I was sayin', showin' up on my territory and all that really threw me for a loop. Can't blame me for overreactin', right? But hey, don't mean we can't still be friends. We can be … if you're smart about it."

Gaijin crap? *His* territory? Oh please, don't tell me this man is trying to say I don't belong here. "I didn't see any 'Japanese only' signs out front," I reply in a cold voice.

"Pssh, yeah, that'll change, hopefully. Ugh, *speakin'* of which, what do you say we get out of here and head up to my place instead? You know, before the flood of *people* take over this place? I can show you a way better time there." He snickers and points at me. "You'll have to ditch the *gaijin* getup of course, 'cuz I don't mess with that. Say, what's with that getup, anyway?"

I sit there frozen for a moment. "You're not serious."

"'Course I am! I ain't walkin' around with no *gaijin*. Besides, this is Jibun Jishin! You're supposed to do away with all that jazz. You know, you're awfully uptight for a half-human."

"A *what*?!" People passing by our table stop and stare, but I don't give a shit.

"Well you *are*." The man tries to cross his legs under the table and gives up. "What? What am I saying wrong?"

Zaniel looks between Akki and I, bewildered. He probably thinks I'm going to punch this dude, but no. I take a calming breath instead. "Okay. I think you've worn out your welcome, sir."

Akki chuckles. "… what is that, some kinda joke?"

"Zaniel and I were having a conversation and you interrupted us. I'm sure you can find a table elsewhere. It's a big restaurant."

Akki's smile slowly turns from lighthearted to menacing without moving a muscle. "I don't want another table. I like this one. After all, that's *my* friend you're sittin' next to. Zaniel hasn't told you who you're dealin' with, has he?"

"He's mentioned you. But I don't care. You can't go around talking to people like that."

"Hmph. *People*. Right. Look, you're obviously new 'round here. If it's entertainment you're lookin' for, don't bother with the kid. He ain't gonna know the first thing about what to do with ya. I'm tellin' ya, my place is more fun." He looks at me like I would be a fool to turn him down. "Plus, I got swords."

I look him dead in his eyes. They seem to have caught the reflection of some neon green light from somewhere. "No."

It's finally enough to wipe the grin off his freaking face. "Fine! Whatever! Didn't want to sleep with you, anyway. Don't fuckin' flatter yourself, I would've been doin' *you* the favour. Come on, Zaniel, let's bounce. This bitch ain't no fun. Stuck-up, just like all the other fuckers."

"He doesn't have to go anywhere," I blurt out.

"He's mine," Akki jerks his girth out of the booth and stands up. "Get your own."

I turn to Zaniel, who has never look so scared. I don't understand his fear. Maybe because I don't feel scared myself. I didn't expect him to defend me — people rarely do. If I was more sober I'd be more fearful of rubbing a guy like this the wrong way. It's easy to guess what sort of crowd he hangs around. But right now, I'm not afraid of anyone or anything. "Are you?" I ask him. "Are you 'his'? You really want to leave with him?"

Zaniel swallows. "No."

"Then, don't," I say quietly, taking his hand in mine again. He relaxes. Even smiles a little.

"Oh *hell*, no," Akki curses. "This stops NOW."

He grabs my shoulder and starts to pull. I'm livid. I don't know what he expects to happen, but this being the third time a man has put his hands on me this week does not sit well. I writhe from his grip and elbow him right in the chest. "Don't TOUCH ME." It's not enough to do much damage, but it does throw him off-balance. He topples against the table.

Something else topples with him. It must have been in the

folds of his *haori* jacket. A small pinkish-grey sphere rolls under the lips of the empty plates and comes to a stop against the soy sauce holder at the end of the table. A large brown circle points right back at me.

It's an eyeball.

"What the hell ...?" Zaniel asks, equally horrified. "You ... you've been ..."

Akki's voice is deadpan. "Oh, don't look so shocked." He reaches for it and straightens himself up. "Geez, you and Hino are two pages out the same damn book. Killjoys."

I'm locked into my seat, gripping the leather, focusing my gaze on something — *anything* — so I don't scream, or vomit, or pass out. *There was a fucking eyeball on the table.*

"How long ..." Zaniel's voice is hoarse. "How long have you ...?"

"Like it *matters.* Geez. Now, are we gettin' out of here, or you gonna hang around with this ... *thing*?"

"*Thing?!*" I start, but Zaniel is suddenly shoving me out of his way to slide out of the booth. I'm about to yell at him, too, until he pushes me behind him in a protective stance.

"Zaniel-*kun*, geez." Akki looks mildly entertained. "Don't run over the girl. Someone's gonna think you got the shits."

"Akki-*sa*—" he pauses. The silence hangs in the air like a dagger. Then it drops. "I quit."

Akki is still smiling. He waves his hands like he's talking to an unintelligent child. "No, dummy. I didn't say 'quit,' I said —"

"I QUIT."

Everything stops. The servers, the dinner talk, the karaoke singers. It feels like everyone is frozen in various poses of stunned awkwardness. "I'm done. Finished. This —" he points between himself and Akki "— is over."

The smile on Akki's face slowly disappears, then morphs into a warped mixture of admiration and respect. "I see. So you've decided to grow some balls. 'Bout time. A good woman'll bring that out in ya."

"Like *you'd* ever know." Zaniel's hand brushes against my hip. Instinctively, I grab it and squeeze. "And this has nothing to do with her. It's about … how you *promised* you would never, *ever* hurt anyone."

"Okay, Zaniel, shut *up*," Akki lowers his voice as a couple passes by with wary glances. "Ain't like the whole planet needs to hear."

"I don't care who hears. I don't mind if the planet knows I'm no longer under Akki's thumb. *I'm done.* And for the record, Cybelle's not a *thing*. She's a person. We both are. Being *gaijin* doesn't make us any less of a human being."

Akki looks at me as if seeing me for the first time. His face goes slack. *"Gaijin?"*

This idiot. What the hell did he *think* I was? "Yeah," I say, trying to summon my drunken bravery back. *"Gaijin.* Duh. It's not makeup; it doesn't come off. Get on the *tokkyuu*, pal."

Zaniel turns to me. "Come on. We're leaving."

A part of me wants to take his arm. Another wants to push Zaniel out of the way and run for it. A third has to go pee again. I honestly have no idea what to do. He takes the initiative by taking my hand. We don't get far with Akki's paw on Zaniel's shoulder.

"The hell you are. Your little jokes have gone far enough, boy."

"I'm not your boy." Zaniel thrashes and shakes Akki off. "I haven't been your *boy* for years. I'm through with this — this BULLSHIT you call … you know what, I don't even know what to call it. I won't help you do it. I don't care about demons coming after me anymore. I'd rather deal with a thousand of them than one of *you*."

Akki stands there, dumbstruck. So does the entire restaurant, for a time. Zaniel gives me a pointed look, turns, and walks away, pulling me along with him. My heart feels like it's going to burst.

It almost does when Zaniel suddenly lurches as he is grabbed from behind, whirled around, and socked in the stomach. Some people gasp as he crumples to the floor, but several more jump up from their tables and booths and scatter to get away. Before I can get down to see to Zaniel, Akki is stepping over his body and grabbing my upper arm, hard, squeezing me like I owe him money and he's about to beat it out of me. I know no one is coming to help me. There's only one thing left to do. I scratch the air like a cat with my free hand until I hit something that feels like a face, and when Akki shouts in pain and releases me, I lift up one foot and drive it right into his groin.

"OW!" Akki goes down clutching himself, looking hurt and confused. "What the hell was that for?!" He staggers to his feet and stands upright. I brace for another attack.

"Akki!" I hear Zaniel's voice behind the large man. He turns just in time to catch the end of a four-litre *shochu* bottle square in the face with a splintering glassy sound. He spins 270 degrees, staggers backward, and flips right over the railing. Zaniel doesn't lower the remains of the bottle neck until we all hear him crashing onto a table a few floors below, followed by the screams of whomever he almost crushed.

All I can do is stand here with my hands on my head. "Shit," I say. "Oh shit, oh shit, oh shit, you killed him. You *killed* him!"

"If only it were that easy," is all Zaniel says. He tosses the broken glass aside like he smacks people with giant liquor bottles every day and takes me by the hand. "This is the part where we run."

"Run?! Run where? There's like a hundred cameras and witnesses in this place! We aren't running anywhere! Holy crap, my whole life is over. My family won't even cross the ocean to visit me — they're not going to come bail me out of Japanese jail!"

He points to the emergency exit he's dragging me toward. "No, we're not going *on the run*, we just have to —"

"Let go of me! You fucking killed someone! What the hell is wrong with you?!"

He smiles. "Oh, how the tables have turned. But seriously, we really should get going before he does."

I didn't think my jaw could drop any lower. I don't know how much time passes with me standing there, covering my mouth like an idiot while Zaniel pulls at me, before the whole room shakes with the scariest noise I've ever heard. It sounds like a pig squealing, but much louder — angrier, too — and it seems to be coming from below us. From what I can see over the railing, everyone on the lower floor is screaming and shoving each other out of the way. Something large and heavy flies into the air and slams into the railing, right where our booth is: an angry, ravenous animal is scrambling, clawing its way back up to the seventh floor. It's hard to see because the restaurant is so dark, but if it wasn't for all those drinks I'd say it was a shadow with neon-green teeth. No, not teeth. Tusks.

Panic ensues. Fights seem to break out on all sides of us as people run for the nearest exits. Crumpled on the floor, an older man laughs himself in stitches. *"FAITOOO!"* he cries with a mouth full of teeth and blood. As if they've prepared for this their whole lives, all servers and bartenders put down their trays and menus and file along in neat orderly lines to the nearest emergency exits. Everyone else pushes and screams. Zaniel grabs my jacket, umbrella, and purse, yanks me into a stairwell, and presses me against the cold stone walls to avoid the barrage of panicked, flailing patrons. Some still have napkins tucked into their shirts, others are still holding chopsticks, and one small woman has a mouth full of what used to be some kind of mousse cake half-spilling from her lips as she shouts for everyone to get the hell out of her way.

"Well, I said I could go for an adventurous Friday night," I gasp. "Never again."

Zaniel is giggling. He's clearly still drunk. "Look on the bright side, at least you don't have to work tomorrow!"

I could slap him. "I *do* have to work tomorrow!"

"What?! Why?"

"*EIKAIWA.*"

He cocks his head, thinking about it for a second, then bursts out laughing. "Oh, right! I completely forgot."

"Oh, terrific. You've snapped. You're violent *and* happy about it. Fantastic."

"Just hold onto me and keep your legs moving. Whatever happens, do not let go. Think New Year's shopping sale. Think rush hour at Shibuya Station!" His voice gets higher the more he speaks, like's he's getting off on the excitement.

"I don't go to either of those things, just to avoid situations like this!"

"Then you haven't lived, my dear. Where's your sense of adventure?"

"Is that why you slugged that guy?! For adventure?"

He grips my hand tighter with a mischievous smirk. "Isn't that what we've both been looking for?"

I groan to myself. "Sweet merciful ... What have I done?" Wait a minute. What *have* I done? Nothing. I don't owe this guy anything. I barely know him. He's only been hanging around me for the job ... right? "Zaniel," I say calmly, ignoring the patrons pushing and shoving into us on their way down the steps. "I'm going to need my hand back."

Zaniel gives me a puzzled look. He doesn't let go, but I can feel his grip relax. I don't bother to wait. I wrench my hand away. Now it's my turn to push and shove my way down the stairs. Someone higher up the stairs, presumably a woman, screams. Another bout of panic ensues as the crowd surges down the steps. I hear my name over the cries of terror. A rogue salaryman tries to shove me from behind. I shove back as we all burst through an emergency exit door into a back alley. I'm carried by the tide of people into an empty *shoutengai* where I run past closed shops and stores until

I see a sign for the Midosuji subway line. I fly down the st
the empty station halls, not even stopping to dig my wa
from my purse and scan it over the ICOCA panel. The train plays
a happy tune as the door slides closed a split second after I run in. I
don't stop to look over my shoulder or catch my breath until I pass
through each car to the last one, where I collapse on the empty row
of seats. I'm alone. I'm safe.

I'll never wish for adventure again.

"Ima oki ... Ima oki ... Ima oki ... Ima oki ..."

I open my eyes to the peaceful sounds of an autumn weekend morning: ambient chatter below my windows, people walking
their dogs, a garbage truck rolling by, announcing to the world that
it's making a left turn. I snuggle deeper into my covers, relieved my
head isn't thumping in pain from last night, content to have the
rest of the weekend to recover from the hell that unfolded in the
blink of an eye.

"Ima oki ... Ima oki ... Ima oki ... Ima oki ..."

Oh, wait. There's another sound I didn't notice before — muffled, staticky. It's my alarm clock lying prostrate on its side, clock
flashing 12:00 p.m. It sounds broken. I don't even have the energy
to shrug. I'm going to need a dozen hotcakes to care. Looks like I'm
going to lie here a while until I'm too hungry to function and I have
no choice but to get out of bed. Ugh. Freaking Osaka. Freaking
Jibun Jishin. I may never leave my house on a Friday night again.

Did I just say Friday night?

"OH FUCK, IT'S SATURDAY."

I launch myself from my futon, dive onto my purse, and dump
everything onto the floor. I snatch up my phone and check the
time.

1:11 p.m.

My heart sinks into my stomach like a rock. If I had anything in my stomach right now, I'd be puking it up.

I'm holding back tears when I get on the elevator of the Zozo building. There's a mantra screaming in my head: *Third time's a charm. Strike three, you're out.* A string of idioms with the number three follows. The first two times this happened, I got fucking lucky. There's no way I'm not getting fired for being three hours late. Not a chance in hell.

The elevator doors slide open; the Zozo lobby is only half lit. I don't hear anything — no shrieking students, no high-pitched singsong voices of teachers, no parent chatter, no rampaging Manager or Bucho spitting fire down my throat, nothing. I'm completely alone.

"Holy *balls.*" It's so quiet the word "balls" echoes down the hallway. If anyone were actually here, they certainly would have heard it. Not again. There's no way I am doing this for the third time in a month and getting away with it by some divine plan. It is a normal day, a normal freaking Saturday, and by all rights and accounts I should be getting the tongue-lashing of a lifetime. "What the hell is going on this time?"

"Morning," a warm cello voice says behind me that makes me jump out of my skin. Zaniel is sitting on the waiting couch right beside the elevator doors. He's scrolling on his iPhone with one hand. One long leg crossed over the other, dressed in jeans, long slim-fit black jacket, sunglasses, and a fashionable scarf, looking like he's waiting for a bus. He grins at me. "Sleep well?"

"Oh no," I groan. "What are you doing here?"

"Meow," he pretends to claw at me. "I thought you'd be happy to see me again. Last night was so much fun."

"If *you're* here, it can't be good." I gesture to the empty lobby and the weird lighting. "Now if you don't mind, I'm pretty sure I'm fired."

Zaniel's eyebrows arch into two devilish-looking shapes. "Are you sure?"

"Aaaaahhh," I hear a voice come from the staff room. "Cybelle-*sensei* ..." It's Manager.

"Oh, sweet mercy," I mutter. I drop my purse on the floor and kick my shoes off, not bothering with my slippers. I won't need them when I'm on all fours, bowing in apology. "Manager, I'm so sorry, my alarm clock —"

Manager is lying on the floor, taking up half the staff room, wrapped in baby blankets, using the broken, twitching Anpanman toy as a pillow. He looks as happy as a just-fed newborn. "Cybelle-*sensei*," he says again, dreamily. "Aaah ... so sorry ... I forget, again. No school. So sorry ... maybe ..." his eyes droop closed.

I stare at him for a long time. There are too many things going on in this room to wrap my head around all at once. "No school? What the hell?" I wait, then clear my throat. He snores. He is out cold. "MANAGER."

"Ah!" Manager sits upright. "Ah, so sorry! Cybelle-*sensei*. Do you know? Maybe, today, typhoon will come. So today, no school. All classes — cancelled. I call everyone. But I forget you. Again. I'm so sorry. But today, you can take a rest!" He grins foolishly. "Like me! I rest, after I call everyone. I ... so tired ..." He wipes his hands over his face like he's trying to wash the exhaustion away and lies back down.

"What the heck are you talking about? We just *had* a typhoon. Manager? Manager, can you hear me?! Fucking hell."

"Everything all right?" Zaniel calls from the lobby couch. He's still playing with his phone.

"No." This is scary. Maybe he's just severely hungover. I kneel down to Manager's level. "Manager, if there's a typhoon coming, why are you sleeping here?"

"Ah, ha ha ..." he rolls away from me. "I'm so sleepy," he says. "*Meccha nemui na ...*"

Zaniel snickers in the staff room doorway. "Well, you heard the man. School's out! Let's go."

"I can't just leave him here. He's an ass, but … but … I don't know, we just can't leave him here." I go back to where I left my purse, to look for my phone, to call Yoshino. Perhaps she can talk me out of this drug-induced dream.

Zaniel crouches down next to me. His hand closes over mine before I can call anyone. "My lady —" he removes his sunglasses "— you just got yourself a three-day weekend. And you're going to enjoy it."

"How can I enjoy anything when —" I pull away a bit. "What's going on with your eyes?"

On cue, they dart back and forth between mine. "What's wrong with them?"

"Nothing. That's just it. They're gorgeous."

Zaniel blushes. "Maybe they're contacts."

"They're not." I squint. "You don't have any circles around the iris. Like you had yesterday."

He rises to his feet and holds out his hands. "Nothing slips by you, huh? I keep forgetting how clever you are. Now, let's leave the little men alone to their sleepy time and get out of here."

"*Oh*, no." I stumble away from him to stand up before my heart takes over my brain, which *should* be shunting me to the emergency exit. Not that I want to see one of *those* again anytime soon. "You did something to him, didn't you? What did you give him? Drugs? Sleeping pills? *Anpan?* What did you do to him?! And who are you calling 'my lady'? I'm not your *anything.*"

"All I said was there was a typhoon coming." Zaniel pouts innocently. "I didn't say it was coming *now.*"

I pause. "So, there's no typhoon."

The corners of his pouting lips begin to twitch. "You might say that. It's funny … I was just sitting there, talking to myself about the typhoon Japan had a few days ago. And he just so happened to be taking a nap at the desk when I did. I guess something in my voice persuaded him to be extra cautious today?"

"Ah, now I get it." I nod. "I'm dreaming. I knew there had to be something. I'm still asleep, in my bed, and this is all a lovely, glorious nightmare."

"Oh no, you're awake. You must be, because I am, too. And from what I can tell, you were fully late for work today — don't look at me, not my fault — but lucky for you, I thought you might be a little worn out from all the excitement last night and figured you might like a day off. Now you've got one! You're welcome."

"Great!" I head straight for the elevator. When I punch the button, it opens right up. "I'm going home."

"*An*-punch! *An*-kick! *Mata ne!*" Anpanman groans from the staff room.

"Oh, no you don't." Zaniel picks something up off the floor — a backpack — and leaps in after me. "We're going out. But," he looks me up and down, "you'll want to go home and change into something else. It's going to be a long day." I glare at him for a long time. He jumps a little, realizing he hadn't pushed the button for the ground floor. I'm still glaring at him. He blushes when he finally notices. "Yeah, I figured you'd give me that look. Come on; follow me."

We go outside where he leads me past the bike rack to a neatly parked scooter. It's large enough to seat two average-sized passengers. Zaniel lifts up the large seat to reveal two motorcycle helmets — one white, with a black dot, and one black, with a white dot.

"Dare I ask what you intend to do with this?"

"I don't know," he sings. "By that growling noise in the elevator I was thinking you might like to get some breakfast first. Maybe you won't be so afraid of me on a full stomach."

Damn. He has a point. I'm also sure I'd be better off eating something for energy when the time comes to pepper-spray him and shove him off a bridge. "Fine. There's a Saizeriya down the street, a Mos Burger, a KFC, and a Mister Donut in the mall, a

McDonald's that way, and a … What's so funny? You're *laughing* at me, now? What's so funny?!"

Zaniel shakes a teasing finger at me. "If we go to *all* of those places, we're never going to get anywhere."

I can't help smiling a little. "Those are your *options*. Don't be a jerk."

He laughs again and tosses the black helmet at me. I almost drop it. "Tell you what. I'll give you an hour. If you'd like to go home and change out of your lovely suit, if you want to grab one meal or ten, it's up to you. I'll wait right here, and if you're too scared to join me on a little trip, I will understand."

I caress the helmet in my bike basket the whole time at the red light while waiting to cross the intersection near my 7-Eleven, and let it rest in my lap as I eat some eggs at my *kotatsu* and watch *Doraemon* on TV for the first time in — wow, I can't remember how long it's been since I had a Saturday to myself. What harm can come from just chilling out here until Tuesday? Plenty of harm can come from a joyride with a cute, possibly homicidal stranger who now knows where I work.

I groan. He *is* cute. And I really don't know what else I'll do with my day.

"Son of a bitch."

I take a quick shower, put on a pair of jeans, an Afropunk T-shirt, my Kuromi scarf, and my favourite hoodie. I also eat a matcha bagel with rose jam after I pack some snacks, gloves, and a small spa bag and throw them all into my messenger bag. If I end up wandering the streets on the run from the law tonight, I'm going to need them.

Zaniel is still where he promised he would be. "So, where would you like to eat?"

"I had breakfast. Let's get this over with."

He smirks, lowering his sunglasses from the top of his head. "Suit yourself."

"You promise you're not going to murder me." It's not a question.

Zaniel takes my hand and locks my pinky with his. "I promise." He pauses. "I'm sorry for what happened last night. I took too long to stand up for you. It won't happen again."

I nod, slightly impressed. "Apology accepted."

"Not yet," he pulls me onto the back seat. "That was just the verbal part of my apology."

Riding on the back of a scooter is smoother than I thought. It's also scarier. I have no choice but to pretend this guy knows what he is doing as he swerves and leans around the compact cars and mopeds we pass on the main roads. Then we hit the highway. I feel the scooter engine shivering between my thighs as it accelerates to match the speed of traffic. I was a little hesitant about touching him before, but all that shyness is gone and I wrap my arms around Zaniel's waist, tighter than any seat belt. The sky is a lovely clear blue, beautiful as any given day in spring, and just as warm. My ass there's another typhoon coming. What am I thinking? Why am I *not* at work? What the hell am I doing on the back of a scooter with some random albeit gorgeous guy I just met yesterday? And what's in this backpack he has me wearing? What if it's drugs? *I should be at work.*

These are the first words out of my mouth when we finally pull over at a rest stop that looks like a space station and my jelly legs can barely get me inside. "I should be at work. And you haven't said where we're going."

"No," Zaniel tousles his helmet-hair and beams at me. "I haven't."

He guides me inside and plants me right in front of a meal ticket *jidouhanbaiki* to get some food (he hands me a crisp 10,000-yen note) while he uses the restroom. My mind is reeling with panic — we are hella far from Nishibe — which gains me the sympathy of several large men in biker outfits who think I don't know how to use the machine and put all their English skills together to order me two chicken *katsu* curry plates. They reluctantly depart when Zaniel returns, but every now and then they wave from their booth and ask me if I like Japanese food.

The curry and the coffee Zaniel treats me to help my nerves a bit. So do our conversations. I have to keep reminding myself that this dude is a complete stranger, because he's so easy to talk to. He's no different from the way he talked during his interview. I honestly can't pinpoint why he doesn't have a single close friend. No mention of killing puppies or vowing revenge on his mother or looking for someone to complete him. Maybe others shy away from him. I can't imagine why. Maybe it's his eyes. He mistakes my deep thought for reluctance to get back on the road. "Ready for round two?" He smiles reassuringly. Teasing me, he pulls out my chair and offers me his arm, like I'm a fragile old lady. He even picks my helmet up off the table with great care, handing it to me as if it were a giant egg.

"See you again!" the biker with the highest mohawk shouts at me. I wave back with my left hand, then I feel something slide against my right pinky and gently pull me away. The biker guys make high-pitched wooing sounds before I can look down to see Zaniel's pinky locked with mine as he nonchalantly guides me back to his scooter. He doesn't even look their way. I have to admit, it's a pretty sly way to tell people to back off, taking handholding to an exponentially high level.

"It's okay," I joke after a while. "I don't think they're going to kidnap me and make me teach them English at knifepoint."

Zaniel studies me with a mockingly unconvinced look. He weaves the rest of his fingers through mine. He grins. "You never know."

Again, my legs turn to jelly. They tremble against Zaniel as the scooter revs to life. "Are you going to tell me where we're going now?" I ask.

"It's a surprise."

All the towns we pass through are small, just wide enough to fit a few houses and a Jusco or two. Everything else is rice paddies and rolling green hills. Then we hit a solid block of traffic and Zaniel guides us down several smaller, one-way streets. I start to worry ... until I recognize the familiar orange-red silhouettes of Fushimi Inari's torii through the trees, and then the telltale spike of the Kyoto Tower antenna as we pause at a traffic light. "See?" Zaniel points at the tower. "We made it one piece. You need to relax. You're officially on vacation from your stressful job today. Now, we should get something to eat ... unless, you're not hungry yet?"

"I'm always hungry," I shout over the revving car engines.

"So I've noticed!"

We drive on a little more, past the tower, some shrines and temples, up and down a couple of side streets, along the Kamo River, whizzing past a group of *maiko* being chased by tourists armed with selfie sticks in front of the Minami-za kabuki theatre. Then we cruise into a big parking lot and the scooter engine stops. Wobbly legged and jittery, I follow Zaniel back to the main street in the direction of an electronic train schedule board hanging over a big expanse of space. People hobble this way and that as they manoeuvre themselves into an old-school-looking building. "Keihan railway, Eizan railway, Demachiyanagi Station" it says in English and Japanese.

"What are we doing *here*?" I wonder, still looking up at the building. "Where are we going?"

"I told you. It's a surprise."

Zaniel takes the change from lunch and buys two tickets for each of us. I make a face at him while the station attendant takes one of Zaniel's tickets and puzzles over mine. "'Happy birthday' surprise, or 'I was the killer all along' kind of surprise?" I ask.

"Happy birthday surprise, silly; what do you take me for?"

I wager a guess. "Someone who hypnotizes a girl's boss into giving her the day off, that's what."

He smirks. "Doesn't make me a killer."

The train is packed, but we manage to nab the last space on the seat. The ride is relatively quiet between Zaniel and I. Our attempts to make small talk about how many tourists Kyoto gets are pointless. It's too loud to hear ourselves over them. At the last stop, tour guides shout in what sounds like Mandarin over the chatter of the train car. We herd off with all the others. Zaniel grabs my hand and pulls me through the violent crowds to a long flight of steps and a cable car. We sit across from an elderly couple who stare at us the entire way up. The cable car dangles precariously over the treetops as it ascends into the mountains. Everything gets quieter the farther we get from the city, which spreads down below us like the sea. *"Keshiki ga subarashii desu ne?"* the woman says to Zaniel, remarking on how much I'm enjoying the view. She asks Zaniel where we're from, how long have we been in Japan, and whether we've been to Enryakuji Temple before. Zaniel blushes and says we're going up Mount Hiei. I sneak a glance at him, which makes him even redder. When it comes time to disembark, they insist on letting us go first. The woman says something to her husband about how she could never do what I'm doing, living in a foreign country. *"Gaikokujin tsuyoi na,"* her husband replies.

"You could have just told me where we're going, you know," I pretend to scold Zaniel. "I've been here before."

"But then," he says, looking around to get his bearings, "it wouldn't have been a surprise. You hungry yet?"

"Um, kind of."

"Good. Come on."

Like I have a choice. "You say that a lot."

He just laughs.

We go to a little 7-Eleven next to the station and take our time selecting bento boxes and *Chu-His*, along with some chilled plums and pickles, then weave through the mob of tourist groups heading for the temple. I'm glad we're not going there, even though I don't understand why he wanted to bring me here. Mount Rokko would have been much closer. Why drive all the way here? Still, I don't question it. If he's here to kill me, I rationalize, I can always push him off a cliff or something.

We talk less and less on our way up the mountain. We stop once or twice, exchanging embarrassed chuckles between us at our own exhaustion, but after some time, the trees thin out and we reach a wide open clearing. We can see the whole city from here. Zaniel takes a thick blanket out from his backpack and spreads it out on the ground for us. Sitting feels great. Digging into my bento feels even better. Zaniel is just as hungry as I am, if not hungrier. He finishes slurping down his last noodles and reclines on his elbows when I've only just finished my *hijiki* salad. I assume he's enjoying the view until I sneak a glance over at him. He's staring at me. I can't help smiling despite the mouthful of food. "*Now* what?!"

He grins back, shyly looks down at his lap. After I finish eating, he hands me a *Chu-Hi* from his backpack. He then takes his phone out of his backpack, pops in an earbud, and offers me one (after a thorough courtesy wipe on his thigh). I shrug *sure* and take it. I can't place the music or the artist, but it's lovely, soothing stuff. Drawn-out organ chords and enigmatic high-pitched lyrics in a language I've never heard before. "What is this?"

"Sigur Rós."

"I love it. And it really goes with the view." We don't say anything more until the song ends. "The colours are so bright up here."

"Some say it's because of all the fires up here."

"The what now?"

"Rumour has it Kurama *no Hi* runs longer than just a day up here. People say these mountains are full of *yokai*. They run about all month long, lighting their own fires, having their own month-long festival … thirty days of feasting and fighting …" He pauses. "Sound familiar?"

"Hmm. Sounds like a thirty-day holiday I could use. Er, without the fighting. Maybe."

Zaniel studies me. "How do you *really* feel, working in *eikaiwa?*"

"I like it. Honestly. Sure, there's a lot of dramatic crap that comes with it, but that's something you deal with anywhere, in any job."

"You think so? You don't think things would be better for you back in Canada?"

"Nope. It's strange, really; you can pick up your life and move ten thousand miles away, and when you get there you're stuck with the exact same situation you ran away from."

Zaniel goes back to studying the horizon. "I guess," he says finally. He doesn't sound happy about my conclusion. I want to change the subject. *Is this a date?* No, that's a stupid question. What do normal people talk about in these kinds of situations? "The view up here is really, um, something." As soon as the words come out of my mouth, I realize I'm repeating myself. *Shit.*

"Nice, isn't it? I haven't been up here during the day since I was a kid. I still can't believe how beautiful it is."

"I still can't believe I'm not at work." The look he gives me in return cracks me up. "Okay, okay! Don't mess yourself. You're right, though; it's quite a view."

Zaniel looks right at me when he says, "It is."

I feel my face get hot. "Um ... well, you seem to know this area really well."

His smile turns grim as he looks away. "I've been up here more times than I'd like to think. It's not really the same, in my dreams. It's ... darker. Colder."

"Oh."

He clears his throat. "When I first moved to Japan, I went to a private international school here. We hiked around these mountains. We made curry together, and everyone was super nice to me.

I thought about it a lot throughout school. How it set the standard of how I wanted to be treated in my Japan life. I started to see it as a cosmic joke that had been played on me.

"A few months after my grandpa died, I came back one night, by myself. I didn't mean to. I didn't have a plan that day, just a wish. The wish for it to all stop. Coming home every day with a new bruise, or a new nickname, waking up every night with a new scratch. You can only take so much abuse from others just for being what you are ... You know what I mean?"

I nod. "I do."

"So, after school I hopped on a train and the next thing I knew, I was up here. I thought I was alone. I wasn't. Akki was there. He saw what I was there to do. He talked to me. We talked for a long time. He ended up saving my life that day. He said he saw a bit of himself in me. But whatever that part is, it's gone now. Last night showed me that. He's not the same guy I met. Maybe he never was that guy; maybe it was all a front to hook me. I don't know. I just know we're done. I don't want to turn out like him."

To turn into a giant, racist, eyeball-collecting weirdo? I don't get it. "What do you mean?"

"I was always looking for someone to make him happy, I think partly because I owed him, and partly because I could see how bad he is at talking to people. You know, you've met him. I thought I was helping him. But in all that time I never thought of looking for someone to make *me* happy."

I nod again. "That's no way to live. You don't think he's going to ... I don't know ... come after you?"

"Nope." His smile returns. "I didn't see a wink of him after the restaurant last night. In fact, I didn't really see *anybody*. Maybe one or two, but they waved hello and left me alone. It was the first peaceful night of sleep I've had in years, and it was fantastic. It makes me wonder if I ever needed him."

I'm not entirely sure what he's talking about, but he certainly looks happy. I don't want to discredit that. "Thank you for sharing your story with me."

"Thank you for listening."

A long awkward silence follows. I cross and uncross my legs. It's starting to get cold. "Okay, I'm going to ask: What were you interviewing me for yesterday? It couldn't have been just to watch the sun set."

With a pause and a heavy exhale, Zaniel rolls up his sleeves, and extends his arms to me. I notice for the first time that he has two bracelets of beads on his wrists, one black and one red. They're beautiful. "I decided a while ago that the time to get rid of these had come ... but I couldn't get them off. Believe me, I tried."

My hands are reaching out to him before I understand what they're doing. My fingers finesse the tiny knots holding each bracelet together. It takes a few minutes, but I finally get them off. Zaniel sighs and clutches his wrists. There are deep red circles where the beads once rested against his skin. Burn marks?

"Okay, you're free. What do we do with these?"

He looks around himself and picks up one of our tiny *conbini* bags. He holds it open to me. Without asking I drop them in. Instead of putting it in his backpack or something, he hops up, jogs to the edge of the cliff, and whips the bag into the air.

"Ah," he says after a beat, like he was expecting the bag to come flying back. "Much better."

"... did we just litter?" I tease.

"More like 'returning,' than littering." He comes back. Those *are* burn marks on his skin.

"Zaniel ...?"

"I know. It's okay," he says, reaching out to me. He helps me to my feet. "I'll explain later. We have to get out of here before it gets dark."

"You don't have to tell me twice. It's gonna be freezing up here soon."

"Yeah. Freezing …"

We pack up our garbage (I'm glad to see nothing else go over the cliff), Zaniel's blanket, and our helmets and head back down the mountain. It's gotten dark so fast. The next cable car won't come for another thirteen minutes, so we wander around the tourist shop. I buy a bag of peanuts from the shop and get a hand-painted postcard of Lake Biwa from a kind elderly man selling art next to the shop. His monkey assistant, "Mon-kyam," accepts my two hundred yen in his tiny monkey hat. Zaniel takes a picture of him on my shoulder with his phone just as the cable car arrives. On the ride down the mountain, the lights of Kyoto shimmer like a starry sky. We get seats facing the city at Yase Hieizan-guchi Station and wait for the train to depart.

I notice after a while that Zaniel's hand is resting on mine. I play it cool and pretend to scan the entirety of the train car. There's plenty of room on his side of the seats, but I don't say anything. In time, he rests his head against mine. He must be falling asleep. I close my eyes. The train jolts to life, but I don't let up the pretense of sleep. Even the scores of people clamouring into the car marvelling at us, possibly taking our photo (I hear several camera clicks) does not faze me. This feels good. *He* feels good. I don't want anything to take this warm feeling away.

The train slows to a stop. A voice comes on the intercom. "Attention, everyone. Please remain calm. There is a boar on the tracks."

Like wildfire, everyone jumps up from their seats and runs to one side of the car to get a good look. Oblivious to the chaos, a train attendant steps into the car and bows. "Attention everyone, attention. We are momentarily stopping the train. Once the way is clear we will move again. We apologize for this inconvenience."

Someone wails. "Geez, look at the size of that thing! What do we do?"

"We just have to wait."

"Look at its eyes ..."

"They're *green*!"

"That is fucking scary. What the hell do we do?!"

"Look at the *size* of him. That thing could rip a man in half."

"Shut the hell up! All of you, get a hold of yourselves. It's just the reflection from the headlights. You wanna scare everyone? Just be cool; it'll have to move sometime."

"Mama, I want to go home!"

"Me, too, sweetie. Me, too."

"Thank you for your patience," says the attendant, who disappears the way he came in.

The giant boar stands its ground as the passengers whip out their cellphones and cameras. A hundred flashes snap at him, but it remains unmoved. It continues to survey the crowd, trotting over to the car doors, sniffing and snuffling. People looking at their phones exclaim, screaming that its tusks are covered in blood, they're sure of it.

Somewhere in the bushes, a voice rings out: "This is stupid. We should go." But the boar does not respond. He is hell-bent on his task. This is the car he is searching for. He can smell it. He parades around a little more, letting the humans push and jostle, and really get their elbows into one another, to point, to take more pictures, to cry for their mothers.

The boar gallops up to the window and smacks its hooves against it. Everyone cries out in terror, fleeing the window, except for a few foolhardy people who just take even more snaps on their cameras of the cloudy fog the boar breathes onto the glass.

The boar looks right at me, narrows its almost-human eyes, green as radioactive material, and slams into the glass, twice. The third time the glass cracks and breaks. The boar leaps through the window and launches right at me with a high-pitched squeal.

I scream.

"Hey." Zaniel has one hand around my shoulder. The other is rubbing my back. "It's okay. You were dreaming."

I'm sitting stock straight. The scream I thought was mine is the gentle screech of the train brakes in front of Takaragaike Station, according to the intercom. A few people look at me oddly — but then, what else is new? "We stopped."

"Yeah."

"There was a boar on the tracks."

The hand on my back stops mid-circle. "You must have dreamed that part," he says. He doesn't look happy when he says it. He reads the look on my face and guides me back to a reclined position. He rests his head against mine again, his arm presses up against my shoulder. "Don't go back to sleep," he murmurs. "Tell me what you're thinking about."

"Hmmm ..." I try to keep my eyes open. "Have you heard this saying? About how if Tokyo were a person, he'd be a cold, stern salaryman, and Osaka would be his glam rock, visual *kei*, gum-chewing, rebellious Lolita daughter?"

He laughs. "Where'd you hear that?"

"I can't remember. But if it's true, I think Kyoto would be a beautiful woman, in *furisode* and everything, but only during the day. At night she'd be something else. Something mysterious. Like those stories you hear about people with no faces running into you at night. But she's not scary or evil or anything. She's just different."

"That's an interesting metaphor. Are you sure you didn't just make it up?"

"I might have. I don't know."

We're pretty quiet until the train arrives at Demachiyanagi Station. We retrieve the scooter and drive along the river, now lit up almost like Christmas, and stop briefly at Kyoto Station. Zaniel lets me wander around the shops decked with giant boxes of fruit cakes, chocolates, baby-pink Hello Kitty stationery with temples and shrines in the backgrounds, black bean *nama yatsuhashi*, and fancy Kit Kats. He buys me a small box of tea cakes that look like flowers and bunnies, which we polish off after a quick selfie on Zaniel's phone, before we hit the road again. I feel high on sugar and fumes all the way home. I don't want this day to end.

Goodbye, Kyoto. See you again.

It's brighter than it was on the mountain when we get out of the city. I cling to Zaniel's waist like a drowning sailor again as we swerve between the cars on his two-seater. I close my eyes again, this time because I'm tired, but the noise of the drive and the vibrating against my ass keeps me from falling asleep. Our matching black-and-white helmets with converse tadpole eyes must look like Yin and Yang snaking down the highway like a stealthy sea creature in the ocean. Schools of blue whale trucks and white bass coaches moan and honk around us. A bus full of teenagers shout *hello* from their windows. They wave, but when some of them stick their tongue out at me I flip them off just as Zaniel guns the engine and the scooter leaps forward. We're both laughing under our helmets.

It feels late when I recognize the distant Saizeriya I sometimes frequent. "Where do you live?" Zaniel asks at a red light.

"Down this way, past the McDonald's and the 7-Eleven. But you can drop me off here, it's fine."

Zaniel says nothing. The light turns green and we take off. He pulls over at my building, safe and sound. My legs don't feel so Jell-O-like when I get off the scooter and hand him my helmet, which he tucks away safely under his seat.

"Thanks. I had a great time with you today. You're *sure* you're not a killer, right? You can tell me. I promise not to get mad. I'd rather you tell me now than tell me ... you know, later."

"I could ask you the same thing. Are *you* capable of killing someone?"

I give him a sideways glance. "I don't like how you sidestepped my question."

"So did you."

"You're interviewing me again."

"Maybe."

We're both trying not to smile.

"Well ..." Zaniel checks his watch. "I should go. And thank you for ... you know, today. Taking me up on such a strange quest."

"I had a great time. When can we do it again?"

"Depends on when Grandma loans me her scooter next. She's going to love you, by the way."

"Why? You gonna set us up on a date?"

"I should! She's always badgering me to teach her English, then never listens to a word I say, so I don't know what I can teach her. She'll listen to you, though. You're pretty and polite, with your tiny hands and your 'healthy' skin ..." He tries to pinch my cheeks in a poor imitation of an old woman. "And the way you're always hoovering down food ..."

"Am not!" We both laugh again. Then it gets too quiet between us. "You really want me to meet your grandmother?" I ask.

"Well, yeah. I think you have to, now. She's been bugging me to bring a nice girl home for years. Don't worry, she's one of those tiny non-threatening *obaachans* who love foreigners. I'm telling you, she's going to eat you up."

"I don't wanna be eaten up," I grin.

"I hope it doesn't sound like I'm rushing you into anything. I mean, we have all the time in the world."

I take a deep breath. "Yeah, that reminds me ... my contract ends in five months, and they want to know if I'm renewing, and ... well, I still haven't decided ..."

"Cybelle —"

"I'd just rather be up front with you. I'm not trying to freak you out or anything, but if we're talking about meeting grand-mothers, I just think you should know ..."

Zaniel cuts me off with a hug. I'm stunned at first, but then his peachy scent overtakes me. My eyes droop and my arms wrap around his body, which feels long and warm. He repeats, steadily: "All the time in the world." He pulls away to look me in the eye. "Trust me. You haven't scared me off, and you haven't seen the last of me."

"Okay. Good. Let me see you off."

"It's fine. Just make sure to lock the door behind you. This isn't Canada."

"Hardy har har."

Before I can stop myself, I throw my arms around his neck. He laughs, staggering against the scooter a little, but his reciprocal hug is stronger than the first. Without another word I run into my building. I can't help peering through the glass of my front door to watch him go. He doesn't move an inch until the door clicks locked. He gives a little wave goodbye with his long fingers, re-straps his helmet.

A sudden thought occurs to me. I throw open the door. "Get home safe," I call out. His smile turns a little sad for a brief moment, but he nods *yes* before he takes off.

Upstairs, I lean against my *genkan* door, feeling tired and giddy all at once. I haven't felt this amazing in years. My body slides down the door as I let out the biggest breath of air I didn't know I'd been holding. What a week. I still don't quite understand what happened today, aside from having the best date I've had my whole life. My eyes close, and I can still see his face — his sharp piercing eyes, his soft-looking mouth — and hear his voice, promising me I haven't seen the last of him. I curl up on the floor and turn on the heater to get some warmth into my fingers and toes. Just a minute or two here, and then I'll take a bath or find something to eat. Just another minute, here, on the floor ...

I'm so sleepy.

But it's okay. I'm home.

Zaniel manages to get the scooter back to his grandmother's place in Fuse, where she makes him a surfeit of food and wants to hear all about why he borrowed her scooter so last minute. She scolds him about why can he not be a real man and get his own car and a house, he is going to have to stop sponging off her eventually, and so on and so forth, the way all grandmothers tend to do. When he tells her about his date, she exclaims in shock. She wants to hear all about her. Zaniel shows her a picture of the girl on his phone. "She dream-walks, like me," he tells her.

"*Bijin!*" his grandmother shouts over and over again. "*Aitai, aitai!*" She demands he bring her over for a meal. "Can she eat tempura?" she asks. "Can she use chopsticks? Can she speak Japanese? I can't speak English! What will I do?" To Zaniel, it is one of those cute displays of youthfulness with which his grandmother spoils him every time he comes to visit.

She sends him on his way with all the leftovers. He gets on a train back to uptown Osaka. He falls asleep. As soon as he does, a very large man gets on at the next station. There is plenty of space for him to sit anywhere but he squeezes himself right next to Zaniel. He watches the young man sleep. For a *hafu,* he is quite beautiful when he sleeps. The large man can see why women warm up to him so easily.

But the women, the ones he met and had Zaniel escort to him ... he never saw them again. They all woke up and left him. The presence of his nightmares is inconsistent. They do not always come when called. And Hino, the closest thing he has to a friend ... Hino, whose intermittent visits can be anywhere from a couple of days to a couple of centuries. She is always leaving him. This one, though, this single, beautiful human who needed Akki once, as a sad, gentle boy; this one he wants to keep. He must keep him. In fact, he decides, he *will* keep him. He is not going to be alone. No.

Not anymore.

Not this time.

The train pulls into Osaka Station. Only the bag of food remains where Zaniel once slept. Both he and Akki have disappeared.

thirteen
EAT ME

地震雷火事親父

Fear those greater than yourself

"Ima okina-EE-to, okurema-SOO, yo ... Ima okina-EE-to, okurema-SOO, yo ..."

"All right, all right, I'm up ..."

I roll over and open my eyes. I'm in a large extravagant room, on top of a score of down pillows piled in its centre. Thin mesh drapes surround me. Beyond the drapes and the pillows, hundreds of candles line the walls and extend far into the darkness. A giant paper lantern hovers in mid-air over the blankets. The fire glowing within it is a deep blood red. Ghostlike wisps of incense hover in the dark air.

I have a bad feeling about this.

I roll across the pillows, to come out from under the drapes. My arms and legs feel heavy, as though something is weighing them down. The atmosphere, perhaps? I don't know. Maybe wherever this place is, it's high up a distant mountain. That would explain why it's so cold. The air feels strange, too, and not just from the thick odour of incense and tatami. I bundle myself in my robe as best as I can, but it is so thin it does little to improve how I feel. I stumble in the dark until my hands find a door that I can slide open. There is more illumination beyond the door, in this strange, narrow hallway; I'm grateful, but still uneasy. I don't recognize these surroundings, either. It is still cold. The tatami under my hands and knees crunch with breaking frost. *What is this place?*

"Cybelle?" The sound of my name is soft, but close. "That *is* Cybelle, isn't it?"

"Huh? Oh. Hey …" My words get lost as a strong pair of arms wrap around me from behind. Instant warmth against my body; just what I needed.

"So, you're here at last. I've been waitin'."

I laugh a little, finding it hard to breath against the arms tightening around me. "Geez, it's only been a few hours. Did you miss me that much? Ow. Zaniel, what's gotten into you?"

"Zaniel, Zaniel, Zaniel … don't you ever think about anythin' else? Come on, this is your chance to be with a real man. Your last chance, if you think about it. Then again, you don't think about much, now do ya?"

"Ow. You're hurting me …"

The arms tighten even more. "Good."

A gurgle comes out of me, a choking sound that cannot escape my body any more than I can escape the arms pinning me. Even my breath feels trapped in my lungs. I can barely scream for help. This is not Zaniel. It can't be; Zaniel would never do this. I lunge sideways and forward, trying to break from the deadly embrace. I'm only able to breathe for a moment before the arms release me and pin my throat between two strong bicep muscles. A high-pitched sound I didn't think I could make squeaks from my mouth. My eyes roll back against their will. I can't see anything.

"Don't bother," says the deep growl that is no longer Zaniel's voice. "He can't help you now. Don't you get it? He's *mine*."

"No … h … he —"

A light flickers in the darkness. A lit cigarette glows. "Buzz off, Hino," the voice growls again. "You don't need to see this."

A high school girl leaning against the distant wall takes a long drag on her cigarette. "I *really* do not understand your actions sometimes, Akki. You got him back; what do you want with her? She cannot do anything for him."

"This don't concern you. This's between me an' *her*. I won't let her take him from me. She ain't takin' him back to America, where they tortured him. They made him suffer!"

"You really believe that is what she wanted?"

"WHY ELSE WOULD SHE TAKE HIS BRACELETS OFF, HINO?"

I croak out another horrid sound. "I —"

"Fuckin' *gaijin*. You destroy what you don't understand and mourn for it when it's gone. Don't think you're special, half-human. They'll just do the same to you." The arms tighten even more around my throat. "Consider this a favour."

"N— no," I choke. I try to pull at his giant fingers, but it's like scratching at thick bands of rope. I gag. I can feel my body has frozen up. It's as if I'm already unconscious, but I'm looking down on myself from high above, and watching my body thrash in my struggle for breath. He is choking me, here, and killing me, *there* …

"You're a tough one," growls a voice in my ear. "I'm gonna enjoy seein' those big brown eyes of yours every day."

As I slump to the floor, he kneels behind me, still squeezing. *What do I do?* I feel liquid running down my cheeks from my eyes and hope it isn't blood. *What do I do?*

Cybelle. It is but a whisper, but it rings so familiar to me it seems to echo off the walls. "Help," I struggle to say. But deep down, I know it is the whisper of someone who cannot help me. The whisperer can only watch. Even before the whisper continues, I know what I need to do.

Cybelle — RUN.

Summoning what little strength I have, I concentrate, shunting it down my body. It hurts to move. But I have to. My right foot shoots out behind and drives hard into the man's groin. He lets out a high-pitched cry as he crumples to the floor, holding himself in his hands.

"Ow! Fuck! Why do you keep kickin' me in the crotch?!"

My only reply is with my other foot, driving right into the giant man's face, knocking him to the floor. Sobbing, coughing, still unable to see, I stumble-run down the hallway for my life. I run blindly down the twists and turns, slipping several times and banging against the walls, down a long flight of stairs to where I see a door — a regular push-and-pull door with a knob.

With a last burst of speed, I launch myself forward and go right through it.

"*Ima okina-EE-to, okurema-SOO, yo …*"

I flail upright in my bed. *Thank God, it was only a nightmare.* I collapse back down onto my pillow and give it a good, tight squeeze. Then I stop, remembering the feeling around my throat. I touch my neck. It even *feels* tender. I wonder if there's a bruise. No, that would be ridiculous. It was just a dream. A vivid, bizarre, fucked-up dream.

"Cybelle!" I hear my name. "Breakfast!"

Downstairs in the dining room, everyone is already seated and digging in. I take the seat next to Bully in front of a short stack drowning in maple syrup and topped with a pat of butter. "Look what the cat dragged in," my twin sisters snicker.

I ignore them, clapping my hands together. "Yum. Thanks, Mom."

"Hey," Dad chides me. "I helped with the bacon."

"Thank you, Daddy. *Itadakimasu!*"

"We're not in Japan," Bully snaps at me. "Just eat, already. We're going to be late, thanks to you."

"Late? For what?"

Bully slams her fists on the dining table. "She forgot about the wedding. Mo-om, Da-ad, Cybelle forgot about my wedding!"

Mom ignores her. "Cybelle, eat fast or we're going to be late. We don't have time for jokes today."

I pick up my fork and knife to start hacking away. "I didn't forget. It's just that ... well, I should tell you. I just had the most horrifying dream. I was —" I look up from my forkful of pancakes. There's something in the kitchen window. "What the hell is that?"

No one seems to hear me. They go on, chatting with one another. Something scratches at the window. It disappears from sight, reappearing at the back door. It's a giant boar. Somehow, someway, it manages to wedge its thick, massive snout into the aluminum side between the door and the kitchen wall. It pushes through the crack, and the door begins to slide open.

It's coming inside.

"No!" I leap from my chair, toppling it over. Again, no one notices anything out of the ordinary. I throw myself against the door, trying to stop the beast. I push my shoulder and my foot against the door, noticing two more creatures in the backyard. They look like shiny gold aliens with bulging black eyes. One is eating plums off a small tree. Its mouth is smothered in dark juice as it crams more and more fruit into its face. Another is fishing in the mint garden, fishing rod in its awkward hands and a small bucket of fresh smelt beside its naked bum. It turns and sees me and smiles a stretched-out row of translucent shark teeth. I scream for help again and again, but no one comes to the rescue.

I look over my shoulder. My family. Where did they go? There's only a gathering of glowing will-o'-the-wisps around our dining table.

"Storm's a brewin'," says a high-pitched voice. "Perfect weather for a wedding."

I turn my attention back to the door. The boar is now a person, two feet taller than me with dead anime eyes and a wide toothy grin. It isn't pushing the door open anymore. It's reaching for me. My last cry for help is cut short, gagging in my throat as the dead-eyed creature smiles, squeezes, and smiles even more. Slowly, I begin to lose the battle for my life. My eyes flutter. My legs kick. Everything goes dark and quiet.

"Ima okina-EE-to, okurema-SOO, yo ..."

"What?" I sit upright.

I look around the big round table, covered in white linen with a huge bouquet of flowers in the centrepiece. At least ten empty dishes lie in front of everyone sitting at the table. All the women are dressed in their finest *kabas*, and all the men sport kente vests under sharp-looking suit jackets. Couples. If they're not engrossed in conversations with each other, they are scrolling and clicking away on their smartphones. No one seems to notice I'm even here.

I'm in a violet-pink lit room full of people sitting at similar-looking tables in heterosexual pairings. The shouting and thumping bass are loud. Somewhere behind me, off toward one end of the room, tables have been moved away to make space for an already-packed dance floor. Several onlookers are snapping away on cellphones or giant cameras on tripods. Something tells me that is the part of the room I should be in. Not here, the only single girl at the table.

I stand up. Someone grabs my hand and pulls me down. I can't place who it is, but the couples on either side of me are now staring at me intently. "Where are you going?" the women ask in unison. "Come on, talk to us. How was China? The food was obviously good there, eh?" I feel fingers jab at my stomach and my sides.

"Leave me alone," I stand up again, violently this time. My chair topples over. Déjà vu.

"Aw, come on! Talk to us. Stay here with us." The chorus of voices follow me down the room as I finesse my way around each table, heading for the dance floor and yet feeling like it's so far away that I'll never reach it. I'm bombarded with questions and gossip and grabby hands pulling at my kimono from each table I pass:

"How did your youngest sister end up marrying before you?"

"Didn't you bring anyone back with you? How sad!"

"You're not going back there, are you?"

"Don't you know how much your family needs you?"

"Wish *I* could pack up and ship off to a foreign country anytime I want. If only I didn't have a husband … You'll see, one day you'll see how lucky you were …"

"Let go," I tell them all. "Get off me!"

It's like wading through thick seaweed, trying to get past. Someone grabs my wrist again. I whip my arm out of their grip and smack into a butler — or something that looks like a butler. It's half my size, and there's a metal block where its head should be. "You-want-some-more?" It holds up a flute full of champagne. I shake my head no and keep going. "You-want-some-more?" I hear behind me. With its robotic voice, it sounds more like a statement of fact than an offering. *You want some more.*

I don't want champagne. I want my family.

That's where I'm going. To see my family. It's my family in the centre of the dance floor. Five women who look like me are all in a line wearing matching bluish-purple bridesmaid dresses, flanking the youngest-looking one in a long, flowing wedding dress. An older woman bumps up against me, forcing me into the dancers.

"There you are, Cybelle! We've been looking everywhere for you. Don't tell me you fell asleep again. I *warned* you about that jet lag. Now, go take your sister's train before she trips."

I squint at the woman. "You're not my mom."

But the woman just rolls her eyes at me and laughs. She pushes me again. I'm in the middle of the throng now. I have no choice, but as I pick up the long wedding train, I grow more and more certain that that woman is not my mother. Something isn't right about all this. I can't keep up with the dancers, or the song: something about stomping and sliding and going to work ... I've never heard this song before in my life. The directions are simple enough, but I can't follow along. I'm always one step behind, coming face to face with angry partygoers. My legs tangle with theirs. They glare at me, but they keep dancing. Something is wrong with everyone's eyes. It's not just looks of disdain. Their eyes are warped, turned vertically. Everyone's eyes are ... except for the bride. She stops dancing and rips the train out of my hands.

"What are you doing?!" she demands to know.

"I ... what?" I'm turning away from her. I can't help it.

She grabs me before I can spin away again. "You heard me. I want to know what you're doing."

Everyone collapses on the floor like rag dolls. The bride and I are the only ones standing.

"I don't understand," I say. I feel numb. But it feels good not to be spinning anymore. "I'm ... supposed to be here."

"You know you're not."

The song is still going, encouraging people to move. No one moves from the floor.

"Now look what you've done."

Tears sting my eyes. "That's not my fault!" There's a giant shadow floating over their bodies now. I look up — there's a massive skylight in the ceiling I didn't notice before, and a giant shape is hurling toward it. The bride grabs me by the arm and pulls me out of the way just in time for the glass panes to break and shatter over the crowd. The dancers get up from the floor in a screaming frenzy, but they are caught in the rain of shards. I slam into a table and fall to the floor. My instincts kick in and I dash under the table to avoid the glass and the impending rush of feet I now hear all around me.

Something gigantic and heavy lands on the floor with a crash. I lift the tablecloth, just to peek. Within that inch of space, I can see everything happening in the room. The floral centrepieces on the tables explode into dancing flames that streak through the air, singeing decorations and the guests' clothes and hair as they swoop down on them. The wedding cake also explodes; fireballs pop out of it like they'd been hiding inside and waiting to make their appearance. The music is eaten up by the sounds of high-pitched cackling laughter. In the middle of the dance floor, the dark, giant shape takes form.

It's a boar. A giant boar with blood on its tusks and flaming, neon green eyes. It rises to stand on its hind hooves. "GET ME THE DREAM EATER."

In front of my table, two women run right smack into each other. Like cats fighting, they claw at each other, grabbing and ripping off one another's faces, exposing torn flesh and veins. They point and laugh at each other.

"No, you are not the *yokai* we are looking for! Oops!"

"Let's look for her together!" Arm in arm, they attack another guest, ripping off the man's face, laughing again. Another rebuff, they laugh and the three go off in search of another face, and another. A gruesome game of Zombie Tag.

I duck back under the table. The tablecloth moves, exposing me, but somehow no one spots me underneath and comes to

collect my face. I feel like I'm in full view of the demonic creatures running around, but for whatever reason they don't see me.
Perhaps they are too engrossed in catching the people running
for their lives to look down here. I can see the bride — my sister?
She looks so familiar now — and her new husband hiding under
another table nearby. She turns and sees me. The bride scurries
past the thundering feet to my table and pulls the tablecloth down
behind her. "What the hell are you doing?"

"I … it's your wedding," I reply. I can hear the tears in my
own voice.

"No, it isn't! Cybelle, you've turned this into a nightmare!"

"How is this my fault?! I didn't …" I'm crying now. "I didn't
mean to —"

"No, Cybelle. Shut up and listen to me. You're HAVING a
nightmare. You need to wake up!"

"Why does everyone keep telling me that?"

Someone screams as a fireball hurtles past the table. The blast
shakes the room, sending guests screaming in all new directions. I
can feel the heat of another fireball as it streaks above and hear the
tinny, anime-like sound effect of something catching fire.

"Come on!"

The bride grabs my wrist and runs out from under the table.
"No!" I say, scared out of my wits. But she's always been stronger
than me. She pulls hard and runs.

We're running through a forest. There's mist and green everywhere. A peaceful, beautiful scene, incongruent to our fleeing in
terror from whatever just happened. Now I really don't understand
what's going on. "You owe me some answers," the bride says without losing her stride. "Who are you?"

*I'm someone who's just been to the stupidest party she's ever been
to.* But I can't say that to my own sister. Wait. No. Not my sister. I
close my eyes and let her pull me through the trees. I think. I think
hard. I've been asked this question before.

Who am I?

I open my eyes. "I'm ..."

Silence. Darkness.

"Bully?"

She's gone. So is the forest. So is the wedding hall. I'm in bed, now. I creep out of the bed, out of the dark room, down a flight of stairs to a dark hallway. There is a small light — a night light — plugged into the wall, here. I think I need to go to the washroom. Yeah, that's what I'm doing here.

A light clicks on. There's blood all over me, soaking into my robe. My period has started. Terrific.

I've just about cleaned up my legs when I hear a squeaking noise just outside the washroom door, like rubber wheels dragging on a rough surface. I stick my head out. There's a little boy standing there, maybe about two or three years old, with a little red wagon behind him. He's looking right up at me as if he expected me to open the door. Maybe he's just waiting for the washroom. "What are you doing here?" I ask. "Do you need to go?"

"Yada," he squeaks. He runs off, leaving his wagon behind. I step out of the washroom. He's already gone, lost to the darkness beyond the night light.

I try to go after him. I think I know him. Maybe he can tell me what's going on here. Beyond the hallway there is a living room with a single couch. Someone is sleeping on it. It's completely dark in here except for something glowing — a pillow under the sleeper's head, I believe? Or maybe it's a folded-up towel. I can't tell. But it's emitting enough light for me to see there is someone sleeping there. I go over and place a gentle hand on the person's shoulder. I think it's my mother. "Mom?" I ask. "Where's Bully?"

My mother moves in her sleep. "She's dead," she mumbles. Her voice is strangely deep. "Bully is dead. And Zaniel is dead. And Cybelle — she's dead, too." She giggles. It's a deep, inhuman chuckling sound. It's awful. I shake her harder; maybe I can wake her up and save her. The harder I shake her, the louder and higher she laughs. It's a squeaking, high-pitched laugh now. Like that boy's wagon.

"Leave my mother alone," I shout. No. Whatever this thing is, it's not my mother. It's something possessing her, making her say these horrible things. I yank the glowing pillow out from under her head and try to smother her laughter, but it only gets louder, ringing in my ears.

"That won't wo-ork," sings the pillow.

I drop the pillow and run out of the living room. Down the little hallway. It's so dark I trip over that kid I saw earlier, curled up in a ball on the floor. "What are you doing?!" I ask him. "We have to get out of here!" I scoop him up without thinking and run. Out the front door. Out of the house. Running down my foggy street, I can still hear the demon laughter. "Fuck off!" I cry, clapping my hands over my ears. Wait. What happened to that little boy? He's gone.

Maybe I shouldn't have left the house. Maybe that *was* my mother. I run back, try to get inside. The front door is locked. The demon laughter grows louder. It's a man's laugh now. It rattles the windows and bangs the front door. I clap my hands over my ears as I scream and cry, half of me hoping it will drown out the sound. Hoping that the demon can't hurt me if I can't hear it. It doesn't work. It's all around me, it's even inside my head.

Then I hear a long, tea-kettle scream. It takes a while for it to register that it's me.

"Ima okina-EE-to, okurema-SOO, yo ..."

I open my eyes to pure darkness. There is nothing here. Okay. This is good. Well, it's better. But not by much. I just need to remember that this is all one big nightmare, and I have to get out or get help. Panicking, I wade through the black, hoping to find something. Someone. Anyone.

There, in the distance. A faint pink light. Taking careful steps at first, in time picking up the pace and running toward it. A giant cherry blossom tree in a tiny courtyard. I throw myself against the trunk. It's real; solid wood. This fact comforts me. I sob against the bark, heart still pumping, grateful to be touching something that cannot hurt me.

"Konbanwa," says a voice above my head. I scramble to my feet. A man stands before me, holding a short candle in his hand. It must be a tea light, because I can hardly see any candle underneath

the flame. *"Jibun Jishin e youkoso,"* he welcomes me with a deep bow and a wide smile. He seems awfully happy to see me. I don't care why. *Someone is here. Thank God.*

"Please," I pant. *"Onegai ... tasukete ...* um ..." It's a struggle to breathe and speak Japanese at the same time. The panic is too much. *"Hashitte ...* running. I'm running ... *nigete imasu ...* Chasing — no, I'm being chased. Attacked. I need help. *Keisatsu.* Can I call the police, please?"

"Attacked? Oh my. That's awful. Please —" the man gestures to a sliding door. It draws open. He walks into the main space of a restaurant. I follow him, nodding my thanks. The restaurant is empty, but the stage is lit up. The man pulls out a chair at the nearest table. "Have a seat. Would you like some ... water?"

I practically jump at the word. I hadn't noticed the lumpy, choking feeling in my throat until now. Water would help. I can taste it already. "Thank you." I manage to sit down. The man leaves and brings a glass full of clear, sparkling liquid. His smile widens with each of my greedy gulps. All I can see is his smile ... the rest of his face is all ... fuzzy ...

"Tell me: What is it you are afraid of?"

"I'm not afraid ... I'm being chased. I was attacked."

"Attacked? Oh, my. That's ... awful." He strokes his chin in deep thought as he repeats himself. "What can we do?"

"Can you call the police? Please?"

"Police." He makes a face, as though the word leaves a bad taste in his mouth. "Ugh. No police. You go to police when you're lost. Are you lost?"

"Lost?" What the hell is he talking about? Has he not heard a word I've said? "No! I'm —"

"Lost. Yes. You lost. I mean, you lose. I mean —" He smiles, enjoying a secret joke. "I mean — you lost someone. Yes?"

I open my mouth to protest. "I ... yes." I pause. "I did." I remember now: the music, the people ... and then, the monsters.

What happened to them all? "I was at a wedding. There were so many people. I lost them all."

"A wedding? Hmm," says the man. His smile widens even more. I can't help noticing how sharp and numerous his teeth are. "How strange. Don't you think? A wedding, in *this* neighbourhood? Are you sure? Sounds like make-believe to me."

"It wasn't. I was there. Just like … I've been here before. I know this place."

"Okay, if you're sure. But then, why'd you leave?"

"I ran away. There was a —" *How can I explain it? He'll think I've lost it.*

"Nah, you can tell me."

"It wasn't safe. I wanted to find somewhere safe."

"So, you came *here*?" the man titters. "To this place? Take a look around, chickie; there's no one here. And there's nothin' around for miles, either. Not at *this* time o'night. Face it, girl: you're in a make-believe place. It's not real."

That's not true, says a voice in my head. *Try to remember — the train station nearby, the 7-Eleven down the way, the supermarkets, your school … they're all real, this is not …*

"You tell yourself that. But maybe you made all that up, too! Maybe you ain't really even in Japan. Ever think of that? Maybe you're at home right now, asleep in your four-poster bed, surrounded by your little anime posters and *Final Fantasy* shit."

How does he know all that?

"Oh, I know. Trust me. I know all about you. I know you're a good cook, I know you like *kitsune* udon, I know you think nightmares taste like lemon, and I know you've wanted to go to Japan oh so badly your whole life. But think. Maybe, just maybe, this is all in your head. You've always had a big imagination, haven't you? You ain't thought this could all be in your head."

He's reading my mind or something. He's in my head. I've got to get him out.

"Want me out of your head, eh? You'll have to do better than that, chickie." He brings his face close. "No one's comin' to help you. The kid sure as hell ain't comin'. He don't exist no more. Hey. Are you sure you didn't make *him* up, too?"

"No! He's real!" The intensity of my own voice suddenly makes me question who I'm trying to convince. *Who? Who is real?* Who am I talking about? I try to draw the image of a face in my mind, but only see an empty outline. An empty outline with piercing eyes.

"See? The kid's gone. Bye-bye. And soon, you'll be, too."

I cringe. "No ...!" *What is he doing?* "Let go — that hurts!" I try to pull my wrist out of his grip, which just makes him squeeze even harder. He twists it backward, pulling me off the chair, down to the floor as if he is trying to crush me under the strong torque of his arm. There's a good chance he can. My knee hits the cold tile of the floor, and it hurts, as well. "Ow! What are you doing?! Get off me!"

He throws his head back and laughs, a laugh as though holding me down is the easiest thing in the world, my pain and terror merely entertainment to him. He twists my arm again, winds up, and cranks it again, and again. There's a popping sound coming from the socket. My screams empty out of me as the sleeve of my kimono, my skin, and my entire arm rips away from my shoulder, like dough. The man raises my detached limb into the air, tilts his head back, and lets the blood and dangling pieces of meat tumble into his open mouth.

"Ooh. Mmm. Salty *and* sweet. And caramel. Wasn't expectin' that. I need more. I need *more*."

Automatically I begin to scramble away with my good arm, but he plants a firm, heavy foot right down on my stomach, pinning me. Kneeling, he grabs the glass of water and pours it on my face. When I open my mouth to scream for help, the tiny trickle of water feels like a gushing faucet emptying into my throat. I am drowning. He is laughing. I have to do something.

My feet kick out and my one hand swipes the air in a fit of fear. My clawed fingers connect with his face, and I can feel the sick sensation of my nails right on his eye. With a yelp he reels back and releases me. I crawl away fast until I can get to my feet. I vomit up all that water. Then, I run straight for the stage. If I can just hop up there, I'll be out of his reach. I plant one foot against the board to boost myself up and swing one leg over. I'm almost there.

Without turning, I can feel the man's pain as he clutches his eye and feels blood trickling down his face. It's like watching a movie, watching myself. He lets out an anguished cry, which becomes a deafening bleating sound. I somehow know it is not the blood he minds — it reminds him he is alive — it is the fact that I'm getting away. He will not let me get away, not this time. His rows of sharp, wide teeth sport fangs and tusks as he wriggles out of his clothes and gets down on all fours. He charges at the stage, knocking over tables in his way, and leaps at my outstretched leg.

I'm too late.

I scream. It feels like sharp metal digging into my calf, the pain so deep it reaches the bone. He hooks his tusk into the flesh and rips off the whole calf at the knee. My high-pitched scream turns guttural. I didn't know such a sound could come out of me. But it doesn't stop me from dragging myself onto the stage where I can hold what is left of my leg and cry in pain. The air, if not the whole room, smells like rotting hamburger mixed with dead fish. The floor underneath me becomes wet with warm ooze pooling around me. I can't even form words to cry out for help.

"Ah!" says a faraway voice. Somewhere in the vast room there's a young woman in a colourful kimono decorated with birds. She steps out from the darkness. "I thought I heard something. See?" A man steps out from a doorway — to a kitchen? — wiping his hands on his apron. He also seems shocked to see someone on the stage. "What do we do?" asks the woman.

"We have to tell them to leave, of course," the man shrugs.

"Excuse me, honourable customer," the woman calls out. I'm still screaming, unable to form coherent words. With a patient sigh, she approaches. Not questioning the overturned tables and chairs; she simply clicks her tongue and picks them up. *"Sumimasen, okyaku-sama,"* she tries again in Japanese.

Then she sees the boar. He stops ramming at the stage boards and regards her with an exasperated look that only boars can make.

"Aw, come on, lady, it's *way* past sunset!"

"Demo ..." she stares at the talking boar, horrified. *"Kyou wa getsuyoubi desu ga ... yasumi desu ..."*

"Oh, for the — You're closed on Mondays?! Since fucking when?!"

The young woman is out of rational thoughts, it seems. She runs, screaming for the man. The boar sighs — "Be right back," he says to me — and chases after the woman with an excited squeal. The clashing of pots and pans in the kitchen and the ear-piercing human screams bring me back to my senses.

I have to get out of here. But how? Half of my leg is gone. The muscles in my good leg have seized up. I can't walk, let alone run, and when I roll over to drag myself with my remaining arm, I feel a hundred pounds heavier. I can't do it. I collapse on the stage, eyes shut. *Think.* Something about what the man-boar said, about make-believe. No, this can't be make-believe. The pain is so real, and there's blood everywhere. It smells.

It isn't. Just think about it. You have to try. You have to get out of here. It's the only way.

All around me, the stage lights get warmer. They're getting brighter. I don't open my eyes, though, not yet. Just a little more. I need to concentrate. I have to imagine any place but here.

The stage lights grow brighter and brighter. The boar trots out of the kitchen and is instantly blinded. "What the fuck?!" His hooves are too short to shield his eyes. Luck is on my side. I squeeze my eyes tighter. I can do this.

Everything gets brighter and brighter, until …

Light. Warm, soothing light of a sepia-coloured sky surrounds me. There's something hard underneath me, not unlike cold, smooth glass. A floor that stretches as far as I can see. Translucent and dark, opaque checkered squares alternate with each other. No walls, no ceiling, only the sky with its misting pink clouds. Down below me, beyond the clouds — green and brown farmland, reminiscent of the grid I'm lying on, on the cusp of a blue ocean. I start to cry at the beauty of the landscape thousands of miles beneath me, on top of my own tears of panic. "Home." It is so far … too far to ever be there again.

Run … run there … run home …

"I can't," I sob. "It's so far down."

You have to … run …!

The comforting, rational voice that may be all in my head is right. I have to run. And perhaps home is the safest place for me to be. I look down at my body. My arm and my leg are back. Why am I lying here when I have perfectly good limbs? I push myself onto my knees and immediately my body buckles under the weight. I cry out sharply as my body connects with the glass floor and cracks it. "I told you, I can't!"

You have to.

Never have I felt so alone. It feels like something has been ripped away, and not just my arm and leg. "Come with me," I weep. "I need you with me."

Don't worry about me. Get out of here!

A horrible bleating noise rips through the silent air. I can feel the high pitch and volume in the wells of my ears, like a loud, deep source of feedback. There it is. The boar. It is far away, miles away, but I know what that shadow in the distance is. Its eyes blaze green like fire. Its fiery bristles quiver in the wind.

"Ah," the boar moans. Blood and bits of coloured kimono ooze from its mouth onto the checkered floor with every sentence.

"Your eyes. He always liked your eyes. I hope they taste like salty caramel things, too. They'll be a perfect addition to my home."

Akki. The voice in my head sounds sad. *Why are you doing this?*

"I have a thousand years to kill. I can do whatever I want!" He stamps his hoof as a stubborn child might stamp their foot. "And you're supposed to be asleep! Leave me alone, can't you see I gotta do this?!" The boar lets out a roar of aggravation, of exasperation, of white-hot rage, and charges at me.

What can I do? If I try to get up again I'll just stumble, and the boar, who is bigger, faster, and stronger will just tower over me, then it will pounce and gore. I could crawl backward on my hands, dragging my sore legs with me, to the edge to throw myself over — if there was one — but the floor stretches out for miles. Now, suddenly, inexplicably, so do I. I do not know what is happening, but I am taking up more squares than I was before. I'm growing, or I've grown. Somehow, through all the pain and suffering, I've grown.

I won't be more feast for the boar. I can do something.

I pound at the floor, cracking two more tiles. Success spurs me to punch and hammer through the pain in my good arm, punching even through the wringing feeling in my wrist and the splintering feeling that travels up my now-giant knuckles. The glass cracks like the surface of an icy river.

I fall for miles and miles. I feel everything. The air being sucked from my lungs, the flailing of my heavy limbs, the wind sharp and cold against my skin. Every muscle in my chest clenches tighter. I shut my eyes.

It won't hurt, hitting the bottom. It won't hurt. Aim for the water. Just like we did before.

No. It will not hurt. It will wake me up. That is all I need. One big burst, one shot of energy to jolt me.

Deep breath.

"I can't ..."

Cybelle.

The sound in my ears is like an explosion. The water is cold. My body, still hugged in a tight ball, descends farther and farther down before unravelling. I have plunged too far down. Now, the sharks come. I must hurry. Every tread of water comes with the sharp, blinding pains of exertion as I fight against the pressure. Every moment hurts. It is so painful, but it is the only way.

Fangs sink into my legs. I can only use my arms now. I paddle and paddle … the surface is so close, and my lungs are about to give out.

I'm sorry, Cybelle. Goodbye.

I burst through the surface, sending water everywhere in a powerful cascade. I'm sitting upright in the dark, coughing the water out of my lungs. Trembling violently with the shock and cold, I haul myself over the rim of my bathtub. The momentum of my own weight does most of the work. Shuddering in my soaking wet nightgown and the pool of water that has flooded the bathroom floor, I let out racking sobs of panic as I try to remember how I got here. My washroom, my bathtub. I remember none of it. It's okay. I drag myself across the tiny floor to the wall to turn on the light. The light will make everything better.

Everything — my nightgown, the water left in the tub and all over the floor — is red.

I want to go home.

PART III

fourteen

LIONS AND UNICORNS

知らぬが仏

Ignorance is bliss

Miso udon noodle soup with shiitake mushrooms
Gomae (Japanese sesame spinach salad)
Ginger Miso Soba Noodle Bowls with Wakame

"Geez. I hope I can make all of these things. This one looks good …
hmm, this one looks hard …"

I'm scrolling through Pinterest, lying on the floor, fully
dressed for work, when my iPhone starts to buzz in my hands and
play gentle, soothing *koto* music. The alarm title "time to move!"
pops up on the screen. I sigh and somehow manage to roll over
onto my side, then push myself up. It's time to bundle into my big
white puffy winter coat and leave my empty-ish apartment. Ever
since my family left, Zozo's apartment has never felt so devoid of
life. They left with most of my clothes and knick-knacks, so I don't
have to worry too much about shipping six and a half years of stuff

back to Canada. And after two weeks of being crammed in here, cooking, shouting, laughing, and fighting, I feel even more relaxed and ready to go back to work. No chance of falling down the rabbit hole of stress these next few months, that's for sure.

The light dusting of snow on the ground means the possibility of ice, but I'm so used to walking from my family's visit that I don't mind crunching my way to work this Tuesday morning. Once again, I don't see my temple friend today, which makes me a little sad. I haven't seen him since I got sick. I only have eleven more chances to see him. After this, I have eleven more Tuesdays, and then I'm home. Unless I find somewhere to travel after my contract is up. Three more months of cold morning snow on palm trees. Three more months of *"Mite, kowai"* as I walk around town or go to work. Three more months of work, period. Things have been so busy at Zozo that I actually look forward to being out of a job for a while.

In the Zozo building, the downstairs lobby is decorated with giant *kadomatsu* and *shimekazari* decorations. I catch the elevator doors just as they close and find myself in a torrent of parents and children in winter gear.

"Belle-*sensei*, Belle-*sensei*!" The bustling mass of kids glomp me with their puffy limbs and chubby smiles. "Hello! How are you?! I'm fine, thank you!"

"Hi, everyone!" I try to high-five them one by one, and when that doesn't work, I let them attack in one big cluster. "Hi, Soka; hi, Mimi; hi, Mami; hi, Sota; hi, Naoki; hi, Kotone; hi, Ai — It's okay, Tomona, squeeze in! 'High touch'! Sotaro, I almost didn't see you there! What's that, a present? For me? Aw, thanks, big guy! I missed you all so much! *Akemashite omedetou!*"

"*Uwaaa! Sugoi! Mama, Papa,* Belle-*sensei nihongo shaberu yo!*" The kids hurl themselves into their parents' arms. "*Sugoi, sugoi!*"

"Oh!" the parents gasp and applaud. "You know *akemashite omedetou! Nihongo jouzu desu ne!* Happy New Year!"

"Thank you. That's right! Have you considered taking one of our parents' classes?"

"Ah, yes ... class with Cybelle-*sensei*?"

"Well," I pause. I hate this part. "It might be with me, but you may get another teacher. It's really up to you!"

"Eh," the parents look around at each other pensively. *"Tabun."* Maybe.

"Okay, think about it! No pressure."

We empty into another sea of children waiting for us in the lobby. Along with the exponential increase of students are the new hires: Yukako, Kana, Yukie, Ryoko, and Shigeyo have replaced Misaki, Yuki, Yuri, and Jun, joining Yoshino in the coolest team of teachers I've ever met. Seri-*sensei*, with her swollen baby bump, is surprisingly still here. My guess is it's just for the week before her mat leave begins.

"Ohayou gozaimasu!" I bow to the teachers. *"Akemashite omedetou!"*

"Ooh," Seri croons. "You know *akemashite omedetou*! *Nihongo jouzu*, Cybelle-*sensei*. Happy New Year!"

"Oh! You know 'Happy New Year!' *Eigo jouzu!*" I applaud back, which makes the other teachers laugh.

"How was your vacation?" Yukako asks me. "Did everything go well with your family?"

"About as well as expected," I shrug. "Packing up most of my apartment was a breeze with seven extra pairs of hands and suitcases. They weren't even sad to say goodbye; too busy fighting about where they were going to sit and just how much duty-free liquor they could sneak in their carry-on bags."

"Did you go anywhere special?" Kana asks.

"Nowhere too far. The big cities were too far and too busy, so we just went to the deer park in Nara, and a bit of shopping in Osaka. Oh, and we went salsa dancing with Yoshino in Kobe!"

Yoshino nods enthusiastically. "Yup! I got to meet them! Her family is *so* adorable."

Everyone oohs and aahs, saying they're jealous that they didn't get to meet them. It feels like a good time to produce the boxes of maple cookies my mom brought for them all. We all herd into the staff room so the teachers can put their cookies away and we can all get ready for our first classes. While we're back here, Yukie reveals her souvenir cookies open on the counter — "I went to DisneySea with my boyfriend!" — which makes Ryoko remember the individually wrapped sweet potato crackers she bought for everyone from Kagoshima.

Yukie playfully smacks her forehead. "Ah! Cybelle-*sensei*, I forgot. Can you eat cookies?" She checks the ingredients. "Ah, no. Butter. I'm so sorry!"

"Oh, that's okay!" I wave my hands. "I can eat them over the weekend. For now, I'll just smell them!"

"Eh? Why, Cybelle, you don't eat butter?" Ryoko asks. "Oh, that's right, you're vegetarian, right? I think the crackers might be okay ..."

"Vegan," I correct her. "But on weekends I cheat a little."

"Oh, I didn't know that," says Kana. "That explains why you never have meat for lunch. Now it makes sense! How long have you been vegan?"

"Since October. I got really sick around the time we had that typhoon holiday from school."

"Eh?! Really? That's too bad. May I ask, what were you sick with? Nothing serious, I hope."

"Mono." When I get blank looks in return, I.get my iPhone out and look it up on my Japanese dictionary app. "Let's see ... *sennetsu?* Wait, there's another nice long word here ... *den-sen-sei-tan-kaku-kyuu-shou?*" No one recognizes it.

"But you call it 'mono' in English," says Shigeyo. "I see!"

"I still don't know how I could've gotten it — none of the kids had it, that's for sure — but ever since then I've restricted my diet. It made my symptoms clear up really fast."

"It wasn't serious, I hope."

"To be honest, I don't remember much of what happened back then. But yeah, I did have to go to the hospital."

Yoshino pats my shoulder. "I still remember it. She came to work in her costume and everything, held on until the end of the day, then passed out. Oh, I was so worried!"

"Ah, I turned out all right. I had an extra-helpful friend that day." I give her a reassuring smile. "And my outfit cheered up some hospital kids, so it wasn't a total disaster."

"Ehhh." Everyone nods and goes quiet.

"How about all of you?" I ask, changing the subject. "Did you all have a good vacation?"

Yoshino replies first: "It was all right. I cleaned a lot. Went to Ikuta Shrine. Slept in. Clocked an *obaachan* for a grab bag at the Earth, Music, and Ecology New Year's shopping sale. The usual."

Think New Year's shopping sale. Think rush hour at Shibuya Station.

I'm glad my back is turned as I return my iPhone to my purse on the shelf. I think my heart just skipped a beat. Where have I heard that phrase before?

"I just rested all day," says Ryoko. "Too tired."

"Me, too," Kana says. "I was so burned out. So many kids!" She shudders. "I'm *already* looking forward to the next holiday."

"February twelfth," Yoshino examines a calendar on the wall. "It falls on a Monday, of course."

"Boo. Isn't there something before that?"

"You're thinking of Setsubun. That doesn't count. Especially since it's going to involve spring cleaning this whole school on a freaking Saturday."

"So, it'll be the exact *opposite* of a holiday." Kana pretends to melt. *"Ah mou, shindoooi!"*

We all laugh, but I find myself rubbing my chest. Maybe I too am looking forward to another holiday. Or maybe I'm weirded out by the mental image of Yoshino laying the smackdown on a grandma half her size. Either way, I psych myself up in time for the sounds of another wave of clients stepping off the elevator. No time to dwell. School has officially begun.

The teachers all gather their boxes from under the counter and head off to their respective lessons. While I arrange my work on the counter, I notice Yoshino is the last teacher to collect her things. "Can't believe it'll only be three months until we're done here," I say to her.

Yoshino pouts. "I know. What is this school going to do without our awesomeness?"

"I doubt they'll even notice."

"Oh, they will. When it's *too late*." Yoshino temples her fingers and steps out into the reception desk just as Manager barks her name. On the other side of the door I can hear them talking about arranging makeup classes from October's "emergency holiday." The holiday our school is still reeling from, despite all the new students we managed to enrol.

I sit down and take stock of the staff room. I feel ... I don't know. Different. Like everything changed so suddenly, and I didn't even notice until now. Yuki and Yuri were sorely missed when they were transferred to the Osaka branch. Jun got married and moved to Yokohama. Misaki quit in the blink of an eye. Yoshino and I are the only teachers who will finish off a complete school year. Seri will be gone soon, now that kids are starting to ask hilarious questions: "What happened to your tummy? Are you sick? A BABY?! But *Mama* says you're not married! Who's your husband? Why doesn't he make you wear rings? How did a *baby* get in your tummy?" Scandalous stuff on top of all the abrupt departures.

Manager slides the staff room door open and steps in, rubbing his neck in a nervous gesture. "Ah, Cybelle?"

"That's my name."

"Cybelle, *ohayou*. You have class with Baby Two babies today, yes? Maybe, *mama* and *papa* will ask about emergency holiday.

They arrange makeup with Yoshino today, so maybe, when they come, they maybe ask you to bring them to Yoshino."

"Sure, I can do that. Oh, that reminds me, I ran into Hiroki's parents during the holiday. They asked if I'll still be his teacher in April."

Manager hisses through his teeth. "Ah ... okay. Maybe, if they ask, please tell them we are still deciding. Maybe, you should not say Cybelle will go back to Canada in April, or maybe they will not return to Zozo in April."

A web of lies; Manager's solution to everything. "Okay, but what *should* I tell them? I'm not comfortable with lying to them." At the time I said I wasn't sure, so it wasn't an outright fib. Thankfully having my legion of a family around me convinced baby Hiroki's parents to keep the conversation short.

"Hmmm ... *ja*, maybe ... hmmm. Let me see."

"You know what? Don't worry about it, I'll just send them to you." No need for this painful conversation to get any longer. "I'll be here prepping if you need me."

"Ah, okay. Thank you for your understanding, Cybelle. You are still so hard-working, even though you will leave. Zozo appreciates this. *Otsukaresama desu.*"

Uh-huh. "*Otsukaresama.*" Once Manager exits the staff room, I stick some old lesson plans into a few textbooks, then retrieve my iPhone and pocket Wi-Fi to finish my vegan Pinterest board. For kicks, I also take a few snapshots of my cats on *Neko Atsume.* I don't have anything to do except take my walk to Tully's at 12:40 and pick up a Snowman soy latte for my Moms' class. Gosh, do I love being over-prepared.

Around noon, Yoshino pops into the staff room and asks if I'll get something for lunch with her. I have my cabbage salad, but I could go for some sushi. We bundle up and head to the supermarket under Daiei.

"So how are things on the admin front?" I ask her.

"Ugh," Yoshino shakes her head. "A big clusterfuck, as usual. We're still recovering from that typhoon day — *still*. I don't know how we're going to make up everyone's lessons by April. Why did it have to happen on a Saturday, of all days? No one knows what happened. We don't have any notes, and Manager doesn't remember what he told parents except that the school was closed. But I guess making everyone come in the midst of a typhoon would have been worse. Better safe than sorry, right?"

"So glad I don't have to deal with any of that." I'm especially grateful that I can finish my last three months without doing any work — I can use lesson plans from past years — which means more time to relax and catch up with people via Facebook on my new phone.

"Oh yeah, did Manager tell you about your makeup lesson at one? You'll have five students to play with today!"

"He *did*, for once! I'm looking forward to it. My own little army of one-year-olds. But the parents still want to know what happened back in October. I also have to convince them to re-contract, somehow."

"I see. It's tough, I know. I don't want to lie to my parents, either. Most of them would understand, I think, but we're not allowed to bring it up first … sucks, huh?"

"Understatement."

We walk down the escalator past displays of winter jackets and *fukubukuro* bags to the supermarket level. The sushi guy remembers me quite well.

"Ah, konnichiwa, gaikokujin-sama! Akemashite omedetou!"

"Akemashite omedetou." I smile at him.

"Vegetarian *futomaki, ne?"*

"Ee, sou desu ne." The colourful display catches my eye. *"Soshite, natto maki to inari zushi, onegaishimasu."*

"Ohhh, *natto maki, ne*! Do you like *natto*?!"

I shrug and nod at the same time. We have a nice little chat about how healthy *natto* is before he takes Yoshino's order.

"Do you *really* like *natto*, Cybelle?" Yoshino asks as she walks with me to Tully's. "Because even I've never been a big fan of it."

"It's okay; not the greatest meal in the world, but my New Year's resolution was to eat more kinds of food. I've been eating the same things for the past two months. I'm surprised my body hasn't rejected anything out of boredom yet."

"Well, don't go telling too many people, or you're going to break hearts when you tell them you're leaving."

I can't help laughing. "How did you know that was my second resolution? 'Don't make any new friends.'"

We're still giggling in the Tully's lineup as I buy my "Moms' class coffee" — we all bring hot drinks so we can chat like we're in a café together. It was Fumiko's idea when she asked Manager and Bucho if we could hang out outside of Zozo in a casual setting (naturally, they said no). My latte won't stay piping hot after my lesson of army-babies, so I use that as an excuse to get a winter tumbler for it.

"Happy New Year!" I greet each of my mom students as they arrive, fresh-faced and ready to take on English conversation again. We talk about our holidays: it turns out they all went somewhere. Fumiko went to Disneyland with her family, Mami spent the holidays with her parents in Kumamoto, and Miyoko went to Todaiji in Nara. Everyone breaks out boxes of goodies they bought to share in class today. Great timing, because I could use the sugar-based "second breakfast," but the box of maple cookies my family left for each of them gets the biggest reaction.

"Oh! *Speaking* of your mother ..." Miyoko tests out a new phrase to all of our admiration. "I wanted to give you these to share with your mother and your sisters. But maybe, they are already back in Canada, so ... I guess ... only, for Cybelle-*sensei*!"

"Aw, Miyoko-*san*! Thank you." I find myself holding a small box of tea with a cartoon deer on it, and a larger box with deer squeezing their eyes as globular brown balls fall from their tails.

"This is Yamato-*cha* — green tea, very famous," Miyoko explains. "And this is … um …" Fumiko and Mami are doubling over, laughing. "No, no, NOT deer *unchi*! It's *choco dango*." They nod and make sympathetic "ahhh." sounds, but they still wipe away tears of laughter.

"I knew, when I saw them, I said, 'Ah, Cybelle-*sensei*, will like,'" she adds. The moms all resume laughing.

"I have trained you well, my young Padawans," I cheer.

"Oh! *Star Wars*! I remember!" says Mami. We laugh some more.

"Did you have fun with your family?" Fumiko asks. "Did they like Zozo?"

"Yeah, we had a good time … eventually," I say. "We didn't really travel anywhere far. We stayed in town for Christmas, but then my sisters got bored of Nishibe, so I took them to Osaka. It was nice to spend time with them again."

"If you will go home in spring, you must be very excited," Mami says. "May I ask, when you go, what will you miss in Japan?"

Eating.

Huh. That was a weird thought.

"The food, mostly," I say, which makes everyone nod and laugh. "And, of course, I would miss all of you!" We all have an "aww" moment there. "But don't worry, you still have me as your teacher for at least a few more months." It's not a complete lie. All of them seem to be expecting me to say whether or not I'll leave, but I've been good about keeping it secret for the past few months. "Oh! I can tell you what I *won't* miss."

"Manager?" Miyoko offers. We burst out laughing.

"The insects." We are still laughing but the subject turns serious as I recount when my cousin came over back in November and I noticed a dead creature that had fallen out of my closet, which meant there were probably more nesting in there somewhere. We had to go to the supermarket to buy the dreaded white powder I'd hoped I'd never have to buy. "I've always been lucky with not having too many bugs, so I guess it's to be expected that I would find one big one before —" Oops, I can't tell them I'm leaving. "Before the school year ended," I say hurriedly.

"Ah! So ... your cousin ... saw a big insect ... was it *mukade?*"

"We weren't sure. It was really long and had lots of legs ... but it was kind of a pinkish-white colour?"

"Oh! So dangerous!" Fumiko exclaims. "Did you kill it?"

"I think it was sleeping," I admit. "Because it didn't move until we got a big piece of paper and tried to push it into a Starbucks bag so we could run outside and throw it in the rain gutter — you know, the *ame doi?* And then, as we were pushing it in, even though it was slathered in *mukade* powder it started twitching, like it was starting to wake up, and it was like 'Huh? Wha? What's going on ...?'" I half-close my eyes and flop around, imitating the insect. My students shriek with laughter. I conveniently leave out the part where my cousin threw the bug, the bag, and the paper off the balcony and slammed the window shut. We were relieved to see that the bag and paper had landed neatly in the rain gutter, and not on someone walking by. "So, yeah! Long story short, I will not miss the insects here."

I feel that there's something else I'll miss ... but I can't remember what. I had this talk with my family before they left, and it was made very clear (mostly by Mom) that I've done everything: I ticked off clubbing, capsule hotels, Mount Fuji, watching a sumo match, and participating in tea ceremony years ago. In the past couple of weeks, I squeezed in Mario Kart racing, fugu, and feeding the Nara deer with my family. So, what else is there? *What am I missing?*

What else will I miss?

"Ah, that's right, Cybelle-*sensei!* I had a dream. I remember, I write ..." Fumiko flips through her notebook excitedly. "Wait, no, maybe I didn't write. Never mind."

"You had dream?" Miyoko asks. She looks just as excited, too. "A dream, about Fuji-*san*?"

"No, not Fuji-*san*. Something else. But, no Fuji-*san*." Fumiko draws a single invisible tear down her face.

I burst out laughing. "Aw, me, neither! I didn't dream about Mount Fuji — again! And I *really* concentrated this year, too! I think I had a dream where I was surrounded by babies ... probably because I was at a capsule hotel with my family and they were acting like babies. But I woke up with this wicked craving for eggplant, so we went to Café Absinthe for baba ganoush."

"Eggplant?" Fumiko tilts her head. They all look it up on their electronic dictionaries. "Ah! *Nasu!* Oh, you are very lucky!"

"Really?"

"Yes! First lucky dream is Mount Fuji, then *taka* — ah, hawk? And then, eggplant is third lucky dream."

Mami nods. "Yes, and you said you had dream about babies? If baby has no hair, is also lucky. 'No hair' in Japanese is *ke ga nai*, but also 'no injury,' so it's good luck, too."

"Cool," I say. "So, what happens if you dream about a bald hawk eating eggplant on Mount Fuji?"

They laugh. "Maybe you will win lottery!" says Miyoko.

"We've talked about dreams together before today, haven't we?"

"Yes! First lesson ... we talked about 'having a dream,'" Fumiko says. "And maybe about babies?"

Miyoko nods. "*Sou, sou, sou.* I remember Cybelle dreaming about babies."

"Really?" I ask. I don't, but I decide not to correct her. Anything that keeps them talking these days is great.

"Yes. You should tell your family. Your mother will be very happy to hear you want a baby, I think." Miyoko gives me a hard but playful slap on the back of my hand.

"Yeah, right! I'm not telling her that! She's already lining up guys to set me up with." This leads to a long discussion about what the term "set-up" means, which leads into a conversation about matchmaking in Japan. We don't even bother with the boring textbook today. At ten to three the students next door burst from their room, cueing the moms to collect their things and thank me for another fun lesson. I escort them to the door, but Miyoko lingers behind, rustling something from her handbag.

"Ah, Cybelle-*sensei*, I forgot another present! I did *osouji* and found a book for Cybelle-*sensei*. Maybe, you will like? It's *yokai* book. In Japanese, but you can study!"

"A *yokai* book?" I take it from her. It's a small, thick book with sketches of monsters on a black background. "妖怪絵" is written on it in thick white characters. It looks brand new. I flip through a few pages. It's an art book, which happens to be my kind of book. "Wow. Ooh, look at this one. It's like a school for demons!"

"Yes!" Miyoko leans in, describing the page. "This is Shoki, and he is teaching *yokai* about Rashomon."

"Like the movie?" I peer at the picture. "No, maybe not. What does 'Rashomon' mean, anyway?"

"Hmm … it's difficult."

"What about this one? It looks like it's teaching English."

"Yes, this is *kappa*."

"Ah, *kappa* I've heard of before. And what does this say? '*Shiri-go-tama*?'" Saying the word makes Miyoko burst into giggles and turn away. I squint at the word, then it slowly dawns on me as I piece together what I know of body part vocabulary. "Oh, wait. I think I know."

"Yes, we do not say this word!"

Enough said. "Thank you! I love it. And it'll teach me to read Japanese. Yay, learning!"

Out in the lobby, I wave farewell to the moms again as they gather around Lieko for a rundown of her lesson with their kids. As per my third New Year's resolution — stop taking crap from people — I pass her without a glance. It's funny, but I never thought Lieko could be *more* passive-aggressive toward me until I got mono. For the past two months she's been weirder and ruder around me than ever. She doesn't even sit in on my teacher interviews anymore. It's like she'll catch it if she gets too close. We have our lessons with mutual students, so there's the odd time when she escorts them to my room; otherwise, we have no real contact with each other. She never sat next to me at lunchtime breaks or responded when I tried to make conversation, anyway, so I guess it's not much of a difference — and yet it feels like there is a *big* difference between pre-Halloween and now. Yoshino chalked it up to jealousy at my family visits and the support I got from the Zozo staff. Strange things to be jealous of, I said, but at the time I didn't want to argue with the only Zozo friend I had. I was mostly curious about her reasons for ostracizing me that she didn't have before. It's not like I had hope for burying any hatchets before I go.

Between lessons, Lieko and I trade places talking to parents. She waits for me to approach the Zone VI students' parents and translates my comments without being asked. I let her come over and translate to my newest kinder student's parents that "Tomohide really does his best in English" when I say he really needs to be told in Japanese not to self-stimulate on the floor. We bow to everyone as they leave with their respective kids and students, and Lieko and I go our separate ways. That's it. No fuss, no cuss. What are the odds of this lasting another three months?

At any rate, I didn't expect the first day back from New Year's vacation to go so quickly and so well. Aside from Tomohide's antics, Riko and Reiji behave quite well, and even Kennichi is a little more upbeat than normal. Maybe it was because I was willing to share the respective *omiyage mochi* and cookies my students gave me. Either way, I'm in quite a cheerful mood when it's time to collect the garbage from all the classrooms.

I walk in on Yoshino in Room Five, wiping down the whiteboards. "Hey, Cyb, we still on for salsa tomorrow night?"

"Sho' nuff. Why?"

"Well, I was thinking, we should invite the other teachers. I think they'll like it. It'll be a much more fun way to get to know them than that awful welcome party we had."

Ah, yes, the *izakaya* dinner before Christmas, where I barely ate because everything Manager and Lieko ordered had some form of animal protein in it. It was unfortunate we couldn't just go back to Pepe, which last I checked had closed down. "That's not a bad idea." I stroke my chin. "But what if they don't like dancing? Won't they be bored?"

"Hmm, good point. How about we skip the lesson and just go for eight p.m.? Or, we can go the usual time and chat before the dance party starts. Then we can eat and hang out, and if they don't want to dance, they can go home!"

"Sounds good to Cybelle. Um, I have to ask … are we talking about *all* the other teachers?"

Yoshino's eyes search the ceiling, then she nods, slowly. "Ah … yeah …" She says after a moment.

"It's okay. It won't be fair for all the girls to go and we don't at least *invite* her. I don't mind. It's not like I have to dance with her, right?"

Yoshino laughs. "You know what? That would be something to see. Let's do it. Let's invite Lieko along! She's going to be the fish out of water for once, not you, right?"

"Please. I don't concern myself with her anymore. Three more months and she'll have some obnoxious foreigner to deal with while I move on with my life. That's what I'm hoping for, anyway."

"That's the spirit, girl!" Yoshino reaches out for a fist bump. "Besides, I've always been curious to see how she'd fare in a real 'English' setting. You know she's always correcting me and the others about our grammar and shit?" She whispers in a quiet voice. "It's annoying as hell, I don't know how everyone deals with her. Especially you. Patience of a saint."

Manager sticks his head into the room, apologizing in Japanese for interrupting us. "*Ne*, Cybelle-*sensei*. I must ask, how is your apartment? Maybe, it is intact? After family visit? Nothing is broken, yes?"

"Yes, Manager. The apartment is perfectly fine."

"Eh? Really? *Really?* Wow! Your family must be very careful people. This is good news. You know, because maybe landlord get scared of *gaijin* breaking the walls and so on. But in your case, this is good news. Thank you for your understanding, Cybelle."

"Uh-huh." That's right, Manager, me and my *gaijin* family didn't destroy everything in sight. The sheer rudeness factor of this guy doesn't faze me anymore.

"And, Cybelle, I must also thank you for your careful attitude regarding our clients. Cybelle is such a good teacher. If only we could find a man like Cybelle to replace Cybelle."

"Yes. If *only*."

My sarcasm goes over his head. "Ah, yes! Speaking of which, here is a letter from Head Office about vacating apartment, paying bills, cutting off internet and phone, and so on. Please read it carefully. Oh yes, and Ayuna will come on Thursday for makeup lesson from October emergency holiday," Manager adds. "She will join Kyoko and Yumi's class. Oh, and Friday, maybe … Hitomu, too."

I say the name a couple of times. "Hitomu … Hitomu … oh. OH. Yeah, I forgot all about him. Whatever happened to that kid?"

"Ah, Hitomu … yes …" Manager draws the word out in a long, unsatisfied hiss. "His mother, ah, she wants him to try English school … again. Maybe, his crying, it will stop?"

"Oh. So, he's gotten better?"

Manager makes a face. "Hmm … maybe, no."

Wonderful.

"Ah, yes! And, Cybelle and Yoshino-*sensei* will prepare for interview with Okamura-*sensei* tomorrow at twelve. Sorry, no lunchtime. Again."

"Another interview?" Yoshino pipes in. "We already have four new teachers!"

"Yes, but Bucho wants one more, and this one ... he is ... maybe, his English, not so good, but, he is ..." Manager trails off again. I'm not surprised; we all know where he's going with this.

"Ah, mou ..." It's the closest Yoshino comes to complaining. "Hey, whatever happened to that one cute guy? Why didn't we hire him?"

"Eh? *Dare?*"

"*You* know ... Cybelle knows ..." she winks at me.

"Which guy? Kuwajima-*san?*"

"The guy with the glasses? No! You know, the cute one!"

"He was kinda cute. He looked like a teddy bear."

"No, that was Nakanishi-*san.*" Yoshino looks like she's going to throttle me. "You know, the *cute* one. He was all over you!"

"... that wasn't Kuwajima-*san?*"

"Cybelle! No! Ugh, I can't believe you don't remember him! I was sure he was going to work here and you two would totally hook up. How can you *not* remember?! Kinda tall, longish hair, big ears? Ring any bells?"

"Yoshino, I don't even remember what I had for breakfast."

She hunches over and mockingly drags herself out of the room, past Manager. I follow her. I'm the wrong person to ask about these things. All our male candidates' names blur together in my mind these days. The guy with the pit stains? No. The guy I saw reading *ero* manga in front of the station? Definitely not. It can't be the dude who pretended to have a heart attack and laughed at me when I rode by on the street (I still relish the look on his face when I followed him all the way up to the school, and the horror when Manager told him I was going to be the one interviewing him). I guess the guy with the lisp last week was somewhat attractive ... "Okamoto-*san?*" I offer.

It's obviously not the answer Yoshino was looking for. "Meh, I guess he was okay-looking," she finally says. "But that's not the guy

I'm thinking of. Shoot, what was his name? The second I remember I'm going to call you screaming it. Have your phone handy at all times."

"Will do. And if you don't remember by tonight, you can let me know at salsa tomorrow."

"Sounds good!" Yoshino winks at me. "If I'm sober enough to pronounce it by then!"

The next day goes by in an equally efficient blur. At the end of the night we all get our sturdiest heels ready for Salsa Wednesdays at Bar Iznt. The best discovery I made since I moved here, six and a half years too late to enjoy it. We hop on the train and take it west to Sannomiya station. Bar Iznt is already fully packed by the time our beginner dance lesson begins. First, our Brazilian instructor Sebastián reviews the basic salsa step so that our new co-workers can catch up. Then we dive right into open holds and cross holds for the rest of the hour. As we move from the dance floor, a man asks Yukie to dance and she accepts, waving goodbye at us before he twirls her away. Kana and Shigeyo partner up. Yukako hangs back to ask Sebastián more about the basic step while Yoshino, Yukie, Ryoko, and I head off for drinks.

"I wonder where Lieko went?" Ryoko asks us.

We all shrug. Lieko was mysteriously absent for the duration of the lesson. Whatever. If she decided to ditch, she saved herself a thousand yen and spared me an hour of her side-eye; of course, I can't say that out loud. My resolution depends on it. "The bar?" I suggest.

"Ooh, that's right! We can use our drink tickets now! What will you have, Cybelle-*sensei*?"

"I'm okay for now." I accompany them to the bar, anyway. One bartender, a young man named Marcy, waves us over. "Hey, you're back! And you brought friends. Welcome! But where are your sisters?"

"They went home."

"Zannen!" Marcy throws up his hands. "And they left you here?"

"For now. I'll join them in the spring."

"You're LEAVING? Oh my Gott!"

We only have another moment to chat about my not re-contracting and future plans back in Canada before the wave of newcomers floods the bar. As much as I love Marcy, I give him the vaguest answers I can think of — to be honest with myself, I have no idea what I'll do come springtime, aside from sticking around long enough to enjoy the *hanami*. I order my usual giant plate of nachos with some mozzarella and cheese sauce on the side for everyone to share back at our usual table in the corner. We pull up a few chairs so us Zozo girls can all sit together. We *kanpai* with our drinks (and my water) and pounce on the nachos.

"Excited about seeing Hitomu again?" Yoshino asks me.

"Makes no difference to me. Zozo gets their money, I get *my* money ..."

"Who is this famous Hitomu I keep hearing about?" Ryoko asks us. "Lieko mentioned something about him being in one of my lessons, too."

"The too-long-didn't-read version," Yoshino says after a swig of her Corona, "is that Hitomu has problems. He's terrified of strangers; it's like an anxiety thing, but to the extreme. And he's only, what, three years old? Anyway, it's pretty scary to witness. But we haven't seen him since Halloween, so ..."

"That's awful," Ryoko shakes her head. "Do you think he might be ... you know ... *gyakutai sarete iru no*? Eh, being abused?"

It's my turn to shake my head. "I don't think so. I mean, the kid obviously has a problem, but the way he scrambles to his mother, I don't think he'd behave like that if she were abusing him. It's like he's genuinely afraid of something at our school. But instead of trying to help him we're trying to get as much money out of him as possible. I get it, that's the business, but it doesn't make it right."

Ryoko nods. "I don't like it, either, but that's *eikaiwa* for you."

They all nod in agreement, turning the topic to child abuse in general. I busy myself with the cheese-less nachos to avoid donating my two cents. I'm leaving in three months; the last thing I want to do is to say anything against my new co-workers' work culture or get political. The truth is that, despite all appearances, something about Hitomu is just ... *haunting*. It goes beyond the whole child abuse aspect.

Shigeyo, Kana, and Yukako join us, drinks in hand, pointing over at the bar to Manager. I had no idea he was coming, but oh well. When he comes over, we *kanpai* again and the subject changes to whether or not they'd like to come back for more salsa lessons. Manager is the only one who refuses to dance or talk about dancing. He seems content to sit and stare down his beer until someone brings up Zozo. Then he lights up.

"*Ne*, Cybelle," he leans over to me, now. "I am so sorry, you have Hitomu tomorrow. *Mama* says he is better, so maybe he will behave."

"I hope so. Thanks."

"Thank you. You have been so hard-working for ... *roku nen* ... six years, yes? *Sugee na!*" His *Kansai-ben* means he's beginning to relax. "Oh, did I not tell you? Soon, you cannot call me 'Kinomoto-Manager' anymore. Soon, our school will have ... new manager." His face turns crestfallen. "I should have told Cybelle sooner."

"Aw, that's too bad. When will this happen?"

"This spring. April. So, maybe, after Cybelle leaves."

So, it won't matter, anyway. Meh. "So, what should I call you instead of Manager, Kinomoto-*san*?"

"Ah, please! We are not at Zozo, Cybelle. You can use my *shita no namae.*"

"Yeah, what is your first name, anyway?"

"Hyuu *to moushimasu*."

"Hugh?!" I throw my head back and laugh. Manager doesn't seem to mind; in fact, he laughs with me.

Halfway through our conversation Marcy comes along with a giant jug of red, sinister-looking liquid that has blueberries and orange slices and something that looks like lotus root floating in it. He says something into Yoshino's ear, gesturing over his shoulder back toward the bar, where an attractive salaryman raises his glass in our direction. Yoshino giggles. "It's sangria!" she yells over the crowd. Marcy goes and returns with several wine glasses. We *kanpai* again. I have about two glasses full before the jug is empty. Marcy is already at our table with a replacement. By this time, the bar is in full swing and everyone is dashing back and forth between the tables, the dance floor, and the long line at the bar. Yoshino stands up and starts dancing right at our table. She grabs me by the hand, pulls me up and twirls me around, humming along to the music. Laughing, I pretend to dip her before taking the lead.

"Nooo!" Yoshino flails away. "I'm too drunk to remember anything!"

"Liar!" I yell back. "It's the basic step. You *know* this!" We hit the dance floor to shimmy and undulate together instead, pretending to know the rest of the words we're singing while our new co-workers stand off to the sidelines, exchanging awkward giggles. Maybe at our dancing, maybe sharing their own private jokes. I don't care.

"You know what we should do?" Yoshino yells against my ear. "We should make every moment of these last few months count — *you* especially! You should be living it up! Who cares if you make new friends or not? If they're smart, they'll *want* to stay in touch with you! And this whole vegan trip — don't take this the wrong way, but are you sure you're not afraid of anything?"

"Afraid of what?" I shout back.

"I don't know! Of getting sick again, maybe?! I know that was a scary time for you but think about it — when is the next time you're going to be back here, Cyb?! If I were you, I'd be eating my way through this country! Stop depriving yourself, girl!"

I laugh. "Okay, okay, I'll think about it!"

The song ends, but not before a tall older gentleman sweeps Yoshino into the core of the dance crowd. A new swarm of sweating bodies flank us on all sides, some of their faces familiar. Same dancers we see every week after the lesson's over.

A young woman shorter than me comes over. "*Sugoi!* You are good! Good dancer! Can you speak Japanese? Where are you from?"

"Canada."

"Oh! Do you know Shakey's? In Osaka? Have you been to Shakey's?"

"Never. I want to, though. I hear they have s'mores and good bubble tea."

"Yes! S'mores is delicious!"

"I wouldn't know, I don't think I've ever tried one."

"*Ehhh?* But you're from Canada!"

I shrug. "Where are *you* from?"

"Busan!"

"Oh, cool! Would you like to dance?"

We dance for one song, then Sebastián comes along and extends his hand to me. After a couple of songs, everyone manages themselves into a big circle where we follow Sebastián's gyrating moves. A couple of girls take the centre of the ring, too. One drops into a perfect split. We in the circle all hold hands, swinging our arms back and forth, making the circle bigger and smaller. Every now and then someone shouts at me, asking me where I'm from, how long I'm staying here, can I speak insert-language-here, and I can't respond fast enough before opening my eyes and realizing they're gone. It's okay; tonight, I'm not here to make friends. Hell, I *can't* make friends. We'll only end up breaking each other's hearts when it's time for me to leave. Regardless, I smile back at people who may or may not be trying to strike up conversations, dance circles around everyone, around speakers and tables laden with food. I don't stop dancing between swigs of sangria, snatches of conversation with the Zozo crew, and handfuls of nachos. I am fluid. This is my weekly stress reliever. It's a secret I wish I had discovered years ago, long before last fall, long before Zozo, maybe even before I toyed with the idea of teaching overseas. All this time I just needed to fucking *relax*. Keep moving. Keep pushing forward. Never stand still. Never stop long enough to think about where I'll flow next. No way in hell am I going back to two months ago. Waking up in my bathtub, nightmares for days ... Nope. Not letting that happen again.

"You're good!" I feel stubble against my neck. "And I like your hair!" The same salaryman who bought us sangria makes a gesture with his hands, like he's rubbing shampoo into his fauxhawk. "Your hair! Cute!"

"Thanks!" I smile. "I like your hair, too! Very hip!"

He falls in step in with me, trying to keep in time with the beat without getting too close to me. He isn't half bad, and it looks like he's trying not to be a creep. It's too dark to see his face, but from what I can tell from the fuchsia strobe lighting, he's a bit older than I am. Still, I'll feel better keeping this conversation short and banal so I don't run out of breath. "Your English is really good!" I tell him.

"Aw, I don't know about that!"

"*Wow*. See? That right there proves it's good! Your accent, too! You've studied or lived abroad, haven't you?"

The young man nodded. "America!"

"California?"

"Yeah! How'd you guess?"

"I have a student who grew up in Los Angeles; she sounds exactly like you!" So much for the short conversation plan; now I want to know more about this guy.

"You have a really good ear!" The man stops bobbing back and forth, placing a hand on the small of my back as he leans in close. "Wanna get a drink?" He offers his arm. We pass by Yoshino on the way to the bar. She pauses in her grinding between two dudes to tap me on the shoulder and press her hand to her mouth, opening in an exaggerated mock gasp.

The salaryman leans up against the bar, murmurs something to Marcy as he holds up two fingers. While Marcy serves us our drinks, it hits me that I have no idea what I'm going to talk to this guy about that isn't the usual line of questioning. When the salaryman asks, "How long will you stay in Japan?" I breathe a huge sigh of relief. We can keep this interaction short and sweet.

"I'm actually going back home in three months!" I take a proud sip of my drink. It's a Fuzzy Navel. My first in months, come to think of it. It's good, but it tastes … funny … almost like real peach juice. I guess after all that lotus-y sangria anything is bound to taste strange.

"What?! Aw, come on! Seriously? Why?! You got a boyfriend waiting for you back home? Nothing good enough to keep you here?"

For the first time in ages, my answer is all tied up in my tongue. "It's just … time for me to go."

The man leans forward, eyes glinting with the neon blue of the overhead lights. "What would it take to change your mind?"

I swallow half my drink to avoid coughing it back up in shock. What a question. "I've already signed the resignation form, dude."

"No. I mean, what if you found a reason to stay? I mean, a *really* good reason. Would you change your mind?"

"Ha! It would have to be a freaking good reason."

He smiles, pleased. Apparently, it was the answer he wanted to hear. "If I tell you something, promise you won't be mad?"

"No."

The man's smile widens, like a Cheshire cat. He leans over, pressing his stubbled cheek against mine. "I have a confession to make: your sister sent me to come and get you. She's waiting for you. Outside."

"My WHAT?!"

"Ah, ah, you promised — oh wait, you didn't promise. Well, she's still outside. Waiting for you. She said you'd be mad." He offers his arm again. "Come on."

At any other point during the week, I would probably stop and think for a moment. If it were daytime, or if I were going full throttle at work, I'd be way more clear-headed than I am now. I wouldn't be under the influence of sangria, peach Schnapps, loud dance music, that foggy dry ice that makes me cough, or my own adrenalin, and I'd be sharp enough to ask questions: "Are you sure this chick is my sister? Which sister? Maybe you have me confused with another woman of colour. Are you a murderer? Are you sure? Hey, insert-co-worker's-name, can you come with me and this rando to make sure I'm not about to get murdered?" and a list of other things to make sure I'm not being led to a black van full of government ninjas who kidnap foreigners. That I'm not about to end up in another situation that makes me (and everyone else I know) question my sanity.

But nope, I don't ask any of those things. Instead, I follow him to the elevator and punch the button for the ground floor.

"I cannot believe this is happening again," I mutter. "Everyone swore Bully was doing great — *especially* her! She's been saying for years that she'd never do something this stupid again. Well, I don't know about stupid … she has this whole taste-for-adventure thing and it got her a husband, so I guess I shouldn't talk. How the hell did she find me all the way out here in Kobe? It's not like she's psychic. This is so weird. Please tell me I'm dreaming."

The salaryman doesn't say anything.

"Okay … that doesn't help. How about this: if you're not going to murder me, say and do absolutely nothing."

No reply.

"Well, at least we've cleared *that* up." Strangely, I don't feel the least bit worried. If he tries anything, I'll just use the power of peach liqueur to punch him and make a run for it.

Outside Bar Iznt the street is completely empty. I look down at the ground and see wet pavement. Bars and restaurants down the way are still open, fluorescent lights glaring, storefront music playing. The sound of *enka* mingles with Shakira's "Loca" playing upstairs. I look up and down the street for signs of life, let alone someone who looks like me. Not a single person in either direction for miles. It must have just rained. That would explain why there are fewer people than normal, but for Sannomiya to be completely barren is still odd.

"Okay …" I begin. "Is *this* the part where you kill me?"

The man drops my arm abruptly. In the blink of an eye he's several feet away, up the street, heading toward a brightly lit building with pictures of pale-skinned women all over its marquee. He's talking to someone crouching down on the ground. I catch a glimpse of black hair and pale skin before the man blocks my view. That is definitely not my sister. He's babbling in Japanese; there's an urgency in his voice. I catch a few words … something about how he's been looking everywhere for whoever he's talking to, and if they can go to a hotel now.

"Um, hey, buddy? You said …"

I trail off. He's talking to a young girl. She wears a dark blue blazer, a black-and-white plaid skirt that exposes her shockingly pale thighs and knees bent over a pair of blood-red Converse sneakers. Her hair is so long it almost touches the filthy pavement she squats down on. Her long fingers jab expertly on a heavily laden *keitai*, even as she rises. She snaps the phone shut and turns to face me, oblivious to the man ranting so fast I can barely understand half of it. My heart feels like it's been submerged in ice water.

"*Hisa-bisa, baku-sama,*" the girl says. Her voice is quite deep. "Do you know what that means?"

This is getting weird. I shake my head. *Hisa-bisa*, of course, I understand, but *baku?* I wonder if it means the same as "*baka*" and start to feel offended.

"'*Hisa-bisa'?!*" the salaryman barks in Japanese. "What the hell you talking about?! We just saw each other ten minutes ago!" He staggers on his feet as if copious amounts of alcohol in his veins have resumed their course. His entire tone and rhythm of speech has changed so much it's like he was possessed by the ghost of a sober, smooth-talking American who has now relinquished his body. "Okay, if you don't want to go to a hotel, let me try to sneak you in again! The bouncer's gone, and everyone's so wasted they won't even notice. Shit, why the hell'd you have to show up in your uniform, anyway?!" He ruffles his hair angrily, and sighs when the girl doesn't respond. She's still staring at me. "Look, I'm sorry, okay? I'm just so horny. Why don't we go to a nice warm hotel, instead of hanging out around here?"

The girl freezes him with a "talk-to-the-hand" kind of gesture. "I apologize for this one. As I was saying. '*Hisa-bisa.*' Do you know what that means?"

I gulp. I know I should be running back upstairs to the safety of the English bar and my co-workers, but I don't. "'Long time, no see.'"

"Of course you do. I apologize; I do not mean to belittle you. It has just been such a long time. I have been wondering what happened to you. I had worried that maybe you had left. Then I happened to see you here, a fortnight ago. You were with your family. I take it they left. Are you leaving soon, too?"

I'm *so* confused. Who is this girl? A former student, or something? I don't know her, and yet I feel compelled to tell her the truth. Like there's no point in lying to her. Something about her demeanour tells me that if I lie, she will know. "Yes," I say finally.

"That is nice," the girl replies without smiling. "They will be happy to have you back, I am sure. But what about him?"

"'Him'? Who? *Him?*" I point to the frustrated salaryman who is now on his phone shouting about the nearest 'hotel.' "I've never seen this dude in my life."

The girl steps closer and closer as she speaks. "I beg your pardon. I have been wondering what happened to you. So, I sent you some help. Did you like it? The humans certainly enjoyed the libations. Anyhow. I wanted to let you know something; while you are still here. He has not forgotten about you, you know. He says your name in his sleep. So, if you plan on leaving, I believe he would appreciate your help, first. It has been months. I do not think anyone else is coming for him. Of course, it is your choice. I just thought you would like to know, one 'minority' to another." The salaryman appears to be returning to her with good news. "Oh, one more thing. About that little boy. The one the *yamauba* is always looking for; rumour is he has been asking about you, too. That woman who left earlier will not help, but you can, just as you can help the dream walker. Please consider it. His grandmother does not know the first place to look. But I am sure you do."

"Who?" I find my voice. "*Yamauba?* Who's that?"

"Sorry; the *oni baba*. She is coming." Without looking, she extends an arm behind her, toward the salaryman. He grabs it without hesitation and pulls her away. Then she turns on her heels and the two of them take off.

Something bounces against my shoulder. One of the Iznt bouncers is taking some velvet ropes away. "Oh! *Sumimasen.*" He bows as he excuses himself. "*Daijoubu?* You going back inside?"

"No — I mean, I'm fine, but —" I swing around. Another employee has materialized, rolling up a carpet. Slowly, like shadows, people are reappearing. In the distance, I see them — the salaryman and the girl, already miles away. "I'll be right back!"

"*Hai, hai,*" says the bouncer, but I'm already running. Like fog fading from invisible glasses, more and more people seem to solidify around me, blocking my path. I'm grateful for all that sangria I had. It spurs me onward as I force my way through this thickening crowd. My feet pound a new chant in my mind: *I'm not losing it. I'm not losing it.* Or maybe they're saying, "*Don't lose it. Don't lose it.*"

But I have a feeling that I already have.

I run up the narrow street choked with neon signs and super-bright LED displays of pale half-naked girls until it opens up to a wide avenue with green hedges in the centre and Dutch-style buildings on the other side. The traffic light up ahead changes yellow. I'm too late. The wall of pedestrians politely waiting for the light to complete its change blocks my path. I jump up and down fruitlessly, trying to keep the couple in view. People back away from me in fear. I see someone with a long shock of hair weaving through the mob, blending in, disappearing. *I'm not imagining things. I'm* not *losing it.* "Wait! H—" Shit, what is her name? It's on the tip of my tongue.

"Cybelle!"

I jump again, startled. It isn't the girl who's calling me. I whirl around and see Yukie coming up from behind me. "Are you okay? Yoshino said she saw you leaving, but your purse is still at the bar. Why were you running? Is everything okay?"

I could bear hug this woman. "Yukie, thank God you're here. Look across the street — do you see that girl, with the super-long hair?!"

"Uh, yes, I think so …" She squints. "In the green coat?"

"No," I sigh, dejected. "No. It's okay. She's gone."

"Who's gone? Someone you know?"

"I …" I don't know what else to think. The crowd flows around us as the crosswalk turns green. "Never mind. It's okay. Let's go see how my nachos are doing."

Yukie smiles. "Okay! But just so you know, we ate them all!"

fifteen
FABULOUS MONSTERS

果報は寝て待て
If you wish for good luck, sleep and wait

I've never been so grateful to work with children. Something about being immersed in their teeming world of germs and boogers and open-air coughing has fortified my immune system. Ever since Wednesday night I've been feeling out of sorts, but nothing like what the others must be feeling. Yoshino took her first sick day ever yesterday, and the other teachers are in various stages of cold and flu. I seem to be the only one unaffected, otherwise I'd say we'd been drugged. I do feel something though. Light-headed. Ever since salsa night I've been walking on the bottom of the ocean; a very relaxed state for the past forty-eight hours. I try to remember the last time I felt so at ease. Before I got mono, that's for sure. It feels like a strange form of déjà vu.

There is more déjà vu waiting for me when the elevator doors slide closed on my Senior students. It is now eerily quiet for a Friday night at Zozo. No kids, no teachers, no light evening chit-chat with live human beings. Sadly, Lieko is the only sign of life I can see. Rather than bothering to make small talk with her, I head back to Room Five to tidy up my things. The only other teacher who isn't sick from Wednesday night, Lieko is solely focused on typing away whatever report she has on the reception desk computer, with a look on her face like she's been drinking vinegar. I think I know why she didn't get sick: my hypothesis is it had something to do with that lotus-laden sangria, but that still doesn't make sense. *I* drank it, and I was fine.

First I clean up my cards and Jenga pieces, then fold up the tables and push them up against the wall, leaving one table in the corner. It's all I need to do to get the room ready for Hitomu. He didn't show up for his makeup lesson yesterday, and after drilling Manager, despite his wicked hangover, I learned that I'd be getting a bonus for Hitomu coming in tonight. That's all I'm going to keep telling myself to get through this last hour of the night.

To kill a little more time (and look busy), I retrieve the "窓" rag from the washroom and go around the school, cleaning up the viewing windows in each room. Still no students, no teachers in sight. Even Manager has disappeared somewhere. Déjà vu, indeed. If the lights weren't on and Lieko wasn't sitting on the other side of the reception desk, I'd grab my things and run home.

I pass through the silent lobby again. Lieko still doesn't look up from the computer, but I'm out of things to do. "Where is everyone?" I finally ask.

"We have a very important meeting with Bucho at eight o'clock tonight," Lieko says to the monitor. "But we have final lesson with Hitomu, so I must stay here until he is finished with you."

That didn't answer my question at all. I study her for a moment. "Lieko, where the heck did you learn to talk to people like that?" I want to add "Bitchy University?" but I've said enough to make my point.

She looks up at me, for once. Her face is like stone. "I beg your pardon?"

Down the hall the washroom door opens. I hear a young woman's voice saying something about behaving so well for Lieko-*sensei*. Hitomu and his mother come down the hallway. Odd. I didn't even hear them come in. They must have shown up during my Senior lesson. And to add to my surprise, the little toddler in the Snoopy onesie is replying with words instead of the high-pitched shrieks I now remember.

"Okay, Hitomu, time for Cybelle's lesson!" Lieko steps out from the reception desk to greet them in her professional, high-pitched voice. "Please do your best, *ne?*"

"Ah, *Sensei, yoroshiku onegaishimasu*," Hitomu's mother says with a low bow. She murmurs something to Hitomu, who gives me a wide-eyed look but says nothing.

"Oh! Cybelle-*sensei*, Hitomu say he missed you!" Lieko kneels down to Hitomu, praising him, grinning her widest without so much as a glance in my direction. His mother bows again and releases his hand to Lieko; they turn down the hall to Room Five as if I'm not even there. I follow, allowing myself a tiny shrug. Fine, whatever. Let's get this over with. Then I can chill out in the staff room while the others suffer through their long-winded meeting. Someone will probably just send me home.

"Ah, *there* you are, Cybelle-*sensei*! Yes! Okay! Let's enjoy English! Do your best, Hitomu!" Lieko strides out of the room, closing the classroom door firmly behind her. I spy her hovering in the window as I grab my things from the box, and I assume she's holding the doorknob on the other side just in case Hitomu makes a break for it. But there's no need today. Hitomu sits like a perfect student on the floor, hands in his lap, eyes downcast. He still looks like he doesn't get much sleep for a three-year-old ... but on the bright side, I can hear myself think.

"Hello, Hitomu, how are you?"

Hitomu's eyes lift to meet mine, as if he's noticed I'm there for the first time. "I'm-fine-thank-you-and-you?" he whispers.

"Wow — I mean, I'm great! Thank you for asking! High-five?" I tease him a little, moving my hand so he has to try and hit a moving target. It makes him smile a little. "Good job, Hitomu! What's that, Jibanyan? You want to sing the 'Hello Song' to Hitomu? Okay, let's do it! *Hello, hello hello hello, hello hello hello, hello hello what's your name?*"

"I'm Hitomu."

"Holy cra— uh, great job, Hitomu! What's that, Jibanyan? Another song? Well, sure, why not? Hitomu, would you like to sing a song with me? Jibanyan, can we sing the 'Welcome Song,' too? *Hello, hello, hello, and how are you? I'm fine, I'm fine, and I hope that you are too!* Good job! High-five! Now let's stand up!"

I make a rising gesture with my hands and stand. Hitomu smiles a little more as he rises to his feet. Shock is an understatement for what I'm feeling right now. He didn't even wipe his hands after my high-five. As I start the song on the CD player, he claps and sways back and forth a little. I wonder how long it took Lieko to teach him the "I'm fine" reply as we dance to "Head, Shoulders, Knees, and Toes" together. Pretty good for someone his age. As we move, Hitomu goes through the motions slightly faster than the song recites the names of body parts. He even seems to know the "Baby Shark" song. Since when did the little guy become such an expert? Maybe ... wait, why does all *this* feel so familiar? Have we done all this before? This déjà vu thing is getting out of hand. I stop the CD player and dig through my teacher's box.

"You know something, Hitomu, you've done such a good job I think you deserve some ... bubbles! Would you like some bubbles?"

Hitomu gasps. *"Shabondama ..."*

"Then let's say, 'Bubbles, please!'"

"Bubble, pwease!" Suddenly, Hitomu crosses his legs. "Ah! *Oshikko.*" His voice is barely a whisper. He has to go pee.

"Oh! Okay, sure, go ahead."

I open the door and peek outside. I can't see Lieko at the reception desk; she must be in the staff room or something. Thank goodness or this would be awkward. Hitomu scoots to the washroom, holding his crotch. When I follow after him, he waves his hand in protest. *"Jibun de dekiru,"* he says at normal volume. He can go by himself.

"Great! Go nuts."

He shuts the door behind him, singing what I understand to be a song about going potty. Impressive. Here I was bracing myself for the screaming of a lifetime. Whatever phase Hitomu was going through seems to have ended. I almost feel sad that he won't have any more lessons here. Oh, well. *Shou ga nai.* With nothing to do but wait for him, I go to the lobby and see if his mother is still there. I'd love to get insight on what cured her son of his *gaijin* terror.

His mother is gone. No one's here except for Lieko, who is no longer sitting behind the reception desk. She's kind of squeezed into a corner, like she's hiding. Afraid of something. Maybe there's a spider on the floor.

"Wow. The business meeting is *that* boring, huh?" I ask as a joke. Of course, she doesn't reply; I don't expect her to. I sift through the foam puzzles on the desk. Hitomu might like to do one of these. Lieko turns her head and watches me so intensely I expect her to yell at me to get back to the room and stop wasting Hitomu's mother's time, but she says nothing.

"What is it? Another spider? Should I get the spray?"

No answer. She just stands there, staring down the hall now, hands clenched so hard her knuckles are turning white. It's like she doesn't even know I'm here.

"Let me guess; you want me to get back to work? Well, you can relax. Hitomu's in the washroom. Listen. Hear him?"

Down the hall the water in the washroom is running. *"Te o aratte, te, te, te,"* Hitomu sings.

Lieko relaxes, slightly. She peels herself from the wall, sits back down in the receptionist chair, and takes a deep breath as she smooths her hair and her suit. "Good. If that is the case … just do your job."

I kinda saw it coming, but it still makes me suck in my breath to hear her say it. "What?"

"We must be professional, no matter what. And so must you. Go back, now."

"Are you serious? You're telling me I can't leave the room even if the kid has to go pee? You know what? No. You're not serious." I find the puzzle I'm looking for, deliberately taking my time to make sure all the pieces are there before turning on my heel. She can't tell me what to do.

Lieko shakes her head. "Never mind," she sighs. "Just return to your room before Hitomu." I turn to leave when I hear her mutter under her breath: *"Yokatta, kidzuite inai."*

Thank goodness, she doesn't get it.

Now I'm peeved. This was so close to being a perfectly good day. "You know something, you've got some nerve. Of course I get it. And I've understood Japanese for the past *seven years.* Just because I'm not Japanese doesn't mean I'm an idiot. You need to chill out, you know. My successor may not be so willing to take your crap."

Something about that last remark makes Lieko open her mouth to say something, but I don't give her the chance. I head back to my room. The washroom door is wide open, which means Hitomu's waiting for me. Good timing. Another moment of standing in this woman's presence and I'd probably take a swing at her. At least, that's what the old Cybelle would have wanted to do. The new and improved Cybelle is still as professional as ever. And for the sake of staying sane for the next three months, I can swallow my words and keep my cool for this little boy.

I stop just outside Room Four to take a few deep breaths. It's quiet in my room. In fact, all of Zozo is quiet. I can barely hear the staff meeting down at the other end of the school. I don't even hear Lieko at the reception desk. All I can hear is Hitomu's quiet, quivering voice, murmuring something. He must be singing to himself again. Poor kid. I've kept him waiting long enough. I continue down the hall to Room Five. "All right, Hitomu! You ready for some bubbles …?"

Hitomu is not alone. There's a woman in here. An old, dishevelled-looking woman. Her back is turned to me, but I can tell by her long, greying hair and her greying rags of a dress that she should not be here. She's standing over Hitomu, who is cowering under the tables pushed up against the wall, squeezing himself into the corner of the room so hard his tear-stained cheeks are turning red.

"*Tabetai,*" the old woman croaks, tottering closer and closer to where Hitomu hides. "*Oishi-sou, yawaraka-sou. Tabetai.*" *So tasty, so tender. I want to eat.*

The puzzle falls from my hands. I don't know what to do. Do I shout for Lieko to call 119? Do I burst in on the staff meeting to get help? Do I tackle the old woman and tell Hitomu to run for it? I'm frozen in place, watching a horror movie unfold before my eyes. I seriously don't know what to do.

"Please," I hear Hitomu whimper. "Don't eat me. Please don't eat me, please don't eat me."

"*Tabetaaaai …*" *I want to eat.*

"No. Please don't."

The old woman wobbles back and forth, moaning over and over again. "*Tabetai. Ta. Be. Ta. I. Tabetaaaaaaaai.*"

"I don't want you to eat me," Hitomu whispers one more time.

The old woman goes quiet. Then something in her snaps. With a wet snarl, she shoots out a hand and grabs Hitomu's short hair, like she's trying to rip his scalp off. "*TABETAI.*"

Option three it is.

In the split second it takes to lunge at her and slam her into the wall, a dozen thoughts go through my head. Most of them revolve around getting arrested, losing my work visa, and being deported over arm-barring a decrepit old woman. The others are about how little I care. The next thing I know, I have the old woman's gaunt wrists bound in my hands behind her back. Hitomu is hiding behind me, still crying. It won't be easy to drag her all the way to the elevator. A faster way pops into my mind. The emergency exit.

"Hitomu-*kun, hijouguchi,*" I tell him.

Without hesitation he runs out the door. I pull the old woman nice and hard (I hope it hurts) and herd her in front of me just around the corner of the hall. Hitomu reaches up on his toes to push the handlebar of the emergency exit. It's too high for him. "Scooch over," I say, not really caring if he understands me or not, but he does. He ducks out of the way as I push the old woman ahead of me, kick the door open, and shove her into the stairwell.

"Hhhhrrrnngh ..." she turns and snarls at me. Now I recognize her. I have seen this woman before. Here and there, around town. She's the same woman who spat at me a few months back, for sure. What she's doing here, how she got here, or why she's attacking my student, I don't know. Don't care, either.

But now that she has seen me apparently she has something to say. "Hrngh ... *gaijin ... kuso, baku-gaijin ...*"

She lunges at me with another snarl. I hiss back at her like a snake. "Put one of those chicken-bony fingers on my student again," I add, "and I'll eat your fucking face."

She reels back, afraid, and retreats into the stair railing. I step back inside and let the door slam shut on its own with a resounding, satisfying clang. The door does not open again.

"You all right, buddy?" I turn and kneel to Hitomu's level. Without warning, he runs right at me. I have no idea what he's doing until I feel his chubby arms wrap tight around my neck and his little feet scrambling up my torso. It feels like a small hyperactive monkey scuttling up my tree trunk of a body. *"Daijoubu?"* He's not crying anymore, but his voice is still unsteady. *"Un. Daijoubu."* I have no choice but to pick him up as I stand. *"Shinpai shinaide ne,"* I pat him on the back. "She's not coming back." I turn to the door just to make sure. I can't hear any gurgling or snarling anymore on the other side, but I don't hear footsteps retreating down the stairs, either. Just silence.

"Cybelle-sensei, arigatou," Hitomu whispers into my ear.

Aw. I rub his back again. *"Dou itashimashite,* Hitomu-*kun."*

He giggles. Then he sits upright in my arms. *"Ah, mite!* Lieko-sensei *da!"*

Uh-oh.

I turn around. Sure enough, Lieko is standing right there, holding Hitomu's bag. She does not look happy.

"Okay, Hitomu-*kun!*" She extends a hand. "Let's play in our colouring book while we wait for Mommy!"

Hitomu turns to be let down to the floor. I comply, still kneeling as I watch him take Lieko's hand and let her escort him back to the lobby. I'm in trouble, I know it. The look Lieko gives me over her shoulder cements it.

I follow them both. Hitomu hops onto one of the stools at the reception desk while Lieko pulls out his colouring book and crayons. Happy as a clam, Hitomu picks up a pink crayon and scrawls all over the picture of Zozo the Clown counting cookies. *"Mite,"* he points to the pink circles. *"Akumu ja nai yo, donatsu da yo!"* They aren't nightmares; they're donuts.

"Good job, Hitomu!" Lieko sings. "Now, Cybelle-*sensei* and I must talk in staff room. Please, keep colouring! Cybelle-*sensei*, will you join me in staff room?"

Nice try. "I think we should wait until Hitomu's mother gets here."

"Cybelle-*sensei*," Lieko's voice drops an octave or two. "I must have serious talk with you."

I look her dead in the eye. "I'm not leaving him here alone."

Her smile flickers and becomes a frown. I continue to watch Hitomu colour, his legs swinging excitedly. I even draw a cupcake with him when he offers me a couple of crayons. Lieko can drop all the hints that I'm in some level of trouble. I've got words for her, too. I have seen and heard some wild shit here in Japan and as time went on things have bounced off me or at least made interesting bar anecdotes. What happened today is different, and I plan to let his mother know as much.

"*Nani shiten no?*" Hitomu asks when I start a new doodle.

"I'm drawing footprints," I answer.

"Eh? 'Pootfrents'?"

"*Foot*prints."

"'Pootfrents'?" He tilts his head. "*Nande?*" ·

"*Nande ya nen!*" I respond. He bursts into giggles, asking "*Nande?*" again and again, laughing harder each time I repeat myself. This goes on for about five minutes. Then, something in his face changes. "*Sawatte ii?*" he asks, reaching for my face. Smiling, I nod. He strokes my cheek, and then the back of my hand. "*Eh ... meccha yawarakai,*" he whispers, holding my hand. *Super-soft.*

Hitomu's mother steps off the elevator. Her arms are laden with a bouquet of flowers and a small paper shopping bag. "*Eh? Hitomu-kun?*" she says at the sight of him peacefully sitting at the reception.

"*Mama!*" Hitomu leaps down from his stool and runs into his mother's arms, chattering away about the stickers he got in Lieko's class and how he did his best today in mine. Lieko jumps right in, interrupting him with deep, polite bows and high-pitched Japanese about how his lesson went. I listen for keywords but hear nothing about a strange woman breaking into Zozo and attacking him. Guess that's up to me —

"Cybelle-*sensei*, *arigatou!*" His mother suddenly turns to me. "*Anou, purezento … sankyuu purezento …*" she hands Hitomu the flowers and the bag. He toddles over and hands both to me. I kneel down to receive them.

"Oh, wow! Thank you!" I bow. I wasn't expecting this.

"Yes. *Eeto …* Hitomu thank you. For lesson. Eh … he loves … Cybelle-*sensei*, so he … *anou …*" she explains the rest in Japanese, that he asked his mother to get presents for me. He picked them out himself. I find it odd that they're both for me, and they brought nothing for Lieko, but I keep my mouth shut and open the bag.

It's a Peanuts pencil case. Hitomu leans over and points at the characters. "Snoopy *da yo*. Charlie Brown *da yo.*" He points to the red wagon Snoopy is sitting in. "Hitomu *no* wagon *da yo.*"

"Aw, thank you, Hitomu-*kun*. I love them! *Purezento daisuki. Arigatou!*"

"Cybelle-*sensei, daisuki!*" Hitomu wraps his arms around my neck, then runs to his mother.

Whoa. None of my young students call me by my full name, let alone tell me they love me. My eyes sting.

Manager steps out of Room Three to bid them farewell as Hitomu's mother puts his Mickey Mouse winter coat on him. Now is my chance. "Hey, Manager," I call to him. "Can you translate something to Hitomu's mother for me? I want to tell her, and you, about this —"

"Ah," Lieko interrupts. "But, Hitomu has an appointment from now, so they must go. Maybe, another time, they will visit Zozo, but for now they must leave quickly." She turns back to Hitomu and his mother, who have already boarded the elevator, and continues thanking them. Maybe Lieko is telling the truth. The mother does seem to be in a hurry, scooping Hitomu into her arms. Lieko and Manager bow several times as the doors close. Hitomu waves at me one more time. And that's it. No more Hitomu.

"How were the lessons?" Manager asks.

"They were fine," Lieko plants herself between me and Manager before I can speak, explaining something to him in rapid-fire Japanese. Again, I don't catch the word *"obaachan"* or anything remotely close to what happened today. Do I tell him? It seems pointless now that Hitomu and his mother have left, potentially forever. It's worth a shot, though.

"Manager, something —"

"Cybelle, please sit and relax in staff room," Manager switches to English. "We will finish meeting soon, and then we can all go home. *Otsukaresama!*" He takes off, back to Room Three, mid-sentence.

"Hai," I reply to the door slamming shut. Although I only have fifteen minutes left on the clock, it doesn't sound like a bad suggestion. At least, not until Lieko steps in, slides the door closed behind her and stands over me.

"Cybelle," Lieko folds her arms. "Do you know what you have done?"

"Let me guess." I stare back up at her, nonchalant. I can't let her scare me. "Is this about me speaking Japanese?"

"It is about more than that. You shouldn't have —"

"Stop. Right. There." I stand up. "First off, my speaking Japanese with a three-year-old is the least of our problems. If you're going to let some homicidal woman off the street wander into our school, you have no right to tell me off about anything. His mother needed to know —"

"His mother would have never believed us. There was no point in worrying her about her son any more than she needs to be. Hitomu has a problem. A problem that he has to deal with himself."

What the hell? "A 'problem'?! You call what happened a 'problem'?! No. Tomohide humping the floor is a problem. The jumping spiders in Room Three are a problem. An old woman trying to rip your hair out and eat you is —"

Lieko shakes her head like *I'm* the idiot. "*Please*, keep your voice down. The teachers are still in important meeting. You do not understand. You were not born here. We're not *like* you. Just stick to what you know from now on and everything will be fine when you go home. We don't need you bringing down this school any more."

On the other side of the staff room wall I can hear the teachers filing out of Room Three. The staff meeting is over, yet for whatever reason Lieko has chosen this moment to vent her true feelings toward me. Well, bring it, woman. "How exactly did I bring this school down by talking to a little boy in the only language he understands? Let's hear it, Lieko."

"You know exactly what I mean. Coddling the students. You give them special treatment and it will bring them down. I wasn't coddled. I didn't have that luxury to have someone rescue me. That child will have to deal with it his whole life. Just like that *teacher* you all fell so madly in love with has had to deal with it *his* whole life. Well, he seemed to be doing just fine. Fine enough to ruin our whole school year so he could flirt with *you*. Now if you'll excuse me, I've said all I needed to say."

I forget all about keeping my voice down. "That teacher …?" Wait. She's talking about the guy Yoshino wanted me to remember. Memories of that strange girl who spoke to me in Kobe flood my mind. "You remember him! What happened to him? Where is he? *Who* is he?"

Lieko turns her back to me, arranging and collecting papers from the workbench. "That's not our problem. Our problem is doing our jobs and dealing with the mess he left us."

The mess? "You mean the typhoon day …?" I think hard. I still can't remember. Everything is so fuzzy. "Lieko, this is important. I need you to tell me what —"

"*No.* I won't talk about him anymore. And don't you *dare* tell anyone about him, either. *I'm* the one who's had to reschedule everyone and deal with everything after it happened. Don't tell me you've seen him again." She glares at me.

"Of course not. That's why I'm —"

"Good. Bring him back and I'll have you fired." She turns away again, talking more to herself as she picks up her things: "I'll do whatever it takes. I've worked too hard to come this far. *Monsutaa* like you are NOT ruining my life anymore, and if Hitomu is lucky, one day he will say the same."

Monsutaa. Monsters. Everything goes numb. "What did you call me?"

Lieko doesn't answer, or maybe she didn't hear me. She's already walking out the door, greeting Bucho and thanking her for all her hard work. She slides the door closed behind her, apologizing for missing the meeting, she had something to deal with ...

I'm left in the staff room, alone and stunned and angry. Not just angry. My blood is boiling. My armpits are sweating, my heart is racing. I want to scream every Japanese profanity I can think of. Not the best idea with all my co-workers and the regional manager on the other side of the door. I want to punch the wall, but it's painted concrete. No. It's fine. I can hold back the tears. I can take my anger home. I can keep it balled up in the hollow of my stomach until I get into the elevator, at the very least. I just need to sign out, pick up my things, *otsukaresama* my way out as I get my shoes and everything will be fine. Professional, polite, and playful. I can do this.

I sign out on the staff room computer. I push in the stool I was sitting on under the workbench. I stomp over to the cupboard. No sign of my purse. "Son of a bitch, not again. Not today ..." I scan every shelf, moving over binders and boxes.

And that's when I locate it. It's been shoved deep into a corner, squashed right under Lieko's giant Louis Vuitton bag.

I CAN'T DO THIS.

With an unrepressed roar, I grab Lieko's purse and hurl it at the staff room door. It isn't until it leaves my fingers that I realize her purse is open. That, or I just broke the zipper. Either way, the spray of cosmetics and pens and wallet and sanitary napkins and notebooks as the bag bursts against the door is the most satisfying exhibition of rage I have ever experienced.

"*Eh?! Nani?* What was that?!" Bucho says on the other side of the door.

Uh-oh.

Lieko slides it open again. She looks at me, then down at the carnage of her belongings on the floor, then back to me. I don't care. I'm ready. Ready for her to lunge at me like that old woman lunged at Hitomu. Ready to physically defend myself. Ready with that list of Japanese curse words running through my head just a few moments ago. I'm ready for this bitch.

"Lieko-*sensei*." Manager's voice is gentle. "Cybelle-*sensei*. Come with me, please?"

With a dignified sniff, Lieko turns and follows Manager to Room One. I step over the mess and follow, maintaining the same arrogant look on my face. I'm about to get it. Not sure how much Lieko will get, but I am definitely about to get it. Three months ago, I would have been in tears. Now, I am defiant. They won't fire me for throwing someone's purse, not if I apologize enough.

Conveniently, there's only one chair in the room. Manager takes it once he closes the door behind me. Arms folded, he first lectures Lieko about everything she said to me, which was all completely audible on the other side of the door. He tries to get the details out of her on what exactly she was talking about, because he couldn't understand it all, but his questions are all rhetorical, so Lieko answers none of them. She simply looks down at her shoes, nodding when appropriate, and bowing with a murmured "*sumimasen*" whenever it seems like it's her turn to talk. I've seen enough Japanese TV shows to know I should do the same.

"Cybelle-*sensei*." Manager then turns to me. "Are you all right?"

"Yes. I'm sorry for what I did. It won't happen again, Manager."

"Good. Good." Manager turns his attention back to Lieko. She peeps up every now and then, but Manager's tone changes completely. Their whole conversation is in Japanese, but from what I can understand, Manager is pissed for various reasons. He's not going to be manager for much longer, and Lieko may have had something to do with it. Bucho and others at Head Office want the changeover come springtime, but she's not going to be in charge for long if she can't keep the *gaijin* under control. She will have to do better. I don't interject because all I can think of is how *she knew*. When Yoshino was talking about that guy on Tuesday, I had no idea. But all this time, Lieko knew. And the mess she said he left us … she has to mean the typhoon holiday. I wish I could remember something, anything about it — everything that happened around that time is still a nightmarish blur — but rather than tell me, she calls me a monster and expects me to deal with it.

"So, from now on," Manager switches to English, "what will you do, Lieko-*sensei*?"

Lieko sniffs. Is she crying? "I will work hard and do my best."

"And Cybelle," Manager turns back to me, his tone of voice is still firm, "what will you do now?"

I know what I'm supposed to say. I know what I'm legally obliged to spout in order to appease Manager, Bucho, and the rest of the Zozo gods and not get myself fired three months early. They want to hear me say that I'm sweeping this under the rug with all the other moments I've had to sweep under the rug working for this company; to turn yet another blind eye to this malevolent woman and keep working at 110 percent like I always have. But there is one thing about all of this that keeps the words locked in my throat.

It's the fact that I am not losing my mind. I never did.

"Cybelle?"

"I'm going to work hard and do my best. And ..." Lieko still isn't looking at me, but I turn to her when I speak, anyway.

She's crying.

I don't care.

"I'm going to get my friend back."

"How the hell am I going to get my friend back?"

My last cube of *agedashidoufu*, swishing around in the small cold pool of *ponzu* sauce at the bottom of my favourite bowl, does not answer. After my having poked at it for the better part of an hour, I pop it into my mouth. For three weeks I've racked my brain over this exact question. I'm just glad I have the privacy of this apartment when I need to wallow in my own stupidity. *What the hell was I talking about?* Lieko could have called my bluff that day, and at least I shut her up, but truth be told I had no idea what the hell I was talking about. With a sigh, I toss my bowl and chopsticks into the sink and go through my giant stack of boxes to be shipped, full of books, papers, even *nengajou* postcards ... not one single piece of information about this guy. The worst part is I don't even remember his freaking name; would I recognize it even if I found it?

I'm hungry again. My appetite has been off the charts all week. I've been able to curb it with big helpings of water and green tea until today, my busiest Friday in years. I had an early start at 10:00 a.m. and my lunch was cut short by another makeup lesson. Then I came home and made a quick *omuhayashi*, starting my meat-eating weekend early. It disappeared in about ten minutes. I thought this giant serving of tofu would satisfy me, but it was like eating tufts of cloud soaked in a delicate soup.

I check my phone: 8:47 p.m. I flip through a few channels. Finding nothing of interest, I go through the cupboards in search of a snack. Nothing really grabs my interest except some microwave popcorn my sisters brought. I don't own a microwave, so I throw my coat on over my pyjamas and head to 7-Eleven to use theirs. Of course, I purchase a few things to make up for it: a bag of barbecue chips, some *umeboshi* and sweet corn *onigiri*, two boxes of Korean brownies, two cartons of vanilla Essel Super Cup, and a carton of Lipton's peach iced tea. I greet the cashier, who is as tall as Lieko, but seems eager to speak English with me. *Three weeks*, I think to myself as I head back home. *Three weeks of a Lieko-free workplace.* Ever since the Hitomu thing, she has been completely ignoring me, and I her. She doesn't even eat lunch in the staff room anymore. It's kind of like she's ignoring everybody. Maybe she plans to do so until spring when she becomes the new manager. Fine by me. I'm *so* glad I'll be gone by then.

The popcorn and brownies are done by the time I finish my *Spirited Away* DVD. Not sure if I should watch something else since it *is* Saturday tomorrow. Busiest day of the week. Curling up under my *kotatsu*, I polish off the *onigiri*, chasing them with the barbecue chips as I boot up the new laptop to watch some good old *Jump! Maru Maru Chuu* episodes. Perhaps Yusuke Yamamoto ducking from *Matrix*-agent-like "hunters" will get my mind off things. It doesn't. Maybe a big bowl of Monkey's Heaven will make me feel better. It means sacrificing my ice cream, and I don't have any grated coconut, but I haven't had it in years and my brain craves distraction as much as my stomach craves … well, it's craving everything right now.

Much to my dismay, hunting for Kahlua and filling the apartment with the scent of burning alcohol and banana does not stop the slew of endless questions racing through my mind like a runaway bullet train: What did this guy look like? How tall was he? How deep was his voice? What colour was his hair? His eyes? I groan. Right. *Japanese. My height. Maybe.* Geez, I sound like Manager. Hyuu Kinomoto: a famous actor's first name and a *shoujo* heroine's surname. Guess now I know why he insists everyone call him "Manager." But enough judging my boss. If I don't figure this out, I'll climb the walls ... and then Manager will complain about all the claw marks.

I soak my frying pan in some soapy water in the sink and pace around, eventually deciding against Instagramming my dessert and opting to chug the last half of my peach tea straight from the carton. Pacing gets tiring real fast in such a small space. Eating a bowl of melty ice-creamy soupiness in bed sounds like a bad idea, so I hoover it down in the kitchen, leaning against the wall and licking my bowl as another episode of *Tosochu — Run for Money* begins. An actress I don't recognize gets tagged by a hunter five minutes into the game. She collapses on the ground, half-crying: *"Maji? Eh, maji?!"* She reminds me of my senior high students when they lose at a game of Jenga. I'll miss that when I go back home. No more Sachina and Meruna to entertain me on Friday nights. Leaving my bowl in the sink, I crawl back into bed and pretend to concentrate on the screen this time. That girl outside Bar Iznt. I knew I'd seen her somewhere before, too. But where? She sure as hell isn't a former student. Her English was perfect, despite her unplaceable accent. Where do I know her from? And if this guy is so important to find, why didn't she give me a name? Who *are* these people?!

"*Ugh*. No more thinking!" I pull my blanket over my head. I need to get off this thought train. Maybe I'll do a little light cleaning in the kitchen.

A third episode of celebrities running for their lives accompanies my rummaging through the cupboards to separate the cans and bottles of food I can finish by March. I collect a few in a bag so that I might be able to donate them somewhere, but also wonder if my successor will want some of them. It would save him or her the arduous task of shopping that first week. I let out a sarcastic laugh. I can imagine the look on Lieko's face when she learns she'll have to take the new NET grocery shopping. It would be the same one if she found out I didn't clean everything out of my kitchen.

I head back into the living room with an opened can of peaches, power down my computer, and turn on the TV again, hoping for something interesting. I've just finished off a meal and a half, but my dessert stomach can squeeze in a little more. The channel I've landed on is airing something called *Yokai Daisenso*. Looks interesting enough. I'm also going to clean out my purse. It's been a few weeks since I've done that. Among the ruin of construction paper cut-outs I want to leave for my successor, I find Miyoko's book. How did I forget about this? I curl back up in my futon to go through it.

What a coincidence. *Yokai* in my hand, *yokai* on the TV.

I flip through the pages. No English; just strange, beautiful paintings on every page. A red-skinned demon with horns holds a burning man, like a cigar. A baby with one eye gets a bath. A person made of ceramics looks ready for war. And then there's the *kappa* teaching a classroom of demonic creatures. My favourite picture so far. One other comes a close second: a creature on all fours with an elephant's trunk and tusks, leopard spots, long hair, and it looks like it's on fire. The kanji is unfamiliar, but I can read the *furigana* next to it. "Baku." That sounds *so* familiar. I crawl back to my purse to get my phone. According to the *Imiwa?* app, it's a Doctor of Philosophy or "a mythological creature that devours bad dreams."

Wait. *Baku-gaijin.* That's what that old woman had called me. But that makes no sense. I'm no dream-eating *yokai*. Unless she meant *"baka"-gaijin.* Maybe I misheard her. Then again, after almost seven years here, I'm not in the habit of mishearing Japanese. Written another way, the app says it can also mean a burst of laughter. "Well, that certainly helps," I groan.

I stretch the book over my head and stare at the picture, hard. *"Baku-gaijin."* She *must* have meant "stupid foreigner." Nothing else makes sense. It's like the time I had to carry a ton of groceries home and this old guy at the station yelled *"Akachan wa fukuro ga ippai!"* at me. Manager and I got into the longest argument later about whether the guy was calling me a "baby with a ton of bags" or not. In the end, I couldn't convince him otherwise, but I was so sure ... still am.

The floor rumbles. Somewhere in the distance, a garbage truck is driving down the street. It's way too late for garbage trucks to be driving around. And it sounds like it's driving awfully fast, heading straight for my building. Shutting my eyes, I find myself bracing for impact. The floor shudders with a ripple, the truck sound fades, and all is silent again.

My eyes fly open. An earthquake, maybe? No. Everything in the apartment is fine. No swinging light fixture, everything still on the shelves. Even the tall stack of boxes in the corner hasn't budged. A real earthquake would have done *something*. Oh, well. I'm fine; that's what's important. There's no way I can sleep now, though. Too shaken up. Might as well watch this movie and see where it goes.

I pick up the remote to press the subtitle button, then stop. The TV is bright white, but blank. "What the hell ...? Come on, NHK, don't do this to me now." It's happened. They're onto me. They've cut my cable after all these years. No. It's the TV itself that's the problem. Or maybe the remote? I look down at the buttons and realize I can't read any of them. The buttons that used to have numbers and Japanese are all squiggles and wiggles.

"Great. Now, I can't read. What's next?"

I get up to turn the TV off manually. My arms and legs feel heavy, sluggish, and it takes some time to get to my feet. I feel unsteady. My knee crashes against the *kotatsu* against the wall. Too much food. Too much peach tea. "Well, now I've done it. I'm too big for my apartment. Great, Cybelle."

The room is suddenly way too bright. No, it's my face almost pressing up against the light fixture when I turn my head. I stagger, try to block the light with my hand. No such luck. I stumble around until I feel my hand run against the wall and flick off the light. "That's better, I guess ..." There's still a bright source of light nearby. The lampposts outside, maybe? I can see them through the open curtains. That's got to be it.

With one reach of my arm I draw the curtains open. The night sky is alive with dragons and monsters and bird-like creatures, all glowing neon pink, purple, green, and bright.

"Whoa ..." Must have been one hell of an earthquake. Did the centre of the earth open up? Have the demons of old been unleashed?

I slide the window open and begin the arduous process of squeezing through it. Only one way to find out.

sixteen

THE CRIME COMES LAST OF ALL

鬼の居ぬ間に洗濯
When the cat's away the mice will play

It is long past the sunset hour, when monsters and demons emerge from their places of slumber to visit upon the human world. Now they are alert and active and wide awake. The Yokai watches in awe as they parade down the street, drumming and singing, leaping from rooftop to rooftop with the agility of gazelles, swinging from electric cables by their monkey-like tails, clawing up and down buildings, gleefully knocking over trash cans and prancing with the goodies they find inside: egg sandwich crusts, fish bones, *umeboshi* pits, and Ghana bar wrappers with bits of chocolate still stuck to them. There must be hundreds. Many demons the Yokai does not recognize; yet they all shout passing greetings to her as if to an old friend:

"Well, well, look who's here!"

"Baku-sama, konbanwa!"

"Hisa-bisa, Baku-sama!"

"Good to see you again!"

"It's been ages. Where have you been?"

"Welcome!"

The Yokai can stand here forever, counting the monsters, the creatures, and the human-looking characters that pass her: umbrellas hopping on single legs, people with *shamisen*-shaped heads walking *koto* dragons on leashes, giant spiders the size of vans, giant-back televisions with tiny legs, a seven-foot tall mountain goat with a cartoonish grin walking on its hind legs, a dog with a human face, electronic toilet seats scuttling along the ground like Roomba vacuums (the Yokai does her best to avoid stepping on those), an androgynous-looking woman with a long swan neck handing out hot spring eggs, a giant cloud of smoke drifting above her head ... The Yokai could spend hours trying to count and describe them all.

A little boy and girl, no more than two years old in appearance, hair and clothes drenched with water, stop at her feet. "Look, sister," says the boy. "It's that *girl*."

"Wait, brother. That's no girl. We know you. You're the one who wants Akki's boy."

The Yokai looks back and forth between the two children. They indeed appear to be children, but judging from the rest of the crowd, the Yokai deduces they are not. "I have to find him again, before it's too late. Do you know where I can find him?"

"Sorry, Miss *Baku*. We don't know where he is anymore."

The boy cocks his head. "Aren't you cold?"

"No," the Yokai looks down at her body. She is barefoot on the snowy pavement, wearing nothing. "I don't feel anything," she adds, mystified.

"Well, we haven't seen him in the woods for months. He hardly wanders around alone there, anyway. Certainly not anymore."

The Yokai sighs. "Okay, thanks." She watches them rejoin the procession, holding hands. Had she and the man ever held hands like that? She cannot remember. She watches them go with a longing that makes her stomach sink.

"You are jealous," buzzes a voice behind her. She turns around to see a giant Japanese hornet floating by on a large velvet cushion, holding cigars in four of its appendages. The other two rest on the cushion for balance. "You wished for that, once. With Akki's boy. Did you not?"

"I think I did — I mean, I do," the Yokai says. "Have *you* seen him?"

"I am afraid not, child. I see nothing these days. It is my time to hibernate until the heat of summer returns that I may terrorize your fellow humans once again."

"But I'm leaving, and I have to find him before I go."

The *suzumebachi* takes a puff of one cigar, exhaling a cloud into her face. "I know. I have known for quite some time. I wish I could be of more help. You charmed me, more than most *yokai*. Perhaps it was our talk of cuisines and dreams that I found thought-provoking. I am glad we were able to meet, and I do not say that often. Take care on your journey, will you not?"

"I will. Thank you."

The hornet floats its way above the procession and off into the distance. The Yokai half-wanders into the street to watch it go, oblivious of the congregation of kettles that stumble into her ankles. One, an electronic model, tilts up on its short legs to look at her. "Bless my wiring! I know that face and hair anywhere. Why, I made your green tea for six years!"

The Yokai kneels down to get a closer look. She squints. "Mr. Kettle?"

"We meet again, young *baku*-lady. Tell me, have they replaced me? You have a younger, better model, I'll bet. One that lights up like a rainbow and sings when the water is ready?"

"Sorry. We're not allowed to get another one."

"Well, I'll be. I've left a legacy. The last Nishibe-Zozo kettle. Hear that, everyone?" The congregation screams and steams. "Fancy a cup, miss?"

"No, thanks. I'm looking for my friend. Have you seen him?"

"'Fraid not, dearie. I don't know much about things that don't have to do with tea. Have you tried asking the air conditioners?"

"No. Thanks, anyway."

And so it goes. The Yokai scans the heads and tails of the long line of demons careening toward and around her as they cavort and caper down the street. The friendly, more intoxicated ones try to lure her into the procession with a not-so-subtle wink or an overly long handshake that turns into a tug on her arm. She refuses each time. *Find him*, she must keep repeating to herself. *Find him, find him, find him …*

"Would you like a bowl, miss?"

A gentle voice at her shoulder makes the Yokai turn. It is someone with an udon cart. She recognizes the sly smile and eyes so sharp they can cut through her.

"*Kitsune-ojisan?* Is that you?"

"Ah, *Baku-sama*! It's been a long time!" The fox man bows. "Huh. You're smaller than I remember. Back for another bowl, eh?"

"Maybe later. Have you seen my friend? Black hair, grey eyes." The words come to her before she can even register the image in her memory.

"Hmmm," the *Kitsune* strokes his whiskers. "No. Not since you two came to my truck. Don't tell me you two broke up?"

Heat floods her face. "I … I just have to find him."

"Sorry, little one. Haven't seen him."

The Yokai sighs. "I wonder who I can ask for help."

The *Kitsune* taps a long, pointy nail against his chin in thought. "When I'm stuck like that, I find it best to ask everyone I can. You never know who has the right information for you."

"I'll try that. Thanks."

"See you again!" The *Kitsune* rolls his udon cart away. *Ask everyone I can.* The Yokai struggles to think. There are so many of them.

Scores, hundreds even. Asking them one by one will take her eons. The Yokai clears her throat. "Excuse me, everyone," she calls out.

The parade stops abruptly. The music pauses. Everyone stares at her.

"Sorry. I'm glad to see you all again, I really am, but I'm looking for my friend. Have any of you seen him?"

Everyone looks down at the ground, at their multitude of toes, up at the sky, at their arms as if they have watches. Everywhere but at the Yokai herself. A scaly blue demon eventually steps forward. "I'm sorry, dear *Baku*," it says. "We haven't seen him in months. Not since the Flight from 自分自身."

"The Flight from what now?"

"自分自身. Jibun Jishin," the creature repeats, slower. "Everyone says you were the cause. Don't you remember?"

The Yokai does not understand. She shakes her head. "I wish I could. Never mind. It's okay. Thanks, anyway."

"Have you tried the mountains?" shouts someone in the back of the parade.

Mountains. Now *that* strikes a chord with her. "I haven't. Thank you!"

"Be careful, *Baku-sama*," the blue *yokai* tugs at her hand. "For if the King of Nightmares knows you're coming, he'll devour your life again and may even take your eyes. That's what he's been doing these days, ever since the disappearance of his boy."

"He has more eyes than ever, now!" someone adds. "For months he's been able to prey on any human he desires!"

"He's more *dangerous* than ever!" another voice trembles.

"Built that moat from all those humans, he did!"

"Join us, *Baku-sama*," begs the blue demon. "Don't go! It's the annual parade! We'll have sake and tomorrow night we'll sneak among the humans!"

"I have to. I'm sorry. It'll be okay." The Yokai is certain of it; *this time,* she thinks, *things will go my way.*

The demon reluctantly relinquishes her space. "Be careful. Have you had any peaches today?"

"Yes. And I had some tea."

"Good. Then it will only take you a few minutes on those long legs of yours, with the power of peach running through your veins and all." The procession giggles at this joke. "Good luck, *Baku-sama*. We wish you nothing but."

The Yokai drifts through many dreams on her way to the mountains. She runs through plains bombarded by red and blue lightning strikes. She wades through a crowded bubble tea shop called Jubilee Irwin, where she is offered a cold minty shake in a small milk chocolate bucket. She listens to the tale of an old piano abandoned in a forest (sadly, the piano tells her, not the forest she is looking for). She crawls through a tunnel of dripping honeycomb, where children no bigger than her thumb lick the walls and beg for her attention as they dance and somersault, high off the sugar. The Yokai traverses through them all. She walks through daylight, through darkness, into the wild, crossing highways, and feeling her way through poorly lit tunnels. She walks for a long time, until she finds herself at the end of the world. Thick white billowing clouds line the cliff before her and stretch into the darkness. When she turns around, she sees a forest.

This is the place. I'm back. Now her hunt truly begins.

She explores the maze-like woods: the oak and redwood trees, wide as miles and tall as the sky, the forest of bamboo stalks, the short little spruce and pine trees that look as if they have just been planted, and all the other trees she does not know by name. Then come the laughing ones: The ones with soft, fuzzy orbs hanging from their branches, bobbing in the silent wind. The peaches. The ones that laughed, even when she sank her teeth into their soft, pliable faces or ate them whole. Her stomach rumbles and her tongue tingles with the taste of fear. The trees are not laughing anymore.

She hears a rustle in the grass. "Who's there?" she calls out.

They emerge from the bush: babies. Hoards of them, toddling on unstable chubby legs. Only one of them speaks. "Ah, the *baku* is back. Welcome, *Baku-sama*, welcome."

"Hello, Mr. ..."

"Please, no names. *Konaki Jiji* will do. So, you have returned to us, and to the forest. To seek your friend, no doubt?"

"Yeah. Have you seen him?"

"I am afraid not. No one has seen the boy since 自分自身. That was three full moons ago, I believe. Only the King of Nightmares can know his whereabouts now."

"I have to find him. He needs help. Someone told me so the other day."

"If the King has him, then yes, help him you must. You are probably the only one who cares about him that can."

"Why me?"

"I wish I had the answer to that question. Perhaps it is your connection, or the red string of fate that brought you two together, and it compels you to search for him. Unfortunately, as old and as wise as I am, I can tell you little. Talk me through your thoughts, child. What do you remember?"

"I remember ... peaches. Eating peaches, the first time I saw him. Walking with a girl to a house. A quaint little cottage. They went inside and I ... I came close. It had a golden-brown kind of smell ... and when I touched it, it was so warm from the sun. The house looked so delicious, like I could eat it. So, I took a bite. Then I wanted more. I want more. I want some more." She grins. "Maybe I wanted s'mores?"

"I am afraid I do not know of these ... 'some mores,'" says the *Konaki Jiji*. "However, by my understanding, your consumption of the *jinmenju* fruit and your manipulation of the boar god's house set off a series of reactions among the more prevalent *yokai* in these woods. Your ability to transform things to food, combined with

your ability to consume nightmares — even demons, perhaps —
is uncanny. Limited only to the *baku* of yore. Oh, fear not, child.
These abilities are good things. They put you, and only you, in the
best position to find the boar god's man, for there are no other
baku in these parts."

"But how am I supposed to find him when no one knows
where he *is*?"

The *Konaki Jiji* produces a small, heavy-looking burlap sack.
"Here. Take these. They were found next to a sleeping priest in a
hut on the small island. They smell blessed. I think you can use
them better than any of us can. Consider it a long-overdue gift for
the time you successfully carried me without dying."

The Yokai accepts the bag with a low bow of her own. She rolls
it in her hand. It feels rough like burlap, and full of small oblong
articles. She opens it and reaches inside. "Beans?"

"Close: *soy*beans. But in your hands, they are not just soybeans
anymore, are they?"

She weighs the bag in her hand. "So, what are they?"

"You tell me. It is your dream."

Are they protection? Weapons? The Yokai does not know what to
say. "Thank you?" she finally decides.

"It is I who must thank you. You saved me. I would be passing
through squid *yokai* bowels were it not for you and your bravery."

The Yokai shrugs in the dark. "I wouldn't call it bravery. I just,
you know, do … whatever."

"Exactly. And do again you must, to save your friend. I will
leave you to it."

"Wait a second! I still don't know how to find him. Everyone
says he's with the King. The King of Nightmares. How do I find
this King?"

"Would that I could escort you there, *Baku-sama*. But anyone who approaches the King's domain now suffers terrible
consequences, human and demon alike. He has fortified his

residence since the Flight. All I can do is offer directions. First you must find the winding path that curves eastward, not westward, through the woods with many names and no names at all. Then you must turn south-wise four times, light incense — I assume you have nothing else for protection — then let the smoke demons guide you through the Rock Treasury Mountain. It is the long route, but the safest."

The Yokai groans. "I can't follow all that! I barely know where I am *now*. There must be a way to — hang on. Do you smell that? Smells yummy."

The *Konaki Jiji* looks over its shoulder. "A nightmare. Get down. *Down!*"

About to inform the creature she cannot kneel down any farther, the Yokai gasps as she feels the sharpest of tugs on her arm. The *Konaki Jiji* pins her to the earth, shushing in her ear. "'Tis the blood-drinker," he whispers.

There is something moving in the dark. A light, bouncing along in the darkness twenty feet away. It bobs one way, then the other, as if dangling from a wire, coming ever closer. A humanoid figure follows it. A girl. A tall, long-haired girl, thin as a rake, dressed in a schoolgirl's uniform.

"What does he want?" says the girl.

"To talk to you, Hino-*chan*! He's been worried."

"Then he should not tarry any longer. He should take the man's eyes and be done with it."

The light and the girl figure pass close to the ditch, illuminating the Yokai's bare legs by mere inches, then turn and continue down the path. They do not speak again. The *Konaki Jiji* and the Yokai hold their breath until the light fades away.

"Forget the directions; follow the nightmare," the *Konaki Jiji* whispers. "Follow the nightmare and the blood-drinker to the King. But beware, *Baku-sama*. Do not let the nightmares spot you, or they will devour you, too. I could not bear that happen."

With a kiss farewell on the *Konaki Jiji*'s tiny hand, the Yokai rises to her feet. Like a leopard, she springs from her feet and scrambles up the nearest tree. She runs and leaps across the tree-top branches over the path, keeping the girl and the bobbing light in her sights. At some point she loses them around a bend but looks up and sees the house just ahead. She continues toward it, confident in her noiseless feet carrying her above the path, confident that she will not be spotted. "I can do this ... I am invisible. I am invisible."

A sudden flash of light shines overhead, illuminating the barren treetops of a multitudinous forest. There it is. The house on the small hill surrounded by brambles and dying gardens and what appears to be a lake. The house that was once a Japanese ryokan, a love hotel, an alley behind a shop, the emperor's palace, the top of a Ferris wheel, an infinite number of other places, and once even had the most decadent chocolate and baked confections for walls and roofing. The house was all of these rooms and places at one point in time or another. Now it is simply a house of wood and tile, ancient but built to stand strong against the elements of time and weather, maintained by some unknown supernatural force to serve its owner. Just above the roof, with its demon- and spike-shaped monuments, several hundred lights like stars hover in the air. *Nightmares.* The Yokai can smell them over the dead-fish stench of the moat, like a breeze of fresh air, but heady and fruitier and delicious. She can feel the urge to grow up to the height of the house, reach out a hand and scoop them into her palm all at once, cupping them to her mouth, feeling the chewy sensations as their flavourful essences burst out of their delicate skins ...

The front door of the house kicks open. "What the HELL? Turn that shit off!" Akki storms down his steps. "What are you idiots doin'? Tryin' to light up the whole mountain?!"

"Sorry, Akki-*sama*!" his nightmares squeal. They dim. It was enough. The Yokai can tell where she must go.

She sidles down the ridge toward the moat surrounding the house. Upon closer inspection, it appears to be blood. Potentially harmless to the touch, the Yokai tiptoes around its edges regardless, careful not to dip a single toe in it. Crouching in the darkness, she notices a light bobbing closer toward where Akki stands. It is the nightmare from before, accompanied by the girl.

"Hino-*chan*! Good to see ya, as always! How's my kid?"

Hino steps over the bridge, over the moat, into Akki's dying garden. "Your 'kid' is fine. But I must tell you — my word, Akki, what happened to you?"

"What? Oh, this?" Akki chuckles, grazing a large knuckle over the deep gouge across one eye. "Guess it *has* been a while since you've seen me on two feet. Ah, ain't nothin' to cry over, Hino-*chan*. It'll heal, give or take a century. But I kinda like it. Shows I've been through some shit. Really adds to the look." He waves a hand through the air. "'The *scarred* samurai.' Pretty sexy, eh?"

Hino ignores his jest. "Akki, I cannot do this anymore."

"Why the fuck not?!"

"I am a demon of night. This is not in my nature. I cannot keep it up."

"Aw, come on, Hino-*chan*. You're the only one I can count on! All my nightmares can do is watch him, and the restaurant trick don't work no more. I need someone who can get their hands on human food for him, and you're the most human-lookin' *yokai* I know!"

"I am the only human-looking *yokai* you know."

"You know what I mean, man. You *know* I'm not like you. You said so yourself! You can touch whatever you want, but I only got one day when I can go out in the real world and have earthly form. And it ain't like I can transform leaves into money, or control humans' minds and get them to buy me shit — no offence. *And* how's it gonna look phasin' through people in downtown Osaka? They're gonna think I'm a fuckin' ghost!" He takes out his topknot and ruffles his hair in frustration. "You gotta do this for me. Pleeease? You've been doin' it for this long already!"

"And had I known it would be three months I never would have started. I am not spending the next year looking after your pet, Akki. He needs food and maintenance *every day.*"

"Aw," Akki whines. "Come *on*! Not even for one more night?"

Hino sighs. "You need to make a choice. Take his eyes or release him, before ..."

"Before what? It's not like anyone's gonna come and get him. I made sure of that."

"What do you mean?"

Akki sports his fangs. "I mean, I took care of that dream-eatin' bitch. That's right. You didn't see it, but it was pretty fuckin' awesome. Ate a good couple of chunks out of her. An arm *and* a leg. She won't be back."

The nightmares in the sky above them snicker. "Yeah, you should've seen it, Hino-*sama*! Akki *nii-chan* ate her good. Worst nightmare of her life!"

"Hmm," says Hino. "I suppose that would explain why she has not ventured into these parts for all this time. And it has not gone unnoticed the manipulations have ceased. Are you sure there are no consequences to your actions, Akki? It is not in your nature to think far ahead. And besides, we know nothing of *gaikokujin baku*. This foreign one, her power ... it rivalled even yours."

"Heh. Shows what you know, Hino. Why you think she ain't been stickin' her nose around here? Why you think she hasn't come for the kid? She's scared shitless, that's why. What? What's with that pouty look?"

"Nothing. You have successfully dashed all my hopes of her staging a rescue is all."

Akki puts his hands on his hips. "Oh, she ain't rescuin' shit. Ain't no more 'stampipulatin' from *her* anymore, now that she knows what I can do."

The Yokai narrows her eyes at the haughty figure. "'What you can do,' eh? We'll see about that, Nightmare King."

While Akki and Hino continue their conversation and the nightmares are distracted, the Yokai takes a running leap over the moat, right into the scaffolding. She lands noiselessly and shimmies up the bamboo poles as though she has done it a million times. It only takes seconds to reach the banister and swing herself over. Once on the other side she peers over the railing. All is quiet, save the *yokai* arguing at the front door. The Yokai notices the ground is higher on this side of the house. She can see a town or two below, and beyond that, the rest of the dream forest under the moonlight. She rests her head against the cool bamboo railing. *No turning back now.*

The Yokai creeps along on her hands and knees and climbs through a dimly lit window. A long hallway stretches before her. She vaguely remembers this place, now. The Yokai fled from red-haired, red-faced women down this hall. The only identifiable difference is the floor. Almost every inch of the once-golden tatami is now splattered with blood varying in degrees of degeneration. Some patches are covered with the thin yet tawny substance, while the rest is soaked in a black inky ooze that still looks wet. The Yokai steels herself and rises to her feet. She has a feeling she is already standing in blood. Reluctantly, she takes long strides over the floor, attempting to make as little noise as possible while making the nearly impossible hops to the cleanest parts of the floor. More than once, she comes close to losing her footing and bringing her face close to the lumpy pools before her. After what feels like ages, she reaches the end of the hallway.

This must be the banquet room, she muses. She can recall it now: the long table buckling under the weight of so much food and so many dishes. Is this the room she wants? *If I were a nightmare king, where would I hide my human?* she asks herself. A silly question, perhaps, but the Yokai is out of ideas. She is still puzzling over this when she hears voices approaching:

"Lost little Yokai
Looking for a friend ..."

"Remember that? That was fun."

"Uh-oh." The singing. The Yokai remembers that song. And the bites. The blood, the needles. "Nightmares."

She scampers along the wall until her hands find the edges of a sliding door. Without hesitation, she slips into the room and gently slides it closed. The tiny voices grow louder and quieter as they pass. The Yokai releases a breath she did not realize she was holding.

She finds herself in a dark massive room in which she can somehow see despite the absence of light. Down pillows are scattered all over the floor, mingled with torn mesh drapery and filthy plates. Hundreds of unlit taper candles line the room, extending for what seems like miles. At her feet lies a crumpled paper lantern covered in a thick layer of dust. The Yokai looks up at the walls. She finds herself surrounded by eyes. Eyes everywhere. They are watching her, noiseless, thoughtless. They all have brown irises and they are all focused on her. The Yokai waits for some kind of alarm. Hearing none, she stands upright. The eyes belong to no one. They are part of the room, etched into the fabric of the door and the walls themselves. The eyes bear varying degrees of coloured sclera: many are freshly white, others are quite yellow, some practically brown with age. All of them are filled with pain and loss.

"What happened to you? Who did this to you?"

Some look away with guilty glances. Others leak fresh tears. None answer. The Yokai feels close to tears herself. This is a room of desolation and suffering. These were once human eyes. Now, the walls have taken a life of their own, comprised of centuries of inconsolable souls. Enmeshed into the walls, the eyes are now resigned to watch over one thing: the young man dozing in the middle of the room, entombed in thick plastic sheets. The young man who never saw them with his own sad, piercing eyes but had felt their presence since his first visit.

"Zaniel!" the Yokai cries. Forgetting all about stealth and silence, she runs to him, throwing herself on the bed, shaking him by the shoulders to rouse him. She calls out his name, over and over again, as if to make up for all the time she has forgotten it. Nothing wakes him. She presses her head to his chest: an audible heartbeat through the layers of plastic. The sound of it seems to reverberate in the room as the Yokai begins to claw and tear at the thick sheets of saran wrap that encase him. Her sharp fingers make quick work of it. Zaniel begins to stir.

"*Baku kurae ... baku ...* Akki? Please ... let me go ... Akki ..."

"No, it's me. I've got to get you out of here. Can you walk?"

Zaniel groans as the Yokai forces him to sit upright. She throws one of his arms around her shoulders and hoists him to his feet. He is heavier than lead. "Damn it ..." The Yokai pulls at his lethargic body. That is when she looks down and sees it. His left leg, stuck to the bed, living plastic slowly but loudly shrink-wrapping around it. The sound of it is deafening.

"Shh, stop it! Get off of him!"

She reaches to pull it off. Zaniel pushes her, hard. She hits the floor. "Stay back!" He stops her with a guarded hand when she tries to get back to his side. "Get away from me!"

"Zan—" his name dies in her mouth. The plastic takes hold of him. It drags him back to the bed, pinning him to the mattress as it slides up his body. "No, no ... I came to save you ..."

"You can't. Not here. You have to go back to the World."

"But I don't know where to look!" Tears start to well up in the Yokai's eyes.

"Yes, you do. Yourself."

"What?!"

"Believe ... in ..." He struggles to say something more, but the plastic squeezes out his last gasp of air.

"Okay," the Yokai nods, sniffling. "It'll be okay. I'll find you. I promise."

With a final *scrunch* the plastic wrap takes hold of him. He is wrapped even more tightly and in many more layers than he was before — it must be a trap that reinforces itself every time he tries to escape. Just watching the process is painful for the Yokai to witness. There is no way she can rescue him. Crying now, the Yokai stumbles back from the bed and goes to the door, oblivious to the now-bewildered eyes blinking in warning at her. Too late — she opens the door. Right in her face is a dragon, tattooed on a broad muscular chest. Its yellow eyes widen, its hackles rise, and it hisses like a threatened cat. She looks up and recognizes the thick black locks of hair, the blazing green eye, and the strong jaw barking at someone unseen. She screams and slams the door on him, leaving Akki confused on the other side.

"The fuck?" Akki tries to open the door but cannot. He realizes the door has become a Western-style swinging door that is now locked. Someone is manipulating his house. Again.

"No, it can't be! It's not *possible!*" Akki throws his head back with a roar and lunges at the door, plowing right through it. Several pairs of eyes fall to the floor, rolling back and forth, crushed under the weight of his feet as he storms around the room. Zaniel appears to be untouched but the room is completely different, filled with furniture that has been thrown around as if to hinder his progress. Strange new cupboards and dressers and tables that were not there before and have never been in this room. Angered, Akki overturns tables and kicks in the doors of the cupboards. He finds no one. The intruder is gone.

"The Dream Eater," Akki growls. "It can't be anyone else."

He must think. Where would she go, where would she hide? He must think like her. She would not stay in the room; she would have created her own method of escape. There are no windows in this room. Aside from the door she transformed, there is no way out. He sinks his fingers into the tatami and rips it up. Flowing in waves, the mats spring up from the floor. "Aha!" He sees it. A trap door that never existed in his true home. He pounces on it, rips it open. She has manipulated his house to her liking once again, and once again it heeded to her. *We'll fuckin' see about that.*

Akki leaps down the hole beneath the trap door, plummeting soundlessly through the air. He lands with a *thunk* on the ground below, one knee bent. He is below the house now, out in the open air, surrounded by bamboo scaffolding and, beyond that, the lake of blood. He sees her. The Yokai is sprinting across the garden, over the bridge, and into the woods. She is fast; powerful, even. Akki lets his tusks grow forth. *But she ain't fast and powerful enough.*

He takes one step forward. His straw-sandalled foot sinks into the earth. It remains stuck there. "What the fu—?"

As if to answer him, the scaffolding buckles in on itself. Then comes the splitting of a thousand bamboo sticks. The groan of heavy infrastructure. A sound like a thousand bowling pins raining overhead. And then the house above his head implodes in a torrent of wood, plaster, and smoky dust. A moment later, Akki's head emerges from the destruction with a cartoonish *pop*. He struggles to pull himself out of the wreckage; even in a pile of cinnamon-and-ginger-scented rubble, the house does not obey him.

Okay, that does it. You've asked for it, bitch.

Hatred courses through his veins, and a hum stirs in his throat. Akki closes his eye and starts to sing.

"Ho, ho, hotaru koi …"

The Yokai runs and runs and runs. Ignoring the path completely, she hurtles through the trees as fast as her legs will take her.

Her bare feet stumble more than once on sharp rock and upraised tree roots, but they do not stop her.

"Ho, ho, hotaru koi ..."

The deep voice booms all around her, shaking the dead trees. She recognizes the voice immediately. Her arms and legs pump faster in a fresh burst of speed. Akki's song stirs the air around her, and with his song comes the sound of rustling paper. *Paper?* Yes. A thousand papers being rustled and rumpled and crushed all at once, all around the Yokai. Ahead of her, behind her, all around her, they come. Tiny little lights stir as if from slumber.

"Acchi no mizu wa nigaizo, kocchi no mizu wa amaizo ..."

The lights fire into the air, screaming like small rockets. They join the crowd of lights already in pursuit of the Yokai.

"What's going on? Who woke me up?"

"Look, down there! It's *her.*"

"After her! Akki-*sama* wants us to eat her!"

"Really? Doesn't he want any for himself?"

"'Eat around the eyes,' Akki-*sama* says!"

The paper sound crescendos into a riotous noise. The Yokai claps her hands over her ears and runs even harder. The nightmares. They are coming, faster and faster. The sound of them racing through the air becomes deafening. The Yokai trips over a tree root; she cries out but does not stop running.

A nightmare dive-bombs on her and nips at her head. She ducks just in time, but she can feel the sting of its teeth. She smacks it. It cries out in terror as it careens into a tree trunk and splatters. The tantalizing scent of it makes the Yokai dizzy, but she refuses to stop.

The Yokai reaches the edge of the forest, where the sky meets the land. Still, she does not stop. She barrels through the last remaining trees, out onto the winding path, and straight off the cliff. The clouds under her bare feet are like sand. They cause her to slip and stumble a little, but she keeps running. She must not stop.

"Ho, ho, hotaru koi ..."

The sky lightens. *Yes. I'm almost there. I'm almost free!* She is wrong, she realizes. It is not the impending arrival of sunlight that is dimming out the stars and turning the sky from deep violet to a warm, burning orange. It is the nightmares, growing in number and proximity. There must be thousands of them. *How many nightmares can there be in the world?* Whatever the number, it seems they are all after her, now.

It is your dream, the *Konaki Jiji* had said. *I'm dreaming. I gotta wake up.* The clouds cause too much traction under her feet. The Yokai stumbles one last time and falls. All around her the horizon of clouds turns the colour of nightmare. The Yokai squeezes her eyes shut. She wraps her arms around her head and curls up into a ball. *Wake up,* she admonishes herself. *Wake up, wake up, wake up ...*

"Acchi no mizu wa nigaizo, kocchi no mizu wa amaizo ..."

"There! She's stopped! GET HER."

Wake up, wake up ...

"I call dibs on her eyes!"

"Ho, ho, hotaru koi ..."

"No way! *I* want her eyes!"

"We're supposed to eat AROUND them."

Wake up, wake up ...

"It doesn't matter who gets her eyes, just GET HER!"

"HOTARU KOI."

Wake up ...!

The world is a deep, dark orange hue. I open my eyes. The living-room light is still on, bright as midday sunlight. I crawl out from under my *kotatsu* and stand up. My heart is racing like I've just run a marathon. *Weird-ass dream.* Probably stemmed from this movie, which is still playing on the TV and now feels all too familiar. I should just forget about it and go back to sleep. No — better yet, I need to calm down first. Get all those images out of my head.

The television lands on NHK. The screen also shows the time: 23:48. That's when it hits me. I know exactly what I must do. And I only have twelve minutes to do it.

The universe is on my side. My speedy biking skills got me on the last eastbound train. I have my choice of seats. The entire train ride, I feel giddy. Even after the train passes Amagasaki and the bay, the adrenalin doesn't subside. Trains always used to make me feel calm. This one doesn't. It feels like it's taking me to a point of no return. Or maybe I'm just still thinking about *Spirited Away*. I wait for the train to rock me to sleep, but sleep does not come. I wonder how much I'll get before work tomorrow. It all depends on how this little urban adventure goes.

"*Tsugi wa* Osaka-Namba. Osaka-Namba. *Shuuten desu.*"

There's no turning back home, now. *It's okay*, I tell myself. It's not the way back I need to worry about. It's the way forward.

Everything is closing up for the night here. The last remaining people on the train all seem to have briefcases or suitcases or are wearing suits of some kind: salarymen, office workers, even the train station attendants are carrying something. I'm the only one empty-handed. I'm the only one wearing pyjamas, too. No one seems to care. Everyone rushes past me, set on their respective destinations, as the station shops close up for the night. It's as if, for the first time in Japan, I'm invisible.

Tourists still taking pictures with the Glico Man, teens dancing to hip hop on boom boxes in front of the closed shops and their reflective windows, some girls in club outfits jogging to get out of the cold. No one gives me a second glance. Maybe I *am* invisible.

A group of breakdancers' heads turn from their mirrors as I walk past. They invite me to dance: "*Ne, ne!* Come on!" When I wave in refusal, one young man shouts, "WHY NOT?"

Nope, never mind. I'm not invisible after all.

As I venture farther south there are fewer and fewer people. I also notice the increase in wheelie carts full of garbage bags, ragged clothes, toes poking out of shoes, and the distinct smells of cheap sake mingled with pee. Something in the back of my mind tells me I won't have to go past Shin-Imamiya station, and when I see the signs for it, I breathe a sigh of relief. I don't have to go farther than this; I remember telling myself I wouldn't when we went out after Zozo that night.

Don't worry, you'll be perfectly safe. Think of me as your "bodyguard."

I walk down the next wide street for a minute or two, stopping at a Family Mart to pretend I'm shopping for food. I do end up buying two cans of hot corn chowder and a bottle of peach water after ten minutes of loitering. Now, if anything happens to me, someone can report to the police that yes, they did see a *gaijin* in pyjamas and a white winter coat tonight. I chug down the peach water and slip the soup into my pockets. They're small enough to fit next to my wallet and pocket Wi-Fi, and they make nice hand warmers.

Now, where did we go from here?

My instincts guide me toward a smaller *shoutengai*. I can hear guitars playing medieval-sounding rock music. It's quite beautiful. Lyrical. Now I feel like I'm truly on some kind of adventure. The music is leading me in the right direction, it has to be. Maybe it's a group of buskers or students playing; maybe they can guide me the right way.

The shops here are all closed. I can't tell where the music is coming from. I keep walking. The music is coming from all around me, mostly over my head. Wait. I've been down this *shoutengai* before, once, when everything was open. I vaguely remember this one sells jewellery and watches, and in that one a man had a pig on a leash. There wasn't any music playing at the time, or maybe there were just too many people to hear. And I remember now; I wasn't alone. I was with him.

Right on cue, the music changes. The light guitar becomes heavy and guttural, cut through with a deep growl and foreboding lyrics. Is that "One" playing? It is. "Great. *Now* I'm scared." This better not be some kind of foreshadowing.

The *shoutengai* turns out to be very short. I'm more than happy to get back out in the open, away from whoever is playing Metallica at one in the morning. Out here, people huddle against the cold. In the backdrop of cityscape, Tsutenkaku Tower glows neon bright.

I follow the main streets in the tower's direction. As a woman living anywhere, I always make sure to get my bearings. I never know when I'll have to make a run for the nearest police box. That's why I remember the tower: Tsutenkaku was my landmark when we got out of the subway station. We walked down this main street — Sakaisuji, according to the signs — for a few minutes. I remember thinking I could go to Spa World if I missed my last train or if he had turned out to be a real creep. If I'm wrong about all this, I can spend the night there and hightail it back to Nishibe first thing in the morning so I'm not late for work. But if I'm right ... if I'm right ...

Then what?

I shake my head and pick up the pace. I'm not going to think that far ahead right now.

I come out of the alleyway and immediately recognize the pharmacy we must have passed on the way. Hard to forget a name like "Love Drug." I hurry past its neon glow, farther down the street. There's a small shrine on the corner. I remember this, too. As I step over several knocked-down trash cans covered in snow, the sound of bamboo knocking against bamboo and trickling water reaches my ears. The noise makes me feel less alone, more courageous, and confident that, when I turn this corner, I'll find what I'm looking for.

And there it is. The torii gate. But there's no one here. Why does it feel like someone should be here?

Because I'm about to do something stupid, that's why.

I walk up to the gate thrown up in the alley between the two squat buildings. I wonder how it even got here. It's covered in black graffiti, as is every inch of the brick walls on either side. To my left, I try to read the colourful gang symbols and kanji. Everything is scribbles to me except for four white spray-painted characters that I instantly recognize:

自 分 自 身

"Jibun Jishin," I read. "Myself." *Yourself.*

Snow begins to fall now, silent as can be. This is the place. I don't feel scared at all. Silence means I'm alone.

I approach the gate with caution and stick my hand into the darkness between the legs of the gate. There's a thick black tarp there. Darkness lies on the other side. This is stupid. This is dangerous. And at the same time, it's exciting. What would my co-workers say? I exhale a blast of white air. Time to manoeuvre my phone out from my pocket and turn on the flashlight. The flight of steps isn't that long. If I run into government ninjas or giant raccoon monsters, I can run back out quick. So down I go, looking back over my shoulder, seeing nothing but snow falling from the night sky.

There is snow down here, too. It looks like some of the roof has been ripped out, or maybe it caved in. Either way, there is enough moonlight for me to see a little bit better. I walk forward a little more, my feet finding their way as naturally as walking around my own apartment without turning on the lights. There's a tree here. It's dead, by the look of the white streaks running through its bark. It must be a *sakura* tree. There is a slight buildup of snow already collecting on its long, thin branches. Past the tree is a doorway, where a rice-paper door lies ripped and broken. It's brighter on the other side. The dim light pulls at me. I put my phone down and head on through.

A giant room with a giant stage. Storeys high. No ceiling, just falling snowflakes and a starless sky illuminated tawny violet by all the city lights nearby. I don't feel so scared anymore. Just sad. This place ... we came here together, and it was packed with people. Now it's abandoned. Like everyone just got up and left in the middle of their meals. The tables are covered with plates and glasses thick with dust. Chairs and tables are knocked over. The entire place smells like age. I'm standing on a small bridge that leads to the heart of the room. Underneath there must have been water running through. Now it's just brick and tile, evaporated dry and white with calcium. The only footprints here belong to me. I walk around the room, past the bar, past a lobster tank now clouded thick with mould. A flight of stairs leads down past the stage.

Ready or not, here I come …

My cellphone is my saviour again. I turn on the flashlight. The shaking beacon leads me down each landing. At the bottom of the staircase is a short, narrow hallway. It's warmer down here, cramped with huge broken sake casks, long bamboo sticks, a washing machine so big I can probably fit inside and sit upright, microphone stands, broken tambourines, and lots of other old junk. There's a thick tatami smell down here, too. And something else I can't put my finger on. Thankfully, it's not a bad smell. Last thing I need is to discover a dead body. I'm already afraid of what I might be stepping on in here. In fact, it smells … delicious …

There's a room at the end of this cluttered hallway — or at least, a door. I can see it just beyond the edge of the light from my phone. I step over the detritus and garbage, fumbling along the walls. It's another sliding rice-paper door, but still intact. The squares almost feel warm. I stroke the gold handle of the door, about to slide it open, when I hear a crash above my head. It almost sounds like thunder, except for the sound of screeching metal accompanying it.

"What the hell?" I whisper. Then I hear another sound. A repetitive tapping sound. It's fast.

Footsteps.

"Shit."

A homeless person who's been squatting here. A cop. Someone else entirely. I don't want to find out. I have to hide. I kick my way through the garbage, trying to be quiet, and reach the stairs. The sound is getting louder. The footsteps are coming this way.

Double shit.

I stagger, bumping into the giant washing machine. The footsteps are definitely coming this way. It's almost like whoever's up there knows I'm here and is heading straight for me. There's nothing for it. I pry open the washing machine and hop in, closing the door as best as I can without shutting it completely. It's surprisingly warm inside and smells clean enough. And I *can* sit upright in here. I hug my phone against my body, covering the flashlight with my hand, there's no time to click it off. My boots squeak against the metal a little, and I can feel a little pool of snow melting against my ass. Well, I *hope* it's snow.

It's too dark to see anything outside of the little drum window. I can only hear sounds. The footsteps come down the stairs, little pitter-patters that slow when the person reaches a landing. They stop at the bottom, just in front of the washing machine. My eyes widen despite the dark. My body tightens every muscle. I brace myself for the machine door to be pulled open from the outside. I can't breathe. For a moment, all I hear is my own heartbeat, and I'm certain whoever's on the other side of this door can hear it, too.

The footsteps crunch through the same garbage I walked over, past the machine. They stop far away. A door slides open. I hear a deep voice. Only one voice, though. No reply. The door closes. The footsteps go past me and the machine again, back up the stairs, on a landing, up the next flight of stairs, another landing, and up the next. After that I don't hear anything. I wait a long time, leaning against the metal drum, curled up to stay warm. It's so comfortable in here. My eyelids get heavy after a while, and I startle awake. I peek at my phone, shielding the light from the window. It's almost two. Surely Jibun Jishin's second intruder has left by now.

Heart in my throat, I push the door inch by inch until it opens all the way. Nothing leaps out from the shadows, nothing attacks. I stick my head out of the drum and use the flashlight app. No one is here. It's like nothing happened; I know I didn't imagine those footsteps, though. *I am* not *losing it.* I grimace in the darkness — okay, so what I'm doing now isn't exactly normal. But I know I didn't imagine anything. And I'm not imagining things now, as I climb out of the machine, trudge back to the door, and carefully slide it open.

Several voices gasp.

I stumble back from the door and whirl around. "The fuck was that?" I shine my flashlight around the hall. No one else is here, but I know what I heard. "Who's there?!" Silence. I step toward the room again. I let out a gasp myself.

The room is lit up by a single light in the ceiling. In the room lies a man. He's curled up on his side in a tiny cot in the room, which is empty except for him, a bedside table next to him cluttered with plastic bags, and a bucket in a corner. Takeout cartons litter the floor beside the bed. The room smells like a subway station washroom. This whole set-up is very strange. But the more I look at the man, the more I recognize him.

"Zaniel!" I run to him, shake him. He's warm, thank God. I shake him harder. "Zaniel. What the hell are you doing here? Come on, get up. *Get up.*"

He rolls over, onto his back. Something flutters onto the floor from his hand. A postcard? I pick it up off my boot. "What is this ...? Lake Biwa?"

"*Baku,*" he murmurs. "*Baku ... kurae ...*"

I shake myself to attention and kneel over Zaniel. "I don't understand. What ...?"

"*Akumu ... akumu ...*"

I know that word. Hitomu's word. *Nightmares.* "Don't worry. I'm getting help." I turn to my phone and start to dial 119.

"No," Zaniel grabs my arm. His eyes are still closed. "No police ... Cybelle ... the *akumu* ..."

"What?" I don't get it. "Ugh. Forget it, then. I'll get you out myself." Again, I thank God for this phone. According to Google Maps there's a hospital nearby, less than ten minutes away on foot. I need to get him there, but how?

Something catches the corner of my eye. I look at the bedside table again. There's a *conbini* bag with more takeout containers and a bottle of what looks like Pocari Sweat. Has he been living down here? Why? And for how long? And *why*? I poke at the bag. There are some things behind it. I move the handles of the plastic bag away. An iPhone, a silver watch, a burlap sack, two bracelets, and a box. The air shudders a little. It's a box of *mochi*, bright yellow balls. Almost shiny. Five of them in a container meant for six. They look delicious.

Oh my GOSH, Cybelle, why are you thinking about food at a time like this?

"Okay, Zaniel. Let's get you out of here." I roll Zaniel over, take one of his arms and wrap it around my shoulder. With my other arm I lift him up. He moans a little but doesn't wake up. He's heavy as hell.

"Shit." I lie him back down. There's no way I can get him out of here on my own. Not that I have a choice. I look at the box of *mochi* again. Why are they so yellow? Are they lemon-flavoured or something? What could be inside it? It can't be ice cream. Red bean, maybe? "You don't look like ice cream …"

Something whimpers above me. My head snaps up. The only thing there is the ceiling light. It's flickering. *Triple. Shit.* If it goes out, I don't know how I'm going to manoeuvre this guy out of here in the dark. I can't sit here thinking about food. I need to summon enough strength to carry him out of here. Preferably now.

But I *am* hungry.

I pick one up. It's so soft, and strangely warm between my fingers. Smells like lemon to me. It almost feels wrong to do this … like I'm about to eat a living thing …

Cybelle. Mochi *is vegan. Everyone knows that.*

I eat one. And another. And another. And the last two. Delicious.

seventeen

THE EIGHTH SQUARE

噂をすれば影が射す

Speak of the devil and he shall appear

Everyone is staring at me. Of course, they are. I'm a *gaijin*. Sitting
in a hospital. In her pyjamas. I've never felt so out of place. Beats
talking to police in my PJs, I guess. Oh gosh, is someone going to
call the police? Maybe someone already has. My fists clench in my
lap. Two more months and I would have been free! I can't have a
criminal record now; I was doing so well ... *No, Cybelle, it's fine.
You're fine.* Why would anyone need to call the police? It's fine. But
I try to play cat's cradle with the handles of the plastic bag in my
lap to keep myself from fleeing out of the hospital waiting room,
into the night.

For someone who bragged about being fluent in Japanese just
a few weeks ago to the world's bitchiest co-worker, it turns out I
have a long way to go. Getting Zaniel out of that horrible place
and into a cab was the easy part — he was surprisingly lighter
than I'd expected — but when we arrived at the hospital, I was

at a loss for words about what exactly was wrong with him. I managed to explain to a nurse that my friend was unconscious and that he didn't look hurt. He woke up just enough to say something to her that I didn't quite catch. Then it was all rush-rush as the nurse hailed a barrage of orderlies to lift Zaniel from my arms onto a gurney and whisk him away with an oxygen mask on his face and an IV in his arm. It was like a TV show — running down the hall with him, holding onto his hand until someone wrenched me away before a set of double doors could smash me in the face. At least I was able to understand that Zaniel would be fine and that I was to sit in the waiting room and fill out some forms for his admittance.

And that is where I am now, what has to be a solid two hours later. Pen still in hand, with the only box filled out reading "ザンイエル" where his first name should go. Or should I write "ザニエル"? "ザニエール"? I don't even know where to begin with his last name, let alone his age, address, oh gosh, his blood type ... No, wait! Yes, I do. I stick my face into the plastic bag on my lap, remembering the smartphone I took with all the other things on that tiny table. The pleather case holds half a dozen cards, and sure enough, one of them is a driver's licence with a handsome photo on it. *Guess I'm not so stupid after all.* I grin to myself.

I happily fill out the basics of the form, which are all I can read at this point. Maybe "friend" was a strong word to use. Still, I can't just up and leave him here. It doesn't feel right, and I'm certain a doctor or nurse will come around asking questions. So instead of attempting the rest of his medical information, I sit and deal with the stares. After that gets boring, I check my phone. It's almost four. Dawn will come soon, and then I'll have to head to Zozo. Maybe I should send someone a quick text about where I am. Yoshino would be the best person for that. Whoa, hang on. I can't tell her what happened. She'd never believe me.

Or she might never stop lecturing me about crawling into an abandoned restaurant like some overzealous tourist. She'll be so worried. But I'm out of ideas. With a heavy sigh I text her some gibberish about being at Osaka General with someone, and if she could give me a rough play-by-play on how to fill out this freaking form for him it would be great. I throw in a couple of screenshots and send it, praying she wakes up in the next couple of hours to see it.

Dumping the forms and clipboard on my chair, I get a drink from the nearest vending machine. Everyone in the waiting room watches in awe. One elderly man in a wheelchair even lets out a small *"Ehhh, sugoi"* as I press the button for a C.C. Lemon water and return to my seat. I chug half the bottle, staring back at him the whole time.

"Oishii desu ka?" he asks me.

I nod. *"Meccha oishii."*

"Eh, sugoi na! Nihongo jouzu da na!" He orders a nearby nurse to wheel him over. We have a nice chat about what I'm doing there (waiting for a friend, earning me another *"sugoi"*), what he is doing there (he maybe broke his ankle slipping on the floor of his local snack bar, he's waiting for his X-rays to be sure), where I'm from, what I do, if I like Japan, can I teach him English, do I like lemons, if the friend I'm waiting for is my boyfriend, and would I like a Japanese boyfriend. A nurse comes by to wheel him away to see a doctor before I have to answer that one.

I check my phone again. That chat killed thirty minutes. Nothing better to do now than take a nap. Maybe in the next hour someone will wake me for an update on whether or not I should stay. Spa World isn't too far from here. I can afford a thousand yen to squeeze in a quick nap there if someone comes along to release me soon. I find three seats without handles in a relatively vacant part of the waiting room and spread myself across them with my nice puffy coat as my pillow, kicking off my boots before lying down. When a nurse passes by, she asks if I would like a blanket. I graciously accept and set my iPhone alarm for 6:30. If anyone needs to find me before then, well, I shouldn't be too hard to locate, being the only *gaijin* here.

I relax, despite the harsh fluorescent lighting and the sporadic announcements on the hospital PA system. The images of that place still float in the darkness of my mind, like photographic negatives: the musty descent down the flight of stairs, the clutter of abandoned sake casks, the hazy lights in that room ... and Zaniel, lying there like Sleeping Beauty. None of it makes sense. My body grows heavy with sleep. Just before I doze off completely, I hear a sound like rushing water, and I faintly smell something like salt. Maybe it's the ocean about to close over my head in a tidal wave.

No ... it's applause ...

"Omedetou, Baku-sama!"

"What?" I mumble. I open my eyes and find myself surrounded by strange faces, animals on two legs, people on all fours, creatures no taller than my knee, animals bigger than cars, monsters in modern-day suits and ancient *yukata* and kimono, and they're all clapping (except for the *tenome*, who wave and twist their hands in the air to sign for applause). "You did it!" they cry. "You found him!" "Hooray, hooray! Callooh! Callay!" *"Omedetou, omedetou!"*

"Huh? Oh, no. It was nothing. I just did what you all told me. I think."

"Good! Now, there is one more thing you must do, Cybelle."

"What's that?"

"Cybelle?!"

"That's my name."

"CYBELLE!"

I sit upright in shock. Yoshino is kneeling before me. "Oh my gosh, you're okay! What happened?" She hugs me without waiting for an answer. "*Are* you okay? Wow, you're so dusty. How'd that happen? And you have something in your hair ..."

"I'm okay, it's just — gah!" I recoil in horror as Yoshino draws a spiderweb from my hair and lets it fall to the hospital floor like it's nothing. "Um. I'm okay. It wasn't me who got admitted; it was my ... er, I ... he's, um ..." I glance at the clipboard just past my feet. It's devoid of paper now.

"Oh, don't worry about that. Lieko has it. She's already filling it out for you." She sits down next to me. "Tell me what happened."

As I wipe my face for drool, I look over toward the entrance. Lieko is talking quietly with another nurse. "What is *she* doing here?"

"I called Manager as soon as I saw your text. I'm sorry, I panicked! I didn't know he was going to call her. I guess it makes sense; she lives closest to this hospital. He figured she could get here faster than I could. We ended up running into each other just outside the doors." Lieko is too far to hear her, but Yoshino drops her voice to a whisper, anyway. "I wouldn't get too friendly with her though. She technically offered, but she's still got a stick up her butt about it."

Lieko heads toward us with her own clipboard as the nurse trots off in another direction. She doesn't sit with us though; she takes a seat back where I was sitting with the old man and whips out her cellphone. Yoshino gestures with her head and we get up to go over.

"So," I begin awkwardly. "Tricky form, eh?"

"Yeah, but you don't have to worry about it," Yoshino cuts in before Lieko has a chance to speak. "We'll wait for him to wake up and he can give us all his information. Hey, we're just glad it isn't *you* in a hospital bed!" She shakes her head. "Who is this person, anyway? A friend of yours or something?"

"What? Yoshino, he's the guy you —"

Lieko looks up from her phone, directly at me, horrified. In all the months I've known her, I've seen this look on her face only once before. She looks like she's about to cry.

"Um, he's ... you know, the guy you see passed out on the street, and you can't, you know, help feeling sorry for? So, I bent down and asked if he was okay. He wasn't, but when I started to call 119 he said not to. So, I did a quick Google search and saw this hospital was nearby. Cab ride took less than five minutes."

"Damn, girl, you're a hero. I would have stepped right over him. May I ask what you are doing in Osaka this time of night, anyway?"

Lieko rolls her eyes like she's back to her old self. "Cybelle *has* been talking about visiting Spa World, Yoshino-*sensei*. That must be where she was. Why else would she be in this part of town?"

"Um ..." I shrug with an embarrassed grin. "Yep, you know me. I'm all about my *onsens*?"

"Oh," Yoshino nods. "That makes sense."

A nurse comes through a set of double doors and over to us. "The man you brought in is awake," she says in Japanese, directly to Yoshino and Lieko. "He'd like to thank you. Please, come with me."

"Just a moment, Yoshino-*sensei*." Lieko stands up abruptly. "Maybe, only Cybelle should go. She can take the form to the gentleman while you inform Manager that everything is all right. He must be worried."

"Yeah." I grin. "Manager's probably shitting himself right now."

"Okay, sure. Good idea."

I bow, thanking her. *"Azassu!"*

Lieko hands me the clipboard as Yoshino turns away on her phone. She holds onto it a second too long, giving me a slight but meaningful nod of her head. It's almost a bow. *"Tomodachi o tetsudatte ... onegaishimasu,"* she mutters under her breath, too quiet for Yoshino to hear. *Go help your friend … please.* I nod back, then follow the nurse. I didn't see it coming, but we've come to some level of understanding. That, or she just wants me to get rid of him. Most likely the latter. Either way, I'll take it.

"Cybelle-*sensei* will be all right, won't she?" I hear Yoshino say behind me.

"She is *gaijin*," Lieko replies. "If *gaijin* cannot do their best, they should not live in Japan."

I groan. Two steps forward, three steps back, Lieko.

The nurse leads me into an already-busy short-stay room. At least a dozen beds are spread around with thick curtains drawn and hushed voices on the other side. The nurse stands in front of one bed, ready to draw the curtains once I step in. She says something very soft and muffled about keeping quiet because many residents are sleeping, etc., etc. I ask the nurse in Japanese what happened to him. She puts her hands together under her face and cocks her head to one side. "Sleep," she says in English. But she quickly adds something in Japanese that I don't quite catch. I don't stop to think about asking her to slow down and repeat herself. I just want to see him.

The nurse bows and closes the curtains around me. Zaniel opens his eyes and looks up at me. They're so clear and piercing I can't help holding my breath. "Hey, look who's here," he smiles. "My hero."

I grin. "Ha, ha. How are you, Mr. Kamisawa?"

"You remember me now, do you?"

"I peeked at your licence. Cute photo. But seriously, how are you feeling?"

"Like I've been asleep for a hundred years."

I take a seat next to him on the bed. "Well, you certainly look well-rested."

"Hmmm," he says, closing his eyes again. Geez, even his lashes are beautiful. I wait a moment for him to say something else. His chest rises and falls. He's asleep again. I nudge him gently in his thigh. "Huh? Who's there?" He stretches like he's waking up from a late-afternoon nap. "Cybelle?"

"That's my name." I laugh a little. "Listen, my medical Japanese isn't great, so this is for you." I plop the clipboard of forms and the plastic bag with his belongings right on his chest. "This is all yours, too. You're lucky I have two co-workers here to help me with translation. Er, I didn't call them here, they just ... um, showed up. Don't worry, I skipped the part where I found you in the basement of an abandoned restaurant."

"I appreciate that." He gives the clipboard and the bag half a glance before moving them next to his leg. "Not that your school is going to hire me anytime soon." He chuckles grimly. "Guess I shouldn't've gone through with that ploy. Could've saved myself all this excitement."

"Hey, you know me. I'm all about excitement. Or maybe you don't know me. I don't know. How did you end up down there, anyway?"

He's still grinning. "Long story. Too long for now. Let's save it for our next date."

"Yeah ... We did go on a date ... didn't we?" I thought that old place looked familiar. The main room did, at least.

"Technically, two dates. There was food and handholding, and long philosophical conversations. Sounds like a date to me. I can't believe you forgot all about me."

"Hey! I didn't! Well, okay, maybe I did ... but I'm here now, aren't I?" I shake my head. "My memories are still pretty fuzzy. Consider that my excuse for not calling you?"

The curtains suddenly jerk sideways. A young doctor steps in and reels back when he sees me. "*Uwaa*! Oh! Sorry! *So* sorry!" He bows. "*Hontou ni sumimasen. Anou, tomodachi* ... uh, friend? You bring ... in taxi?"

"That's me."

"*Anou* … Japanese, okay? *Anou* … friend … needs rest. So, please, excuse us. Home, okay?"

I turn to Zaniel. "You gonna be okay?"

"Yes, dear. I don't think any demons are coming to kidnap me anytime soon. And I have you to thank for that." He takes my hand and presses it against his lips.

I shrug, grateful I'm not blushing. Whatever drug they have running through his IV drip, it's working wonders. There's nothing more I can do by staying. Zaniel is still holding me as I get up to leave. "Phone, please."

"It's in the bag."

"I mean *your* phone, silly."

Confused but entertained, I hand it over. He sends a text, then types his number into my contacts and hands it back to me. "I promised to explain, and I will. In time."

"Okay. Keep me posted, eh?"

Zaniel chuckles. "You said 'eh.'"

Yup, that IV drip is definitely working its magic. With a bow to the doctor, I let the nurse (who is already shooing at me to leave) guide me back to the lobby where I inform Yoshino and Lieko that all is well. We walk together in comfortable silence to Tennoji station, just a few minutes from the hospital. I thank them again for coming out to help when I get off at Namba. Yoshino squeezes my hand, Lieko focuses all her attention on her phone, of course. It's still pretty early in the morning, so I pop into a Lawson for two beef *onigiri* and wolf them both down before getting on a train to Nishibe. My stomach begins to growl again two stops later.

Thank goodness it's still super early on a weekend: my reflection in the window looks like I just rolled out of bed and I'm grateful there's no one around to see it. I'm the only one in the train car again. I could stretch out on the seats and take a quick nap if I wanted, but the last thing I need is someone boarding at the next stop and taking pictures of me or something equally awful. Instead, I lean back and watch the bay pass by the opposite window, and let my mind catch up to everything that's happened in the last twelve hours. The weirdest part of it all is how I thought running into Zaniel again would recover that piece of myself I felt was missing all this time. But it hasn't. How the hell *did* I find him, anyway? What made me think I'd find him when I first stepped out the door last night? What led me to that restaurant in the first place? I shudder at the thought of October repeating itself. I only have two more months to survive the rest of my contract and leave with my last shred of sanity. If that's my problem to begin with. He said he'd explain it all to me in time. When? What time? I don't have time. I'm too busy and I'm leaving in the spring. Which I didn't tell him. It never came up. Not that it's any of his business … right?

I also wonder what he meant by "demons"; maybe it was just the morphine or whatever they gave him, but something about that statement of his still haunts me. *Weird guy.* What am I talking about? *Weird night.*

The door connecting my car to the next slides open. A giant cloud of fluff with tiny black horns waddles through, down the aisle, straight to me. It takes a moment of staring to realize it's Yagi-*sama*, Nishibe's mascot. How cute. *"Baku-sama."* A pair of fluffy white-gloved hands extend a sheet of thick pink paper to me. *"Onegaishimasu."*

"Oh. Thanks, bro." Yagi-*sama* bows and toddles away, off to the next car. Good old English, the number one conversation killer. Wait a second — what did he just call me?

My head lurches to one side and my eyes open wide. They take a moment to adjust to the Japanese sign outside the open doors of the train that reads "Nishibe" in kanji. Shit. It's my stop. I must have dozed off. With two agile strides I make it just in time for the doors to slide closed behind me. Phew.

Something crinkles in my hand. It's a flyer, for a festival at a shrine I've never heard of. Hang on. I squint at the kanji characters and a tiny map. This place is all the way back in Osaka, near Shin-Imamiya station. I was just there. No thanks, local shrine. As promising as you sound, I can just go to the one down the street from me. I fold up the flyer and stick it in my pocket without a second thought. I've got to get home.

My mind plays through the whole evening as I shuffle down the empty streets. I don't feel the slightest bit sleepy, and my bike will be fine at Zozo; it's too old and crusty for anyone to steal. Relief washes over me stronger than the hot shower I'm dying to take when I get inside my apartment. The living room is still a mess from whatever I was doing before I ran off into the night: a big empty chip bag, *onigiri* wrappers, a carton that used to hold my favourite brand of peach iced tea, and then some. I ate and drank it all, watched *Spirited Away* and that weird *yokai* movie ... then I must have fallen asleep. Is that all that happened? That doesn't help. *Think, Cybelle. This isn't something you can "oh well, shou ga nai, Japan!" your way out of this time.* Something *happened* to me last night, and it brought me straight to him. But ... what?

Hold up. What am I doing? I have the rest of the weekend to wallow in my thoughts and figure out this whole thing. Right now, it's time to get ready for enjoying English. It's still Saturday. If last night's adventure is the strangest thing to happen all day, it'll be a major win.

I make some eggnog from scratch and add it to some instant pancake mix for breakfast. Then I change into a professional-looking red sweater and dress pants and watch some *Doraemon* on TV as I devour my pancakes. Before I bundle up into my winter coat, I catch my reflection in the *genkan* door. I look pretty decent for someone who went spelunking in an abandoned restaurant and didn't get a wink of sleep last night. Professional, polite, and playful. That's all I need to be today. Then I can worry about food and rest. I walk to Zozo with only my coin purse and my phone, ready to plow through another busy-ass Saturday.

The lobby is as busy as ever when I get there. The walls are now covered in red paper hearts over all the neon orange, yellow, and green everywhere. Yukie and Shigeyo say good morning as they run past me, arms loaded with boxes of teaching supplies. Ryoko and Kana are handing out 100-yen sheets of red, creamy orange, and pink papers to a grabby crowd of young children at their feet. Yukako and Yoshino are behind the reception desk. *"Ohayou gozaimasu!"* They bow in sync to me.

"Ohayou gozaimasu." I smile. "Busy day!"

"Busy day," Yoshino sings. "Watch out for the demons," she adds.

My eyes widen. "The who?"

Right on cue, someone down the hall screams. The cries get louder and louder. Two young children appear, chasing down another crowd of kids, wearing red and blue masks covered in straw. They stop at my feet. *"Oni wa soto, fuku wa uchi!"* I hear their muffled cries.

"Oh," I laugh. "You mean *these* demons. Ha, ha. Who's under there?" I stoop down and touch the red-masked child's nose. "Is that Reiki?"

The one in the blue mask rips it off. "I am Reiki!" he beams. "He is Honoki!"

"Fukumame choudai," the red-masked boy growls.

"Ah, he wants you to throw beans at him," Yukako calls out to me. In the second it takes to turn back around, the twins are already gone, running to the reception desk and demanding Yukako and Yoshino hand over whatever beans they're hiding. Another surge of people emerges from the elevator, and the boys terrorize them, too. I watch, fascinated, hoping this will be the hardest my heart beats today. I can't believe I forgot all about Setsubun being today. That explains Yagi-*sama*'s flyer. How time flies.

The day speeds by without any mishaps. Even my trip to Daiei to get sushi for lunch is uneventful, with maybe the exception of how excited the sushi guy gets when I order the lucky Setsubun *ehoumaki*. That earns me a few good stares. Back at Zozo, I'm so busy getting organized for my classes and running back and forth between rooms that I forget about what happened last night until my Zozo Zone 2 class. Twins Reiki and Honoki are sprawled on the carpet in Room Five with me and another student, Mako, colouring in our homework books. I notice Reiki is vigorously using a lot of red in his picture of Zozo the Clown jumping into a giant rain puddle. The two aren't related, but when I liken Reiki's picture to a scene from a horror movie, I can't help thinking about how last night could have ended differently. I was lucky. *Very* lucky. "What colour is that, Reiki?" I ask, mostly to disengage from morbid thoughts.

"I know, I know!" Mako shoots her hand into the air. "It's red!"

She always precedes her answers with the phrase "I know." Today, I'm ready for her. "Okay, Mako. How do you know it's red?"

Mako bares all her baby teeth in a wide smile and a serene voice. "Red is the colour of Jesus blood."

I blink. "Well, you're not wrong." She giggles, and proceeds to colour her puddle red, too.

Sakura and Ayuna come and go for their respective private lessons. I catch Sakura with a notebook where she has written the world's cutest "cheat notes" on how to ask me how I do my hair, and Ayuna reads me a short fanfic she wrote about our most recent chapter in *The Two Towers*. After translating for my parents, Kana informs me that Mana hasn't arrived for our trial lesson yet. That's cool. It gives me a good ten minutes to hide in the staff room and sneak in some downtime. I check my phone and see a single message on the lock screen. It's from Zaniel, from several hours ago.

The hospital let me go. I need to see you.

Wow, that was fast. Guess there couldn't have been anything seriously wrong with him. Good news. In a way. *Wanna go to a festival?* I type. I don't know why this idea pops in my head. There's a voice in there, telling me to meet him somewhere public, that I can't argue with. Low-key, I'm way overdue for some festival fun, too. I start to type in "Nishibe Shrine," then the voice in my head deletes it all and adds the name of the shrine in Osaka instead. It'll be easier for him to get to that one. That's probably it. I add that I can get to Shin-Imamiya station around 7:30 if I get out of work in time. He replies with a thumbs-up. Easy-peasy.

Mana comes two minutes late but leaves right on time. I collect all the garbage from the empty classrooms, sign out, and bid everyone farewell. Outside, the sky is dark as midnight, as if the whole day never happened. There are a few snowflakes floating down. That will be a nice touch, tonight. Since I don't have time for a full dinner (the festival is bound to have tons to eat, anyway), I just grab a couple of lemon Baumkuchen cakes from the *conbini* and devour them. They're wonderful, but oddly, not as good as all that *mochi* I ate last night. Must have been a while since I had *mochi*, that's all. The cakes at least somewhat dampen my craving for lemon. Just a bit. Man, this shrine better have food nearby. That *ehoumaki* did not last nearly as long as I'd hoped.

My stomach is itching on the inside when I arrive at Shin-Imamiya station. Zaniel is easy to pick out among the commuters in his long black winter coat, his head peeking three to four inches above everyone else's. For someone who spent the morning in the hospital after being dragged out from someone's basement, he looks pretty damn good. I march right up to him and poke him in the arm. He jumps but looks pleased to see it's me. "So, what's the verdict? No alien eggs in your stomach, I take it?"

"Nope. For a guy who's been asleep for three months, I'm perfectly fine." He reads the look on my face and laughs. "You look surprised."

"Well, *yeah*. I'm surprised because that's freaking impossible. If you've been comatose for three months, what are you doing out of the hospital? Shouldn't you be hooked up to a dozen IVs or walking with a cane or at least somewhat *suspicious* about your state of health?"

"I wasn't comatose. It's a little more … well, complicated than that. Let's just say they couldn't find any reason to keep me. But to make sure …" He unzips his coat a little and takes out a bag of pills from an inside pocket. "They gave me souvenirs, naturally."

"Naturally. Hold up. Have you not gone home yet?"

"No. I've just been hanging around Namba, charging my phone and shopping." He gestures to his coat. "I wanted to see *you*, remember?"

"Hmmm … I don't know. You're sure you're okay for a festival?"

"I think I'm in good hands." He playfully nudges me with his elbow. "Besides, you and I need to talk."

He says this, but he doesn't elaborate. The shrine is about five minutes from the station — maybe ten, with all the people around — but the air above us is already thick with smoke from the fire rituals that must be going on. I can hear the ominous beating of drums and the reedy sounds of *shou* when we leave the station, joining the herd of people all bundled up as they shout *"Uwaa, samui"* and pat themselves on the backs for dressing for the weather. Snow is really coming down by the time we get there. Scores of people line up around food and sake stands nearby. There's a decent-sized crowd at the shrine. We join the short line to wash our hands at the *temizuya* and stroll through the gate to the main grounds. Photographers with massive telephoto lenses position themselves atop stepladders throughout the grounds. Small children sitting on their fathers' shoulders cry at the men dressed as scary red-faced *oni* in paper armour running around yelling and growling at everyone. The older kids approach some of the *oni* to smack them and run away before they can catch the sharp ends of their prop spears. Around the shrine building itself, large crowds of people yell and laugh as they try to catch packs of soybeans thrown from the upper floor by gorgeous bundled-up *maiko* with silver *kanzashi* ornaments in their hair, shimmering from the glare of giant spotlights everywhere. There are giant speakers set up around the grounds, too, and a woman somewhere is chanting *"Oni wa soto, fuku wa uchi"* as the crowd goes wild. It's pretty easy to walk around because most of the shrinegoers who aren't jostling each other for the *fukumame* are huddled around all the giant bonfires to warm their bare hands.

The fires make me wish I brought some marshmallows and sticks. I suddenly have the worst craving for s'mores.

"You hungry?" Zaniel asks. His words are thin white clouds of carbon dioxide.

"Starving."

"Looks like we can beat the lines before the *mamemaki* ends. Unless you want to join in?"

"No, thanks," I wrinkle my nose. "I'm not really in the mood for *obaachans* elbowing me for beans."

He laughs lightly as we head back to where all the food stands are. He doesn't eat much — understandably, since he was in the hospital this morning — but I can't suppress my hunger. What starts as a few polite, tiny bites turns into me hoovering down the beef *yakisoba* we agree to share, followed by a round of *takoyaki* and two warm, fresh *taiyaki* (Zaniel insists he doesn't want his anymore).

"Zenzai!" I grab Zaniel's arm as we pass by a stand serving out heaving bowls of steamy dark-red soup. "I didn't think I'd see any after New Year's! Can we get some, *pwease?"*

He laughs at my puppy-dog eyes. Unfortunately, they've also attracted the attention of an old man with a giant camera. The man takes our photo, then winks at me and holds it. Yuck.

Zaniel skirts me away as I'm handed my soup. "Well, that was exciting," he says with a big grin.

"That's one way of putting it."

He chuckles. "Some sake will cheer you up."

He lets me find us a bench while he goes to another stand and returns with a box of something called *Oni-koroshi*. He offers me the straw first, winking. "Sorry, there's only the one."

"You're not sorry," I grin back, but the sake is so disgusting it makes me gag. "*Ugh.* Gross! That certainly got the taste of that guy out of my system." Zaniel laughs at that, making a face when he takes a sip, too. I inhale my bowl of *zenzai* as best as I can, endangering my heat-sensitive tongue but effectively washing out the taste of bad alcohol with the sweet, thick *adzuki* soup and *mochi*.

Two elderly women plop down on the bench next to Zaniel, squeezing themselves in although there isn't much room. "*Samui desu ne,*" they say to him. He agrees with a shy nod. Then they notice me. "*Eh?! Gaijin? Zenzai o taberu no? Sugoi na! Shusshin wa? Eh, tabun nihongo wakaranai na. Nee, anata no koibito na no? Kanoujo ni kite mite!*" They poke at Zaniel with sharp-looking knuckles, tittering.

He turns to me. "They want me to ask you where you're from." Poor boy.

"Is that *all* they want to ask?" I tilt my head, intrigued he left out the fact that they think I'm his girlfriend. He blushes. "Canada *desu,*" I tell them.

"*Ehhh, nihongo jouzu desu ne!*" the *obaachans* applaud. One of them asks if we can all take a picture together with her phone, but the other smacks her, saying they should let me finish my soup first. As they wait, they barrage Zaniel with the history of the shrine and force him to act as my translator. Then they go into more detail about Setsubun itself, prodding Zaniel to translate how it's the day before the beginning of spring on the Japanese lunar calendar, and how the beans we throw are meant to drive away the bad spirits and bad luck and bring in the good.

"Did you know that eating *ehoumaki* started in Osaka?" Zaniels interprets politely.

"Honestly, I had no idea," I reply.

The *obaachans* seem very proud of this fact. Then they change the subject and start talking to Zaniel directly. They ask where he's from and why his eyes are so pale, and that they've never seen a foreigner with such pale eyes. They're shocked when he tells them he's half-Japanese. They insist our relationship must be difficult, but seeing the two of us together is "beautiful" and we will have spectacular-looking children. We have to do our best together, especially in a world where everyone is so afraid of difference. My ears and cheeks warm as they say all this, and it's not from the *zenzai.*

Then they start talking about something else that's too fast for me to catch. "Okay, now they're getting political," Zaniel murmurs instead of interpreting.

"Sorry. I'm done!" I put my empty bowl down on the ground and we all squeeze together for *Obaachan* #1 to take several selfies. When they get up to leave, the second woman insists we take all the packs of soybeans she caught in the crowd. The first notices my bowl on the ground and insists she take it to find a garbage can for it. *"Ookini,"* I thank them both, earning another round of cooing and *"nihongo jouzu."* Once again, they make Zaniel and me promise to *ganbare* for the sake of our future children before they take off and disappear into the crowd, which looks like it's starting to thin. The shrine workers must have run out of beans to throw.

"They're not wrong," Zaniel raises his eyebrows at me. *"Issho ni ganbarimashou, ne?"*

I give him a haughty look. "Slow your roll, young man. We're not in relationship mode yet!"

"What are you talking about? This is our third date. Whether you remember the first two or not."

"Ahem. I did *not* ask you out. You said you had to see me."

The smirk disappears from his face. "Right. About that."

"What?" His seriousness wipes the grin off my face. "What's wrong?"

"I need you to explain something." He takes the plastic bag he's been carrying from his arm and opens it up. I'd forgotten he was even carrying anything. "I thought the worst was over. But then I found these."

He reaches in and produces a small but heavy sack. It looks like something you'd get from a health food store and spins in the air a little when I take it from Zaniel's hand. It reeks. "Mmm, pungent." I sniff again. "Beans?"

"*Soy*beans." He pauses. "Why do you think you got these?"

"Me? You're the one holding them."

"They were in the plastic bag you gave me with all my stuff in it. The things you picked up from that table next to me, right? Only *this* isn't mine."

"Well, they're certainly not mine!"

He waves a hand. "Never mind. Blessed soybeans are the least of my concerns. Look inside."

He opens the bag up and lets me lean in to take a peek. "The bracelets? Yeah, I thought those looked familiar."

"… you don't remember them, do you?"

"Um … aren't they for praying, or protection?"

"You have no idea how they got there?"

"Why would I? I have no idea how *you* got there. Or even how *I* ended up there …"

He studies my face for so long I squint back at him, waiting for him to break. "Why do you think it wasn't until Setsubun that you were able to find me?" he finally asks. "Convenient, don't you think?"

I smile. "You're beginning to scare me, guy. What, are you saying that springtime demons led me to you? You sure the morphine they gave you this morning wore off?"

He ignores my questions again. "How did you find out about this festival?"

"I got a flyer from Yagi-*sama*."

"Who?"

"Oh, he's Nishibe's mascot," I reply, digging through my pockets. "I got it from some guy in a costume this morning. Shoot, where did I put it? I could've sworn I just had it … unless I left it somewhere at work …"

Zaniel doesn't seem to care. He's looking around at the people, now. "Makes perfect sense they'd tell *you* about this festival." He sounds like he's talking more to himself. "They know you, now. They've seen what you did. What you *do*. They wouldn't want you here unless it was for a good reason." He stops me in my futile search by taking both my hands. "It's okay. I don't think you'll find it." For someone not wearing gloves, his hands are strangely warm. "Listen, Cybelle, I … I wanted you here to say thank you, in person. You saved me. I owe you my life."

My face warms up again. "Don't mention it?"

"I think I have to. I don't know where I'd be without you. No, scratch that. I *do* know where I'd be. Hell, I'd still be there if it weren't for your little nighttime adventure."

"Pouring it on a little thick, aren't we? And by the way, I am *done* with adventure. No more for me. I'm going back to a normal life in Canadian suburbia, where nothing happens. After seven years of adventure, it'll be great."

Zaniel laughs, then stops. He lets go of me. "Wait, you're going back? For how long?" he asks, slowly.

I raise my hands in a shrug. "Forever?"

"What do you mean, 'forever'? You can't! We just — I mean, you just — you've never talked about leaving before."

"Okay, I may not remember much, but I'm pretty sure I never said anything about staying in Japan forever."

"I guess." He looks down at his feet. "I just, I don't know … maybe I assumed you felt like you belonged here. Last I saw, you seemed happy."

"Yeah, well, I wasn't when I signed my re-contracting form. I really wasn't." He wouldn't know. He wasn't there to see. No. I'm not going to think back on it. "Whatever. It's fine. It's not like I'll *never* come back. I can always visit."

Zaniel doesn't look up. "You don't know that. A lot can happen. People change, places change. The things you can do now, there's no telling if you'll be able to do them again. *Ichigo ichie*, remember?"

I didn't think I'd have to deal with this feeling until I got on my plane home, this hollow drop in my stomach like the last time I went on the Do-Dodonpa roller coaster. "So, if we're different people when we meet next, what's the problem?"

"You say 'when.' You're being optimistic. I'm thinking about *if* we see each other again at all."

"Why wouldn't we?" The words come out sounding angrier than I meant them to. So many things are reeling through my mind, but I'm too scared to say any of them. So, I tell him what I've told countless others, hoping it'll end the discussion: "I've already signed the contract. The plane ticket is booked. I can't do anything about it now."

"Of course, you can! You can do anything. You're ..." He stops and rubs his naked fingers into his eyes like he's fed up with trying to explain something to me. "Okay. I get that you weren't happy before. How do you feel now?"

I shrug again. I can't help it. "Fine, I guess." It's an aloof response, but I don't really care. This whole conversation has gotten too weird and too deep, too fast.

"If that's the case, why go back? Why leave *forever*?" Zaniel shakes his head. Snowflakes fall from his hair. "I don't understand."

"I don't know, okay?! I don't know. I thought I did. But now ..." I sigh. "It just felt like the right thing to do. I mean, look at me. *Look* at me. I don't belong here. Maybe I never did, and I just stayed so long thinking I could change everyone's minds, but I can't. I'll always be treated like I don't know the culture, or understand the language, or follow the rules. I'll never be normal here. Don't get me wrong, people are nice to me — finally — and the students I teach are adorable. But when Zozo asked if I wanted to stay ... I couldn't say yes because something has been missing. Some part of me just ... *vanished.* I don't know who or what took it, but I need to get it back. I need to feel whole again. I need things to go back to normal."

"And you think you'll find that part of yourself ... by leaving?"

Zaniel's voice is gentle. Almost sad. Feeling defensive all of a sudden, I'm unsure of myself for the first time in months. "I hope so," I finally say.

But what if you don't? That's the question I know he wants to ask, it's as clear as day on his face. I'm grateful that he doesn't, but what he says next really hits me, harder than his piercing gaze. "I guess I'm not in any position to convince you to stay. And consider it an understatement when I say how much I'll miss you. But you said it yourself: you can pick up your life and move ten thousand miles away but still be stuck with the same situation you ran away from."

My blood runs cold. I *do* remember saying that. Or at least believing it.

"And I don't know what you think is missing from yourself, but take it from me: you're never going to go back to 'normal.' Your life will be the farthest thing from it. Trust me on that one."

What the hell is *that* supposed to mean?

I leap to my feet, trying to look distracted by the crowd so I don't cry. "It's freezing out here," I snap. "I'm going to find some *shougazake.* I'll be back ... I guess."

Zaniel calls out after me as I storm off, but he doesn't pursue. Good. My heart is pounding too hard for me to think. Now I really *do* feel like I'm on a G-force roller coaster; one ill-timed word and I'd probably throw up on him. I don't know why I'm angry and nervous and dizzy all of a sudden. Maybe it's hunger. No, it isn't any of those things: It's fear. Fear that he's right, fear that circumstances will change so much we won't see each other ever again. I couldn't handle that. And he's right about one thing: I was happy here. I mean, I *am*. Especially with him. But I get the feeling he wants me to stay for his own sake. That's nothing new. He's not going to miss me. I've met tons of guys just like him, three this past month alone, looking for someone to replace the ever-revolving door of *gaijin* they befriend over time. Unless he really *does* see us as more than friends. But it's not like we have the time to do anything about it.

Wait. Why am I even talking like this? There was never any "we" to begin with. Three dates don't make a "we."

I wander around the other food stands to see what's left: corn dogs, cotton candy, and other stuff no one wants because it's hardened by the cold exposure. Everyone seems to be getting ready to close up for the night. I'm ready to head home myself. This was a bad idea on the tail end of a string of bad ideas. I head back empty-handed to our bench. Zaniel is now standing beyond one of the bigger bonfires, looking cold and irritable. His face brightens again when he sees me, then goes slack like he is about to see a small animal get hit by a car. "Cybelle!"

"*ABUNAI!*" someone shouts behind me. *Look out.*

Something large and heavy crashes through the giant bonfire next to me. A burst of flames sends bits of charred wood and hot embers into the air. I duck and curl up on the ground. Everyone around me screams. Then the crowd starts to surge toward me, running for their lives. I scramble on all fours and hide behind a bench. I hear a woman scream something, her voice high-pitched and frail, followed by the sound of an animal growling as it tears through what I assume is flesh.

"*Inoshishi,*" someone screams. "*Inoshishi! Minna, nigero!*" It's a boar. Everybody, run.

Someone collapses right into me as they take shelter behind the bench. "Did you see the size of that thing?" a man next to me says in Japanese. "It's bigger than my damn car!"

There's a family hiding against a neighbouring bench. "Did someone call the police?" the mother cries.

"Cops?! What are *they* gonna do? We need the *zoo*, bitch!"

Another explosion through a bonfire sends a fresh wave of heat through the air. Even behind this bench I can feel it above my head, up my back. I turn around to look under the space of the bench and scoot away just in time to avoid the pool of dark liquid coursing through the dirt toward me.

Now, I scream.

The man next to me hauls me to my feet and pushes me ahead and out of the way from the crowd fleeing the shrine grounds. He disappears before I can even try to thank him. Zaniel is nowhere to be seen. I yell his name over the tide of frightened people herding me toward the street. The sky opens up again and I am standing on the main road, pushed and shoved by the people streaming around me with shocked, tear-stained faces. Standing there in a daze, I wonder what my own face looks like. I can barely fathom where I am or what I should do next. All I can think about is the fate of those two elderly ladies.

Something grabs my arm and practically pulls it out of the socket. *No! Not again!* flashes across my mind. I scream and try to shake it off.

"It's okay," Zaniel doesn't release his grip. He keeps running, away from the shrine, away from the crowd. "I've got you."

A guttural sound quakes the ground and people scream in response. Those who are running pick up an extra burst of speed while the people standing around to catch their breath or take out their cellphones lose composure and join them. It had started to snow, but everything feels hot, like a wave of fire is coming toward us. A tsunami of heat. The idea of such a thing makes me hyperventilate. Zaniel doesn't let me stop to catch my breath. His hand is strongly clutching mine as we duck down a short alley.

I remember this alley. *Metallica.* "Where are we going?"

"You'll see. Come on."

It's a rhetorical question. Deep down, I already know the answer.

We've slowed down, but it's still hard to keep up with Zaniel's long-gaited speed-walking as we pass the flickering lights of Love Drug and the tiny shrine on the corner. We hurry down the empty road with that skewed torii gate. Zaniel abruptly turns and pulls me through it. We're trapped between two short buildings now, in the same dark cul-de-sac I found myself in less than twenty-four hours ago. Zaniel finally lets me go and slumps against the wall, all colour drained from his face. I take this as my cue to lean against the cold brick and catch my breath. What are we doing back here?

"It's him. He's here."

Right on cue, a shriek pierces the air and echoes into the night. I'm afraid to ask who he's talking about. And yet, deep down, I already know the answer to that question, too. "No." I shake my head, backing away from Zaniel, from the dark hole he's already heading toward. "I don't want to go back in there." Something tells me I won't be coming back out.

"It's going to be okay. Trust me." He extends a hand. "Please," he begs. The solid comfort of his grip seems much more promising than the prospect of running through the empty streets of Osaka with some feral creature on the loose. So, I take it.

Zaniel takes out his phone and uses the flashlight to guide us down into the dark remains of the decrepit restaurant. The dead *sakura* tree I trip over does not comfort me, but I feel somewhat relieved when we reach the main room. There's enough light coming in from where there used to be a ceiling that Zaniel doesn't need his phone anymore. I'm less comforted when he pulls me deeper into the room, approaching the giant stage, and ducks under a clothed table. "What the —? Ow!" He reaches up and pulls me down with him. "What the hell are we doing now?"

"Listen, Cybelle. I know you don't believe me, and I don't have time to explain, but what happened to you three months ago … it's going to happen again if we don't do something about it. As long as we're both here, he's just going to keep coming. This has to end. Right now."

I have no idea what he's talking about, but I only have one pressing question on my mind. "How?"

Zaniel bites his lip, steeling himself. "You have to go back to sleep."

I blink. "I have to *WHAT*?!"

"You heard me," he gasps. I can practically hear his eyes lighting up. "The room downstairs. You can sneak down there to sleep. I'll buy you as much time as I can while you —"

"Ew, *no*! Have you completely lost your mind?!"

"It's the only way to get to a place where you can defeat him. You can do this." He proceeds to rip off his coat and wrap it around me like a blanket. He's got to be kidding. "This might be the last thing that'll convince you of anything … hell, I won't be surprised if it makes everything even worse for you. But at least you'll be in a position to finally understand."

Uh-oh. Understand what? "Zaniel … what are you about to do?"

He leans across the space between us and wraps his arms around my neck, pulling me into him. As weird as this all is, I allow myself a moment to rest against him. He smells amazing.

"Here. Take this."

He digs something out of his coat pocket. For some reason I half-expect him to produce a weapon. But no. It's the small, burlap sack I took from the basement.

"The fuck? Your soybeans? *What am I supposed to do with these?!*"

"ZANIEL," says a deep, growling voice, its echo so loud that it sounds like it's right behind me. I hear sniffing, snorting, and then: "Ceeeeeeebelle ..."

My eyes water in fear. "Zaniel, what the hell —?"

"I'll distract him. Stay here," Zaniel commands me. He doesn't give me much choice, dropping the cloth back down over the table after he slinks out from underneath. The *clop-clop-clop-clop* on stone stairs gets louder and closer. I'm sweating and shaking, hot and cold at the same time. What the hell am I doing? I don't have to stay here. I should make a run for it. I can shout for Zaniel and we can get the hell out of here, instead of whatever he thinks I'm about to do with these freaking beans. But why would he give them to me when running away would be the logical thing to do?

A deep, clear growl ringing through the dark restaurant freezes me in place. "Well, well, well ... look who's up and about, eh?" I know that voice.

"No thanks to you," Zaniel's retort echoes off the walls.

The resultant laughter sends chills up my spine. "You know," the voice continues, "I gotta hand it to that bitch. Crossin' my territory, gettin' past the moat, all the way to *you*. And then she goes and eats my fuckin' nightmares — AGAIN. You picked one hell of a *yokai* to be on your side, kid. Now, tell me where she's hidin' so I can kill her nice and slow."

There's a scuffling sound, like someone bumping into a far-off table, and the sound of utensils and glass being jostled. The voice snickers, then bursts out laughing. "A fork? Seriously, kid? Who do you think you are now, Momotaro or somethin'? Please. Zaniel-*kun*. Look at me. *Look* at me. I'm not your enemy."

"Oh, really, Akki? Was it some other demon who took three months of my life?"

Akki. I *know* that name.

"Hey, you wanted my protection, and I fuckin' gave it to you. Did anyone bother you all those three months? I fuckin' did you a *favour*, kid. I protected you, just like you asked me to, all those years ago."

"Right. And that whole time, you were lying to me. Stealing souls behind my back. And like a sucker I helped you do it. Well, it's over, Akki. You're going to leave us alone from now on."

Stealing *what*? Am I hearing things right?

"What? You're leavin' me? For what — HER?"

Zaniel lets out a breath. "Yes," he says steadily. "But mostly for myself. Let's face it; you were never going to let me live a normal life. In the end you would have taken my eyes, too, when my looks faded and I'd outlasted my usefulness. I was just a fool not to see it coming."

"Guess you're not as stupid as you look, kid. But you've forgotten one thing. Momotaro needs *three* creatures to help him win against the demons. And he doesn't defeat them. He just makes them promise to behave. Well, hate to break it to ya, but I have no plans to behave! Once I'm finished with your new friend, her eyeballs will be the least of her problems."

What the hell are they talking about? Who is Zaniel even talking to? Something on the floor skitters across my hand. It feels like a giant cockroach. No. I'm not sticking around to find out any of this. I'm out of here.

A high-pitched screech, like the sound of metal being torn, pierces the air. I clap my hands over my ears and try not to cry out. It almost sounds like a wild boar, bleating, but it's way too loud and too close. There's the sound of scuffling, and tables being knocked over. I hear Zaniel shout, as if struggling against something. "No, no!" he begs, and then there is a moment of silence before the air whistles and something heavy crashes into the table next to mine. Someone groans in pain. I peek out from the tablecloth and see Zaniel lying on a broken table. It's like something threw him across the room.

"Zaniel ... get up!" I forget about everything he said before and scramble out from under the table to his side. His coat falls from my shoulders, and I drop the bag he gave me to touch his waist, to gently shake him. He cries out in pain. He must have broken a few ribs. "Shit ..." Why do I have to keep getting him out of this godforsaken place?

"Cybelle ..." he moans. "Run ..."

His warning comes too late. Someone grabs the neck of my coat and pulls, hard, dragging me away from him. I choke out a scream, grabbing the cuff of my coat and kicking out my legs in panic.

"YOU. DON'T. TOUCH. HIM."

The words echo all around me. My flailing arms catch the legs of nearby chairs and tables to slow my attacker down. Bad idea. With an angry roar, my attacker reaches down to grab my belt buckle and jerks upward, hard. I find myself hoisted at least seven feet in the air like I weigh next to nothing. I already know what's going to come next.

I scream, anyway.

And then I'm flying, sailing over all the tables and chairs, praying that I land on something soft. In the dim light, I can see the stage getting closer and closer, and I briefly think to myself that the curtains look like they might soften my landing.

Unfortunately, I don't make it — not by a long shot. My body twists in the air and the first thing I feel in my back is the solid slam of hard wood before I bounce off and land on a table, breaking my fall, and everything goes black.

Sweltering heat and the scent of trees hit the Yokai as she steps off the plane, grateful to finally be out of that cold, stale, boxy compartment. She bows to the flight attendants who bid her farewell, and saunters down the metallic staircase that leads straight into the heart of a tropical jungle. Palm trees and coconut trees sway above her in the ocean breeze. *The ocean.* She can hear it nearby. Waves … and music. *Better change here, while there's no one around.* She drags her giant suitcase to a shady spot and digs out a black bikini from among the massive bottles of water, clothes, sandals, and a heavy orange block that appears to read "American Cheese." She quickly puts the bikini on before anyone can spot her, shy despite the fact that there is no one around, and continues on, abandoning the suitcase. It will be fine out here.

The jungle makes way and opens up to a long, cement building that looks like an abandoned bubble tea shop. "Om Nom Nom Nom," a crumbling sign reads. "Oc—n C—nti-a." The Yokai ventures inside, meandering through dozens of neatly arranged circular tables, toward the other side of the building. The wall here is missing, exposing a crowd of creatures dancing on a gorgeous beach. She has found the source of the pleasant tropical music: a giant pink octopus in a red loincloth with the biggest head she has ever seen towers above the crowd, playing several adequate-sized marimbas. There appear to be other, smaller octopi nearby playing accompanying instruments, but it is the giant that has the crowd moving and shaking. The Yokai takes up an empty reclining chair as the octopus sings:

> *"I suck*
> *Submitted by 'Isaac'*
> *Admitting that I suck*
> *I suck*
> *I suck"*

The Yokai wrinkles her brow. "What an odd song." Then she bursts out laughing. "Oh! He sucks because he's an *octopus.* I got it! Speaking of octopus, man, am I hungry. *Garçon!*" She flags down a nearby waiter in board shorts, carrying an empty tray.

"Yes, miss."

"Do you have any *takoyaki?*"

"No, miss. Only chicken and tropical foods."

"Okay. I'll start with twenty chicken nuggets, and all the sweet-and-sour sauce you can give me, please."

"Sorry, miss, we don't have chicken nuggets, anymore, but we do have a new chicken sandwich — it's only twenty bucks."

"What's my tab now?"

"With the sandwich, altogether it'll be $88.89."

"Charge it," says the Yokai; she pours a handful of sand onto the waiter's tray. He leaves, confused but silent, while she produces a large pair of sunglasses out of thin air and leans back to take better stock of her surroundings. Funny how she is one of only three human-looking creatures on the beach. On either side of her lie two gorgeous *futakuchi-onna* in bikinis fanning themselves and sticking maraschino cherries on toothpicks under their hair for their extra mouths to enjoy. A gaze of *tanuki* emerge from the water to ogle them at a closer distance. A herd of gigantic green cows, all with three eyes, now wander onto the sand from the cantina, looking confused and out of place. A large black lacquered Daruma with two eyes rolls up behind them, followed by a pack of huge, scruffy-looking cats with forked tails. More odd-looking animals and people and demons appear to be playing and relaxing all along the beach. But no one, not even the *futakuchi-onna*, look anything like the Yokai. For once, she thinks as she lies back with a peaceful sigh, this does not bother her so much.

"Whoa, ho, ho," says one of the cats, looking around. "Where the hell are we? Okinawa?"

"I don't think so," says one of the three-eyed cow demons, its eyes trained on a waitress with a heaving tray of steamy, caramelized plantain. "I have a feeling we're *way* farther from our neck of the woods."

"Don't you mean, neck of the *mountains*?" says the fan in a *futakuchi-onna*'s hand.

"Whatever, *Sensu-sama*. How did we get here?"

"Forget about us! What is *she* doing here?" Another fork-tailed cat points a claw at the lounging Yokai. "What are you doing, freaking sunbathing?"

"Yes. *I sunbathe.* So what? You know, y'all are really messing with my vibe. I'm supposed to be on vacation."

"You're *supposed* to be fighting the Nightmare King!" the Daruma wails.

"Who?"

"*Akki!* You know, the King of Nightmares? The boar god that's been after you? Hello?!"

"Akki?" The giant octopus stops mid-chorus. "Oh, *hell* no." It drops its sticks and slithers away as best an octopus can slither across a sandy coastline.

"You guys are weird. I don't see any boars." The Yokai looks up and down the beach, then reclines back against her chair. "Besides, this place is all sand. Boars don't — whoa, what's up with that? Sunset, already?"

. The other *yokai* turn to the sky. It is indeed changing, muting from a light tropical blue to a deep orange and, following that, it dims to the blood colour with which they are so familiar. Many breathe a sigh of relief and exchange smiles. Then a few voices cry out in horror. "Look! *Mite, mite!*" The ocean horizon has become a string of fire, blazing from one end to the other like ignited kerosene, and it is climbing up the blood-red sky. A tsunami of fire accompanied by the telltale screech of a bleating boar.

It is Akki, and Akki is angry.

"*Chikushou!* I knew this wasn't over!"

"It was too good to be true!"

"Fuck, we're all dead!"

"*Nigero!* Run, run!"

Everyone scrambles for the shore. The now-bewildered Yokai finds herself tumbling into the sand as the burly cow creatures crash into her chair. A *futakuchi-onna* is kind enough to help the Yokai to her feet, but not patient enough to stay. The Yokai lets the tide of monsters carry her through the abandoned cantina, into the jungle where there is enough open space for her to run. Here, the ground is still covered in hot thick sand, slowing her down. Struggling to breathe, she braces herself behind a thick coconut tree as multitudes of *yokai* stream past her. She braces herself for the wave of heat to come crashing down on her, and is thankful when the waves that rush over her legs are not flames, but water, albeit a disturbing shade of red. She cannot outrun the tsunami, whether it consist of fire or water. She has to think of something else. If only she could get higher —

"That's it."

The Yokai runs once again, but instead of fleeing farther into the jungle behind the others, she breaks off from the group and heads uphill. The trees here are farther from one another, and much, much bigger. Or perhaps it is she who is getting smaller. It makes perfect sense. She is getting hungrier.

"Damn," she pants. "This sucks. I'm *starving*." She kisses her teeth. "I never got my sandwich." Alas, there is no time to wallow in remorse for chicken sandwiches that could have been. She pushes onward as hard as she can, the sounds of monsters crying out in pain as the presumable wall of fire reaches them, creating more and more incentive to climb. She too can feel the heat, all the way up here ... No. The heat is not in the air. It is under her hands and feet, radiating from the ground itself. It rumbles with power. The Yokai looks up; sure enough, the blood sky has become dark with ash and soot. "A volcano. Great." But it is better than whatever is happening down below.

The Yokai's ascent ends at a sharp cliff. She pulls herself up over the face and finds the air is much clearer here. She can even see the top. "What the ...?" There is something already up there. A majestic-looking hawk-eagle with a bald patch perched in a nest, unceremoniously shredding a freakishly large, oblong vegetable with its beak and talons. "Weird," says the Yokai. "Not the weirdest thing I've seen today, but still —"

"Hold it right there, tiny missy!" A muffled voice shouts. "This is *my* volcano!" With an echoing screech, the hawk-eagle flies down, landing with an impressive thud and a dramatic spread of its wings to block the Yokai's path. "I don't allow climbers. If you want to get to the top, too bad. Go find your own volcano, now. Shoo! Shoo!" It flaps at her.

"I'm sorry. I didn't mean to intrude on your volcano. It's just that there's a fiery tsunami down below and a possible boar on the loose. Everybody made a break for it. Maybe you should be, you know, fleeing like the others?"

The hawk-eagle makes a shrugging gesture with its outspread wings. "Well. You know what they say: *kuu ka kuwareru ka.* Now beat it."

"What on earth does that mean?"

"It means I want you to leave."

"No, the other thing you said. *Kuu wa … nandakke?*"

The hawk-eagle sighs. "Kids today. It means, 'Eat or be eaten.' Take my eggplant, for example —"

"'Eat or be eaten'? By an eggplant? I doubt you have to worry about that."

The hawk-eagle looks about to offer a surly retort, then points a trembling wing at her. "Behind you!" it squawks, a moment too late. It takes to the air while the Yokai's hair is pulled so far back behind her she loses her balance and tumbles into her attacker. They roll a painful, pointy journey down the volcano, all the way back to the valley. Gasping, Akki crawls toward the prostrate Yokai.

"Well, fuckin' well. Looks like someone's little nightmare snack's been all digested up — nothin' for you to chomp on, now. Look at ya, you're already shrinkin' down to nothin'. And I thought killin' ya was gonna be difficult!"

A giant hand shoves the Yokai's face down into the sand. She lashes out with a high-pitched squeal and twice connects an elbow with Akki's shoulder. He grunts and reels back, giving her the split second required to gasp for air and cough. He kicks her in the stomach, winding her further. When she rolls onto her back, Akki does not waste time. He tackles her, pinning her still-shrinking arms to the ground.

No! The Yokai squeezes her eyes shut, struggling to think straight. *There has to be a way out of this before the flames hit. Think, damn it, think.* Her mind begins to steel itself. The flames. The fiery tsunami. What happened to them? It didn't make sense. None of it made sense. The beach, the giant octopus, those other creatures, the hawk-eagle. How could any of it be real?

It can't be. It isn't. It's a dream.

Akki barks a laugh in her face. "It's a dream, all right. *My* dream. You're in *my* world now, ya puny little bitch. Once I've eaten the rest of ya, the kid's mine. His eyes are mine. This world is mine. I'm takin' 'em all back, and there ain't a fuckin' thing you can do about it this time." He sees the Yokai is about to make some kind of scathing response, but he will not entertain any witty comebacks this time. Still pinning her down, he smothers her face with his body.

Nope, not a dream!

The Yokai tries to scream, but Akki only hears a muffled cry underneath him. His laughter is a deep, evil bellow of triumph. The upper hand is finally his. How long can half-*yokai* half-humans go without oxygen? *Ah, who cares?* Another minute or two of suffocating against his stomach ought to do the trick. All he has to do is wait for her to stop struggling and die, and then her salty caramel flesh and eyes will be his to consume.

Winning has never been so easy. Almost easier than the last time.

"Ow." Akki feels a pinch in his stomach. He almost reaches to scratch at it. No. He cannot get up yet. Thirty more seconds ought to finish her off. But something is wrong. "Ow ...!"

Very wrong.

"Ow, ow, ow, *ow, OW*!"

He tries to get up and finds he cannot. Something has attached itself to his stomach. It is the Yokai. More specifically, it is the Yokai's teeth. Thirty-two long, sharp needles, all puncturing the skin, sinking into his flesh, and trapping him to her. Akki does not know what to do except panic. Even when he releases her now-growing arms, she does not let go. Blood pours from his wound and spills down his leg, into the pale sand. She does not let go. She is growing longer, heavier, amassing to the point where she could be twice his size, and still she does not let go.

Frantic, he starts screaming for help, for mercy. "I give, I give! Uncle, okay?! *Uncle!*" He tries to pry her off by pushing against her shoulders. The Yokai smacks his hands away as if batting a fly, then does the unthinkable: she wraps a hand over his face as if to silence him, grits her teeth, and wrenches her head to one side. Akki's flesh gives way. A substantial chunk of meat goes flying through the air with a spray of red. More in shock than in pain, Akki collapses into the sand, watching helplessly as the Yokai sprints away on all fours and pounces on what used to be part of his torso.

"Aw, yes," the Yokai sings. "Pork belly!" Even at her size she needs both hands to pick it up and eat it. She savours every bite — the chewy texture of soft, smooth fat yielding to her teeth, the sizzling warmth against her snaky tongue, the sensation of juices dribbling down her chin as much as they course down her throat — she cannot even remember the last time she had braised pork belly. *That's what this is, right?* She pauses in her devouring. "Yup, looks like it. Close enough." The last strips of meat disappear in seconds. The Yokai knows it is impolite but sucks the last shred of meat from her finger and thumb. She already craves more. She looks around, her face slathered with boar blood, her pitch-black eyes twinkling with the prospect of more of that salty, succulent flesh. But all she sees is a wounded baby pig, squealing for all it is worth. Or perhaps it is not a baby; yes, she concludes, it looks like a full-grown adult. She is just that much larger than this particular animal. The Yokai examines herself. How did she get so big so quickly? (She does not remember being this size at the start of her day, but now it feels appropriate.) It does not matter. She wants that boar, the apparent source of that delicious morsel of meat. The way it whines as she stares at it almost brings pity to her heart. It must know what the Yokai wants. No, she should not … but on the other hand, she reasons, if that boar gets the chance, it will most likely do the same and take a bite out of her. She shrugs and gets down on all fours.

"EAT OR BE EATEN."

Her voice is a deep, throaty, feline growl. Her words cross Akki's *yumego* threshold. He understands every one of them, and the intention behind each one. He is screwed.

"Eep!"

Holding in what remains of his side, Akki summons the last of his dream strength. He crawls away with very little haste. In fact, he only gets about three feet before the thundering sound of the Yokai's footsteps reaches his ears. He flips over onto his back and tries to drag himself, but it is a fruitless endeavour. He collides up against a coconut tree, sending a few down to earth.

The Yokai stalks toward him. "Here, little piggy! Come here, little guy!"

Akki hoists a giant coconut into the air with his good hand and launches it in the Yokai's direction. She catches it one-handed with a sharp *snap*. Akki squeals again and throws another. She catches that one, too, and to his horror sinks her teeth into it, ripping out a chunk of the diamond-hard shell, tilts her head back and lets the milk flow into her mouth. She gulps and laughs victoriously.

"Is that the best you've got? You'll have to do better than that if you want to — uh-oh."

A third coconut hurls toward her. She does not drop the other two in time. It smashes the Yokai in the face, knocking her out instantly.

"Ow ... shit ..."

It hurts to open my eyes. I feel like I've been kicked in the face. My back is killing me for some reason, too. Somewhere close by, someone is breathing heavily. It's a raspy, gaspy, old-man-on-his-last-legs kind of breath. I jerk upright, surprised at the sensation of hardwood under my palms, wet and sticky with some unknown substance.

This isn't my living room, and I'm not dreaming.

There's a man kneeling next to me, naked as the day he was born. He's clutching his side and staring at me, hard. His one good eye burns green into mine. I scuttle back on my hands as he stumbles to his feet. He balls up the fist of the hand not holding his torso and gestures in my direction, a bleating sound gurgling in his throat.

In the back of my mind, I know what I should do. I should run away from him, run away from wherever the hell this place is, whip out my phone, call the police, let someone else take care of this giant, messed-up dude who is clearly about to punch me in the face, if not worse, and tell myself it's all a dream. Just a long, realistic, and horrible dream. But I don't. Instead, I get far enough away to scramble to my feet and swing around, ready to face him with a growl of my own. Ready to punch, kick, scratch with all my might. I'm not going down without a fight.

Not this time.

But something happens. The man's giant fist stops halfway in its follow-through, and the sound of beans scattering across the stage floor bounces off the rafters like applause. The man has stopped moving completely, frozen on the spot. His head is turned away from me at an awkward angle, like he's just been slapped. Then his head snaps back to look down at his chest. He touches it and pulls back a blood-drenched hand. Did someone just shoot him? Am I missing something?

"F ... fucking ... *gaijin* ..." he croaks before slamming hard into the stage floor face first, unconscious. Good.

"Cybelle?! You okay?!"

"Zaniel ..."

I hop over the man's naked figure, kicking him in the side for good measure. Then I make my way over the edge of the stage and leap down. The massive room is spinning, but I manage to stumble over the broken debris of restaurant furniture, right into Zaniel's arms. I've never felt so relieved. "I'm having the weirdest day," I pant.

"It's okay. We did it," he mumbles against my neck. Then, he doubles over. "Ah! Shit, I think I broke something. Yep, I broke something. Definitely a rib. Maybe two."

"Let's get the hell out of here, then."

I'm still breathing hard as we half-guide, half-drag one another through all the detritus toward the torn rice-paper doorway. "It's okay," he keeps murmuring. "It's over, it's over."

There's a good chance I'm concussed because I can barely put together what just happened. I just want to get out of this awful place. "It's fine," I eventually say to calm Zaniel down. "Everything is going to be fine. We just need to get out of here. Careful. Watch your foot. That's it. Now, we just need to tackle these stairs and —"

I freeze. Someone is already at the top of the stairs.

"You can't come in," Zaniel's voice is sharp. He's not talking to me. "I'm not inviting you in."

"Nor do you need to," echoes a soft, deep voice. "This was always technically a public place. Besides, you are mistaken; I was just leaving."

Zaniel pushes me back behind him, ready to protect me despite his injury. The shadow blocking the doorway seems to shudder but does not move out of our path. "Relax, dream walker. I am not here for either of you. I always wondered what those beans would do to our kind. Now I know. You would do well to make your escape from this place while you can. You are welcome for this advice, no need to thank me."

"Thank you? For what?"

"A great many things, human. Did you not wonder who took care of you all those months? Akki imprisoned you without any idea of how to keep you. He does not remember what it is like to be human. Perhaps he never was, even in his youth. I too had forgotten how much food and care humans require. It has been so long since I was one myself. At any rate, grateful as I was for Akki allowing you to sleepwalk about that little room of yours, keeping you alive was tiring. So, I went searching for *her*. It was not easy. You are welcome."

Zaniel is quiet for a moment. "Must I guess what the great Hino-*sama* wants in exchange for my care?"

"My only request is that you do not destroy me, too. It is only fair. Right, *Baku-sama*?"

The shadow is no longer addressing Zaniel. I find myself pushing Zaniel away, approaching the dark shadow in the entranceway. It's that girl from weeks ago. The one outside of the bar. And the girl who sat across from me when Zaniel and I came here on our first date. It doesn't make sense, and yet it makes all the sense in the world. "Hino?"

"You remember. I am honoured." The shadow bows low. "Take care, *Baku-sama*, and why not? You, too, dream-walking human. I would hate to see you both end up on cereal boxes one day. Now, if you will excuse me, my search for the perfect lighter continues. Farewell."

Cereal boxes? The perfect lighter? I don't get it. But the dark figure of the leonine, long-haired girl is already turning away, a ghostly figure heading into the dimly lit night, disappearing forever.

"That was weird," I mutter. What am I saying? What out of this whole day *hasn't* been fucking weird? "Come on. Put your weight into me." Zaniel groans as we climb the steps and step out into the open air. "There, see? We made it."

"Yeah …" Zaniel turns to me, then stops in his tracks. "Uh, Cybelle? You … you've got something …" He gestures to his mouth.

"What?" With my free hand, I wipe my chin and it comes back sticky and dark. "The hell …?"

Whatever this stuff is, it's all over my face. I carefully let Zaniel go and step farther out into what little light there is out here. My eyes begin to blur. Something is *very* wrong. I look down and my stomach roils. Behind me, leading all the way up to my feet, is a thick, greasy trail of red fluid and clots in pristine white snow. That's what's all over my face, all over my white coat. The scent on my fingers that's like the time I left hamburger meat de-thawing for too long. Or dead, rotting fish.

It's blood.

And none of it is mine.

I did this. This is what I did to that naked man. I remember sinking my teeth into his stomach … eating his flesh … and *liking* it.

I don't scream. My voice doesn't go high or loud enough. I just let out this soft moan as my body tilts to one side. Everything goes very dark in a split second. Somewhere close by, Zaniel shouts my name as I slip into unconsciousness; I feel his body against mine before I hit the cold, snowy ground.

"It's okay." I hear his soft voice all around me. "I've got you."

Passing out isn't so scary. It's just like going to sleep, but very, very sudden. I don't mind it. It's kind of nice. Safe, in this darkness, in Zaniel's arms, out of my own body, away from the blood. Even if I could think straight, I do not need to dwell on any of it. All I can do now is sleep.

"Zaniel?"

Zaniel raises his head, eyes widening. He is not surprised to see the Yokai above him, emerging out of the dark entranceway. He is more concerned about her freezing, being naked in such cold. She does not seem to notice. She simply takes a deep inhale of the crisp winter air, minty and refreshing in comparison to the dank inside of what is left of Jibun Jishin. "Ooh," she shivers. "It's nice out here."

Zaniel tries to roll over onto his knees. Every movement sends spikes of pain shooting through his torso. The Yokai rushes to his side to assist him. That is when she notices the unconscious body next to him. "Is that … is that me?"

"Well —"

"Why am I saturated in blood?!"

"Y … yeah, about that —"

"Am I DEAD?"

"No! No, you just passed out. And I … well, I didn't want you to be alone."

"Oh. Well. Um. That's very kind of you. Are you…?"

"Yeah. I'll be all right. Eventually." He lets her gingerly help him to his feet. "But it looks like we have to make another trip to the hospital."

"Oh, brother. You can't seem to stay out of trouble, can you?"

"Like you said earlier: I think my days of 'trouble' are over."

The Yokai slowly smiles, remembering: "I never said, 'trouble,' I said, 'adventure.'"

"Oh. Right. Well, how about you? How are you feeling?"

Her arms wrapped carefully around him, the Yokai gazes up at the night sky, then closes her eyes. "Full."

Zaniel starts to laugh, then winces, and clutches his broken ribs. "You? Not hungry? That's a first."

"Yes." The Yokai gives him a sly grin. "But it won't be the last."

"What do you mean?"

"Ah, nothing. Just a feeling. I thought I was done with Japan; now, I'm not so sure." She glances down at herself. She strokes her naked arms and legs, as if she has not seen them in a long time. "Maybe I *do* belong here. But maybe I won't really know until I leave. Does that make sense?"

"Does *any* of what goes on around here make sense?"

"Hmm. Touché. Makes about as much sense as me eating a demon twice my size. Oh, speaking of which, where are those bracelets of yours? I have an idea."

"They were in my ... Damn, I forgot my coat. Again."

"I got you." The Yokai gently props Zaniel up against the graffitied wall and dashes back into the restaurant. She re-emerges with the young man's coat, which he gratefully dons, as she removes the plastic bag from one of its pockets. She unceremoniously dumps the bracelets from the bag onto the snowy pavement and tosses the bag into the burned-out trash can. She then picks up each bracelet from the ground, wipes off the snow and potential germs against her naked thigh, then lifts each one above her head and lightly drops them into her mouth, swallowing them in two gulps.

"There. They won't be back anytime soon. That's three good deeds I've done for the year. You're welcome." She points a stern finger at him. "By the way, this changes nothing between us. This does *not* make me your new bodyguard. I already know what you're thinking."

Zaniel smiles, trying not to laugh for fear of his ribs again. "It's okay. I have a feeling I won't need one anymore, but I'll keep it in mind. Come on; let's get as fucking far away from here as possible."

"Wait," the Yokai says. "I know you're in a tremendous amount of pain and all, but … I *have* been running around for twenty-four hours on no sleep. More if you consider I've been bouncing between two worlds. Would you mind if I … if we … um …"

Zaniel braces himself. "What do you need?"

"I need to sleep. No dreaming. Just sleep, just for a minute or two. Then I'll fireman-carry you back to Osaka General if you want."

"Ha — ow. Why do you keep making me laugh?" He looks down at the figure sleeping peacefully on the snow-dusted ground. "Sure you won't be cold?"

"Cold?" The Yokai cocks her head. "It's not even ten degrees!"

Another bolt of pain shoots through Zaniel's fractured bones. "Fine. If it's just for a minute or two. I'm not in a rush to go anywhere. Except the hospital, but you already —"

The Yokai kisses his cheek. "*Ookini*, Momotaro."

Zaniel blushes. "You're welcome." He lets gravity do the work as he slides down the wall to a comfortably seated position, trying not to stare at the Yokai as she walks away. He turns suddenly, to say something else, but she has already disappeared. He does not mind; he can wait.

Deep in the darkness, the Yokai feels the snow melt under her naked feet, rising inch by inch past her ankles, up to her knees. She steps backward into the restaurant entranceway, disappearing from view. Now standing waist-deep in opaque black water, the Yokai leans back and lets the tide take her to sea, floating on the surface like a starfish, out into the sweet, peaceful oblivion that is sleep.

終章
AND A MOST CURIOUS
COUNTRY IT WAS

老いては子に従え
The old generation must make way for the new

There is a quiet town on a chilly spring day. The sky is blue, the grass is green, and the sun is shining. Along the main road there are no living creatures, save three. There is a young man and a young woman, walking in silence. The third, another woman who is almost as tall as the man, talks in a high-pitched voice:

"I will explain your apartment and how everything works. I will also introduce you to Landlord and he will show you where to take garbage and that sort of thing. And then we will meet the old Manager, Kinomoto-*senpai*, at one o'clock. And Kinomoto-*senpai* and I will show you supermarket, post office, and bank, so you can get your account, and get you a cellphone. Kinomoto-*senpai* is very excited to meet you."

"That's cool," the dark-haired young man rubs a fist into his blue-green eyes. "I'm kinda tired, though. I mean, I did just land here a week ago, Lieko. Can't we do all that bank and phone stuff tomorrow? I already rented one from the airport."

"But ..." Lieko trails off. There is a strange man, standing on the sidewalk, looking up at Cybelle's apartment window. He grins at Lieko as they walk by. Yoshino and the other man walk right by him, waiting for her to finish her sentence. Lieko unlocks the front door with Cybelle's key and ushers them in and up the stairs, ignoring the strange man. "But that phone is temporary. It is very important that you have your *own* cellphone, because —"

"Lieko. Relax. I have a phone, and Cybelle already told me about the pay phone out front. It's fine! It's not like I'm going to have a big emergency my first night here."

"Oh," Lieko shoots a pleading look to Yoshino, who shrugs. Lieko clicks her tongue, wondering why she even bothered. "Then, I will call Kinomoto-*senpai* and ask him if we can wait. We don't want you to be so tired."

"Is this it?" The man points to a door.

"Yes, one moment." Lieko searches for Cybelle's key in her purse. "Sorry, I just had them in my hand. I don't know what made me put them away ..."

"Sheesh, big enough purse huh, Yosh?" The man elbows Yoshino. "What does she carry around in there, her first-born child?!" He laughs so hard it rings down the hall and makes her cringe. She turns away to hide the pained look on her face. *Good luck*, Yoshino wishes the young man's new neighbours. She pretends to admire her surroundings and the heavy metallic doors to the adjacent apartments. Not much difference between now and the last time she was here two weeks prior. She remembers Cybelle saying other than Halloween and other holidays, there are no decorations on the walls to show that anyone lives behind those doors.

Lieko fishes the key out of her massive purse and unlocks the door to the apartment. "Please, Andrew-*sensei*, after you. Ah, ah!

Wait! Here, Andrew-*sensei*. We must take off our shoes before we go in."

"I don't care, you can come in with your shoes on. You don't have to be so uptight. It's my place." Andrew trudges on inside. Lieko and Yoshino grimace, but remove their shoes regardless. "Holy shit, this is tiny."

Now it's Lieko's turn to cringe. "Actually, it's much bigger than many apartments in Japan. Cybelle liked its size. Anyway, you have television, *kotatsu*, which I will show you how to turn on later, the kitchen is here —"

"You call *this* a kitchen?!"

"Yes, I'm sorry it is small, but it has everything: sink, toaster oven, fridge, and cupboards. And over this way, here is the washroom. See? Toilet room is here —"

"*Geez*, things just get smaller and smaller around here, don't they?"

"— and, uh," Lieko laughs nervously. "Here is sink to wash hands and brush teeth, and all cleaning supplies are in this cupboard underneath, and across is your washing machine. And this room is your shower. There are many buttons in Japanese, so I will show you —"

"Well, I know a bit of Japanese. And Cybelle emailed me all the instructions already."

"Ah, I see. But ..." Lieko folds her arms. "This apartment will not have internet until you get your bank account and cellphone. It takes a very long time to —"

"Isn't there a Starbucks nearby? I can just use Wi-Fi. Or the one at the school."

"*Eeto* ... well, the nearest Starbucks was at the station, and Zozo does not have Wi-Fi, so you would have to —"

"What? Are you kidding me?" Andrew swears. "Oh, well. I'm sure I'll figure them out. You know, aside from everything being way too small, it's not bad. I thought Cybelle lived here for years. This place looks brand new."

"Yes! As you can see, Cybelle cleaned very hard, so please, maybe next time, you take off your shoes?"

Yoshino lingers in the living room as Andrew and Lieko argue in the washroom over the shower buttons, vaguely paying attention. She looks around at the remaining furniture, the walls stripped of their travel posters and farewell cards to Cybelle. They really gave her apartment a homey look when Yoshino was here for her farewell house party. Yoshino already misses her. It is hard not to think of the apartment as Cybelle's home. Now, it is Andrew's home. All signs of Cybelle ever existing in this part of the world are gone.

With one exception.

"Found you," Yoshino says out loud. On the *kotatsu* — with the single reclining chair that Andrew will certainly have complaints about — held together with a rubber band, is a small collection of letters in envelopes. Stubs from Cybelle's most recent bills and cancellations, to prove that they had been paid for. Yoshino chuckles, recalling the row Lieko and the former manager had with Cybelle about leaving bills for the "new teacher" to deal with. "It will not be a good impression if you leave Japan without paying. It will make things very difficult for new teacher," Kinomoto-*senpai* had scolded her. And they all knew how important it was to make the new male teacher happy. A part of Yoshino wants to stay with Zozo. *Just to see how much Lieko will kiss this Andrew guy's butt.* However, Zozo has no say in Yoshino's future anymore.

"Hey," she notices her own name on the front of an envelope. "What could *you* be?"

It is a letter written on Sentimental Circus stationery. It explains the contents of the other envelopes: utility bills, phone, and internet, her original plane ticket itinerary marked with the changes Cybelle requested for her new flight date. Lieko-Manager should know what they are, and Yoshino shouldn't have to explain, but you never know. Yoshino definitely agrees there.

There is more:

Let me know how the new guy is! Judging by our emails he kinda sounds like a jerk, but who knows? Maybe he's not the biggest prat in the world? ^____^ If he's cool, we can take him out when I'm back in town! (If not, it'll just be the three of us. Feel free to bring one of your American gentleman callers along, heh heh heh.)

Yoshino snickers. Then her eyebrows furrow. "Um, does anyone smell something?"

"*What?!*" Lieko storms out of the bathroom and starts opening and slamming the fridge and cupboard doors, angry that maybe Cybelle left something rotting. She flies into a brand-new rage when she finds the cupboards full of soy sauce, Costco-sized ketchup, and other condiments. "Why am I not surprised?! Cybelle, *saitei* …"

"Relax, dude," Andrew laughs at her. "I asked Cybelle not to throw these out. I told her I don't want to run around all week trying to buy stuff. Man, she wasn't kidding when she said you'd freak out."

"I — uh, I see," Lieko composes herself. "So, Cybelle did not throw them away because you and she discussed them. Okay. But, please, when it is time for Andrew to leave, please try to throw away, because maybe it will be a burden on the next teacher? Ah, but please, don't leave for a long time!" She adds quickly.

"Ha! Don't worry. I got *nothing* to go back to. I'm staying here as long as I can. I mean, I'm getting paid to teach a language I already speak, and I got four phone numbers my first week here! I'm living the life already. Now, what were you saying about the tub? Cybelle told me there's a way to fill it up, and I've been thinking, might be nice if I ever have someone over who digs bathtubs, know what I mean?"

Andrew disappears into the bathroom. Lieko tries her luck with Yoshino a second time, desperate. "'Digs bathtubs'? Do you understand what he's talking about?" she asks in Japanese.

Yoshino shrugs again with a doe-eyed, vacant look. "I'm so sorry, Manager, I don't."

"*Saitei,*" Lieko repeats under her breath and follows after him. "Ah, Andrew-*sensei*! Don't play with the buttons like that, please! Oh, now we must find towels to clean up ..."

Yoshino hides her smirk with the letter. *Call us "the worst" as much as you want. It's going to be a long year for you, girl.* She returns to the rest of her letter:

... heh heh heh.) We'll be in Thailand for a while, maybe swing by Cambodia one weekend, then Hong Kong for our stopover. We're playing it by ear but kanarazu *we'll be back in time for peak* sakura*! This isn't goodbye yet, Yoshino-*sama*! My adventure in Japan isn't over. I just wanted to thank you for everything you've done for me. I couldn't have survived without you. You kept me going at a time when I wasn't sure if I would make it ...*

Yoshino's eyes start to sting. She will have to read the rest later.

She pulls the letter away, then brings it back to her nose. She has located the source of the strange aroma. Yoshino closes her eyes and takes another deep inhalation. She can feel her knees turning into jelly. She could spread herself on the carpet and drift off to sleep.

"What the ...?" the new teacher steps out of the washroom area. Seeing Yoshino, he laughs. "Are you getting high?!"

"Mmm, maybe," she teases back. "Where'd Manager go?" Yoshino had not even heard her leave.

"I dunno, something about finding the landlord to get some towels. She's a little uptight, isn't she? Must be a joy to work with. You seem cool, though." He leans against the kitchen counter, looking her over. "Are you full-time, too?"

"I was — until yesterday." She stuffs the letters into her purse. "Now that I've gotten you here in one piece, I am *done.*" She dons her jacket and runs to the *genkan* where she left her shoes.

"Congratulations, welcome to Zozo, and tell Manager I had to take these to the school."

Andrew follows after her. "Wait! All of a sudden, you're in a rush to leave? Come on, aren't you going to take me out on the town or something? I thought the Japanese were supposed to be polite."

Yoshino puts on her shoes, saying nothing to dignify him. The building is so quiet she can hear Lieko's voice, way down the hall, mingling with that of the landlord as he locks his door. She only has a few seconds to make her escape.

"So, I'm not going to see you again, ever? Come on, Yosh, you can be nicer than that. Why don't you give me your number and we can meet up later when you're not in such a hurry?"

"Oh, Andrew." She smiles as politely as she can. "I wish I could be here to see how far you go."

Andrew blushes. "What a sweet thing to say. *Doumo arigatou,*" he says with an awkward bow. "So, how about that number?"

"Nope. I'm off! Oh, you can toss the envelope."

"The envelope?"

Yoshino is already gone, running down the hall as fast as her heels will let her — which, by the sound of it, is pretty fast. Andrew grins to himself. *Must be a Japanese-girl thing. They all wear such loud high heels here. Lots of practice.*

"Aha," he spies the envelope on the *kotatsu*. A simple, cartoon-covered thing with Yoshino's name on it in very flowery writing. He finds the remote for the TV. There is a talk show on, something about food. Lots of exclamations and words flashing at the bottom of the screen, but it is all gibberish to him. He flips through the rest of the channels. "Seven channels, not one of them in English. Fantastic." So, this is his new life. Tiny apartment, nothing on TV, a ton of condiments and spices he can't read, and a bitchy manager instead of a super-cute co-worker who can actually speak. *It's going to be one hell of a year.*

Andrew examines the envelope in his hand. *It smells weird, otherwise what's the big deal?* He brings it closer to his face. No — it smells amazing. It is a sweet, warm scent ...

Andrew's eyes grow heavy. It gets harder to keep them open.

... *sweet, yeah. But a little sour.* He hears Lieko's footsteps echoing down the hall. Andrew's head tilts forward ... *peach ... and lemon?*

"Okay, bathroom is wet, so we must — Andrew-*sensei?*" Lieko steps into the room. "Andrew-*sensei?*" She scowls at the unconscious man sprawled on the living room floor. With a despondent sigh she takes out her phone as she slips into her shoes, closing the *genkan* door behind her. "Kinomoto-*senpai*. The new teacher ... yes, I brought him but ... No, he's asleep ... No, I tried to —"

Lieko closes the front door as her superior continues to berate her on the phone. She leaves the man in the apartment to begin her petulant walk down toward the apartment entrance. She steels herself with a deep inhale and opens the front door. The man from the shrine is still there. Well, perhaps not a shrine of this world, she thinks to herself. But he does don a shrine worker's uniform and holds a pair of clacking wood blocks in his hands. He is still smiling. "Good afternoon," he says, each syllable pronounced with slow, sharp consonants.

Lieko glares at him for only a moment before she turns on her heel and heads back toward Zozo. "But Kinomoto-*senpai*, how can we — Yes, yes, I *understand* but ..." She does not give the man a second glance, nor does she return his salutation. The man giggles behind her back. He does not need binocular vision to see she has given up speaking *yumego* long ago; she will not speak it now, not to him. But he is a kind creature, and it was worth a shot.

As the woman walks down the long, wide street, the wind picks up. It stirs the baby-pink and white buds on the *sakura* branches in front of the post office and bank. Their scent mingles with those of French fries and thawing palm trees as the wind blows a little harder, rattling the windows with gentle pulses. The tall, thin woman ignores it all for the sake of concentrating on her superior's voice, focusing on the reality of her situation: that she is not dreaming, she is not dreaming, she is not dreaming ... She continues her journey, unaware that the man she left behind is slipping deeper and deeper into the world of dreams until ...

"Gotcha!"

Andrew's eyes fly open. His mouth forms a perfect, round O but no words come out. His body is hoisted into the air by his throat. Clutching at the strong grip around his neck, he looks down to see a man. The biggest man Andrew has ever seen, with eyes bright as copper flame. He is naked. There are scratches on his face, which only has one good eye, and bullet-hole scars all over his chest, upon which a dragon slithers and hisses. Most of the skin above his dangling penis is gone, exposing a dark, gaping hole where his vital organs ought to be. A hole that could not, and can never, be filled. Andrew tries desperately to pry the man's fingers from his throat and scream at the same time.

"Nice haircut, ya little jackass. Thought you could fool ol' Akki, eh? Hang on ... you're not the kid. Where is he? And where's that *yokai* chick? I traced her scent all this way. She's *gotta* be here!"

Andrew chokes. He can feel his feet dangling in the air. He looks down and sees his own body, stretched out on the floor of his new apartment. Is he sleeping? Is he dreaming? Then why does this feel so real?

"Tough guy, huh?" The giant man laughs. He licks Andrew's face and neck. "You're not the boy," he concludes. "You taste nothin' like him." And this is undoubtedly not the demon girl in disguise. Akki can still remember the salty caramel tang of her flesh and blood. He ignores the feeble fingers that leave no claw marks on his skin as the human wriggles and gasps in his grip. *What to do, what to do ...*

Andrew's eyes roll back into his head. Akki pulls him in close. He homes in on the young man's features with his one good eye. "Hang on. Your eyes. You've got his eyes. Well, not *his* eyes, but … yeah … lookin' at you just right … almost the same colour." Akki licks his lips. "I could … Why not … After I missed my chance with the kid … didn't take his eyes when I could've. Then that bitch went and … yeah. Heh. You know what? I changed my mind. Looks like you'll do after all, human."

He presses his lips against Andrew's face. Andrew croaks in lieu of screaming.

Akki releases his grip. The human slips from his fingers. Coughing violently, Andrew looks up at the demon who savours the gristly flesh between his molars as he chews, and chews, and chews. Something is wrong with his vision. He can only see half of Akki's face: a demonic, devilish face, with a toothy grin like a shark. "Not bad. Awful chewy, though …" The demon regards Andrew as one might look down upon a squashed insect. "Ah, what the hell? My walls still need a *little* splash of colour."

Akki plunges his hand into the human's face.

Andrew thrashes awake on the carpeted floor. "Oh, thank God." It was all a horrible dream. He presses his hands over his face. Something feels wrong. His eyes. "What the fuck?" He feels around in the dark until his hands meet the wall. The wall comes to a stop. The bathroom. He pulls himself in, fumbling for the light switch to look — or try to look — in the mirror. He sees nothing. For there is nothing for him with which to see.

"No … no!" He feels around in the empty sockets. "It's not possible!"

But it is. The demon had taken a perfectly good pair of eyes.

ACKNOWLEDGEMENTS

First, I gotta give props to God for bringing me in the presence of all the influences (human or otherwise) that led to 夢, and for carrying me through the toughest times. Me da Nyame ase.

Second, I want to acknowledge the driving forces behind the books that helped me get the *yokai* names and details just right: *An Introduction to Yokai Culture: Monsters, Ghosts, and Outsiders in Japanese History* by Komatsu Kazuhiko, *Even Monkeys Fall from Trees: The Wit and Wisdom of Japanese Proverbs, Volume 1* by Jun Hashimoto and David Galef, *The Book of Yokai: Mysterious Creatures of Japanese Folklore* by Michael Dylan Foster, *Yokai Attack!: The Japanese Monster Survival Guide* by Hiroko Yoda and Matt Alt, *ARTBOX* ゆるかわ妖怪絵 by Toshinobu Yasumura, and Lewis Carroll's *Alice's Adventures in Wonderland* and *Through the Looking Glass*, which inspired me to shape my dreams and experiences into something comprehensible and shareable. Japanese Wikipedia helped a lot, too.

Finally, I have several humans to thank:

Team 夢 at Dundurn Press, with an especially big fat thanks

to Whitney and Cheryl for their patience and advice, and to Scott for taking the risk!

My translation team and my creativity crew: Nina, Atsuko, Megumi, Hiroko, Norie, Eileen, Heidi, Hamish, Michael, Jessica, Amanda, Christina, Richard, Candace, Katie, Marion, Tamara, and Sarah, who all cheered me on at some point in the process and never made fun of me once.

Marcia and the JET Programme, for giving me the chance to go back.

Lora, for re-introducing me to the world of writing.

Jesmond, for his expertise and generosity.

Everyone behind the well-timed "From Eery [*sic*] to Endearing: Yokai in the Arts of Japan" exhibit at the Edo-Tokyo Museum in 2016, and the patient staff and security who let me wander around until closing time.

The Toronto Horror Writers for their critiques that helped me in making certain scenes nice and gruesome.

Laura, for taking an awesome photo of me.

Last but not least, I want to thank my mother, Angelina, my sister Liesl, and (again) my best friend Nina for withholding all major judgements about me and the contents of this book, as they have always done with all my weirdness — hopefully they read this page first.

ABOUT THE AUTHOR

Sifton Tracey Anipare was born in Windsor to Ghanaian parents and raised in the Greater Toronto Area. An avid reader before she turned three, her favourite stories have always included fairy (and faerie) tales and paranormal accounts. After a self-independent study of Japan that she did in the fourth grade, she made it her life goal to go there at least once. While at university, she began to study Japanese independently and post-graduation applied to teach English in Japan, where she lived for four years. When she is not in the classroom or writing, Sifton will rewatch her favourite movies or play video games for hours on end. She turns to bubble tea, Japanese coffee mixes, and pumpkin spice to fuel her creative fires. She has no plans to stop collecting stickers or stamps, both of which are essential to her writing process, and hopes that stamp rallies and point cards will one day become mainstream worldwide. 夢 (*Yume*) is her first novel.